Paul Doherty was born in ██████████ ████ History at Liverpool an██ ████████ ████ obtained a doctorate at Ox███ ████████ II and Queen Isabella. He is now the Headmast██ school in North-East London, and lives with his wife and family near Epping Forest.

Paul Doherty's Hugh Corbett medieval mysteries - SATAN IN ST MARY'S, CROWN IN DARKNESS, SPY IN CHANCERY, THE ANGEL OF DEATH, THE PRINCE OF DARKNESS, MURDER WEARS A COWL, THE ASSASSIN IN THE GREENWOOD, THE SONG OF A DARK ANGEL, SATAN'S FIRE and THE DEVIL'S HUNT - are also available from Headline, as are his other novels of mystery and murder - AN ANCIENT EVIL, being the Knight's Tale, A TAPESTRY OF MURDERS, being the Man of Law's Tale, A TOURNAMENT OF MURDERS, being the Franklin's Tale, and GHOSTLY MUR-DERS, being the Priest's Tale, all told during the evenings on a pilgrimage from London to Canterbury. He is also the author of THE ROSE DEMON.

Acclaim for Paul Doherty's medieval mysteries:

'Medieval London comes vividly to life . . . Doherty's depictions of medieval characters and manners of thought, from the highest to the lowest, ringing true' *Publishers Weekly*
'I really like these medieval whodunnits' Sarah Broadhurst, *Bookseller*
'. . . this is one of those books you hate to put down' *Prima*
'A powerful compound of history and intrigue' *Redbridge Guardian*

Also by Paul Doherty and available from Headline

The Haunting
The Rose Demon
The Mask of Ra

An Ancient Evil
Being the Knight's Tale
A Tapestry of Murders
Being the Man of Law's Tale
A Tournament of Murders
Being the Franklin's Tale
Ghostly Murders
Being the Priest's Tale

Hugh Corbett medieval mysteries
Satan in St Mary's
Crown in Darkness
Spy in Chancery
The Angel of Death
The Prince of Darkness
Murder Wears a Cowl
The Assassin in the Greenwood
The Song of a Dark Angel
Satan's Fire
The Devil's Hunt

The Sorrowful Mysteries of Brother Athelstan
The Nightingale Gallery
The House of the Red Slayer
Murder Most Holy
The Anger of God
By Murder's Bright Light
The House of Crows
The Assassin's Riddle
The Devil's Domain

Under the name of Michael Clynes
The White Rose Murders
The Poisoned Chalice
The Grail Murders
A Brood of Vipers
The Gallows Murders
The Relic Murders

THE
SOUL SLAYER

Paul Doherty

HEADLINE

First published in 1998
by HEADLINE BOOK PUBLISHING

First published in paperback in 1998
by HEADLINE BOOK PUBLISHING

10 9 8 7 6 5 4 3 2 1

ISBN 0 7472 5872 4

Typeset by Palimpsest Book Production Limited,
Polmont, Stirlingshire

Printed and bound in Great Britain by
Clays Ltd, St Ives plc

HEADLINE BOOK PUBLISHING
A division of Hodder Headline PLC
338 Euston Road
London NW1 3BH

To Patrick Moule, a very brave student of Trinity Catholic High School, with every good wish for the future.

The Gates of Hell are open night and day.
Smooth the descent and easy is the way.

Virgil
Aeneid: VI. 126.

PROLOGUE I

The road outside Chelmsford: December 1564

The rider cursed. He turned his horse's head and peered through the misty gloom at the makeshift signpost planted at the crossroads. The night was bitterly cold. A sharp biting wind seared the flat Essex countryside, piercing his clothes, cooling the sweat on his neck and back. Andrew Cavendish, close friend of William Cowper, a member of Secretary of State Walsingham's Office of the Night, pulled the vizard across his face so it protected his nose and mouth. He tugged at the soft-brimmed hat and, yet again, secured his cloak more tightly around him. He leaned over and patted his horse's neck.

'Now, now, girl,' Cavendish murmured.

He dismounted, dug into the bag hanging from his saddle horn and took out a fistful of oats. The horse nuzzled his hand, nipping his fingers.

'I know! I know!' Cavendish let his horse feed. 'You are cold and hungry, so is your master.'

Cavendish peered up at the clouds racing across the starlit heavens. He thanked God for the full moon; without it the countryside would be as black as a pit. He still had a long journey ahead of him. Perhaps he

3

should stop for the night? In that case he'd probably enter London tomorrow afternoon. Once there, he was safe.

He wrapped the reins of his horse round his hands and glared up at the signpost tilted drunkenly to one side. He was not sure whether it was the wind or some tinkers' trick but now he had no clear direction which road to take. His horse whinnied and started back, its hooves scrabbling at the pebbled earth. Cavendish, alarmed, reassuringly patted the great horse pistol pushed into its saddle holster.

'Whoa there, girl!' he soothed. 'Whoa there, now!'

Cavendish remounted, his arms and back still aching from his long ride. He cursed as his horse whinnied again, moving restlessly beneath him. Cavendish unbuckled the pistol pouch, whose weapon was loaded and primed. Was his horse fearful because the crossroads were cursed? After all, malefactors were hanged here and, beneath the packed earth, the rotting cadavers of suicides lay buried, small wooden stakes driven through their hearts. A haunted, ghostly place! Or was he being pursued? Cavendish turned his horse and faced the trackway he had come along. He had not heard or seen anything suspicious, yet, ever since he had left Chelmsford, a prickling between his shoulder blades, a suspicion that he was being closely watched dogged him.

He'd supped at the Turk's Head on a meaty pottage and a jug of ale. The taproom had been warm and inviting with its roaring fires, its onions and hams hanging from the rafters. The locals were friendly, being used to travellers. Nevertheless, Cavendish had felt certain he was being scrutinised.

He had to reach London. He must inform Secretary

Walsingham and Master William Cowper about the priest and, more importantly, about the Soul Slayer, that hideous warlock. Cavendish was a graduate of the Halls of Cambridge. He always accepted the tasks assigned to him. Nevertheless, he'd found it difficult to accept what Secretary Walsingham had whispered to him in that secret, velvet-draped chamber in the Tower. He would have risen and left but William Cowper, sitting so silently beside Walsingham, had, by his presence, verified what their master was saying. Walsingham, with his piercing, glass-hard eyes, sensuous mouth and neatly clipped goatee beard, had seized Cavendish's wrist, nipping the skin until he winced.

'Andrew, dear boy.' Walsingham's upper lip had curled back over his teeth, a common gesture when Secretary Walsingham was excited or about to impart some great secret. Indeed, Walsingham only dealt in secrets. He was the Queen's spymaster with a finger in every man's pie, a nose for seeking out traitors, those who opposed the rule of the great Elizabeth.

Everyone feared Walsingham, even Cowper, the albino, Cavendish's friend. Walsingham sifted amongst the secrets of men's souls. With his sharp brain and ever-faithful memory, the Queen's Secretary recorded and registered the most minor details of each individual he dealt with. William Cecil, the Queen's principal secretary, was wary of Master Walsingham while, so rumour had it, even the Queen, ivory-faced, red-haired Elizabeth, secretly feared Walsingham and his cabinet of secrets. 'Black Tom' she nicknamed him: black in face, black in heart, black in soul.

'Find the Soul Slayer,' Walsingham had ordered. He pushed a scroll across the table and gave Cavendish's wrist one last nip. 'Read what is there, memorise, then return it.'

Cavendish had. He could scarcely believe it. The Soul Slayer was a warlock of great magic and terrible power who had the ability to take a man's heart and, when dead, hold that soul in thrall.

'I don't believe it!' Cavendish had stuttered.

'He's in Essex.' Cowper had spoken up. 'The Soul Slayer, Henry Frogmore, has returned to England as he has done before.' Cowper's strange eyes gleamed, his voice shot through with anger. 'I have hunted him through Europe and beyond, studied the reports of merchants, travellers, spies at foreign courts. He is here, a master of disguise. We want him captured, brought to London. Uncover his disguise, his whereabouts, his description. Come back here and I shall do the rest.'

Cavendish lifted his head as an owl hooted from a copse further down the trackway.

'You'll not find yourself alone,' Cowper had continued. 'The popish Church also wants the Soul Slayer: a Jesuit priest, Michael St Clair, has now entered the eastern shires. He moves in disguise from this house to that, given protection by the great Catholic families. We want him caught as well.'

'Find him, Andrew!' Walsingham had ordered. 'You are the Queen's own agent. You work for the Office of the Night. You deal in shadows, those things which hang between heaven and hell. The Queen herself is deeply interested in this matter.'

Cavendish had agreed. The Queen, Secretary Cecil and Master Walsingham had a great fear of witchcraft, warlocks and the power of magic. He felt tempted to ask why but a good agent, or scurrier as

Walsingham nicknamed his men, never asked, they simply obeyed.

Cavendish gathered the reins in his hands and suppressed a thrill of excitement. He had been successful! St Clair was on the road somewhere outside Colchester while he had a description of Master Frogmore. Walsingham and Cowper would be delighted at his news. Cavendish leaned down and patted his horse's neck.

'You've had your rest, girl!' He took one look at the crossroads. 'We'll keep heading south, stop at the next farm or village.'

Cavendish dug in his spurs and the huge, deep-breasted gelding cantered along the moonlit trackway. Cavendish forced himself to relax. If his horse kept up this quick pace, he'd travel as long as he could despite the cold and loneliness. They passed a gallows, the horse shying at the crumbling skeleton in its iron gibbet.

'If there's a gallows,' Cavendish joked, 'there must be a manor house or village nearby.'

He turned a corner. The trackway dipped as it ran between the enclosing hedgerows. Cavendish was about to ride on when, out of the trees along the side of the road, slipped a horse and rider. Cavendish immediately reined in, his hand going to the horse pistol.

'Stand aside!' he shouted. 'I bear the Queen's commission!'

'And I bear the Lord of Hell's!' came the mocking reply.

Cavendish fumbled at the pouch but horse and rider were on him. Cavendish glimpsed eyes gleaming behind the mask, the glint of a dagger; even as he tried to move, the razor-edged blade caught him neatly across the neck, biting deep into the skin and bone. Cavendish, choking on his blood, swayed in the saddle. Images teemed through his dying brain before he toppled into the cold, waiting darkness.

His opponent seized the reins of Cavendish's horse, murmuring to it quietly. He dismounted and turned Cavendish over, carefully searching the dead man's wallet and pockets for documents. Once he was satisfied, he cut away the man's leather jerkin and shirt so the skin above his heart was exposed. The Soul Slayer stared up at the sky; he mouthed a prayer and, as carefully and as expertly as a barber's surgeon, he thrust his dagger into the warm flesh, digging deep for Cavendish's heart.

PROLOGUE II

The Tower of London: December 1564

Elizabeth I, Queen of England, sat at the top of the great oaken table in a chamber above St John's Chapel in the soaring keep of her country's principal fortress. Elizabeth had pulled back the veil which protected her white, painted face and carmined lips: her red hair was held in place by a small, jewelled cap which her ladies had pinned so expertly before her yeomen of guard had escorted her from Whitehall to her black galley for a journey up the Thames to meet this, her Office of the Night, at the Tower.

Elizabeth was not pleased. The black galley was comfortable; she had been wrapped in furs while small warming-pans had been placed in the muffler covering her feet and legs. Nevertheless, the river wind had been biting cold and Elizabeth had to miss the elaborate masque so carefully prepared for her by the love of her heart, sweet Robin Dudley. She really should be with him, leaping high in the galliard or allowing Robin to sit on a sequinned stool beside her and whisper subtle flatteries, contrived conceits about how he loved her, how she was his mistress, the queen of his heart, the ruler of his soul . . . Such pleasantries were a welcome relief from the tedium of Council business! As Elizabeth pulled at the fur doublet over her black damask dress, the starched ruff around the collar caught at her chin and made her wince.

'It's cold in here!' she snapped.

'Madame, madame.' William Cecil, sitting on her left, pointed to the log fire crackling merrily in the hearth. 'The room is stifling warm.'

'More braziers could be wheeled in.'

'Perhaps you have a chill?'

Elizabeth's green, cat-like eyes blinked. She looked away.

'I have no chill!' she retorted.

She smiled dazzlingly at her principal Secretary of State. Cecil beamed back, but his smile faded as the Queen leaned across, a vicious pout to her lips, and tugged his small goatee beard spitefully.

'I am your Queen, Master Cecil. My health is good; indeed, it has never been better!'

Cecil forced a smile. 'Of course, your majesty,' he whispered. 'I was just concerned.'

Elizabeth withdrew her hand and slouched further down the great throne-like chair. She looked up at the roof.

'I hate this place,' she whispered. 'My good half-sister Mary brought me here. I came through Traitor's Gate. I thought I would never leave.'

The room fell silent as the Queen pretended to become lost in a reverie. Furtively she glanced across the table; Walsingham was dressed, as usual, in black from head to toe, apart from the white ruff at his neck. The Queen studied those hooded eyes, swarthy skin and carefully dressed hair, the neatly cut beard and moustache. Walsingham could be taken for a popish priest or puritan. He caught her gaze and winked. 'Black Tom' was not frightened. In these matters, he whistled up the tune and was master of the dance.

Elizabeth's gaze shifted to the man on Walsingham's left, William Cowper, with his boyish, clean-shaven face, white hair and deep-set light-blue eyes. Cowper was an albino yet his strange looks hid a sharp brain and even keener wits. A veritable limner, Master Cowper: one of Walsingham's best hunting dogs, he always flushed out his quarry and never left the hunt until it was brought down.

'Well, well!' Elizabeth rapped the table with her knuckles. 'Here we are in the Tower at the dead of night to discuss the affairs of the Office of the Night.'

The Queen smiled thinly at her play on words but the three men stared stonily back. Elizabeth hid her annoyance. This was 'Black Tom's' idea, yet one she had taken up so fervently. She was safe against spies, conspirators, traitors' plot and counter-plot, but magic? The work of warlocks, the practitioners of the gibbet rites? They were a different matter. Hadn't her own mother, so rumour claimed, won her place in Henry's heart by witchcraft only to be destroyed by the same means? Catherine de Medici of France had a whole gaggle of astronomers and astrologers; Elizabeth was no different. She was not concerned about the fortune-tellers, the quacks who sheltered in their booths at St Bartholomew's Fair. The real wizards and witches were those who could perform the three-day fast and summon up powers, and they had to be controlled. The Office of the Night had been set up to scrutinise anyone who might threaten her or the throne.

'The Soul Slayer.' Walsingham decided to waste no more time.

Elizabeth moved quickly in her chair; the spymaster knew he now had her full attention. No more games, teasing or coquetry.

'What about him?' the Queen hissed.

'He is in England, we know that!'

Elizabeth let her breath out in one long gasp.

'Why?'

'We don't know.'

'What's his disguise?'

Walsingham pulled a face, his heavy-lidded gaze never leaving that of the Queen.

'He has probably taken another man's identity . . .'

'Do, please tell me,' the Queen beat her fist on the table, 'what you know rather than what you don't!'

'We know he came from the Baltic lands. A captain of a ship out of Oslo believes he landed in Ipswich. We sent one of our best men, Andrew Cavendish, into Essex.'

'And?'

'Cavendish is dead.' Cowper's words were soft and sibilant. 'Murdered by the Soul Slayer. His corpse was found under some bracken in a ditch on the road from Chelmsford. His throat was cut, his heart scooped out like a child would cream with a spoon.'

Elizabeth blanched. 'And what else?' she asked.

'We don't know,' Cowper continued, 'why the Soul Slayer has returned to England. He may be here to do a mischief, to strengthen his powers or simply hide before travelling on elsewhere.'

'And you have no evidence as to his whereabouts?'

'We have done some searches.' Walsingham spoke up. 'By a system of elimination we think he is still in Essex. It's only a matter of time before we hunt him down.' He pointed at his companion. 'Master Cowper has been keen in the hunt; for months, years, he has pursued this warlock from afar.'

'But why should he come here?' Elizabeth insisted. 'Unless he's to be used by our enemies?'

'That may be so,' Cowper replied. 'But he could also be here for his own nefarious purposes.' He saw the questioning look in the Queen's face. 'The Soul Slayer,' Cowper hurried on, 'is a remarkable warlock. He is a true follower of Satan. He made a compact with hell and, in return, has received certain powers.'

Elizabeth sat back in her chair. She watched this strangest of men pick at a loose sliver of wood on the table. Outside the wind beat against the mullioned glass and shook the shutters, while one of the ravens cawed fiercely against the growing night storm.

'We are waiting, Master Cowper.'

'It is hard to believe,' her agent continued, 'but the Soul Slayer is a warlock who has entered into a contract of blood with the powers of darkness. He chooses his victim and kills him or her. He plucks out the heart and uses this in horrid sacrifice to develop and strengthen his powers.'

'So, these powers have to be replenished?' Cecil intervened.

'Oh yes.'

'And so he needs a steady trickle of victims?'

'Stream would be the correct word,' Cowper asserted. 'The more victims, the greater the strength!'

13

'And what are these powers?' Elizabeth asked impatiently.

'From the little we know, the Soul Slayer's physical and mental strengths increase. He is impervious to cold, hunger, thirst and enjoys great physical and mental prowess.'

'The same,' Elizabeth snapped, 'could be said for a horse which is well fed!'

Cowper ignored Cecil's titter of laughter.

'Your majesty, can a horse become a greyhound?'

The Queen's jaw dropped. She even forgot to cover her blackening teeth.

'Master Cowper, you jest?'

'Your majesty, I do not. We know that the Soul Slayer can, for a short time, adopt the guise of one of his victims.'

'So, how can he be pursued?'

'With great cunning, your majesty. The only real sign is an inverted cross above his own heart.'

'What else?' Elizabeth asked. She pressed her hands against the table to fend off a feeling of unreality as well as the hell-spawned horror now being described.

'He is well named a Soul Slayer.' Cowper ran a finger round his collar.

Elizabeth noticed that, like Walsingham, the albino was dressed in black from head to toe except for the high-collared white shirt under his leather doublet.

'Apparently the Soul Slayer is interested only in certain victims. He wishes to take men and women whose lives, whose moral state has made them vulnerable. Once he has killed them and plucked out their hearts, he can not only take on their form and shape but call on their soul to do his bidding.'

14

'Like a noisome spirit?'

'Yes, your majesty.'

'And what can this spirit do?'

'Wreak havoc. Tip a pot of oil onto a fire, weaken the structure of a bridge, dislodge a stone or boulder so it falls on the rider below. Arrange for a tree, half-rotten and bending, to topple at a precise time. The list is endless.'

'You know a great deal about him.'

Cowper just smiled thinly.

'He can be hired?' Elizabeth asked.

'We suspect,' Walsingham replied, 'that there are powers in Europe, and beyond, who would pay heavily for his services.'

'And these could include our enemies?'

'Your majesty, you have said it.'

'And can this Soul Slayer be destroyed?' Cecil asked, glaring across at Walsingham.

'We don't know,' the spymaster replied. 'We think he can. We do know others are hunting him.'

'The Jesuits?'

'Yes, the Jesuit, Michael St Clair.'

'Who, what is this?' Elizabeth asked.

'Madame.' Walsingham displayed his teeth in what he considered a grin. 'The Jesuits are no strangers to you.' He sniffed. 'They are a highly organised, well-trained society of popish priests. They have allegiance to their superior general and to the Pope. Their main task is to preach and use all their powers to check, and eventually destroy, our Reformed Faith.'

'Yes, yes, I know all about the Jesuits!' Elizabeth snapped. 'They slip into my realm and hide like rats in this house or that. We've hanged enough, and we'll probably hang some more, but what have they to do with this Soul Slayer?'

'Cavendish did despatch one letter to us.'

Walsingham glanced quickly at his lieutenant.

'He stumbled on the fact,' Cowper declared, 'that a Jesuit, Michael St Clair, was also pursuing the Soul Slayer. Shortly after the warlock landed in England St Clair followed. He, too, is disguised and, being a Catholic priest, moves from one Catholic family to another. He probably uses his priesthood to acquire knowledge on the whereabouts of his quarry. We believe St Clair has been sent by the Jesuit Order in Rome to hunt down and destroy the Soul Slayer.'

'So, if we hunt St Clair,' Cecil remarked. 'He will lead us to the Soul Slayer?'

'He might also,' Cowper added, 'inform us how to destroy him.'

'Destroy him?' Elizabeth rapped the table. 'Who said, Master Cowper, that this being was to be destroyed? And if he is to be,' she added hastily, 'I would like to see him first.'

'So, what do you propose?' Cecil asked Walsingham.

'Master Cowper here will leave London for Essex tomorrow. He will bear her majesty's commission, a warrant to carry out her will in whatever matter be assigned to him.'

Elizabeth agreed.

'Cowper will hunt down both St Clair and this Soul Slayer,' Walsingham continued. 'If he has good fortune, this will happen soon.' Walsingham clicked his tongue and hid his own secret doubts. 'Master Cowper has a passion for capturing this warlock.'

'Let it be done,' Elizabeth whispered. She pointed down the table at Cowper. 'And, Master Cowper, remember Cavendish's fate. You are only to return with the Soul Slayer either dead or in chains, nothing else!'

PROLOGUE III

The Lion Hall: the Imperial Ottoman Palace in Constantinople: January 1565

In his great marble council chamber, Suleiman, Emperor of the Ottoman Turks, Allah's Vice-Regent on earth, a True Descendant of the Prophet Mohammed, Conqueror of the World, Possessor of all men's necks, sat on his pure-gold, peacock throne, studying the amethyst ring on his finger. On either side of him, hosts of slave girls, beautiful as houris, lifted light feather fans soaked in perfume so that the nostrils of Allah's anointed might catch nothing but fragrance. If only statecraft was so simple! Suleiman ran a finger down his hooked nose, his black unblinking eyes fixed on the three men kneeling before him. They looked nondescript: dressed in Frankish costume, they had posed as sailors, merchants. They had been given his gold, his blessing and his protection to achieve one thing and one thing alone: the capture of the Soul Slayer, that great follower of Satan, that man of magic whom Suleiman so desperately wished to use.

'You failed,' he whispered. 'You were sent out with a task, given to me by Allah, to perform.'

To the men's right, Suleiman's Grand Vizier made

19

to protest as did his two favourite generals on his left, Dragut Rais and Mustafa Pasha. Suleiman snapped his fingers for silence.

'I know what you are going to say,' Suleiman murmured. 'These were your best men yet I sent out seven. Where are the other four?'

'The Soul Slayer killed them.'

One of the men spoke up, desperately wishing he had not returned here. The cold marble floor was hard beneath his knees. Despite the luxury of the chamber, the mother-of-pearl studded pillars, the gold embossed walls, the pots of smoking incense, the thick woollen rugs, the man caught the stench of death. He and his companions had been promised their lives. Now he was not so sure. The man couldn't take his eyes off the Emperor's footstool, a grisly reminder for all who opposed or failed Suleiman. It was the embalmed corpse of a Moldavian prince who had dared to rise in rebellion. Suleiman's Janissaries had captured him, the imperial executioners, the Gardeners, had strangled him in the dungeons below, then his corpse had been cleaned and stuffed with spices to serve as the Emperor's footstool.

The council chamber was now deathly silent. Suleiman stared hard at each member of his council. The Grand Vizier in his cloth-of-gold gown; the Chief Cook wearing a pointed cap in the shape of a bottle; the Chief Armourer who always bore a crimson satin cushion on which rested Suleiman's sword in its jewel-encrusted scabbard; the Overseer of the Sultan's purse; the Keeper of the Nightingales and the Custodian of the Heron's Plume. All stood rigid like statues in their flowing robes and silken pantaloons, their turbans decorated with ostrich feathers, their shoulders covered with fur-lined pelisses. Suleiman lifted his little finger. A white, plump Circassian slave girl immediately raised a jewel-encrusted glass goblet of ice-cold sherbet. Suleiman gestured at her, and the girl drank. She nodded and handed the goblet to her Emperor, who also sipped.

'I sent out seven men to bring back the Soul Slayer.' Suleiman's lips hardly moved but his voice boomed, even reaching the marble courtyard beyond.

'He was as elusive as the wind.' The man kneeling in the centre before him lifted his hand beseechingly. 'He has powers we do not have.'

Suleiman sighed, the sound echoing long and hard, like the evening breeze which springs up at the end of the day.

'A great magician,' Suleiman declared. 'But where does he come from, eh?' He now deigned to look at the kneeling men. 'Where does he come from? Where does he go?'

'We lost him in the German states! Disappeared in the snows!'

'And?' Suleiman asked.

'We were tricked by another, a popish priest, Michael St Clair. He approached us as a friend and gave us false information . . .'

Suleiman's mouth puckered in disdain. He made a sweeping movement with his bejewelled, ringed hand.

'You are no more!'

The three men flung themselves on the floor, their sobs and lamentations echoing through the court but, already, Suleiman's monkey-faced Vizier had turned, snapping his fingers. The black eunuch of the harem opened a door. The courtiers dared not move; they heard his sibilant hiss and the Gardeners, in their tall, conical hats, slipped like shadows into the room. The Grand Vizier pointed to the three prostrate men. The Gardeners went and stood over them. In the twinkling of an eye the garotte strings were round their throats; Suleiman watched them gyrate in their dance of death. Other Gardeners appeared, the three corpses were picked up and quietly removed.

Suleiman leaned his elbows on the arms of his throne, gently stroking his white moustache and beard. His sharp eyes flitted round the council chamber. Had they learned their lesson? Did they not know this his word was law? How dare such men, the mere dust under his feet, return to tell him that they had failed? Was the Imperial Court becoming too relaxed? Did they really believe that Suleiman had grown soft, lost in the perfumed pleasures of the harem while dreaming of further conquests? Suleiman closed his eyes. He had smashed the princes of southern Europe. On the field of Mohacs, the Hungarian kingdom had ceased to exist; his corsairs now controlled the Greek isles and patrolled the Middle Sea up to the gates of Hercules. Only one small rock remained, Malta, with its Hospitaller knights. He glanced sideways at his Grand Vizier. If they could take it, if they could drive the Hospitallers into the sea! From Malta he could attack Italy, France and, once again, pitch the banners of Islam on Spanish soil. Suleiman had dreamed of seeing the green silken banners of the Prophet floating over the Frankish kingdoms of the west. To achieve this he would use everything in his power. He glanced at the Grand Vizier.

'Perhaps more should die?' he asked. 'Perhaps

others should learn not to fail the will of the Emperor.'

The Grand Vizier did not flinch. 'A mere setback, your excellency. Those miserable wretches were both unfortunate and unlucky.'

'They were certainly unfortunate!' Sulemain snapped, his voice high in petulance. 'But unlucky?'

'They had little experience of Frankish lands, unused to their customs.'

'Who chose them?'

'You did, your excellency.'

Suleiman threw his head back and burst out laughing. As he did so the court gave a collective sigh. The great officials, the Circassian girls relaxed. Suleiman rose to his feet, his falcon-like face wreathed in a generous smile. He wagged a finger at the Grand Vizier.

'Never let it be said that Suleiman cannot crack a joke or take one.' His face turned sour. 'Even if it is at his own expense.'

The Grand Vizier bowed again and kept his mouth shut. He knew he had gone far enough.

'I have, your excellency,' he murmured, 'taken steps to hire another.'

Suleiman picked up the goblet and took another sip of sherbet.

'A mercenary,' the Grand Vizier continued. 'A Venetian, Theodore Ragusa.'

'Can he be trusted?'

'For gold, your excellency, such men can always be trusted.'

Suleiman nodded then walked down the golden steps of his throne.

'Bring me this Ragusa!' he ordered. 'But not here.'

He pointed to the small courtyard at the far end of the throne room. 'I wish to listen to the music of the fountain. Bring two of my nightingales. Let them soothe my soul.'

A gong clashed. The courtiers prostrated themselves as Suleiman, the Possessor of their Necks, surrounded by a crack corps of Janissaries, swept through the council chamber and out into the courtyard, to watch the water splash and listen to his nightingales sing.

Theodore Ragusa was a young, thickset man, his face burned almost black by the sun, his well-oiled black hair caught up and bound in a quiff behind him. He slouched in a padded chair and stared across at the four Janissaries dressed in their yellow coats and white turbans. They gazed implacably back.

Is it true, Ragusa wondered, that these soldiers of the Emperor eat hashish and forget all fear? The Janissaries looked all the same with their clean-shaven, olive-skinned faces: rather pretty in a way, with their large liquid eyes, thin noses and sensuous mouths. Perhaps they were brothers? Ragusa stretched out his arms along the back of the quilted couch. One of the Janissaries wrinkled his nose and Ragusa smiled to himself. His hose was sweat-soaked, his boots scuffed, his white shirt was dingy and the leather doublet, together with the cloak he wore, had both seen better days. These were now slung on the end of the couch. Ragusa glanced quickly at a peg on the wall behind the Janissaries. His true possessions hung there: the leather war belt with its sword, dagger, money purse, as well as the small arbalest and the pouch of quarrels he always carried. Theodore patted his thighs and leaned forward.

'I am very thirsty,' he declared. 'I must stink like a dog but I was given little chance to eat and drink, never mind wash and shave.'

The Janissaries stared bleakly back. Ragusa sighed. He had arrived in the city only two days before, having come to collect the final payment for a task he had accomplished. Then, as was customary, Ragusa had celebrated. The money he had received was considerable but, there again, he had earned it. He had travelled all the way to Florence to carry out an assassination, the removal of a business rival, much resented and feared by a merchant banker with houses in Constantinople, Rome, Paris and London. Ragusa had been fast asleep, lost in a drunken stupor, when these Janissaries had burst into the tavern. They'd kicked him out of bed, urging him with signs to dress and come with them as quickly as possible. Theodore never protested. The sight of the Janissaries' razor-edged sabres had persuaded him to cooperate but he didn't like it. Ragusa liked to keep out of the sunlight.

The assassin hid his nervousness. To these men, the only sin was cowardice. If he was in trouble the last thing he should do was beg or plead for mercy. Footsteps sounded outside and the Aga of the Janissaries, wearing a golden sable pelisse, walked in and snapped his fingers at Ragusa.

'I suppose you've come to invite me to the banquet?'

The Aga stared stonily back.

'I was jesting.' Ragusa forced a smile.

'Your jokes, infidel, do not concern me.' The Aga spoke fluent Italian. 'Our beloved Emperor Suleiman wishes, for his own noble reasons, to speak to you.'

He looked the Italian assassin from head to toe, noticing the scuffed, dirty boots, the darned hose and stained shirt. 'Put your jerkin on and a cloak!' he ordered. 'You have no hat? Good!'

Ragusa obeyed. He went to take his war belt off the peg, and a scimitar pricked the back of his neck.

'No one carries arms in the presence of Allah's Chosen One!'

'Of course.' Ragusa's hand fell away. 'I apologise.'

'When you go into the imperial presence,' the Aga continued, 'you will go down on your knees and bow till your brow touches the ground.'

'I will not . . .'

'You will keep your brow to the ground until you are noticed. You have a choice,' the Aga continued. 'Either bow your head or have it taken.'

Ragusa, the Janissaries marching behind him, was led into the palace: his mouth watered and fingers itched at the treasures he passed. Marble floors were covered with rich textured carpets. Gorgeous Persian tapestries hung on the walls; they entered chambers full of plush velvet divans covered with tasselled gold hangings and satin silk fabrics. Exquisite vases and other ornaments stood in niches. Glowing pots full of fragrant perfume hung from the ceiling. The palace was like a mausoleum, where only the sound of their footsteps broke the silence. Soldiers stood everywhere. Janissaries on the stairs. In the corridors and entrances to rooms, Mamelukes, dressed completely in white, broad scimitars pushed through the red cords round their waists. In the courtyards mailed Sipahis lounged about with archers patrolling the parapets. Officials, in their different turbans and hats, flitted by, quiet as mice.

They passed through the council chamber. As they did so, a side door opened and Theodore's mouth went dry. He recognised the imperial executioners, the Gardeners, who were carrying stretchers. Each bore a sack tied at the top. These were corpses, to be taken down to the quayside and tossed into the Bosphorus. The Aga smiled at Ragusa's concerned look.

'Tread warily, foreigner!' he whispered. 'Your life is my master's and your neck simply a stalk in the wind!'

Ragusa decided he would behave himself. They went out into an enclosed marble courtyard. In the centre a fountain sprayed coloured water high in the air, the sunlight transforming it into a brilliant rainbow of colours. Janissaries stood on all three sides, shields in one hand, drawn sabres in the other. Against the far wall a low-slung divan had been set up, piled high with silken cushions. Ragusa glimpsed the Emperor's harsh, brown face and neatly clipped white goatee beard. He was led past the fountain. The Aga stopped and pressed him on the shoulder. Ragusa immediately fell to his knees and pressed his forehead against the wet marble stone. As he did so, Ragusa became aware of the silence, broken now and again by the lucid song of a nightingale.

'Beautiful, is it not?' The voice was low and carried. 'It catches the heart and soothes the mind.'

The Emperor was speaking the lingua franca Ragusa would understand. He felt the toe of the Aga's boot in his ribs.

'You may approach,' the man whispered. 'On your hands and knees but, keep your eyes down!'

Ragusa did, swallowing his pride as he scurried like a dog. He stopped before a cushion.

'You may sit there,' the Aga commanded. 'Do not lift your head until his excellency deigns to notice you.'

Ragusa obeyed with alacrity.

'I have noticed you, foreigner.'

Ragusa raised his head. Suleiman was sitting directly opposite him. On either side two slaves wafted two huge perfumed fans. Standing behind the Emperor, Ragusa recognised the small, wizened face of the Grand Vizier. The assassin's eyes fell away; he and the Grand Vizier had done business before but not in such opulent surroundings.

'How does he know you?'

Ragusa's heart skipped a beat. Suleiman was now looking over his shoulder at the Grand Vizier.

'I saw it in his eyes. He recognised you.'

'He is someone.' The Grand Vizier's eyes never left Ragusa. He talked slowly, choosing his words. 'He is someone who can be trusted with a delicate task.'

'Then come round and sit before him,' Suleiman teased. 'And tell him about our delicate task.'

The Grand Vizier obeyed. Ragusa let out a sigh of relief.

'You are not to be punished.'

The Grand Vizier squatted on a cushion before his master's divan. Ragusa caught the look in his eyes – the Grand Vizier did not want the 'delicate task' entrusted to Ragusa some months earlier to be mentioned.

'Tell him about the Soul Slayer,' Suleiman retorted. 'Or, at least, what has happened so far.'

'Master Ragusa.' The Grand Vizier spoke the lingua franca, lifting his voice so his master could hear his words. 'Have you heard of the djinn?'

'Your name for demons?'

'Very good.' The Grand Vizier pushed his hand up the voluminous sleeve of his gown. 'In our legends we believe such creatures live out in the desert places. They are lost souls but, now and again, such demons enter the world of man by offering powers, gifts, bribes.' The Grand Vizier sighed. 'The Soul Slayer is one of these. Only Allah knows where he comes from. Legends abound about him. Many years ago, on the edges of our empire, along the road to the great kingdoms of the east, where the yellow-faced men rule like lords, this demon appeared: a great magician or magus. At first it was gossip in the marketplace, rumours in the bazaar. Our envoys reported him in Tashkent on the banks of the Tigris, in Cairo and even further south in the hot, searing deserts beyond the Nile. Then he disappeared.' The Grand Vizier lifted one elegant shoulder. 'Vanished from the affairs of men, only to reappear in the snowy wastes of Russia. At first these reports provoked little interest at our court. However, the more we learned, the more our interest grew.

'A short while ago as our armies came back from another victorious foray against the infidels to the north, one of our prisoners, an orthodox priest, gave us details about this demon and his powers. A man who can shift his shape or appearance, who has entered a compact with Satan himself. A man who kills, taking the heart of his victim then calls upon the soul of that victim to do his bidding.' The Grand Vizier waved a hand. 'This is the least we know. He may be even more powerful but that would be only speculation, not fact. Now, my master,' he bowed his head, 'whom Allah bless, chose seven Janissaries, men skilled as spies, to hunt this Soul Slayer down. They pursued him through the country of the German princes across the frozen seas. He is now in England but we guess that one day he will return.'

'And what has that to do with me?' Ragusa asked.

The Grand Vizier looked over his shoulder. Suleiman, leaning against the cushions, nodded imperceptibly, watching this western mercenary from under his heavy-lidded eyes. Suleiman was assessing the worth of the man. He had scrutinised this foreigner from head to toe: the Grand Vizier had chosen well. Ragusa was a mercenary and a killer, his deep-set eyes, the cruel twist to his mouth showed that. He might assume the graces of a dandy, a court fop with his oily hair and tidy moustache and beard, but Ragusa was deeply interested in the Grand Vizier's tale: it showed in the toying with the buttons on his jerkin, the constant licking of the lips as if Ragusa could sense the lavish reward which would be on offer. A man without a soul. Suleiman smiled. A most suitable hunter for the Soul Slayer.

The Grand Vizier gestured at an official who approached bearing a small casket. The Grand Vizier opened this and Ragusa sighed. It was crammed with pure gold coins which winked and glowed in the light of the sun. His hand went forward. The Grand Vizier knocked it away.

'This is only half,' he murmured, 'of what you will earn if you bring the Soul Slayer back.'

'Alive?' Ragusa asked.

'Alive,' the Grand Vizier confirmed.

Ragusa's eyes never left the gold. 'I want expenses.'

'You will be well furnished with silver as well as

with letters of credit. Merchants are only too willing to advance coins on behalf of our master.'

'I know what you are thinking.' Suleiman didn't even bother to lift his head. 'Master Ragusa, you may be tempted to take the treasure we give you and disappear.'

Ragusa shook his head.

'Well, if you are not thinking of that now,' Suleiman added drily, 'you will when the hunt begins.'

'You have my oath.'

'I'll have your head,' Suleiman replied softly. 'If you take this commission, if we accept your oath, if we pay you gold and you fail. You shall see how long our arm is. Whether you hide in the frozen wastes of Russia or the boiling sands of Arabia!'

'I am to bring the Soul Slayer,' Ragusa declared, ignoring the threat. It wasn't the first time such menaces had been uttered. Ragusa lived for each day; he would cross that bridge when he came to it. 'Why,' he added drily, 'do you need him?'

'The doings of my master,' the Grand Vizier replied, 'are not your concern but, first, let me assure you, his threat is not an idle one.'

'If this Soul Slayer is such a powerful warlock,' Ragusa looked at the Grand Vizier and not Suleiman, 'how can he be captured?'

'He is still a man, of flesh and blood. He must sleep and he must eat. He can be strong but he grows weak. His pact with the powers of darkness is based on murder and sacrifice. His victims are many for he must kill often. How you capture him,' the Grand Vizier pulled his hands out of his sleeves, 'is a matter for you. To do so you must first get close. However,' the Grand Vizier went on, enjoying himself, 'you are

31

not the only one hunting him. You see, the Soul Slayer must cross this prince's territory and then another. As he does so, he kills. He would prefer to do this secretly but, of course, as time passes, he brings himself to the attention of the authorities. The Prince of Moscow, who calls himself the Tsar, now knows of him.'

Ragusa smiled. Ivan the Tsar would have more than a passing interest in such a demon-possessed man. Was not Ivan himself a man of the devils?

The Grand Vizier paused and beckoned a young slave boy over. He took the cup of sherbet from the gold-embossed tray and sipped from it.

'However, others hunt the Soul Slayer. A popish priest, Michael St Clair?'

Ragusa shook his head. The name meant nothing to him.

'This Jesuit has had more success than anyone in tracking him down. Those who return here having failed, decided that, if they followed Michael St Clair, he would eventually bring them to the Soul Slayer. In the beginning it was a wise decision but, in the end, the popish priest fooled them and led them astray.'

'And why should the Jesuits,' Ragusa asked, 'be so interested? At the behest of the Pope in Rome? Surely this would be a matter for the Inquisition?'

'From the little we have learned,' the Grand Vizier replied, 'this Michael St Clair is secretive. His aim is not to capture the Soul Slayer but to destroy him: that must not happen.'

'How?' Ragusa interrupted.

'We know very little about Catholic practices,' the Grand Vizier sneered, 'but the destruction of the Soul Slayer can only be carried out by a virgin. A woman who has no carnal knowledge of a man, pure in body and pure in soul.'

'In which case,' Ragusa jibed, 'his task of finding one in the cities of Europe will be most difficult.'

The Grand Vizier did not smile. 'St Clair is a redoubtable opponent as our agents have found to their cost. Tell me, Ragusa, where will you start?'

The mercenary narrowed his eyes against the sun.

'I have to think, plot,' he murmured. 'But, if our quarry has fled to England, then he must visit London. I'd wager my head that I'll find him there.'

'Master Ragusa,' Suleiman declared. 'Your wager has been accepted!'

Part I

Death only this mysterious truth unfolds.
The mighty soul, how small a body holds.

Juvena
Satires X

1

Dunmow, Essex: January 1565

'Hare-shotten! You've run with the hares and you've kissed them under a full moon!'

Rebecca Lennox turned in exasperation at the two scruffy urchins following her along the cobbled road leading up to the parish church of St Michael's in Dunmow. She moved the basket of herbs from one arm to another and stared soulfully at these imps from hell.

'Hare-shotten!' One of them stepped forward, his face spiteful and mean.

Rebecca pulled back the napkin covering the basket. She took out two thin pieces of sweetmeat.

'You are right,' she said. 'But, hare-lipped or not, I still bake the sweetest marchpane.'

The imps looked at her in astonishment. They did not expect this response. When they baited old Mother Wyatt, the half-crazed witch who lived along the forest path on the other side of Dunmow, she always wagged her stick at them. Rebecca held her hands out. Both urchins went to grasp and she caught their fingers. They gazed up, fear replacing insolence as Rebecca squeezed.

'Why are you so cruel?' she asked. 'Does it give you such comfort to see a maid cry?'

'You are hurting us,' one of them whispered.

He stared at this tall, elegant young woman. She was dressed in a brown smock which covered her from neck to toe, an old, round hat on her head. The boy was mistaken: her upper lip was twisted but she wasn't ugly! Her face was ivory pale; her auburn hair, soft and freshly washed, falling down to her shoulders. Yet it was her eyes which fascinated the boy, sea-grey, much at variance with her colouring. The boy's stomach rumbled in fear. He recalled the stories, how Rebecca Lennox had the second sight. Her eyes were now boring into his, not sharp and cruel like Master Thackeray's the schoolmaster, but sad and thoughtful. She let go of their fingers.

'Take the marchpane,' she told them. 'And, if you come back tomorrow, I'll give you some more, on one condition.'

'What's that?' The boy asked.

She stroked his greasy, spiked hair. 'Don't play down at the river!' Rebecca glanced up at the grey, lowering clouds. 'There's been much rain and the water's swollen.'

The boy backed away, glancing fearfully at his companion. How did the woman know that? They were planning to go there later to catch an eel or a fish without being noticed.

'It will be dangerous for you,' she warned. Rebecca smiled, trying to hide the image of these young boys swirling in the treacherous whirlpools. 'Promise me you won't. Indeed, if you come to the Silver Wyvern just after dark, I'll give you some more marchpane.'

The boys nodded and backed away. Instead of

running towards the river, they scampered away in their ragged smocks to see how far they could bait old Mother Wyatt.

Rebecca sighed and pushed open the four-gabled lych-gate. For a while she sat on the corpse stool. She put her basket down and rubbed the side of her head.

'I wish that wouldn't happen. Yet it comes so quickly!'

One moment she was clasping those boys' fingers, the next she saw them being tossed about by the water, the green slime rushing through their mouths, choking off their breath. Rebecca sighed, picked up her basket and stared along the path leading to the main door of the church, a serene place with the lime trees on either side. Through these Rebecca could glimpse the tumbled gravestones and the outstretched arms of the ancient yew trees, planted, so local lore had it, centuries ago to keep the cattle out as well as provide the wood for the bows and arrows of the archers.

Rebecca studied St Michael's church. A long, simple affair with crumbling steps going up to the iron-studded doors, it boasted a few rounded windows, the rest being mere arrow slits. They said the church had been built long before the Conqueror came, the transepts added later as well as the high, square tower that housed the bells, Mary and Clarence, which always tolled, summoning the people of Dunmow to God. Old Mother Wyatt had told her many stories how, before King Henry had broken with Rome, markets used to be held in the cemetery, church-ale was sold and the nave was often used for pageants and plays. Now all had changed. Henry had died and the Duke of Northumberland's men had come and smashed the painted windows and taken down all the statues except for one, the reason why Rebecca had come here.

She walked up the pathway. The main door was locked so she went to the small postern door which stood opposite the ossuary or charnel house which ran along one side of the church. A grim, stark building, the charnel house, with its small doors and shuttered windows, was a place of dread. The cemetery was so old and filled with so many victims of the plague and other tribulations which visited Dunmow that, every so often, the cemetery was cleared: old coffins dug up and their bones tossed into the charnel.

Rebecca had visited it on a number of occasions. She had seen the skulls stacked along the shelves, the bones and other fragments piled high in shabby wicker baskets. Many in the parish wanted the place to be burned down. They saw it as a grim reminder of popish practices and the charnel house, so the whispers said, was often used by warlocks and magicians who stole the bones and ground them down to powder for their philtres and potions.

Rebecca pushed down the latch and sighed in relief as the door swung open. She walked into the sombre, eerie atmosphere of the gloomy church, across the transept and into the area before the sanctuary. The old rood screen had gone but she could still see the gaps in the floor which had once held the posts. The altar had also been demolished. The niches around it, where statues had once stood, were now empty, dusty shelves. The tabernacle and sanctuary lamp had gone; now there was only the communion table, the priest's chair and the lectern carved in the shape of an eagle. The paintings on the wall, which old Mother Wyatt had described as brilliant and full of life, had been whitewashed over.

In the side chapel to the left of the altar, the statue of the Virgin and Child had been pulled down and smashed with hammers. Now it was used to store pews, benches, and the old cracked stools which were put out in the nave for Sunday service. Rebecca walked down the nave. It was dark except for the slivers of light coming through the windows. She always closed her eyes when she reached a certain spot, and she did so now, before turning right.

'One, two, three, four . . .'

When she had reached ten, Rebecca opened her eyes and sighed with satisfaction. Her statue was still there. For some strange reason, when Northumberland's men had removed the stained-glass windows and other remnants of popery, the villagers had stopped them when they came to this, a life-sized statue of St Michael the Archangel. It stood on a plinth between two windows in the transept, carved out of wood and painted by an artist long buried in the churchyard outside. The statue was so lifelike Rebecca felt the young man depicted there was flesh and blood and, if you stared long enough, those brown eyes would move, the lips would speak. The sculptor had fashioned Michael not with wings or shining, white gown; instead he was dressed like a knight in chain mail over which a surcoat with a red cross on it was placed. Around his slim waist was a jewel-encrusted sword belt carrying sword and dagger. One mailed hand rested on the hilt of the sword, the other was held out as if about to offer help to someone.

Rebecca had never seen such a beautiful face with long black hair hanging down just above the shoulders and well-formed features but it was the eyes, full of affection and compassion, and the mouth . . . Rebecca glanced away. Now she was being fey! She could be accused of talking to the bees as they buzzed around their hives but she did wish she could climb up and kiss those lips, touch that olive skin.

'I love you,' she whispered.

The statue gazed back.

'I'm Rebecca Lennox.' She always made the introduction. 'My mother has died but, when I was a child, she used to bring me here. My father is Bartholomew, landlord of the Silver Wyvern. I wish I could light a candle.'

Old Mother Wyatt had told her about the custom. How, before Northumberland's men came, you could always buy a small candle and place it in front of your favourite statue or patron saint. Rebecca gazed over her shoulder down the darkened church. She had to make sure she was by herself.

'I've brought you a gift,' she said. 'As you are my Valentine.'

She took out the bunch of freshly cut snowdrops from her basket. She placed these at the base of the statue just above the inscription carved from the Book of the Apocalypse.

'I saw a young man coming out of the rising sun and on his head he bore the mark of the living God'.

It was written in Latin but Rebecca could understand it. Her father had been most generous in sending her to the village school equipped with quill, inkpot and horn book, yet it was her mother who had translated this. Rebecca screwed her eyes up. How old was she now? Just on the verge of her eighteenth summer. Mother had died when she was five but Rebecca still had clear, precise memories of her, tall and elegant, always smelling sweetly of herbs and spices. Her favourite colour was blue, sometimes murrey, and she always wore a crisp white apron round her waist. They would walk here, just about now, in the mid-afternoon when the village was at its quietest.

After she died, as Rebecca grew older, she'd question her father but Bartholomew Lennox had, over the years, grown more sour and tight-lipped about his dead wife. Rebecca learned what she had from those who gathered in the huge taproom and, as she helped her father, would ask questions or draw others into conversation.

Father was, by birth, a Scotsman with distant ties to the great Lennox clan. He had been a priest but, when John Knox had purged the Kirk, Bartholomew Lennox, with a pot of silver, had fled south across the border. His wife Margaret Hardwicke had been of good yeoman stock with lands somewhere in south Lancashire. Bartholomew had wooed and wed her before travelling south to Dunmow where he had bought the Silver Wyvern tavern. Rumour had it that Margaret Hardwicke was a papist and, every so often, would slip away to a house Mass or some other secret meeting of her coven.

Rebecca looked up at the statue. Mother had told her all the legends about Michael. How his name was Jewish for 'who is like unto God'. How, at the beginning of time, before God had created the world, Michael had led God's armies against Lucifer and the rebel angels.

Rebecca sighed and got to her feet. She patted the snowdrops once more and glanced up at the

Archangel's face. She was going to say something else, talk about Mother, when she heard the door of the church open. Doddering Parson Baynes, dressed in his shabby gown, his ash cane tapping the flagstones, tottered into the church.

'Who is there?' He called querulously.

Rebecca hid behind a pillar.

'Who is there?' Parson Baynes came closer.

Rebecca repressed her giggle. Parson Baynes had grown so old, it was true what the village children said of him: with his balding head and scrawny neck, he looked like a chicken and walked like one. Yet he was kindly and did his best for the souls in his care.

'Come on now!'

Rebecca cupped her hand round her mouth.

'I am a ghost!' she called, trying to make her voice sound hollow and sepulchral. 'I am the ghost of Vicar Thirkle!'

Old Thirkle's tomb was at the back of the church, a hideous affair with an effigy of a skeleton over which poisonous toads, maggots and vermin slithered in chiselled stone sculpture. Thirkle was supposed to have died insane. Many claimed to have seen his shade amongst the tombstones and yew trees in the grave yard. Rebecca peeped round the pillar. Parson Baynes gazed wonderingly about.

'Oh for goodness' sake, it's only me!'

Baynes stepped out of the shadows, tottered closer, head out, eyes peering.

'Goodness girl! Goodness! Why, Lord save me, it's Rebecca.' He fumbled in his dirty jerkin and placed a pair of spectacles on the end of his nose. 'Why, Rebecca Lennox, that's a terrible trick to play on an old man.'

44

'Oh, parson!' Rebecca laughed. 'Thirkle's long dead and you know it. Though, there again,' she added mischievously, 'he might always come back.'

'Well, I won't be here. I'm off to live with my sister in Royston.'

He opened his mouth to speak again, then closed it. He trusted Rebecca, who could be mischievous but was kindly. She always brought him fresh bread and spicy cheese from the tavern and, whenever he went there, thanks to her, rather than her surly father, he ate free of charge. He looked across at the statue of St Michael.

'You are a strange one, Rebecca.' He walked by her, resting on his cane, and inspected the statue. 'You brought the snowdrops?' He turned slowly. 'You know that's forbidden, to pray before statues and images?'

'I wasn't praying. I was talking. It's such a beautiful statue!'

'It was once a beautiful church.' Baynes hobbled back. 'Beautiful, Rebecca,' he whispered. 'I was here, you know, as a young curate, many, many years ago. The windows were full of glass.' He pointed to the sanctuary. 'Mass was celebrated, the clouds of incense rising like small puffs of prayer to the Almighty. Now it's all gone. We were told it was wrong. We had to take the oath.' He studied Rebecca's face, he felt so sorry for her. She'd be quite pretty if it wasn't for that twisted upper lip. Sometimes Parson Baynes felt like rubbing his finger along it as if he could wipe out that terrible crease.

'I shall pray for you, Rebecca.'

'Do I need it, parson?'

He drew closer, dragging his cane.

'Sometimes, Rebecca, I wish you were more careful.'

'About what?'

'Don't be pert!' Parson Baynes snapped, banging his stick on the floor. 'You know full well what I am talking about! Your father is a wealthy man, that's envy! Some men would like to tumble you. Aye, I won't spare your blushes, and, because of your poor mouth, they think they'd be doing you a favour, that's lust. But, there's something worse than these, Rebecca, fear!'

'Fear?'

Baynes studied her troubled, sea-grey eyes. Rebecca was no longer smiling or being impudent.

'Yes, Rebecca Lennox, fear! People are frightened of you with your hare-lip, your solitary ways, your wandering in the woods. And you know . . .?'

Rebecca stared icily back.

'Your second sight,' Baynes declared. 'It's common knowledge you have it, Rebecca. The list is growing by the month. John Smallwood, remember him? You warned him not to take the journey to Codwood Hall, to be wary of outlaws. Knocked senseless the poor man was, beaten and bruised for months. Or old Mother Repton? You told her to be careful with fire in that cottage of hers.'

'That was just common sense.'

'Was it really? Was it common sense that you warned her to be most careful around Michaelmas and, on the eve of the 24th of September, her cottage was engulfed in flames?' Parson Baynes pointed to the statue. 'And there's that, the popish relic they call it. Oh, the villagers know you come here to talk to it. They say you are fey, hare-bitten. Be

46

careful, Rebecca, I have also heard the word "witch" whispered!'

Parson Baynes had told her nothing new. She had heard such tittle-tattle in the inglenook of the tavern, the strange looks, the whispers behind the hands, the mice-eyed stares of some of the women as they passed her in the high street. But what could they do?

'Go on, Rebecca.' Parson Baynes grabbed her hands. 'Would you tell me my future?'

Rebecca thought he was jesting but the old, rheumy eyes were pleading.

'Will I ever get away from here?' Baynes asked.

'Parson, you're going on Saturday.'

Rebecca squeezed his fingers. As she did so, she saw a room in a house, white-plaster walls interspersed by black timbers. Parson Baynes was lying on a bed. A woman in a brown smock with a large mole on the side of her cheek was feeding him broth. She was chatting to him, and in the far corner was a wooden statue of the Virgin and Child. It was so clear, like a memory of something which had recently happened.

'Your sister will look after you,' she replied enigmatically. 'She'll fuss you. Bring broth soup up to your room.'

'Is that all?' Baynes asked.

Rebecca wished to be more prudent but she caught the challenge in the old man's tone.

'Has she always had the mole on that cheek?' she asked. 'And, like you, Parson Baynes, is she a secret follower of the old faith? Is that why she has a statue of the Virgin in one of her upper rooms?'

Baynes' face paled. 'How did you . . .?' He gasped.

'A mere picture,' Rebecca replied.

She rubbed the side of her head. She wished she could tell this old priest her real dreams.

She went and sat in the bench beside the pillar of what the old folk called the 'shriving pew'. Years ago the priest would sit on the other side and listen to confessions. Rebecca wished there was someone to hear hers. The parson followed her over and sat down. He knew this young woman was no witch but he was old, his bones ached, his nose was constantly stuffed, his head ached with the rheums. What solace could he offer? He felt like a stranger in his own parish.

Parson Baynes had never really left the old faith. In the early hours his apostasy weighed heavily on him, deadening his soul, troubling his spirit, but he would be gone in a few days. The new parson would be arriving soon.

'Be careful, child.' Baynes patted her on the hand. 'Just be careful.'

'I have dreams,' Rebecca said before she could stop herself. 'Sometimes at night I have hideous nightmares. I am in a land where the snow stretches as far as the eye can see. I am walking with someone through the snow, fleeing from dark green-fringed trees where demons dwell. A wolf comes out, slipping like a shadow at eventide, low and menacing. Others join it . . .'

'Just a nightmare,' Parson Baynes intervened.

Rebecca shook her head. 'No it comes back too often, too precise. The air is cold, biting like a knife. We fear those trees. The wolf comes loping towards us and the air is shattered by its horrid howls.'

'And then?'

'The dream changes. I'm in a fortress built amid a sea of grass. The air is filled with the noise of battle.

48

Men are standing on the walls of the castle. A sea of yellow-coated men, huge swords in their hands, are racing towards us.'

Parson Baynes tapped his stick on the stone floor.

'One day, Rebecca,' he sighed. 'One day it will all be explained!' He wheezed and got to his feet. 'But come now. Oh.' He touched his forehead. 'I forgot to tell you the news.'

'About the new parson?'

'No, not about him, I'll be gone by then. I've hired a carter to come on Saturday afternoon to load my baggage and take me away.' He sighed. 'I don't suppose anyone will come to see me off. My parishioners will be as glad to see the back of me as I of them.'

'I'll come.'

'Thank you.'

'But your news?'

The old man gazed sadly up at the altar.

'The Queen's man has come to Dunmow.'

Any other time Rebecca would have been mildly interested but she went cold as if the church door had been opened and an icy blast blown in.

'He's not a scurrier,' Baynes continued. 'He's a Judas Man.'

'What?'

'A Judas Man.' Baynes' face grew harsh, his eyes took on a faraway look. 'The Judas Men are royal agents, they hunt down Catholic priests and those who harbour them. Cart them off to Colchester, or London, so they can dance on the gallows.'

'And is a Catholic priest around here?'

'Aye, a Jesuit. You've heard of them?'

Rebecca nodded. Who hadn't? The news-sheets

from London proclaimed the activities of these sly, subtle priests of the Roman Church. They slipped into the country to spread sedition and treason, or so it was said. They enticed people from their faith and worked to bring the country back under the influence of Rome and the power of Spain.

'So, there's one in the neighbourhood?' Rebecca asked.

'According to the proclamations posted on the gallows and the market cross, Michael St Clair, a Jesuit, is wanted dead or alive. A reward of one hundred pounds silver for his capture.' Baynes glanced back towards the sanctuary. 'I did not realise saying Mass was so dangerous,' he jested. 'I wonder what he's really done? They never offer so high a price for a man's head. Ah well, this is a wicked world.'

'Parson Baynes?'

He turned. 'Why yes, child?'

'What would you do if St Clair was hiding in your church?'

Baynes bit his lip. 'I'd go back to my priest's house and bring some bread and wine, then I'd tell him to be gone by morning. Do you know what happens, child, to those who help a priest? Taken to the gallows in Colchester; hanged till they are half-dead before being cut down, their bodies sliced open, their heart and entrails plucked out like a flesher cleans the carcass of a pig. Afterwards your corpse is cut up, put in a barrel of pickle and, together with your head, exposed over the city gates.' He shook his head. 'It's no way for an old man to end his life. And it's not a story for young ears. I have to go. I must lock the church. I don't want any Jesuits hiding here!'

Baynes was already at the door when Rebecca turned.

'What?' she called. She had heard the words so clearly, not in her mind, as if someone were chanting.

'What's the matter, girl?' Parson Baynes came back into the church.

'Didn't you hear it?' she asked. 'It came from the sanctuary.'

'What did?'

'The words. They were in Latin: *'Confiteor Deo omnipotenti. . .'*

Baynes tried to hide his nervousness.

'I confess to Almighty God,' he whispered. 'To Mary ever a virgin and to Michael the Archangel . . .' He paused. 'Are you sure, child? They are the words a priest used to say at the beginning of Mass.' Baynes, troubled, insisted that Rebecca accompany him back into the gloomy sanctuary to search about; they found nothing.

'Just ghosts,' Rebecca laughed.

Parson Baynes didn't hear her. He was looking at the statue of St Michael and, though he didn't tell the young woman, he noticed that her white snowdrops had disappeared.

The young tavern wench in the Merry Pig tavern which stood on the road leading into Chelmsford bustled across the busy taproom, a brimming tankard in each hand. She swung her hips provocatively and flounced her long red hair. She reached the table and put the tankards down, allowing the men a good view of swelling breasts under her low-cut bodice. She loved to see men lick their lips, their fingers itch to hold what they couldn't. She kept herself to herself. Red-haired Meg could be accommodating but for a price and only for gentlemen of quality, like the one sitting in the far corner watching her intently. He was young and sallow-faced, his greasy black hair swept backwards, his moustache and goatee beard neatly clipped. Meg considered him a foreigner but his English was courtly, his manners correct. He was dressed in dark clothes but the quilted jacket was slashed to display white satin while the shirt was clean and the collar crisp and edged with lace. Meg thought he was a parson except for his hot-eyed stares. No parson should look at a woman like that!

Meg moved around the tavern, bringing tankards, joking with the customers, smacking hands that clawed at her bottom or tried to dip down her bodice. Meg knew she was a fine figure of a woman with her white, swan-like neck, trim ankles and body every man in that tavern would love to play with. Yet Meg was oblivious to all this. She felt like a hawk flying above a corn field: her quarry was that silent man in the corner with his heavy, jingling purse and courtly ways. Sooner or later Meg must swoop. If it wasn't him then it must be someone else before that drunken constable staggered into the tavern to tell the landlord to douse his fire and put the shutters up.

'Do you want another pot of ale, sir?' Meg stopped in front of his table.

The man's black eyes studied her carefully.

'Aye, I'd like a pot! And, perhaps, a pie but let the rabbit be freshly cooked. I can tell filth as soon as I sees it!'

Meg bridled at the imputation but smiled sweetly enough. Now was the time if this stranger was to rise to the lure. Later on, as he struggled to push back her petticoats, she would have her revenge.

'Is there anything else, sir?' Meg's green eyes rounded in innocence.

'What else could I want?' The stranger picked up his purse and shook its silver into the palm of his hand.

'You shouldn't do that, sir!' Meg was genuinely alarmed. 'Brigands and thieves prowl the roads.'

The man pointed to the leather sword belt on a stool beside him.

'It would be a brave man indeed, Meg, a real roaring boy, to come hunting me. And yes, I would like something else, a little company.'

'I'm busy, sir.'

'If not now, then afterwards?'

'I have a garret upstairs.'

The stranger glanced by her at the greasy-aproned landlord standing behind the large tuns of wine outside the scullery.

'I'll wager you have,' the stranger replied. 'And a bed to match with little peep-holes in the wall, eh?'

Meg blushed. The stranger could read her thoughts: Taverner Melton allowed her to entertain strangers, provided he took a share of the silver and a good view of what happened.

'There's the stables,' she whispered. 'Across the midden yard, it's warm and dry, the straw is freshly laid.'

'Then I'll meet you there,' the stranger replied.

Meg spent the rest of the evening in a dreamy, absent-minded way. She couldn't believe that pile of silver. Recalling the stack of logs in the stable she smiled to herself: it wouldn't be the first time one of her customers woke up with a cracked pate and an empty purse. Indeed, with Taverner Melton as a witness, who would bring charges? Who would even be bothered to listen?

Meg was relieved when the constable staggered in, blowing on his whistle, drunkenly tapping his staff on the ground. The customers ignored him until Taverner Melton brought in his two great mastiffs then drained their tankards and went out, shattering the night air with their cries and good wishes.

Meg slipped out of the postern door at the rear of the scullery. The cobbled yard was deserted, empty, but she hadn't seen the stranger leave. Surely he would be waiting for her? Meg prided herself on her looks and her skill. It was not every night that she made herself so available. She went across to the stable door and opened it yet she couldn't see anything in the warm, musty darkness. She turned and stifled a scream. The stranger was standing behind her, hat on, cloak about his shoulders.

'You're looking for me, Meg?'

She slipped her arms round his waist, pressing her body against him.

'Of course,' she whispered. 'I thought you'd be here.'

'I've prepared a better place,' he replied and, taking her by the hand, led Meg out of the yard across the lane. He helped her over the ditch into the field. She could make out the faint outline of the copse. 'I have a nice warm bed there,' he murmured, nibbling at the nape of her neck.

Meg slipped her hand down towards his groin but he deftly knocked her away.

'Come!' he urged. 'Into the trees!'

Meg paused. 'Are you sure?'

Despite her work in the tavern, she had never visited the copse.

'There's a woodcutter's hut, derelict but warm enough.'

He grabbed her hand and they entered the trees. The stranger's horse was hobbled outside the hut, a lantern beside it. The stranger picked it up.

'I borrowed this from your tavern.'

In the flickering light, his face looked even more handsome, white, even teeth, eyes dancing with merriment. The woodcutter's hut was warm and dry with a bed of straw in one corner. Meg was soon lying on her back, skirts pulled up, her legs round the stranger, gasping and struggling beneath him. When he had finished, Meg got up and picked up her woollen cloak.

'I'd best go back.'

She didn't feel so confident now. The stranger had been strong as a stallion, showing no signs of drunkenness while his sword belt and purse had never been out of his sight. Meg pulled her hood up.

'My favours aren't free,' she declared crossly.

'Who said they were?'

Meg was spun round. The stranger's hand was across her mouth as his other thrust a dagger deep into her neck.

2

Rebecca took her broom and walked out of the main door of her father's tavern. The morning mist still hadn't lifted. It swirled about obscuring the market cross, the gallows, whipping post and stocks and even the stalls at the far side. Rebecca breathed in. It was the same every morning, only the weather changed. Up before light, then down to the scullery supervising the maids and slatterns, cleaning up the mess from the night before, firing the ovens, so the bread could be baked. The taproom had to be swept and scrubbed, the great fire lit and meats prepared for the spit.

'I'll be out in the brew house!'

Rebecca turned. Her father, Bartholomew Lennox, was standing, tally book in hand, ink horn and quill strapped to his belt.

'You look tired and harassed.'

Rebecca crossed the taproom. She was about to ask him why he hadn't slept well but bit her tongue. What her father did at night was his own business. She had heard the whispers and wondered which maid he'd been tumbling.

'You are drinking too much.'

Rebecca rubbed her finger along the stubble on his chin. People often said how, in his youth, Bartholomew Lennox had been a handsome man, but now he was running to fat. His square face had become podgy, the determined chin loose with fleshy jowls. His eyes were red-rimmed and weary; his black hair, streaked with grey, was dishevelled and unwashed.

'What's the matter, Father?' Rebecca grasped his hand but Bartholomew refused to meet her gaze.

'Nothing, nothing at all.'

Rebecca pointed to the tally book.

'Is all well? Are the accounts in order?'

Her father turned away, muttering under his breath.

'You shouldn't listen to them.' Rebecca followed him across the taproom.

'Listen to whom?'

'You know full well! The customers and their mad-cap schemes of investing in this, investing in that!'

Rebecca paused as a pot boy scurried across bearing a tray of empty tankards.

'Father, you are a taverner and a good one. The Silver Wyvern makes a handsome profit. So, why invest in futile ventures?'

'You are just like your mother.'

'What does that mean?'

Bartholomew made to turn away but Rebecca seized his wrist, thick and strong, digging her nails deep into the skin. Her father's troubled, light-blue eyes filled with tears.

'She used to do that, you know. Grab my wrist and, if I didn't listen, dig her nails in.' He sighed and sat down at a table, Rebecca opposite. 'I am worried,' he began. 'I and a few others, merchants from Ipswich, fitted out a ship for the salt-fish trade in the northern seas. It's a costly venture but the returns could be good.'

Rebecca's heart sank. Her father was a shrewd

businessman when it came to running the Silver Wyvern yet he was attracted to risky schemes like a mouse to cheese.

'And the venture failed? Oh, by the way,' Rebecca tapped him on his chest, 'before you do anything, Father, go upstairs: wash, shave and change.' She sniffed. 'And rub your teeth with some salt and a little vinegar: I can still smell the ale on your breath. So, the venture's failed, hasn't it?'

'Scottish pirates,' he replied. 'They attacked the ship off Leith. The captain and crew are dead. The ship's a prize in the port of Edinburgh and there's little we can do about it.'

'Promise me, Father, any further ventures and you'll ask my advice first?'

Bartholomew was no longer listening. He was staring at a point behind her. Rebecca turned. A man stood in the doorway, cloaked, booted and spurred, a black broad-brimmed hat in his hands. Rebecca stood fascinated. The man's hair was as white as snow. He had the face of a boy except when she looked closer and noticed the lined, harsh mouth, the furrows in the cheeks.

'Can I help you?' Bartholomew Lennox got to his feet. 'I am the landlord here. Heavens, sir, you move like a cat!'

The man smiled but the eyes constantly flickered about as if memorising every detail in the taproom. He walked slowly forward, the spurs on his leather boots jingling. He threw his cloak over a table and unhitched the broad sword belt.

'William Cowper,' he said. 'And you are the landlord?'

'I've said as much!'

Cowper's strange ice-blue eyes moved to Rebecca.

'My daughter,' Bartholomew explained. 'Rebecca.'

'I need a chamber, stabling for my horse and food whenever I require.'

He flicked a silver piece. Bartholomew let it fall on the rushes before him. Cowper seemed amused by this. He scratched his chin and, leaning down, picked up the coin.

'I meant no insult, sir.'

'None taken.'

Cowper took another silver coin out of his jerkin pocket.

'I'll be staying for some time.'

Rebecca could see her father did not like the stranger. She rose and deftly plucked the coins from Cowper's fingers.

'You must be tired, sir.' She led him to a bench. 'It's still early in the morning but we have . . .'

'Roast chicken,' Cowper requested. 'I'd like the meat neatly shredded, a goblet of watered wine and something hot, broth, yes?'

Rebecca agreed. She gave her father the silver and hurried off into the kitchen. At the doorway she stopped and threw Bartholomew an angry glance but he had already turned away.

Rebecca herself prepared the meal. She sliced the white meat, sprinkling it with a few herbs, and took from a linen cloth some of the bread they had baked the previous evening. She found a jug of watered wine and filled a goblet. When she returned to the taproom, Cowper had loosened his doublet and was studying a piece of parchment which he put away as soon as Rebecca appeared.

'You have travelled far, sir?'

'I was going to ask that question.' Malbrook the parish constable waddled into the taproom, a pompous, red-faced, little man, full of his own importance. 'I'd heard there was a stranger here.'

Cowper didn't even lift his head. Malbrook raised his cane, slamming it down on the table only inches from Cowper's hand.

'Do that again,' Cowper said, 'and I'll take that stick and thrash you within an inch of your life!' He took out the piece of parchment and held it up for Malbrook to see. 'I am the Queen's officer, William Cowper. Last night I stayed at Lord Fitzwarin's.'

Malbrook swallowed hard and blinked at the name of one of the country's most powerful and ruthless magistrates.

'I am sorry, sir,' he gabbled.

Cowper took a sip from the goblet. Malbrook backed away.

'No, no!' Cowper pointed to the stool beside him. 'Do sit down, the girl will . . .'

'My name's Rebecca.'

Cowper's eyes smiled. He studied her hare-lip and Rebecca wondered if it was compassion or curiosity in his eyes.

'We are rather alike, you and I, Rebecca,' Cowper mused. His gaze went to Malbrook. 'A tavern wench with a hare-lip and a Queen's officer who is an albino.'

'My daughter is no tavern wench.' Bartholomew came back in. He threw the tally book on the table. He nodded at Malbrook and went over to one of the barrels where he filled two blackjacks of ale and brought them back. 'I thought you were a Queen's

61

man.' Bartholomew sat down at the other end of the table, sipping at the ale.

Malbrook gulped his, as he sat, furtive as a rabbit, mesmerised by a stoat closing in for the kill.

'You are sharp-eyed, taverner.'

'That's why I came back,' Bartholomew declared. 'I knew you would want a word with me. Oh, and by the way, my daughter doesn't take orders, she's the lady of the house.'

Cowper glanced at Rebecca and smiled.

'I'll remember that.'

'You are a Judas Man,' Bartholomew continued. 'We heard you were in the area. You can always tell a Judas Man, Master Cowper, by his walk, the arrogant way he throws silver like others would sprinkle herbs. You are hunting a priest, aren't you, the Jesuit?'

Cowper leaned back and burped gently, patting his stomach.

'That's the best chicken I've eaten for many a day, fresh and tender.' He licked his fingers. 'You are correct, master taverner! I am hunting Michael St Clair, a Jesuit priest who, contrary to the law and customs of this realm, has come to draw her majesty's faithful subjects from their allegiance. Last night I rested at Lord Fitzwarin's manor. He is organising the sheriff's posse. They will be arriving later and be quartered in other taverns and alehouses either in or around Dunmow. You, Master Malbrook, will now answer directly to me. I want the names of any papists, strangers or anyone who arouses your suspicions. I will be quartered here.'

'What makes you think St Clair is in Dunmow?' Rebecca spoke up.

'Just a feeling,' Cowper answered, sipping at the watered wine.

'It's more than a feeling,' Bartholomew said. 'Dunmow is a resting place for those travelling to and from London yet it's also surrounded by fields and woods, a good place to hide.'

'The very truth!' Cowper broke up the bread in his hands.

Rebecca noticed how long and slender his fingers were, like those of a woman. His skin was soft and white but the wrist was muscular. A swordsman, she thought, and repressed a shiver. Many men stopped at the Silver Wyvern, soldiers, merchants, sailors from the eastern ports, beggars, even outlaws, men who lived in the twilight of the law. Cowper was different and dangerous, a man totally sure of himself, confident in the power he wielded. He wouldn't threaten or bluster, he'd simply act. Was it because of his strange looks, Rebecca wondered? Did he see himself as different and therefore superior to the rest of human kind?

'Well spoken, taverner.' Cowper ran his tongue round his teeth. 'Always trust a taverner, they know the roads. You, sir, will be of great assistance to me.'

'I, sir,' Bartholomew got to his feet, 'will be running my tavern.'

'Is it true you were once a priest?'

Bartholomew turned round. 'I am the Queen's faithful subject.'

'Of course you are.' Cowper toasted him with his wine cup. 'And make sure you stay faithful!'

'Rebecca!' Bartholomew called, choosing to ignore Cowper. 'Your horse Minette, it needs feeding, doesn't it?'

Rebecca took the hint and walked out into the great cobbled yard behind the tavern. One side was the back of the Silver Wyvern, the other three sides comprised outbuildings and stables with a small wicket gate in the wall, the rear entrance into the village of Dunmow. The place was a hive of activity; barrels and vats were being rolled out of the brewing house. The wash house was busy with the slap of cloths, the shouts and laughter of the women. Grooms were leading horses out, hitching up a cart so they could journey to the village to buy supplies. One stable boy was walking a huge, black destrier up and down, cooling it off before he put it in one of the stables. This, Rebecca surmised, must be Cowper's horse.

'A veritable steed for the devil,' she murmured.

She stopped at the door where she kept her own horse Minette, a brown palfrey Father had bought at last summer's horse fair in the fields outside Dunmow. She undid the lock and went into the warm, sweet-smelling stable. Minette snickered as she came in; eager for its morning food, the palfrey nuzzled its mistress. Rebecca laughed and relaxed, stroking the horse between its ears. She kept Minette separate from the rest, her father's one small indulgence to her. Rebecca went across and opened a chest and filled a leather bucket full of feed. She was about to go back when she noticed the ladder leading up to the hayloft to one side of the stable had been pushed away. Rebecca froze: no one came in here, only she had the key. She stepped back and looked up. Above the hayloft was a window, usually shuttered, but this now hung loose. The window was large enough for a man to squeeze through.

The back of the stable overlooked the fields leading

to the stew ponds where her father, to the delight of local poachers, bred his carp and tench. It would be easy for someone to cross that field at night, climb the wall using gaps in the brickwork, slide a dagger under the bar, open the shutters and crawl in. Rebecca put the bucket down, listening carefully. She wanted to run out, call her father, even that dreadful Judas Man feeding his face in the taproom.

'Is there anyone there?' she called. 'You have a choice. Either show yourself to me or I go back to my father. He's the landlord and he'll bring the Queen's man who's staying in our tavern.'

Silence.

'Of course,' Rebecca continued, feeling rather foolish as she might be speaking to no one. 'You can wait till I am gone and then crawl back through that window but, I assure you, you won't get very far. I am going now.' She turned, her hand on the latch.

'Wait!' The word was whispered.

A dark shape appeared at the top of the hayloft. She made out closely cropped hair, a youngish face. He was dressed in peasant's clothing, a brown jerkin and breeches.

'I daren't come down,' he whispered. 'But, mistress, I mean you no harm. For the love of God, don't deliver me into Cowper's hands!'

'You are Michael St Clair, the Jesuit?'

'Yes. I am also very tired and very hungry. For the love of Jesus Christ, help me!'

Rebecca went and moved the ladder.

'I am coming up,' she whispered hoarsely. 'But, if you hurt me, I'll scream!'

Rebecca, heart thudding, climbed the ladder. The man helped her into the hayloft, almost dragging her back against one of the bales. His face was unshaven, his eyes red-rimmed and puffy from lack of sleep. He had cuts on his hands and face, his hair was dishevelled but Rebecca could only stare. It was astonishing. It was as if the statue of St Michael in the church had come to life. If the Jesuit was washed and shaved, the similarity would be even more striking: the same black hair, those soft and gentle eyes, the full lips and firm chin, the youthful yet wary look on his face.

'Are you frightened, mistress?'

Rebecca noticed the priest staring at her lip.

'Do I frighten you?' she teased. 'They call me hare-lipper, a witch.'

Her hand grazed the priest's. Abruptly Rebecca's dream came flooding back, those images which haunted her; the great open white expanse, the dark-green forest and then that fortress in a sea of grass. She rocked backwards and the priest seized her by the arm.

'Mistress, are you all right? I didn't mean to frighten you.'

'I'm well.' Rebecca rubbed her face. 'It's nothing.'

'Can you help me?'

'If I do, I'll hang.'

'And, if you don't, I will.'

Rebecca knew what she was going to do.

'What do you need?' she asked.

'I need food and drink.' The man pushed back his sleeve and displayed the red, angry gash on his left wrist. 'I'll need some ointment and a bandage. Above all, I need to rest. If I could stay here one, two days?'

Rebecca stared open-mouthed at this strange young priest. If Cowper took him he'd die horribly on the gallows at Colchester, his body racked and broken, cut up like a piece of pork into collops while people stood and bayed for his blood.

'My name is Rebecca Lennox.'

'Yes, I know.'

'What do you mean?'

The priest shrugged. 'Nothing. I gained intelligence about the area from the Catholics I've stayed with. Tell me, Rebecca, has Parson Baynes left his church yet?'

She shook her head.

'Please!'

He grasped her hand, his touch warm and soft. Rebecca felt a tingle of excitement in her stomach. If he came any closer, if he tried to kiss or touch her, she wouldn't resist. She felt guilty, for the man was a priest and weren't papist parsons sworn to a life of chastity?

'I also have another great favour. After Parson Baynes leaves, a man will come to his church, the new vicar Henry Frogmore. When he arrives, you must tell me. You must take me to meet him.'

Rebecca drew back. 'I must? I must do nothing, sir!'

'Please!' He seized her wrist again. 'For the love of God, Rebecca!'

Rebecca became alarmed. Behind the priest, in the far corner, she saw the leather war belt carrying dirk and sword in their sheaths.

'I'll think about it,' she replied. 'But stay here. I'll bring you some food. Only I ever come in here.'

Rebecca climbed back down the ladder. Halfway down she paused.

'If the worst comes to the worst and there's danger, I'll sing a song.'

'What song?'

'Summer is icumen.' She smiled. 'I will be singing it outside, then you'll know it's time to leave. If you have to flee, go down past the carp pond, across the trackway into the woods. If you travel for about half a mile, you'll come to a clearing. Stay there and I'll come to you.'

'You are very brave, Rebecca. You are right, they could hang you.'

'They'll have to catch me first,' she replied impishly and scampered down the ladder.

Rebecca opened the stable door and locked it behind her. She felt excited rather than frightened. For the first time in her life something very dramatic was going to happen. She could understand now why men played hazard or dice. The losses might be great but the game and the throw were all. She couldn't forget that face, the gentleness of the Jesuit. She could no more hand him over to Cowper than she could Minette to the slaughterers. So, agitated and yet fearful of Cowper's strange scrutiny, Rebecca went out across the field and sat by the carp pond. The day mist was still heavy, cloaking all sound, making her feel as if she was cut off from the tavern and the rest of the village. She hitched her cloak around her. The Jesuit needed three things: rest, food and information about the new parson Henry Frogmore. Now why should he need that? Rebecca stared down at the reeds, watching the bubbles as the perch, tench and carp nosed to the surface hunting for food. Perhaps Frogmore was secretly a papist? Or he might know the way of getting the Jesuit out of danger? Yes, it must be that!

Today was Thursday. Baynes was leaving on Saturday. Frogmore would probably arrive either just before or after that, which meant the Jesuit might stay two, perhaps three, days. Rebecca swallowed hard. She recalled catching a butterfly years ago and taking it back to her house. Her father had told her to let it go. Rebecca knew she should but it was so beautiful, so precious that she wanted to keep it. The same was true of the Jesuit. Because he looked like the statue, her favourite saint? Or was that just her imagination? Was she bored with the Silver Wyvern; her father's troubles, the petty tedium of each day? The arrival of the two strangers had shattered that. The Jesuit was definitely her friend but was Cowper her enemy? In a way Rebecca felt a strange kinship with the Judas Man. He was disfigured. Perhaps being a Queen's officer was his way of breaking out, building a barrier against the insults and the finger-pointing of others.

Rebecca rose and walked slowly back over the field. When she returned to the taproom, Cowper had gone. A slattern said that he had hired the best chamber and taken Malbrook up to wring as much information out of the constable as possible. Rebecca nodded. She collected her basket from inside the scullery door and said she would cut some more herbs but she felt a little hungry so she would take some food. Surreptitiously, Rebecca went round the kitchen, filching a piece of bread, some dried meat and cheese, and took a small wineskin off a hook on the back of the door. She filled this from a tun and went back into the stable yard, even busier now the farrier had arrived to shoe horses.

'Do you want me to look at Minette?' he bawled,

his fat, red face glistening from the heat of the forge.

'No,' she shouted back. 'Perhaps next time.'

Rebecca walked into the stable and, holding the basket carefully, climbed the ladder and put the food out.

'It's the best I can do for the moment,' she told the priest. 'Tonight I'll bring ointment and fresh bandages for your cut. Till then, wash it with the wine, that will help.'

She was going down the ladder before St Clair whispered his thanks.

'If you need to use the jakes,' she hissed back, 'I am afraid you'll have to wait until dark and leave by the window.' She blushed. 'For the rest, you'll be safe. I won't betray you.'

Rebecca went back into the tavern, deliberately busying herself with different tasks, keeping an eye on Cowper who was now making his presence felt. Malbrook had been busy bringing in villagers with the reputation of being recusants, those who refused to go to church. Despite her father's protests, Cowper insisted on questioning these in the taproom. He was curt and sharp though it was apparent these villagers did not concern him. All he wanted was information about St Clair and someone else. At first Rebecca couldn't discover who. However, by coming in and insisting on sweeping or polishing, as well as offering a goblet of watered wine or a blackjack of ale to those poor unfortunates waiting for Cowper, Rebecca realised the Judas Man was, in truth, hunting someone else, a mysterious stranger.

Friday came and went. Rebecca visited the stables a number of times, taking ointment and bandages in a basket as well as more food. She even managed to smuggle across a razor, a piece of their precious Castilian soap and some hot water. Her conversations with the fugitive were always hurried and short. Rebecca was fearful of Cowper, especially as some of the sheriff's posse had joined him, hard-bitten, tough characters used by the shire court to hunt down outlaws and those who tried to abscond beyond the reach of justice. They swaggered round the tavern exercising their petty power but deferring obsequiously to Cowper of whom they seemed terrified. The Judas Man himself was courteous to Rebecca though once, as she came back from the stables carrying her basket, she caught him studying her closely. His pink-rimmed eyes seemed to bore into her mind and Rebecca wondered if he had begun to suspect.

By Saturday morning she was more guarded in what she did, often waiting till Cowper was fully immersed in his business before entering the stables. Thankfully her father, whose routine had been completely upset by the new arrivals, hardly paid her any attention. He spent most of the day grumbling under his breath and, at night, sat with his cronies around the fireplace at the far side of the taproom. No one liked papists, that was the common gossip, but Cowper was equally unpopular and becoming more feared by the day.

'There's more to this than meets the eye.' Constable Malbrook winked and tapped the side of his fleshy nose. 'They are not just hunting a renegade Jesuit priest but someone else. For the life of me I don't know who. Cowper knows but all he asks is about strangers, anyone who has provoked suspicion.'

Rebecca listened and wondered if there was a closer

connection between St Clair and his pursuer than he had revealed.

Late on Saturday afternoon, Malbrook informed her that a cart had drawn up behind the priest's house and Parson Baynes was preparing to leave.

Rebecca hurried along the high street to St Michael's church. She crossed the cemetery and hastened along the narrow, rutted lane which led to the priest's house. The front door was open. Parson Baynes was supervising the loading of chests and coffers onto a cart pulled by the sorriest looking nag Rebecca had ever seen. When the parson espied Rebecca, he smiled and raised his hand.

'I'll be gone soon,' he explained, his tired face wreathed in smiles. 'I'll have a good supper on the road and I'll be in Royston by tomorrow.' He stared across at the dark mass of St Michael's. 'I'll be glad to leave here.' He whispered, drawing closer. 'I've met the Judas Man. He came here to see me but I had little to tell him. Will you come and visit me, Rebecca?'

'Of course. Father can take me there.' Rebecca tried to sound honest but felt guilty because she knew she was lying. She would never see Parson Baynes again. 'And has the new vicar arrived?' she asked.

'Yes, my child.'

A man stood in the open doorway. He was tall and slim built, his black hair hanging down just above his shoulders, lank like dyed flax. In his narrow, pointed face, the beard and moustache closely cropped, cavernous eyes were accentuated even more by the high cheekbones, and his swarthy skin was pitted with scars. Rebecca shivered. Those eyes were like glass, hard, unblinking; the smile on the lips was false and twisted. He came down and grasped her hand.

'You are the first parishioner I have met.'

'Master Henry Frogmore.' Baynes hastened to make the introductions though he kept his distance as if nervous of his successor.

Frogmore's eyes never left Rebecca's face, a lewd look, as if he was assessing her worth. Rebecca was sure that, if Baynes hadn't been there, he would have touched her breasts.

'I must be going.'

Rebecca stepped back and fled up the narrow lane, her face flushed with embarrassment as she heard Frogmore's low, throaty laugh behind her.

3

Rebecca locked the stable door behind her and climbed the ladder.

'He's here!' she exclaimed.

'Frogmore?' St Clair came out of the gloom, his eyes bright with excitement. He looked younger, stronger since she had first met him. 'You are sure it's Frogmore?' he added excitedly.

'Yes and I don't like him!'

St Clair took the basket. 'Why not, Rebecca?'

'I'm no judge of character but I think he's an evil man, lewd in look and manner. But, it's not just that.' Rebecca leaned against the hay bale. 'Despite my lip, there are those who come to the tavern and look me up and down as a farmer does a heifer at a fair.'

St Clair drew closer. 'What then, Rebecca?' he asked softly.

'He's mocking. Yes, you have the impression that he's laughing at you.'

'Sharp of wit and sharp of eye.' St Clair took the basket. 'You are a rare woman, Rebecca. Keen-witted, brave and beautiful.'

Rebecca found she couldn't stop the tears pricking her eyes.

'They say flattery is a perfume,' she retorted. 'You smell it but you don't drink it.'

75

St Clair edged closer. 'I don't flatter, Rebecca, I tell the truth.'

'Then,' Rebecca teased back, 'are you going to say my beauty is more than skin deep? I heard a merry chapman tell me a similar tale.'

St Clair leaned forward, grasped her chin in his hand and squeezed gently.

'I never lie, Rebecca Lennox. You are the most beautiful woman I have ever met.'

Rebecca stared, dry-mouthed. The priest's hand was warm and soft.

'I don't want you to leave,' she whispered, the words out before she could stop them. 'Please!' The tears brimmed in her eyes. 'Don't go! Don't leave me here! I get tired of cleaning the house, putting vinegar down for the fleas, serving the ale and doing the accounts.'

St Clair took his hand away and lifted the napkin on the basket.

'What are these?' He picked up the small bunch of snowdrops wrapped in a blue ribbon.

'A posy, my gift to you!'

St Clair looked away. 'I want one last favour, Rebecca. When it is dark, I will leave. I want you to saddle a horse and bring it into the cemetery at St Michael's. Leave it near the charnel house. It must be saddled, ready for use, but hobble it carefully.'

'At what hour?'

St Clair looked towards the shuttered window where the streaks of daylight were dying.

'When the candle reaches its twentieth ring.' He grasped her shoulder, his other hand going to the back of her head; he pressed her forward and kissed her on the brow. 'God be with you, Rebecca Lennox.'

She went down the ladder a little faster than she intended and landed with such a thump, Minette, startled, neighed in protest. Rebecca, blinking furiously, pushed open the stable door and, slamming it shut, locked it behind her. She turned and almost walked into Cowper. He was just standing, dressed in his black leather jacket, the shirt beneath open at the neck. He had his cloak slung behind him, and his sword belt clinked as he stepped back.

'Why the haste, girl?' He grasped her by the shoulders. 'You visit your horse a great deal.'

'It's not a horse,' she declared defiantly, breaking free. 'It's a palfrey, her name's Minette.'

'I'd like to see it.' Cowper walked towards the door.

Rebecca found it hard to control the thumping of her heart. Her stomach pitched so violently she felt nauseous, weak in her legs.

'She's not well,' Rebecca replied, coming after him. 'I, I nurse her myself. Tomorrow she will be better and you can watch me ride.'

Cowper stared at the door.

'Rebecca! For the love of God, must you daydream all day?'

Rebecca's heart skipped with joy as her father came out of the tavern, sleeves pulled up.

'For heaven's sake, girl, it's Saturday evening. Master Cowper, you may dally with the maids but not with my daughter!'

Rebecca ran across the cobbled yard. She embraced her father and smiled up at him.

'I'm glad you came out,' she whispered.

Her father looked sadly down at her.

'So am I,' he murmured. 'You seem to spend a lot

77

of time tending Minette. Is it safe?'

He narrowed his eyes and Rebecca realised her father suspected the truth.

'I'll not see a man hang,' he warned. 'But, for my sake, Rebecca, be careful!'

Rebecca heeded her father's advice. Cowper followed her back into the taproom where Rebecca busied herself making sure her father's flagon and those of Cowper's posse were constantly replenished. She kept an eye on the hour candle, its flames edging slowly downwards. When the time was right and Malbrook and his gaggle of cronies were busy flattering Cowper, Rebecca slipped out of the tavern. She quickly saddled one of the mares and left by the postern gate. She carried no lantern. Once she was away from the tavern, Rebecca crouched down and used rags to muffle the horse's hooves. When she reached the church, the horse, a docile mount, became restless, rearing its head. Rebecca had to soothe it by letting it nibble at the sugared apple she carried.

The church was shrouded in darkness. In the light of the full moon the yew trees with their outstretched branches looked stark, frightening creatures against the night sky. Near the charnel house Rebecca had to calm her own fears and anxieties. Both she and the horse jumped as a crack echoed from inside. Rebecca remembered how the place was overrun by rats and other vermin with skulls and bones being constantly knocked off the shelves. She hobbled the horse, gave it the rest of the apple and stole across the cemetery, making her way carefully past the weather-beaten headstones and crosses. She reached the priest's house but the place was in darkness.

Rebecca crouched, puzzled. Surely Frogmore was

here? And where was St Clair? She was certain the
Jesuit had used the cover of darkness to steal out of
the stable. Rebecca listened to the sounds of the night:
the scratch of some bird, the crackling amongst the
bracken at the far end of the cemetery. She turned
and glimpsed the light glowing from the church. She
hurried back to the horse, which was quietly cropping
the grass. She checked the saddle and the leather bag
of food fastened over the saddle horn. All was in
place. Rebecca then stole along the side of the church
and, using gaps in the brickwork, climbed one of the
buttresses and stared through the arrow-slit windows
into the sanctuary.

Parson Frogmore was seated at the communion
table singing softly to himself but this was no divine
service. The altar was a banquet table. The candles
had been lit, the cross had been removed and the
new parson was sitting in the high-backed sanctuary
chair feasting and drinking. Rebecca moved so she
could get a clearer view. For some strange reason
she feared for her statue but it was too dark to see
what the new parson had done. The more she stared
the more frightened she became. The priest's house
was spacious enough yet Frogmore had chosen the
communion table for feasting and revelry, a mockery
of everything he should hold sacred. The parson had
taken off his long, black cloak; his sleeves were
rolled up, his collar open at the neck. He bit into
a piece of chicken, smacking his lips as he slurped
from the chalice now used as a wine cup. Every so
often he would rock himself backwards and forwards,
humming and smiling to himself. On at least two
occasions he glanced quickly at the window. Rebecca
crouched down, sure that this strangest of parsons

knew she was there. He must have heard her with the horse in the cemetery yet he seemed more concerned with his blasphemy than anything else.

Frogmore knew he was being watched but he didn't care. When the sacristy door opened behind him, he didn't even bother to turn.

'I like it here,' he declared quietly. 'There's nothing I like better than an empty church, a spacious communion table and a silver chalice to drink your wine from.'

'You commit blasphemy, Frogmore.' Michael St Clair walked into a pool of candlelight.

'Blasphemy?' Frogmore turned slightly, the goblet held ever so delicately between his fingers. 'How can I blaspheme when I don't believe one jot, one tittle about what prating priests like to mumble?'

He looked at St Clair from head to toe and smiled at the way the Jesuit kept his distance, sword and dagger in his hands.

'What's this, Michael? Have you come to kill me?' He raised his eyebrows in mock fear. 'But you can't do it by yourself. Or have you brought the virgin, that maid with the hare-lip? Is she the person I heard outside?' Frogmore put the chalice down. 'Have you told her to come?' He whispered. 'And aren't you frightened, Michael? Master Cowper might pursue me but he's also hunting you. I know what,' he continued playfully, pointing at the chicken and wine. 'Shall we say a Mass? Somewhere round here there's a little bell. You can be the priest and I'll be the altar boy. I've always wanted that job, Michael, to be kneeling behind you.'

St Clair crouched in a fighting stance, sword and dagger coming up.

'Oh, St Clair.' Frogmore sighed. 'Why do you have to spoil things? I come to the wilds of Essex for a rest, rejuvenation and yes, some mild recreation. I want to be a pastor for a few weeks. I could teach these noddle-pates a thing or two.'

'You're a demon,' St Clair retorted. 'You're a demon who loves the darkness. You came here for the blood, the sacrifice.'

'How long have you been hunting me?' Frogmore refilled the goblet. 'Year after year. You are becoming a nuisance, St Clair, you know that? You are an arrant knave. I can give the others the slip but, when I stop and look over my shoulder, there's always St Clair.' He pointed down the church. 'Have you seen the statue? A lovely piece of popery!'

'Get up!' St Clair ordered.

'I'll be with you in a minute,' Frogmore sighed. He was easing himself off the chair and then, with one quick movement, he knocked the chalice sideways in the direction of St Clair. Frogmore threw himself across the sanctuary, picking up his own sword and poniard which he'd left on a bench. By the time St Clair was round the communion table Frogmore was waiting. He stood languidly, watching St Clair out of the corner of his eye.

'When was the last time we fought, Michael? Kiev, wasn't it? Or am I getting it mixed up? Was it Cologne where the so-called one thousand virgins are buried? Not like that time outside Rome, eh?' He moved, sharp and quick, striking out with his sword.

St Clair blocked this, sword and dagger coming together. The church rang with the slap of feet and the clash of steel, the quick indrawn breath of the combatants.

Outside, Rebecca watched, heart in her mouth as both men parried and thrust, moving swiftly round the sanctuary, each looking for an opening. She knew little about swordsmanship but she recognised both men were master duellists. Frogmore, particularly. That long piece of pointed steel seemed an extension of his arm. Rebecca found it difficult to control her breathing. What happened if St Clair was wounded or killed? The combatants drew apart. Frogmore moved his dagger to his sword hand and he did something so quickly Rebecca couldn't believe it.

'Those things done in the dark,' he mocked, 'will one day be seen in the light. Not now, eh Michael?'

Raising his hand, Frogmore pointed at the candles. They were snuffed out, plunging the church in darkness. Rebecca heard a shout and the clash of metal. She jumped down from the buttress, wiping sweaty hands on her smock, and ran to the front of the church. The main door was open. She heard a sound and looked over her shoulder to see pinpricks of torchlight moving up the trackway. Had Cowper suspected something? Was he bringing members of the posse here? Rebecca threw herself inside the doorway and ran up onto the steps where the bell ropes hung. She seized these, the coarse rope scoring her hands. The bells, Clarence and Meg, began to toll, splitting the night air with their clanging, the peal of the tocsin. In the church the sound of fighting died. Rebecca came out of the bell tower: the candle had been relit. Of St Clair there was no sign though Rebecca glimpsed the side door open. Frogmore was now hurrying about clearing away the mess, sweeping up the chalice, the traunchers and plates, bundling them into an altar cloth. Rebecca ran outside. By the time she reached the charnel house, St Clair had already unhobbled the horse and was mounted.

'Michael! Michael!'

St Clair urged the horse forward. He leaned down, his face drenched in a sheen of sweat.

'You rang the tocsin, Rebecca?'

'I watched the fight but people were coming from the village. I was frightened the Judas Man would take you.'

'If I had wounded Frogmore it would have been worth it. You were there, weren't you?'

Rebecca nodded.

'I thought you would be. In fact.' He sat back up in the saddle and muttered something.

Rebecca was sure that he said: 'You had to be there.' Voices carried on the night breeze.

'I was worried,' Rebecca said. She tried to seize the reins but St Clair moved away. 'I was worried about Frogmore, what he did to the candles.'

'Petty tricks, Rebecca.'

St Clair urged the horse forward then, in one swift fluid movement, he leaned down, picked her up, kissed her full on the mouth and let her down gently.

'Au revoir, Rebecca.'

Turning his horse, St Clair made his way out through the rear gate and into the country lanes.

Rebecca climbed up the crumbling buttress and stared through the window. Frogmore was now dressed in his dark-grey priest's gown. He stood quietly by the lectern; of the feasting or the fight there was no sign. Rebecca moved and watched the others come up the nave, Constable Malbrook, Cowper and members of his posse as well as her father and other menfolk from the village.

'Can I help you?' Frogmore's voice was soft and welcoming.

Cowper stepped in front of him.

'We heard there was trouble here, parson. Someone said they saw a light in the church window. I thought we should investigate. When we reached the bottom of the lane the bell started tolling.'

Frogmore stepped down from the sanctuary and walked towards them.

'Yes, yes, that was me. I came into the church to say my prayers. Two men were hiding here.'

'Two men?' Cowper queried curiously.

'Yes, I couldn't see who they were. I shouted out: What were they doing here? Why had they lit the candles?' Frogmore shrugged. 'I am a man of prayer, not a thief-taker, so I decided to sound the tocsin.'

'And these two men?' Cowper asked.

'Fled into the night, probably ruffians, outlaws. I'm glad you came. Now, sirs, this is God's house, I must prepare the church for divine service tomorrow.'

Rebecca could see that Cowper would have liked to stay and question the vicar more closely but Frogmore deftly shooed them away. Rebecca climbed down and hurried across the cemetery. She hid behind the tombstone. When the church fell silent, she stole out and, following her own secret route, returned to the Silver Wyvern.

Rebecca avoided the taproom and fled up to her own chamber on the third floor. Locking the door, Rebecca took off her dress, which was dusty and stained. She washed her hands and face, put on her night shift and climbed into the small poster bed her father had bought from a carpenter in Chelmsford. For a while she sat staring into the darkness remembering everything she had seen and heard.

Why had St Clair tried to kill the parson? What was so important that he was prepared to sell his life, provided Frogmore himself was killed? And how could Frogmore extinguish the candles so quickly? Some mummer's trick? A fairground ploy? Both men had apparently met before. Kiev? Yes, that was it. Rebecca recalled a sailor who had sailed the Northern Seas talking of such a place while Cologne, so her father had once told her, had been a great place of pilgrimage in the old days when the Pope had ruled Europe. Rebecca chewed her lip. And did Frogmore know she had been there? She recalled his hooded, brooding eyes and repressed a shiver. What had St Clair meant, and she was sure he had said it, that 'she had to be there'? Rebecca remembered being lifted up. St Clair kissing her. She laughed softly to herself: that was her dream. When she sat beneath a tree and fashioned a buttercup chain, she would narrow her eyes and pretend that a knight, very similar to the statue in the church, would come over the lea of the hill, gallop down, pick her up and passionately kiss her. But the dream had always continued. The knight would always put her on the crupper of his saddle and take her to his palace.

Rebecca nestled down between the blankets. What sort of palace? Where Mother was? Where the sun always shone? Where she didn't work in a tavern where men drank till they dropped or knelt vomiting into the rushes? Where Father was good and upright as he once was, and did not sit with the other topers in a corner until, his belly full of ale and his crotch full of lust, he would lumber up the stairs to pester one of the maids? Would St Clair return? He had said 'au revoir'.

Rebecca's eyes grew heavy with sleep. She heard the door creak and opened her eyes. A figure stood there. At first Rebecca thought it was her father but the man turned and, in the candle light on the stairwell, Rebecca glimpsed Cowper the Judas Man.

Everyone was much taken by Parson Frogmore. The service the next morning was clear and well ordered, not like old Baynes who mumbled the psalms and leaned against the pulpit, droning on until most of the parishioners nodded off to sleep. Frogmore came down the sanctuary steps, his robes clean and smart, his hair well oiled. He moved along the nave nodding to his parishioners, his face wreathed in a smile of welcome. He caught Rebecca's glance where she and her father sat on a bench near one of the pillars; he grinned mischievously and winked. Rebecca couldn't believe his impudence. Here was a man who, last night, had sat here mocking this place, drinking and eating as if it were some taproom before provoking a fight to the death with that fugitive St Clair. Now he moved amongst his flock like the Good Shepherd. Rebecca realised Frogmore was making fun of them all. Indeed, the reading he chose was Christ's words about wolves in sheeps' clothing. After he had finished, Frogmore launched into a vibrant, colourful sermon about the dangers of those who preyed on Christ's flock. He must have glimpsed Cowper and other members of the posse at the back of the church. Frogmore exhorted his parishioners to assist the Queen's justice in hunting down heretics and schismatics, those traitors who entered the Queen's realm to suborn the allegiance of her subjects.

Now and again Rebecca caught her father looking at her strangely, as if he sensed something was wrong.

At the end of the service Rebecca made her father stay while she went up and stared up at her statue. People passed her. She heard their muttered curses about 'Romish practices', Malbrook loudly declaring that it was time that statue went once and for all.

Frogmore was standing on the steps outside shaking the hands of his parishioners, promising that he would visit them at his earliest convenience. He laughed and joked with Osbert the fuller, Jack and his brood of ploughmen, even old Mother Wyatt.

'We'll have a feast soon,' Frogmore declared. 'A banquet to celebrate my arrival! A new beginning for the parish of St Michael!'

The parishioners, gathered at the foot of the steps, cheered him so loudly the crows whirled up from the black, gaunt trees around the church. Rebecca, holding her father's hand, went to slip by the parson but she felt a hand on her shoulder. Frogmore smiled down at her.

'It's Rebecca, isn't it? Rebecca Lennox?' His other hand came out. 'You must be Bartholomew, her father. I've heard so much about your tavern.'

Bartholomew clasped the parson's hand and shuffled his feet in embarrassed pleasure.

'I'd like a word with you, Rebecca.'

'I need you in the tavern,' Bartholomew muttered.

Frogmore's grip tightened. 'I won't be long, I assure you.'

'I'll be back soon,' Rebecca said, not wishing her

father to be drawn into a confrontation with this sinister stranger.

Bartholomew made to object.

'Go on . . .' she continued. 'I'll be back before you know it. And check the cheese in the buttery! It should be ready for use. Remember to use yesterday's bread first!'

Bartholomew walked down towards the lych-gate. Rebecca followed Frogmore along to the priest's house. She had been here before. Old Parson Baynes had kept an untidy house. Now it was swept clean, the stone-flagged passageway was scrubbed. The same had happened in the small kitchen at the far end of the house. A merry fire burned between the two ovens, the kitchen table looked as if it had been freshly washed and the air was sweet with the smell of roasting.

'Do you have a maid?' Rebecca asked.

Frogmore pulled back the bench alongside the table and gestured at her to sit down.

'You'd like some wine?'

Before she could answer, he brought her a cup with a jug of water. Rebecca poured in a generous mixture. Frogmore sat opposite. Crossing his arms on the table he watched her.

'You rang the bell last night, didn't you?'

Rebecca sipped carefully; the wine tasted warm and rich.

'Yes I did.'

'So, you know St Clair?'

'I never said that, I just became frightened. I saw two men fighting.'

'So you don't know who brought the horse?'

Rebecca refused to meet his gaze.

'And will you tell people what you saw?'

88

'Parson Frogmore, I may have a hare-lip but I am not hare-brained!' She put the cup down. 'Why did you fight?'

'Oh, Michael and I were old friends. Once we had a bitter falling out. We wouldn't have really hurt each other.'

'That's not what I saw. At least, before the candles went out. How did you do that?'

'Oh, a trick, a breeze, a draught.' Frogmore shrugged. 'Would you like something to eat?'

'I'm not hungry. I really must go.'

'Are you a virgin?'

Rebecca stood up. 'That is my business.'

Frogmore leaned across and gripped her hand. Rebecca noticed how long and clean his fingernails were. They reminded her of the talons of a hawk her father once owned.

'Sit down, sit down, please.' He smiled. 'I meant no offence.'

'I am not betrothed and no man has known me,' Rebecca answered tartly.

Frogmore stared round the kitchen.

'You asked if I had a maid, Rebecca. I could do with your assistance. You are intelligent, sweet . . .'

She hesitated. 'I have duties in the tavern.'

'There'd be other things as well,' he added. 'Do you resent your hare-lip, Rebecca?'

'I was born like that.'

'I saw a picture once. I think it was in Rome when I was on my travels. When Michael and I were comrades in arms.' Frogmore lowered his eyes and smiled to himself. 'You remind me of that picture, Rebecca.' He leaned across the table and, before she could stop him, stroked her hare-lip, soft like the touch of a butterfly wing. 'Such things can go, Rebecca. They can be cured.' He got up and came back with a small burnished hand mirror. 'Look, Rebecca, see the future. A future in my service.'

Rebecca gasped at her reflection. The hare-lip was gone, her lips were full and red, the rucked skin above her forelip was no more. She stared up.

'What?' she exclaimed.

'You are looking at what might be.' Frogmore's voice had a dream-like quality about it. 'All things are possible, Rebecca. All dreams can be made real.'

Rebecca stared again. She couldn't believe it and felt a thrill of excitement.

'Rebecca!'

Her father had come into the house and was standing in the doorway. He held out his hand.

'Come on, girl!' he said. 'There are tasks to do in the tavern, better that than sitting mooning over your face in a mirror! What God has made, God permits.'

Rebecca looked back at her reflection: the hare-lip was still there. She felt like crying at the cruel illusion. She put the mirror down, pushed back the bench and went to join her father.

'Rebecca.' Frogmore was sitting where she had left him. 'You didn't believe anything I said, did you?'

'No,' Rebecca replied.

4

Cowper and his posse left later in the week. The air of excitement they had caused was now replaced by something more ominous. On the day after their departure Malbrook the constable went missing. At first no one was really worried. The constable was a toper and sometimes wandered off for days on end. However, by the beginning of the next week not even the itinerant pedlars and tinkers who roamed the roads said they had seen him. A short while later, old Mother Wyatt also vanished and people wondered if some ill fortune had visited the village. At first they blamed Cowper the Judas Man but, when the villagers assembled in the Silver Wyvern taproom, they recalled the night the parish bell had sounded the tocsin and wondered if the Jesuit, who had probably hidden in the village, had left his ill luck with them.

Bartholomew kept his own counsel. He didn't discuss Frogmore with Rebecca but just gruffly advised her to leave the new parson well alone.

'Why?' Rebecca asked.

'I don't know. There's something strange about him.'

Bartholomew seized Rebecca's hand between his hands. 'I am a taverner, daughter. I deal with people every day but once, years ago, I was a priest, a very good one. Once a priest, I suppose.' He sighed. 'Always a priest. You have your gift of second sight, or so they say. Did you know that when I was a priest I, too, had it? Not as clear and precise as yours.' He let his hands fall away. 'But there's a rottenness in Frogmore, I detect it, the smell of corruption. He doesn't wish you well.'

Rebecca was only too willing to obey her father in this matter. Moreover, her mind was full of St Clair. She questioned the chapmen, pedlars and visitors to the Silver Wyvern if they had news of whether the Jesuit had been taken or not. These just shook their heads, unable to confirm or deny any rumour. Bartholomew, after he had given her his warning about Frogmore, stayed away from the parish church: he made no attempt to hide his dislike of the new vicar. The rest of his customers loudly disagreed, claiming Frogmore was a welcome relief after the boring, dishevelled and forgetful Baynes.

Perhaps it was Taverner Lennox's slightly blasphemous attitude, or so gossip said, which brought about his own ill luck. One night a huge vat in the brew house inexplicably split, pouring its precious contents out, flooding the house and causing further ruin. The next evening a fire started in the stables: the horses were saved but sacks of precious oatmeal and bran were consumed in the flames leaving Bartholomew to buy fresh stock at a time of high prices.

Rebecca did not escape this ill luck. One morning she went to check on Minette. She would feed the palfrey then climb the ladder and sit where St Clair had hid. The Jesuit had been most careful, no trace of his stay remained, but Rebecca, if she closed her eyes, could pretend he was still there and revel in his company. On that particular morning she did not climb the ladder. Minette was lying on her side in the straw, her flanks coated in a sheen of sweat, her breathing fast and uneven. Bartholomew called the horse leech, Furnival, a man skilled in potions and poultices, but there was nothing he could do.

'Some sort of fever,' he declared, grasping Rebecca's hands. 'All I can do is make her comfortable.'

By evening the palfrey was dead, its carcase loaded onto a cart to be taken to the slaughterers. Rebecca, despite her father's best efforts, would not be comforted. She cried most of the night and mourned for her palfrey the rest of the next day. She fought hard against self-pity and busied herself in different tasks around the tavern. By late afternoon it was too much and, although old Mother Wyatt had been missing for days, Rebecca decided to walk down to the old woman's cottage. Just going to a place where one of her few friends had lived might ease the pain.

The afternoon was chill, and heavy, dark clouds hung low over the Essex countryside. Rebecca put on her cloak, a pair of strong boots and took one of her father's ash canes. She walked into Dunmow up the high street, past the half-timbered houses and cottages and down to old Mother Wyatt's. The cottage stood by itself under the shade of a sycamore tree near a small stream. Years earlier a ford had been built, where old Mother Wyatt used to while away her time by telling the fortunes of travellers or selling them herbs and posies. The cottage itself was quite a spacious affair. It was built of stone and wood by old Mother Wyatt's only son, a carpenter who had been seduced by the glory of war: he had marched to join the musters at Ipswich never to return.

Rebecca knocked at the front door. She pushed hard. Mother Wyatt never left it locked but this time it was. The windows were shuttered but, surprisingly, she found the back door open, probably forced by urchins and children from the village. Inside Rebecca found a tallow candle. She lit this with a tinder and searched about. The cottage had been ransacked. In the kitchen jars and pots had been overturned and Rebecca realised that some of the villagers had begun to help themselves to old Mother Wyatt's property, including her collection of fine pewter dishes. Rebecca felt the ash in the fire grate. It was cold and wet. She wiped her hands on a rag, went out of the back door and up the lane, lost in her own thoughts about St Clair, the death of Minette and the disappearance of old Mother Wyatt. Where would the old woman have gone? Rebecca heard a sound further up the lane. Through the gathering gloom, a figure was slowly making its way towards her, a woman small and squat, the cowl of her cloak pulled well over her head. Rebecca stood rooted to the spot.

'Old Mother Wyatt!' she called.

The figure stopped and waved. Rebecca, forgetting her troubles, ran to meet her old friend.

'Lord save us, girl!' Mother Wyatt's eyes danced with merriment.

'Where have you been?' Rebecca demanded. 'It's been the talk of the village for days. You disappeared! Your house is ransacked! Now you come strolling along the lane as if you have simply been out for an evening walk.'

The old woman grasped Rebecca's hands. 'That's

my business, Rebecca.' Her voice was firm and low.

Rebecca went to kiss her on her white, seamed cheek but paused. A chill of apprehension seized her. This was Mother Wyatt but her eyes seemed much larger. Though she was a vivacious old soul, Rebecca had never seen Mother Wyatt look so bright-eyed. Yet this was different, a malicious mocking, a sly twist to her face.

'What's the matter, girl?' Mother Wyatt tilted her head back, a lock of grey hair falling out from beneath the hood.

'I don't know.' Rebecca laughed nervously. 'Maybe it's the fading light, but you seem different.'

'Different? How can an old woman seem different? And I've been hearing stories about you.' Mother Wyatt came closer.

Rebecca sniffed a fragrance which brought back memories of the church, beeswax and incense.

'What stories?' Rebecca asked defensively.

'About that Jesuit, the priest on the run from the law officers? They say you hid him?'

'Who says?'

'Gossips. They say you hid him in that stable where you kept Minette. Gave him food and sustenance. Is that right, girl?'

Rebecca was now alarmed. Here she was on a darkening track, the hedgerows rising high on either side of her, talking to an old woman she no longer recognised. Rebecca stepped back, grasping the walking stick. How could Mother Wyatt know what she had done? And, even if she did, she would have too much common sense to raise it in such a fashion. Mother Wyatt was strange, different exuding a threat which Rebecca couldn't understand. It was there in the posture of her body, head slightly tilted, arms hanging down by her side, holding the cane as a man would a sword. Rebecca felt slightly light-headed as if this were all part of some dreadful dream.

'I think I'd best go,' she said. 'I'm glad to see you are safe.'

Mother Wyatt was now coming towards her but Rebecca fled up the lane. She burst into her father's taproom, her hood pulled back, her hair dishevelled.

'Hog's teeth!' Peter, her father's principal scullion, snapped. 'What's the matter, Rebecca?'

The clamour and chatter stilled, as all the customers turned to look at her.

'Old Mother Wyatt!' Rebecca replied.

She was about to continue but something in Peter's eyes warned her to be prudent.

'What about her?' Callerton, Malbrook's replacement, got up from where he was sitting in the corner playing Pass the Dice with Simnel the church sexton.

'Has she been found?' Rebecca stammered.

'Heavens, daughter, you look as if you have seen a ghost!'

Her father came out of the scullery, his hands bloodied from the carving knife he was carrying.

'It's Mother Wyatt,' she said. 'I wonder . . .?'

'God rest her.' Callerton spoke over his shoulder, going back to his seat. 'Haven't you heard the news, girl? She was found in Demdyke Woods barbarously murdered.'

Rebecca's legs went unsteady; her heart seemed to jump into her mouth. She hurriedly sat down on a stool.

'What do you mean?' she whispered.

Her father came and crouched beside her.

'What's the matter, girl? Callerton spoke the truth. Old Mother Wyatt was found by a farmer out with his dogs. Her throat had been slashed, her chest was one mass of wounds.'

'Tell her the rest,' Callerton called out.

'Her heart had been removed!'

Rebecca's hand flew to her lips. Bartholomew asked if she wanted something to eat or drink but, shaking her head, she pushed by him and went up to her chamber. A few minutes later Lucy, one of the chambermaids, came up, a hot-eyed, buxom wench who walked with a swagger because Bartholomew had taken her into his bed. She pushed open the door without knocking and slammed a cup of mulled wine on the small table beside Rebecca's bed.

'Your father said you were to drink that.'

Rebecca just glared up at her. Lucy spun on her heel, pouting her lips, and slammed the door behind her. Rebecca was sure she heard her say 'hare-lip' but she didn't care. Rebecca realised her homely, rather boring world at Dunmow was coming to an end. That had been no illusion, or even a ghost, out on that lonely trackway. She had met old Mother Wyatt and yet that had not been her.

Rebecca picked up the mulled wine. It was hot to the touch; she took a kerchief out of the chest near her bed and held it more carefully. The wine was strong, heavily tinged with the honey and herbs her father had distilled. Rebecca walked to the window. She stared down at the trackway in front of the tavern; the shadows danced on the edge of the pool of light thrown by the lantern horns fixed on hooks beside the main door. A man stepped into the light. He made as if to go in then stopped and looked up. Rebecca felt the cup slip between her hands. Malbrook the constable stood there, his face a ghastly white, a strange smile on his face. Rebecca backed away and, throwing herself on the bed, began to sob.

The next morning Rebecca felt calmer though her father commented on her pale face and the dark rings round her eyes. She muttered she had nightmares and, when Bartholomew asked her to go into the village to shop among the stalls, Rebecca refused. She felt unsafe. Evil had come to Dunmow. Her father was correct. Master Frogmore had the rottenness of death about him and Rebecca believed the new parson was the cause of what was happening.

Over the next few days Rebecca felt the oppressive evil grow. Frogmore, however, became even more courteous, charming and popular. Only her father wasn't convinced. When the parson came down to the taproom to buy blackjacks of ale and cups of wine and sat joking with the menfolk, Rebecca kept to her chamber. When her father came up to see her, he described the parson as a Herod dancing amongst the innocents.

'He's a bad bugger, Rebecca, but I don't know what to do about him.'

The rest of the villagers appeared to be taken in. Rebecca was about to ask her father to send her to a distant kinsman in Norwich when a chapman, who sold trinkets and gewgaws in the villages and hamlets along the Essex coast, arrived at the Silver Wyvern. He loudly announced that the Jesuit St Clair had been taken.

'Caught in the woods he was.' The chapman

licked the white foam from the top of the tankard. 'Apparently he had a horse but it became lame and the sheriff's men ran him to earth.'

Rebecca fought to keep her face impassive as she caught her father's warning glance.

'Is he dead?' The words rushed out.

The chapman smacked his lips and looked at his half-empty tankard. Rebecca filled it at the butts and brought it back.

'He's not dead. They shot the horse. I passed villagers cutting up the carcase. The Jesuit's in Colchester Castle. He's to remain there until the next Assizes.'

'Was anyone taken with him?' Bartholomew asked.

The chapman shook his head. 'But God save those who helped him. Colchester has deep dungeons, red-hot pokers and pincers to draw the truth out of a poor man.'

Rebecca picked up her cloak and, ignoring her father's shouts, walked out of the tavern. She pulled the hood over her head, not only because the evening was cold and blustery, but so that any she passed would not see the tears streaming down her face. She paused on the corner of Ratgar Lane and watched the bare, gaunt branches of the trees sway backwards and forwards like giant arms against the grey, blustery sky.

Rebecca had never felt so hopeless. Here she was, a taverner's daughter, pining for a man she'd hardly met, trapped in a village by a parson who dabbled in the most evil games. Rebecca walked on lost in her own thoughts. When she looked round she realised that, unwittingly, she had taken the trackway to the church. The side door was open so she went in. The sanctuary was gloomy and empty. Rebecca went along the nave; as usual she closed her eyes but, when she opened them, the statue of St Michael the Archangel had gone from its plinth.

'Oh no!' she gasped.

She ran towards it, feeling with her hands. Perhaps she was suffering from some illusion? She ran round the church. Perhaps it had been moved? She looked in the bell tower, the alcoves at the back, tears stinging her eyes. Without knowing it, she blundered into Parson Frogmore as he stepped from behind one of the pillars.

'Why, Rebecca, what's the matter?'

'You know what's the matter! Where's the statue?'

He clicked his tongue in a tutting noise. 'Rebecca, Rebecca, such popish nonsense!'

'Where's the statue?' she insisted.

Frogmore was fighting hard to control the laughter bubbling inside him.

'You want to see the statue, Rebecca, come with me!'

Before she could object, he grasped her hand and took her out across to the charnel house. Throwing open the door, he thrust her inside. Rebecca staggered about in the darkness, tripping over the bones and skulls which littered the floor. She should have felt frightened but she was angry. Frogmore struck a tinder and lit one of the sconce torches: he took this out of its iron bracket and handed it to her.

'Oh no!'

She crumpled to the floor. In the torchlight the statue lay smashed in pieces. On the shelf amongst the other battered skulls was the decapitated head. Rebecca got up and took this down, stroking the dark, plaster hair.

'Why?' She walked back to Frogmore. 'Why are you so cruel? You don't believe in God or man! You know that and so do I!'

Frogmore bowed. 'The wishes of the parish, Rebecca, as well as the law of the land. Now, I'll tell you what. You can keep the head.'

Frogmore walked out, his whole body shaking with laughter. Rebecca took the head and looked at the way it had been disfigured: the nose broken, one of the eyes gouged out. She went back into the cemetery and walked to her mother's grave. She knelt down, clawing at the hard-packed earth and, when she had scooped out a hole, placed the head in, covering it up.

On her return to the Silver Wyvern, Rebecca would have slipped up the stairs to wash and change but her father caught her by the sleeve.

'What's the matter, girl?' He grasped her fingers. 'Did you fall?' He stood back. 'Rebecca, your dress is covered in mud.'

'Frogmore smashed the statue!' Rebecca burst out, her eyes bright with tears. 'I'm sorry. I appear a woebegone maid but there was no need . . .'

'The statue of St Michael?' Bartholomew's face suffused with rage.

'He took it into the charnel house. He smashed it up and put the head along with the other skulls.'

'Go to your room!' Bartholomew ordered.

'Father?'

Rebecca had never seen Bartholomew so angry: his face had gone pale. He lost that red-eyed, toper look and, for a few seconds, Rebecca caught the features of a handsome young man.

'Your mother loved that statue.' Bartholomew chewed

the corner of his lip. 'I hired a guildsman from Ipswich to paint it specially. He had no right to do that! It was cruel. Go on girl, go upstairs!'

Rebecca did so. A few minutes later Bartholomew came up carrying a tray of diced meat covered in an onion sauce, some fresh bread and a cup of wine.

'Stay up here for the night.' Bartholomew stood over his daughter, stroking her hair. 'I love you, Rebecca.'

She glanced up.

'I've done two good things in my life. I married the woman I loved and she bore me the daughter I always wanted.'

Rebecca seized her father's rough-chapped hands and pressed them against her cheek.

'I don't want to stay here,' she told him. 'I don't want to be part of Dunmow or anything to do with Frogmore.'

Her father crouched down and grasped her face gently between his hands.

'You helped the Jesuit, didn't you?'

Rebecca nodded. 'And now he's taken.'

'Aye,' her father replied. 'And, from what I saw of Cowper, they'll try to make him talk. If the Jesuit mentions your name, Cowper's men will be back here with warrants. Perhaps tomorrow I'll send you away. I have friends near Kenilworth in Warwickshire. But eat your food Rebecca, drink the wine. I have got business to attend to.' He turned in the doorway. 'Do you love me, Rebecca?'

'More than life itself.'

'Remember me!'

Before Rebecca could ask what he meant, Bartholomew had closed the door and she heard him clumping down the stairs. The chamber was now full of the fragrant smell from the meat. Rebecca went across and ate, gulping at the wine. Only as she finished it did she realise Father must have put a potion in. She felt so tired, so warm, the last thing she remembered was curling up on the bed.

Rebecca was roughly awakened the next morning.

'Mistress, mistress, you had best come down!'

Rebecca sat up on the bed. She felt thick-headed, her mouth still tasted of the wine and meat.

'What's the matter, Peter?'

'Your father went out last night and hasn't returned. We are all gathered in the taproom below. He's never done this before.'

Rebecca pulled herself out of the bed. She told Peter to leave and swiftly washed and dressed. Downstairs the maids and servants were gathered round the table; the fire was not lit, the place had not been swept.

'We've been waiting, mistress. Master Bartholomew never returned and you slept late.'

'Where did he go? Did he take a horse?'

Peter shook his head. 'He came down here, oh, it must have been six of the clock. He took his cloak and walking cane. Said he had business to do.'

'Maybe he stayed somewhere?' Lucy shouted, an impudent smile on her face.

'Father would never do that!' Rebecca snapped. She felt apprehensive. Bartholomew had probably gone to see Frogmore. 'Peter, do as Father would. Clean the grate, have the taproom cleaned!'

'We take orders from your father, not you!' Lucy sneered.

Rebecca strode across the taproom and smacked the wench across the mouth.

'Get out!' Rebecca hissed. 'This is my father's tavern. I am his daughter. I am tired of your insolence and your impudence!'

Lucy's lower lip began to quiver. 'I didn't . . .'

'Yes you did!' Rebecca retorted. 'You are as lazy as you are insolent! My father should have dismissed you months ago!' Rebecca felt torn between anger and fear yet she had no regrets at what she had done. 'I am going out!' she shouted. 'I am going to look for my father! When I return, I want you all either working or gone!'

Rebecca strode into the kitchen. She helped herself to cheese, bread, dried meat and a tankard of ale. She ate and drank quickly, trying to curb her fears. St Clair was taken and Cowper might return but she would cross that bridge when she had to. What was more serious was that her father had gone to see Frogmore and had not returned.

Rebecca took her cloak and walking cane and went out into the still deserted square. She turned to go left and abruptly stopped, grasping the tavern wall to steady herself. For a few seconds Dunmow had disappeared. She was standing on the edge of a field of snow which stretched up to a green, sombre forest. Somewhere in her mind rang the clash of weapons.

'Mistress Rebecca, are you well?'

She opened her eyes. Simnel the church sexton was peering at her, his white, doughy face framed by straw-coloured hair.

'I am well.'

He grasped her arm. 'Are you sure, mistress?'

Simnel forced a smile, showing a blackened row of teeth. Rebecca tried not to flinch at his stale breath.

'I am looking for your father,' Simnel stammered.

'So am I.'

'I need his help,' Simnel continued.

Rebecca could now see he was agitated, dancing from one foot to the other.

'My Margot, she has disappeared.'

Rebecca's stomach clenched. She remembered Margot, a dark-haired, plump, merry girl with a reputation for stealing off into the woods with this young man or that.

'How long has she been gone?'

'Since the night before. She said she wanted to pick some herbs for our meat is fairly rancid.' Simnel's watery eyes blinked. 'Oh, I know that was her excuse for meeting someone but she always came back. She never stays out, not all night.' Simnel rubbed his unshaven cheeks. 'And there are the others who have disappeared. Old Mother Wyatt, Malbrook.'

Rebecca, trying to control her own panic, patted Simnel on the shoulder and told him to go and sit in the taproom.

'I am sure when Father returns, he'll help you.'

Rebecca took the quickest route across the cemetery. She hammered on the priest's door but it was Constable Callerton, not Frogmore, who threw it open.

'Why Mistress Lennox.' He refused to meet her gaze, but gave a shifty look and was about to close the door in her face.

'Where's my father?' she snapped.

'Rebecca, Rebecca, come in!'

Frogmore appeared behind Callerton, gently pushing the constable away.

'I don't want to come in. I want my father.'

Frogmore raised his eyebrows. Rebecca thought it made him look even more like a satyr.

'I know he came here!' she accused.

'I didn't say he didn't. He came here just after dark. He talked about the statue. I explained how it had fallen off its plinth. He offered to buy a new one. I said I'd think about it and he left.'

'Well, he hasn't come home.'

Frogmore taunted Rebecca with his eyes.

'Are you saying that he's still here?'

'Why should a taverner disappear into thin air?'

'He hasn't disappeared,' Callerton snapped.

'What do you mean?'

'He came to my house this morning.' Callerton tapped the roll of parchment peeping out of his wallet. 'He said he wished to make a statement.'

'My father came to you?'

'Yes, he made a statement written in his own hand and then he said he was leaving.'

'But he never came home.'

'He said he was going to Colchester. He wanted to see the Queen's man, Cowper, as well as confront the traitor St Clair.'

'Let me see this statement.'

'In my own good time.' Callerton slammed the door in her face.

5

Rebecca's sense of dread deepened over the next few days. Callerton came down to the tavern but he sat with his cronies, heads close, whispering together. Whenever Rebecca approached, they fell silent. Peter the scullion had ensured Lucy left and this quiet, hard-working man proved to be a tower of strength. Nevertheless, he was worried by Bartholomew's disappearance as well as the attitude of Callerton and the others. He eventually took Rebecca aside.

'You should be careful, girl,' Peter warned, his thin, anxious-eyed face becoming even more mournful. 'Something dreadful has happened to your father. I don't believe he's gone to Colchester,' he added gruffly. 'Callerton is stirring up mischief, so is Lucy in the village.' He gripped her by the shoulders. 'I've always liked you, Rebecca. Your father was a fair man.' He bit his lip as he realised what he had said. 'I am sure,' he stammered, 'that he will come back soon but I wouldn't stay here. Look, I have friends in Hallingbury. You go and hide there.'

'I won't hide anywhere!' Rebecca retorted. 'I've done nothing wrong!'

'You've done everything wrong,' Peter replied. 'Rebecca, you and your father are strangers here. You own a prosperous tavern, that prompts envy.

They whisper that you are a papist. They talk about your hare-lip and your second sight. I must speak bluntly, such hatred can lead to murder.'

Rebecca chose not to heed his warning. However, whenever she went into the village, she found Peter's words were prophetic. Some of the tradesmen were kind but many were guarded. Women turned away when she passed them. A few smiled quickly but others cursed and muttered under their breath.

Of Bartholomew there was no sign. He had been gone five days and Rebecca suspected something dreadful must have happened. She could not eat and her sleep was troubled: nightmares where she and St Clair were hunted by wolves across icy, snowy wastes or locked in unseen battle with a hideous army of demons and gargoyles. Rebecca also experienced visions during the day about others missing in the village. Old Mother Wyatt's corpse had been quickly interred in the corner of the cemetery but Malbrook and Margot seemed to have disappeared like puffs of smoke. On one occasion Rebecca had been roused by a tapping on the cobbles outside and, when she looked out of the casement window, the bloody face of Malbrook leered up: a bloody wound covered his chest and his head hung askew as if some one had slashed him with a knife.

On the following morning Rebecca went out to take some bread down to the poorhouse. She passed Simnel's cottage and was about to walk on, when a face at an upper window caught her gaze. Margot was staring down but her face was blueish-white, dark rings circled her eyes, and, as she pressed her body against the pane, Rebecca saw the great bloody mess in her chest. Rebecca felt faint and crouched down, pretending there was something wrong with the heel of her boot. When she looked up the apparition had gone. She hastened back to the tavern.

She spent the day working hard in the kitchens as if the clatter of pots and pans, the homely smells of cooking, the hard work and chatter around her would drive away the demons. As it was Friday, the taproom was full that night and Rebecca could face no more. She drank a goblet of wine, told Peter she would be retiring and went up to her chamber.

Rebecca did not bother to undress but lay on the bed, pulling the coverlet over her. She left the candle alight and stared across the room at a small music box her mother had bought her. Rebecca's eyes filled with tears. She remembered how they used to walk along sun-dappled paths and her mother would sing a tune or teach her a poem as well as point out the different herbs and their properties. The music box had been brought from Norwich and given as a present on her fifth birthday. Rebecca used to love to listen to the lilting tune. Now it might prove too much. She closed her eyes and tried to pray then guiltily realised that, apart from the statue in the parish church, she had never really believed in anything. The words of the scripture, the sonorous lectures of Parson Baynes, the gabbled prayers had only been a ritual, like scrubbing the traunchers or scouring the alehouse: tasks to be completed as soon as possible and quickly forgotten.

Rebecca drifted off to sleep. When she awoke it was dark. No noise came from the taproom; Rebecca felt the hair on the nape of her neck curling. Someone was in the room, she was certain of that. The candle had gone out. Rebecca went to take a night light down and, clumsily holding the tinder, scraped until a flame struck and the wick glowed with life. As she held this up and turned round her mouth opened to scream but it wouldn't come. Bartholomew was sitting in a chair, just to the left of the door. A place where he would always sit when he came up to talk to her; but her father was much changed. His hair seemed greyer, his face was pale and his eyes simply stared ahead of him. Rebecca saw the gash in his neck, the blood stains on his jerkin which was cut and rent round the great gaping wound on his chest. Rebecca sat down on the bed. She must be dreaming.

'Daughter.' The word came in a soft hissed whisper.

'Daughter.' Now the voice was stronger, hoarser.

Rebecca glanced slowly over her shoulder. Her father was now staring at her. He opened his bloodied mouth.

'Daughter, will you listen to me?'

Rebecca curled back on the bed, pushing up against the headboard, staring in horror at this dreadful apparition.

'Father, I must be dreaming!'

'Rebecca, we all dream. I dream now.'

'Father, what is happening?'

Rebecca wanted to pull up the blankets but she was too terrified to move.

'Killed before my time.' Bartholomew was talking as if in a trance. 'My soul snatched out and, because of evil done, unable to travel on.' His hands came up, folding across his lap. 'I hang in darkness, Rebecca, in the great chasm between heaven and earth.'

'Father?'

'Hush now child.' The words seemed to come

from a great distance. Rebecca noticed the trickle of blood curling out of the corner of her father's mouth. 'Frogmore rules me!'

Rebecca stared in horror.

'The parson is no man of God, a great demon. He means you ill, Rebecca, but he cannot touch you. Others hold him back, those who could not protect me because of my life.' He stretched out his hands, placing them together like a priest conferring a benediction. 'Once a priest,' he intoned, 'always a priest. I gave that up for a woman I loved. I could have received pardon but, to besmirch that love with lust and the envy of money! We make our own hell, Rebecca! A demon like Frogmore simply catches us in his net as a hunter does a hare.'

Rebecca felt some of the warmth return to her body. She took the wine cup and sipped at the dregs.

'What must I . . .'

'Hush now!' her father interrupted. 'My time is not long. You must go, Rebecca, flee this place!'

'To where?'

'To St Clair.'

'But he's been taken.'

'Go to St Clair! Kill Frogmore! Release me from the darkness! You must go now.'

Her father was gliding towards her, lips moving. Rebecca could bear it no longer. She closed her eyes, grasping the goblet until its pewter handle bit into her skin.

'Rebecca!'

She opened her eyes. Her father stood at the foot of the bed.

'This is no nightmare. In the pit at the back of the charnel house . . .'

Then he was gone.

Rebecca sat staring at the candle flame until the side of her neck ached. Wrapping the coverlet about her, she walked to where her father had sat. The wine she had drunk now took effect. She felt warmer, stronger. She wondered if it could have been a dream; then she noticed the brass button lying on the chair. It was decorated with a wyvern, a small conceit of her father who had ordered the buttons from a pedlar and had them sewn on the leather jerkin he always wore.

Rebecca was suddenly seized with activity. She dressed, slipped the button into her purse and stole down the stairs. The taproom was in darkness. Peter had hung a small night lantern over the hearth. Around the room Rebecca could see the scullions and tap boys sleeping on the rushes under the tables. From the kitchen she heard a gasping and grunting, a muffled squeal and the sound of a smack of a hand on flesh, a love-tryst between one of the maids and a customer. Rebecca ignored this as she slipped out into the night.

The darkness was cold. A hoarfrost had turned the cobbles slippery but the sky was cloud-free and a full moon lighted the trackway along to the church. Rebecca was determined to prove once and for all that either these visions were a figment of a tired brain or final proof that the Devil had swept into Dunmow.

Then she reached the cemetery wall. The church and house were in darkness. Only the hoot of an owl and the flurry of some animal in the bracken and gorse around her broke the silence. Rebecca's hand went to her mouth. She traced the hare-lip and recalled old Mother Wyatt's belief that, if she went out in moonlight and rubbed the fat from the corpse

112

of a hanged man . . . Rebecca closed her eyes. All such nonsense was over. Dunmow and her life here were finished. She would flee, but not before she had found the proof, and confronted Frogmore with his bloody work.

Rebecca climbed the cemetery wall and crawled on all fours past the derelict crosses, over the wet, soggy burial mounds. A dark shape floated above her, but it was only some bird of the night. At the side of the church, keeping to the small gulley, she crept down to the door of the charnel house. She pushed this open and went in. She remembered Frogmore lighting the sconce torch; taking the tinder out of her purse, Rebecca lit the piece of candle she also carried. The small pool of light revealed the terrors of this place. The skulls and bones of those who had been tossed there glistened in the light. Rebecca's throat and mouth were dry but she kept her hands steady as she held the candle to the pitch-coated torch until it caught the flame, then she took it out of its clasp and made her way across the charnel house. The bones underneath her boots crunched and snapped. Rebecca closed her eyes. She must not think of this place. She must think of her mother and some warm day in a dell full of flowers. She must find the proof.

Her father had talked about a pit at the far side of the charnel house. The shelves on the back wall stopped about three feet above the ground. Rebecca crouched and went under these. She found the gap in the wall and, putting her hand out, felt carefully within. Her fingers touched cold flesh. Rebecca moved her hand. She felt leather and, pulling the torch down, repressed her screams as she stared into the sightless eyes of her father's corpse. Heart thudding,

113

her body coated in sweat, she moved a little to the side. She put the torch down and stared in horror at the terrible wounds in her father's throat, the bloody soggy mess from the gaping wound in his chest.

'God have mercy on you! Oh, Lord, have mercy on us all!' Rebecca moaned.

She drew back. The charnel house now possessed no horrors worse than this. Again she grasped the torch and, squeezing down, almost lay beside her father's corpse. She hadn't the strength to pull it out of the gap. She put her hand gently on his cheek and, summoning up her courage, let her hand go down to the jerkin, where there had been seven buttons. She slowly began to count and, when she reached the bottom, realised there were only six. Rebecca pushed herself away.

The door to the charnel house suddenly slammed open and shut in the night breeze. Rebecca jumped and dropped the pitch torch, extinguishing the flame. She staggered to her feet, hands flailing, trying to remember where the door was but the blackness closed in around her like one of those terrible marsh mists which rolled along the Dunmow high street on winter evenings. Rebecca wanted to scream. She stumbled across, the bones beneath snapping like cracks of thunder. Now and again she fell, her fingers grazing sharpened bone or the eyelets of a skull.

At last she reached the far wall, muttering and praying, banging herself against posts and shelves, Rebecca heard the door open and shut again. She made her way towards it. At last she was outside, crouching in the mud. She stayed, trying to calm the hammering of her heart. Only when her sweat began to cool in the icy night breeze did she stagger to her feet. She was halfway across the cemetery when a dark shape loomed up before her.

'Why, girl, what are you doing here?' Malbrook the constable with his terrible face and horrid wounds blocked her path.

'In Christ's name!' Rebecca screamed.

The apparition disappeared. Rebecca reached the wall, clambered over and fled into the night. So terrified, she was oblivious of the dark, hooded figure, perched like a huge crow on the top of the church tower, watching her every step.

Rebecca had a troubled night's sleep but she woke early before dawn. She looked round her bedchamber, staring at every object. In her heart she knew that life was about to change. Her planned confrontation with Frogmore would alter her life for ever. She went down to the taproom but ignored the scullions and slatterns who were sleepily beginning their duties, sweeping the floor and cleaning the grates. She had her hand on the latch when Peter the scullion caught her by the shoulder.

'You are going to morning service, mistress? I'll make sure the others come. We'll stand at the back.'

Rebecca nodded. 'I want to be early. I want to sit at the front.' She was going to turn away but then grasped his hand. 'Peter, Father will not be coming back. Look after this,' she added, 'whatever happens!'

Rebecca went out into the square. Now and again, through the mist, she glimpsed figures also making their way to the church. As usual there were two services, one just after dawn, the other mid-morning. She made her way along the trackway.

The church was cold, uninviting. Rebecca sat at

the foot of the pillar just beneath the pulpit. Simnel the sexton, still looking doleful, had lit the tapers and candles on the high altar and was now opening the Bible on the lectern, preparing the sanctuary for Frogmore. Rebecca leaned against the pillar and closed her eyes. She heard other people come in and either crouch or stand along the nave.

The light pouring through the windows grew stronger. Simnel tolled the bell. The nave hummed with conversations as neighbours greeted each other. Children fought or ran up and down only to be hushed to silence by their elders. Rebecca concentrated on the tolling bells, which sounded as if they were summoning people to a funeral, low and mournful.

When Rebecca opened her eyes and looked over her shoulder most of the villagers were now present but no one had sat near her. More ominous still, Callerton and the crew who acted as his deputies were gathered across the nave. They sat in a group along the transepts glowering over at her. The bells stopped. Frogmore came out of the sanctuary and bowed to the cross on the altar. Instead of moving to the lectern, however, he walked straight up into the pulpit. He looked down the church and stole a glance at Rebecca, a sly smile in his eyes.

'I have chosen a different text today,' he began. 'Thou shalt not suffer a witch to live!'

Rebecca stiffened as Frogmore's words provoked a murmur of agreement. The church was now silent; even the children had stopped their chatter. The families seated on the benches or the cold flagstone floors were like statues, heads straining forwards, all eyes on Frogmore.

'Thou shalt not suffer a witch to live!' Frogmore repeated sonorously. 'And we have a witch, a traitor and a rebel in our midst!'

'Burn her! Burn her! Burn her!'

The words began as a muted chorus from the back of the church.

Rebecca controlled her fear. Frogmore had arranged all this! Callerton, his deputies and that claque at the back of the church.

'Parson Frogmore, what is this?'

Beddoes the brewer was on his feet. Rebecca recognised him as a good, honest man, a friend of her father's.

'This is God's house!' Frogmore thundered. 'Sit down man!'

'It is a church!' Beddoes bawled back. 'Not a court!'

Frogmore remained unruffled. 'The people of this parish,' he retorted, 'have the right to assemble and seek out traitors. Be they witches, those who harbour the Queen's enemies, or both!'

Beddoes, crestfallen, sat down.

'You,' Frogmore pointed down at Rebecca. 'You, Mistress Lennox, are a witch and a traitor!'

'And you sir!' she screamed back, springing to her feet, 'are a foul assassin!'

Her words were so dramatic, so unexpected, the claque at the back of the church faltered in their chorus. Rebecca turned a fierce glare on the rest of the parishioners.

'What has happened since he,' she jabbed a finger at Frogmore, 'came to Dunmow? Strange sights! Strange disappearances and strange deaths, including that of my father!'

'What nonsense is this?' Callerton walked across to confront her.

'Go to the charnel house!' Rebecca snapped. 'Search the pit at the back and you will find my father's corpse.' She glanced up at Frogmore. He was mocking her with his eyes and her heart sank.

'You've heard the accusation,' Frogmore replied quietly. 'Are you saying, Mistress Lennox, that someone has murdered your father and buried his corpse in our charnel house?'

'Yes I am, and that person is you!'

Suddenly Constable Malbrook, old Mother Wyatt, Margot, even her father were clustered round one of the pillars. Their hideous faces glared at her, horrible wounds in their throats and chests. Rebecca felt herself grow dizzy. She leaned out to grasp the pillar.

'Have you been drinking?' Parson Frogmore mocked.

'You know I have not!' she gasped. 'You know what's in the charnel house.'

'This is nonsense!' Frogmore insisted. 'Constable Callerton, take your men and search the place.'

Rebecca looked down the church. Those living dead, the ones she had glimpsed, were now seated on the bench Callerton and his cronies had vacated.

'This is all wrong,' Rebecca murmured.

She felt her stomach pitch, her legs turn weak. The parishioners were staring at her strangely. An age seemed to pass before Callerton swaggered back into the church, knocking the dust off his cloak with his leather gauntlets.

'Nothing but bones!' he shouted.

Rebecca could do no more. She slid down the pillar, folding her arms across her chest.

'What is more,' Callerton went on, pulling a piece

of parchment out of his wallet, 'I have here a statement by Bartholomew Lennox, drawn up before he left Dunmow for Colchester. He accuses his daughter of witchcraft, of causing the deaths of those she dislikes but, above all, of harbouring the Queen's enemy, the Jesuit St Clair!'

Rebecca grabbed the piece of parchment, Callerton hovering close to her lest she try to destroy it. As she read, Rebecca went cold. The letters and words were her father's, the signature at the bottom was certainly his but the accusations must have come from Frogmore.

Rebecca could barely continue reading it. Her father told the most outrageous and filthy lies. How he suspected she was not really his daughter. How the hare-lip was the mark of a demon. How she conjured against those she disliked and how she had aided and abetted the escape of the Jesuit St Clair.

'These are lies!' she shouted, throwing the parchment to the ground. 'My father would never have written that!'

'Never?' Callerton's beer-sodden face cracked into a grin. 'But you can see it's his writing and signature. He came to my house, made that deposition and then swore to its truth on the Bible.'

'This is trickery!' Rebecca screamed. 'Magic at its worst!'

'Magic at its worst!' Frogmore scoffed. 'You come into this church, Rebecca Lennox and, in the presence of the Lord, you say your father's corpse lies in our charnel house. You call your pastor a murderer, the constable a liar. What sentence should be imposed on a wicked woman like you?'

'Burn her!' Lucy the chambermaid now pushed

her way through the crowd, her florid face a puce red. She smacked Rebecca in the face, throwing her back so hard she knocked her head against the pillar. Rebecca, half-conscious, slipped to the ground.

She was aware of shouting and yelling like the roar of breaking waves. She was pushed and pummelled then dragged to her feet, gaping in horror as Callerton wrapped a rope around her, pinning her arms. She saw others object. Beddoes pushed his way through but he was dragged aside. Peter the scullion tried to restrain Lucy but someone knocked him on the back of the head and he collapsed on all fours to the floor.

The church was now in an uproar. Callerton's men were dragging her towards the main door. A sea of faces swum about her, hate-filled, mouths snarling. Callerton was now in charge of her life. He swaggered in front, pushing people aside with his staff of office. Rebecca tried to catch the eye of her father's friends but they looked away. The shouts to burn her echoed through the church. Try as she might, she could not stop shaking with fear. The ropes bit into her body and she found it difficult to breathe. Surely this was one of her nightmares and she would soon wake up?

'Help me!' she cried.

Her request was greeted by guffaws of laughter. She was being pushed out of the church, into the cold reviving morning air. She had heard of similar occurrences in other villages plagued by a witch craze, of summary justice being carried out, of women being hauled into the market place and either hanged or burned without appeal to anyone. This was going to happen to her.

She was pushed along. On one occasion she stumbled and fell. Her leather boots were ripped off her,

the ring on her little finger snatched away. Other
people plucked at her woollen dress, tearing off the
linen collar. Clods of earth hit her, a piece of dung
caught her on the mouth. She coughed and retched
to the amusement of those around her. Surely, she
thought, someone would come to her help?

They reached the village, dragging her over the
cobbles which tore and cut at her bare feet, then into
the square. She saw the sign of the Silver Wyvern.
People thronged in the doorway, blackjacks of ale
in their hands. A cart trundled by. To her horror it
stopped near the whipping post. Twigs and bracken
were thrown out to build a pyre round it.

'For God's sake!' she screamed. 'I'm innocent!'

But the blood lust was up. A stool was placed
next to the whipping post and she was forced to
stand on it. More ropes were lashed about her and
the bracken was piled high up to her chest. In
the sea of faces around her, she saw men, women
and children she had known all her life. Some
of them she regarded as friends, others she and
her father had helped on many an occasion. Surely
her father would come running out of the Silver
Wyvern? Or some of his friends? Someone was standing on the small balcony above the main door:
Malbrook, his blood-filled eyes glaring malevolently
down at her. Beneath him, on the corner at the
alleyway leading to the back of the tavern, old Mother
Wyatt stood waving a posy of flowers. Rebecca
smelled smoke and stared in terror at the men bearing
pitch torches now surrounding the pyre. She closed
her eyes.

'Christ Jesus!' she pleaded. 'Oh Mother, Mother
of God!'

Abruptly all sound, the furious shouting and terrifying clamour, disappeared. A man on a white horse had ridden into the square. He was dressed in the costume of a knight, his face was that of Michael St Clair, no longer hunted or unshaven, but full and beautiful.

'Help me!' she called.

A plume of smoke rose. She coughed as it tore at her throat and made her eyes burn till they watered. She heard the crackle of the flames as they caught the bracken. Then there came a shout.

'In the Queen's name!'

Rebecca felt the bracken being pulled away, the smoke clearing. Horsemen were now milling about the square, laying about with the flat of their swords. People were running into the tavern or to hide in the alleyways. Men were throwing buckets of water from the horse trough over the flames. Rebecca sagged against the ropes. A man in a brimmed top hat appeared before her.

'Michael!' she breathed.

She glimpsed a knife as it slashed at the ropes. She collapsed into the man's arms but, when she looked up, she was staring into the harsh, impassive face of Cowper the Judas Man.

6

Parson Frogmore whipped his horse, urging it along the tree-lined track out of Dunmow. Now and again, his hand would go down to the saddle horn ensuring the bags slung there were still secure. When he reached the crossroads, Frogmore reined in. On either side stretched the remains of a great primeval forest which had once covered the eastern parts of the country. Frogmore scanned the sky: the day would be a cold and lonely one. He breathed in.

'Snow,' he muttered. 'There'll be snow by nightfall.'

Frogmore let his horse have its head, still snorting against the cruel pace of Frogmore's flight from the church of St Michael. The parson ripped the white neckbands from round his throat, then tossed them into a thicket. He listened for sounds of any pursuit but realised the Queen's men would be too busy with the confusion in the market square.

'Ah well!' Frogmore sighed. He leaned down, patting his horse's neck. 'What a pity!'

He was certain Rebecca Lennox had been the reason St Clair had come to Dunmow, not just to hide, but to seek out that young virgin in his own relentless pursuit of Frogmore.

'And I nearly achieved it.'

Frogmore smiled bleakly at the tall scaffold posts on one side of the crossroads. If the Judas Man had been late, or that stupid mob in the churchyard had acted more quickly, Lennox would now be charred flesh. Frogmore sighed and urged his horse at a slower canter along the lane leading onto the highway to London.

Being Sunday, the trackway was devoid of farmers, peasants or labourers; even the pedlars and chapmen would rest up for the day. Frogmore relaxed, lost in a reverie. He had been to this place before, many, many years ago, when there had been no Silver Wyvern and Dunmow had only been half its present size. He wouldn't have come back except that he had to hide, replenish and refresh himself as well as discover what St Clair intended.

He recalled that violent sword fight in the nave of St Michael's church. He never confessed to, or felt, fear but St Clair was becoming a problem. Years ago Frogmore had been allowed to roam the roads of Europe. He'd even been to the new lands across the western ocean. No one dared oppose him. Oh, busybody magistrates, the occasional incorruptible law officer had been a nuisance but Frogmore always shook them off. Most men could be bought, a few had to be killed, the rest offered no opposition to his skill, cunning and power. St Clair was different. Frogmore reined in and looked up at the crows nesting in the long black branches of the trees.

'Birds of the night,' he whispered.

If only he had their power! But he must wait. Everything had to be developed, one new faculty leading to another. But what about St Clair? He was a bird of ill omen. Where Frogmore went,

St Clair always followed. How long had this been going on? Two or three years? Yes, about that, if he included the time St Clair had inveigled himself into his company. And that was where it had begun, in that violent duel outside Rome. Frogmore was convinced St Clair had fallen to his death but, within the year, he had re-emerged, dogging Frogmore's footsteps.

At first Frogmore had not been concerned. The Jesuit was no more noisome than a fly in summer but, as the weeks passed into months, St Clair appeared indestructible. Paid assassins struck from prepared ambuscades yet St Clair always evaded them. Courtesans were bribed to seek him out with flasks of poisoned wine but St Clair, that prude, refused both the gift and its carrier. Recently, Frogmore, unable to flee any further, had turned and fought. St Clair proved to be a superb swordsman and that worried Frogmore. A master duellist himself, he recognised that, on one or two occasions, St Clair had the advantage but the Jesuit had refused, as if the priest was aware that Frogmore could not be killed in such a way.

Frogmore had become worried and, using his powers and the wealth he had amassed, had gone to study in the great libraries: the Duke Humphrey in Oxford, the well-endowed scriptoria of different abbeys and monasteries, searching out those precious books on the practice of magic and the power of sorcery. A suspicion had been planted in Frogmore's mind, one he dare not admit to. He'd travelled to Moscow to read certain tracts and treatises kept under lock and key in iron-bound coffers of the Monastery of St Michael, in the Kremlin Palace.

Frogmore had always believed he was invincible.

He had made a compact with hell, signed his bloody treaty with the Dark Lords of the Air but, as he had been warned by those who could conjure up the spirits, everything in life was vulnerable, nothing was totally free. A bill would be drawn up, payment demanded. Was St Clair his reckoning? Frogmore had communicated with the Jesuit's headquarters in Rome but he had received no reply. He had even tried to discover St Clair's antecedents but with little success.

Frogmore gathered up the reins in his leather gauntlets. St Clair was proving to be a great danger. He could throw off any pursuers. Frogmore could change his appearance and slip through the tightest cordon but, with St Clair constantly yapping at his heels, he was a magnet for others who pursued him. These had soon stumbled on the fact that where St Clair went, Frogmore was also in the vicinity. Like those fools from the Ottoman court who'd hunted him through the cold lands of the Baltic.

Frogmore heard a sound and his hand went beneath his cloak to the long stabbing dirk he carried. The trackway stretched in front of him. He heard the clip-clop of a horse. As the rider came into view, Frogmore gripped his dagger handle more firmly. Even from this distance he could recognise a fighting man. The approaching stranger was covered in cloak and cowl but the horse was a destrier, a fighting steed and, besides the clink of harness, Frogmore could hear the jingle of a sword slapping against the saddle. Moreover, the way the man sat, hands concealed, meant that his fingers were not far away from his crossbow, pistol or dagger. Frogmore studied the sun-burned face, the oiled moustache and beard, the hair in a tight queue at the back, the earring in the right lobe and, beneath the cloak, the quilted leather jacket.

Frogmore held his right hand up in a gesture of peace.

'*Pax et bonum*, stranger!'

Theodore Ragusa reined in. He pushed back the dagger half-pulled from his scabbard. The man in front was dressed like a parson though he was like no priest Ragusa had ever met. His calm poise, the way he kept his hand on the weapon undoubtedly hidden beneath that black cloak.

'*Pax bonum!*' Ragusa murmured, his sharp eyes scrutinising Frogmore from head to toe.

Frogmore gripped the reins of his horse more firmly.

'So, I pass in peace?'

Ragusa shrugged but, when Frogmore moved his horse, Ragusa blocked his way.

'My name is Henry Frogmore, parson of Dunmow. I mean you no ill, sir.'

'I am Theodore Ragusa, a merchant, and I am sure you don't.'

Ragusa clicked his tongue against his teeth. He could still savour the wine he had drunk and the sweet taste of that tavern wench on his lips. He lifted one gloved hand and wiped his nose on the cuff of his jerkin. He only wished this damned island was not so cold.

'I wonder if you could help me, Parson Frogmore? I bear messages for the Queen's man William Cowper. I understand he's in these parts to arrest a Jesuit, Michael St Clair. From what I gather St Clair has been seen in the vicinity.'

Frogmore relaxed and smiled. 'If that is true, sir,

you are on the right track.' He gestured over his shoulder. 'At the crossroads ride straight on. This will take you into Dunmow.' He urged his horse nearer. 'But, haven't you heard the news?'

The so-called merchant just shook his head.

'The Jesuit has been taken, lodged in Colchester Castle.'

Ragusa nodded. 'And?'

Frogmore fought to control his temper. It would be so easy to lean across and slash this man's throat, drag the corpse into the trees and offer his heart in sacrifice. Yet Frogmore was wary. He always took his victims by surprise.

'Apparently, St Clair had accomplices in Dunmow. Master Cowper will be lodged there until they are all taken.'

'And so why does the parson leave his flock on a Sunday morning?'

The more Ragusa studied this stranger the greater his disquiet grew. There was something wrong, yet Ragusa couldn't decide what and he couldn't afford any trouble. He was a stranger, an alien in this freezing, godforsaken land among people who hated foreigners. He had to be careful; the most petty infringement of the law might mean his arrest, weeks languishing in some smelly gaol, before being taken down to some port and thrown onto the nearest available ship.

Ragusa knew the Soul Slayer was in England because St Clair was here. But St Clair was taken prisoner so where could the Soul Slayer be? He stared at the hooded-eyed parson travelling on a Sunday when these cold-blooded islanders gathered in their grey, grim churches.

'My business is my own,' Frogmore replied quietly. 'I carry messages to the local magistrates. Cowper will need help and, sir, if you go to Dunmow, I will be more than prepared to answer further questions upon my return.'

Frogmore dug his spurs in, tipped his hat at Ragusa and rode leisurely on. He half-expected the man to pursue him but, when he looked over his shoulder, Ragusa was already riding on. Frogmore reined in. He knew a mercenary when he saw one. Ragusa was no more a merchant than he was a priest. Frogmore was sure he had heard his name before. A Venetian wasn't he? So what was he doing in England looking for St Clair? If the mercenary was looking for St Clair, he must also be searching for him.

Frogmore rode on until ahead of him he saw the smoke from the tavern where Ragusa had stayed the night before. He closed his eyes, his mind steeped in wickedness, calling on those powers ever ready to help. Then he dismounted, walking along the track until he found a small pathway into the woods. He led his horse into a small clearing which would serve his purpose well. He hobbled his horse, pulled off the saddle bags and, walking across, squatted before a moss-covered boulder, where he undid the buckle and took out the blood-soaked cloth. He unfolded this and put the severed heart in the centre of the rock. He placed candles stolen from the church on either side and lit the wicks, protecting them against the breeze until they grew strong.

Now Frogmore squatted down, legs crossed, hands out. Breathing deeply he cleared his mind. He opened his eyes and watched the mist shift about him. The cold breeze had now gone. The small glade filled with a rich smell like that of a newly opened spice box. Frogmore chanted his quiet hymn to the Dark Lords, calling on their power.

A hundred yards away, Mariotta, a wench from the tavern, was out collecting kindling. She moved slowly, dreamily. The merchant who had used her so lustfully the night before, entering her time and again, had left her weary and aching but two silver pieces richer. Consequently, Mariotta had been only too pleased to escape from the taproom and the sniggers and taunts of others. Ostensibly, Mariotta always came out to collect dry bracken and twigs; really it was to hide the silver she had earned beneath the trunk of an old oak tree burned by lightning. Mariotta didn't trust the taverner, or anyone else who worked there; this place was more secure than any strong-box or secret cavity around the tavern. She had hidden the silver away and now she was busy collecting fallen branches and twigs, enough to lull any suspicions.

Mariotta smiled to herself. One day she would show them all. She would leave that tavern, the greasy rushes on the floor, the slop-strewn tables, and vermin-ridden bedchambers. She would collect her monies and go into the great city.

Mariotta slowly made her way back, then paused. At first she thought she was imagining it but, no, it came again: a fragrant smell, like those expensive perfumes the high-born lords and ladies used whenever they stopped at the tavern. But here, in the middle of a wood? And what was that other smell? Beeswax candles? Mariotta stood motionless as, on the morning air, she heard the faint chanting. She repressed a shiver. Her curiosity getting the better of her fear, she put down the bundle of kindling and stole quietly forward.

Mariotta reached the edge of the clearing and stared in wonder at the man squatting before the stone, hands extended, the candles burning free and fiercely. She'd heard stories of warlocks and wizards but, surely, these were only fables to frighten children? She watched the man intently, her mouth dry. It was as if a mist was shifting around him. Or seeing someone through rippling water, like that groom at the tavern who became so sottish he'd drowned in the carp pond.

The man was changing. He got up, and Mariotta crouched back. She recognised him from when he came to see her own landlord. What was his name? Bartholomew Lennox, but Mariotta had heard the rumours, Bartholomew had disappeared. What was happening here? How could one man change into another? It was Lennox, tall and broad with balding head. Mariotta couldn't breathe because of the tightness in her chest. She stepped back. Her ankle caught in some trailing briar, bringing her crashing to the ground. When she turned over, Bartholomew Lennox was staring down at her.

Rebecca regained consciousness. Her body ached in every limb. Her head felt thick and heavy, her mouth acrid as if still full of woodsmoke. She was lying in the corner of a barn, a blanket tossed over her. Some distance away her rescuers were sitting round a fire. Rebecca licked dry lips. She craved a drink and blinked her sore eyes. She knew this place! It was the old tithing barn on the outskirts of Dunmow. Rebecca peered through the slats; daylight was fading. The smells from the fire made her stomach turn, bringing back memories of the mob and flames dancing around her.

Rebecca felt herself grow faint. She struggled against the ropes which lashed her ankles and wrists. A figure rose and walked through the gloom.

'Rebecca Lennox!'

'Master Cowper. I need something to drink. The smell from that fire!'

Rebecca threw herself to one side, retching violently. When she had finished, he pulled her up and held the pannikin of watered wine to her lips.

'Drink it slowly,' he urged. 'It will ease the pain. There is something in it to make you sleep.'

Rebecca greedily licked in every drop. Cowper pulled her down so she lay on the ground, placing a smelly horse blanket beneath her head and another to cover her.

'You'll be warm enough.'

He returned to his companions. Rebecca's eyes grew heavy. When she awoke it was dark with a faint glimmer of light from outside. She realised she must have slept through the night. She struggled to sit up. The fire had burned down. Around it her captors snored and muttered in their sleep. Peering through the gloom, Rebecca could see at least two guards: one near the door, the other at the far end of the barn sitting with his back to the wall, head nodding. Rebecca's aches and pains had faded. The smell of cooking no longer turned her stomach but her raging thirst returned. She tried to wet her mouth as she reflected on what had happened.

Cowper had apparently returned to Dunmow but her fortunes had not improved. She was being taken to

Colchester and had to control her panic at what might happen there. She had sheltered a Catholic priest; she was still accused of witchcraft and sorcery. Father might be in Colchester!

Rebecca closed her eyes. Bartholomew was dead, foully murdered. So intent and so foolish had she been in her determination to confront Frogmore, the realisation only now dawned. Bartholomew was gone and their life at the Silver Wyvern was over! Rebecca couldn't stop the tears and, the more she tried, the more her body shook with sobs. Here she was aching, dirty, trussed up like a pig for the slaughter. For a few seconds she felt like cursing St Clair but was it his fault? A shadow moved beside her and she looked up to see Cowper draw his knife and cut her bonds.

'That was stupid as well as cruel,' he observed, his eyes still full of sleep. 'I should have cut them earlier. After all, where can you go, Mistress Lennox? The people of Dunmow would either hang you or turn you in for the reward. You are cold?'

'I don't know what I am.' Rebecca rubbed her wrists and her ankles.

Cowper picked up the blanket and put it over her shoulders, tenderly, like a mother would a child. He went across and started kicking his companions awake. The fire was built up and Cowper returned with ale as well as dried bread and bacon. He squatted and watched her eat.

'When you get on the horse,' he said. 'I'll tie your feet beneath its belly. Otherwise you'll be comfortable. Promise me you won't escape?'

Rebecca agreed and stared into his strange, light-blue eyes, the lids devoid of lashes. She couldn't decide whether he was comforting or taunting her.

'Where are we going?' she asked.

'Colchester Castle.'

'Why?'

'You know why, Rebecca. St Clair is our prisoner. You aided and abetted him.'

'Did he tell you that?'

'Come, come.'

Cowper picked a piece of bread up and popped it into his mouth, chewing it carefully. Rebecca noticed how his teeth were white and strong.

'St Clair told us nothing but we found the wineskin you left, that and the saddle on the horse all bore the imprints of your father's tavern.'

'He stole them.'

Cowper smiled. 'A wineskin? He just walked into your kitchen and took a wineskin and then into your stables for a saddle and the best horse? And, I suppose, up to your bedchamber for that piece of Castilian soap?'

Rebecca glanced away.

'St Clair has not implicated you,' Cowper said wearily.

'I haven't thanked you for saving me at Dunmow.'

'I had no choice. The Queen's justice is the Queen's justice.' Cowper cleared his throat. 'I would have liked to meet this Parson Frogmore but, by the time we reached the church, the hen had flown its coop.'

'Who is he?' Rebecca asked before she could stop herself.

Cowper sniffed and pinched his nostrils.

'This place stinks,' he said, ignoring her question.

'I'll be glad to be back on the road. Do you want to relieve yourself?'

Rebecca was conscious of the cramps in her stomach.

'Go outside,' Cowper advised. 'Keep your dignity, well away from the men. If any of them trouble you, tell me!'

Rebecca struggled to her feet. She walked out of the barn past the leering guards. A short distance away was the trackway along which they must have come. She went behind this and squatted down. When she had finished, she washed her hands in a pool of rain water and stared up. A faint coating of snow must have fallen through the night but the day was going to prove a fine one. The sky was clear, already lighted by the rising sun. Above the trees she glimpsed faint smoke rising from Dunmow village. She wondered how Peter the scullion would be coping? Then Rebecca realised she would never return. She let her body relax and walked back through the hedge into the barn. Cowper shooed the rest of the men away, ordering them to see to the horses, sending two of them back into the village to buy provisions. The fire now burned merrily and he made Rebecca sit down next to him.

For a while she just enjoyed the warmth. Cowper was correct. Where could she flee? How long would she last? She studied the men picking up saddles, talking and joking amongst themselves.

'They are from the sheriff's posse,' Cowper remarked, following her gaze. 'Scum of the earth, Rebecca. They'll rape you, cut your throat and steal your clothes without a second's thought.'

'And I suppose you are different,' she retorted.

'Yes and no. If need be, I'll cut your throat. I'd do it quickly, without you knowing.' Cowper ran his fingers through his white hair, pushing it away behind his ears and tying it with a black ribbon. He turned suddenly and pressed a finger against her hare-lip. 'How does it feel?' he whispered. 'To be strange, to be hare-lipped!'

Abruptly Rebecca found herself no longer in the barn. She was behind a large wall, part of it broken down. Smoke rolled backwards and forwards, the dead and dying lay thick around her. Terrible screams rent the air. Banners, red and gold, flapped above her as men fought hand-to-hand in bloody combat. Cowper watched this young woman, her face even paler, her eyes glazed.

'Mistress Lennox!' He shook her. 'Get on with your work!' he snarled at the staring men.

Rebecca sighed and put her hands down on either side to steady herself. She was in the barn with Cowper. She could smell hay, oats, familiar odours. It was a Monday in January; the weather was cold, she was being taken to Colchester, Father had been murdered.

'Mistress Lennox, are you well?'

She laughed. 'I am cold and bruised, Master Cowper, being taken to a hideous death and you ask me if I am well!'

'You still have your courage,' Cowper muttered. 'You also have the second sight, do you not?'

'So men say,' Rebecca replied guardedly.

Cowper edged closer. 'We are alike, Rebecca.'

Again he touched her hare-lip. He undid the top of his jacket and the cambric shirt beneath; the skin of his neck and chest were ivory white.

'I was once like you,' he continued. 'I was born in Stroud in Gloucestershire. My parents were prosperous yeomen farmers, raising the sheep, tilling the land: good soil, fresh grass and sturdy barns. I was the fourth and last child. My two brothers and sister were as pretty as flowers in a pot. And then comes Master William, white as a shroud, no eyebrows, no eyelashes, pink-rimmed eyes. They called me "Rabbit".' He hawked and spat. 'My mother couldn't bear the sight of me. I was put out to foster with a good man, Ralph Cowper, shoesmith, a trader in leather goods. He sent me to Gloucester Cathedral school where I learnt my horn book.' He bit his lower lip. 'Every day, Rebecca,' he whispered, 'was a living hell. The boys used to chase me, their "Rabbit", up the wynds and narrow alleyways of Gloucester. By the time I was twelve, I was a most accomplished street fighter. By the time I was fifteen, I could hold a sword and dagger against any man.

'I finished my schooling; Master Cowper had the money to send me to the Halls of Cambridge. By then I was quite a curiosity in the city, like some freak at a mummer's fair. Whores used to give me their favours free because they had never been with someone like me before. My kind usually die or are strangled at birth.'

He picked up small twigs and tossed them on the fire. Rebecca watched him intently. At the Silver Wyvern she had been so immersed in St Clair, she hadn't realised Cowper had been studying her. Did he see her as kin because of her deformity? A sister in spirit? Rebecca forgot her own aches and pains, the bubbling grief over Bartholomew's death and her anger at Frogmore. Deep in her heart she was pleased she was going to Colchester. Whatever happened she would meet St Clair and, perhaps, this man could be used?

137

'I've never told anyone this.' Cowper studied her as if making sure she wasn't mocking him. 'One day Master Cowper said my mother was coming to the village. My real father, I won't tell you his name, had died already. It was a June day. I couldn't sleep and I was up long before dawn. I went out into the fields to collect wild flowers. I picked the best, the freshest. I took them into Master Ralph's workshop where I fashioned a leather pot with silver medallions around the side. I bathed and changed, strode up and down in my new pair of shoes. My mind was all a jumble with strange fancies: Mother would take me home. Perhaps she'd explain why I had been put out to foster? Anyway, she came at noon, quite the lady in a carriage. She came into Master Cowper's shop.' The Judas Man stopped. Rebecca felt a twinge of compassion at the sadness in those strange eyes.

'I went and knelt before her, going down on one knee. She was beautiful, Rebecca, hair like spun gold, light-blue eyes. Any man would love her. I also saw the disdainful twist of her lips, the revulsion in her eyes. "Mother", I said and offered her my present. "Mother, are you taking me home now?"'

Cowper picked up a piece of straw and bit on the end, rubbing his finger and thumb along it. Most of the men were outside now, dinning the air with their cries. Cowper made to get up.

'What happened?' Rebecca asked.

'She laughed. I repeated my request. She stroked my hair as if I were a dog. She kissed Master Cowper on the cheek and walked out into the street.'

'And you never saw her again?'

'If I did, Rebecca, I'd kill her.' The blue eyes were now icy cold. Cowper laughed, an eerie, throaty noise. He leaned closer. 'Rebecca, you asked about Frogmore? I hunt a man who takes men's souls. And do you know why I am not frightened? Because I haven't got one to take!'

7

After a bone-jarring ride, Cowper's party eventually reached the outskirts of Colchester. Sudden squalls had swept in over the flat Essex countryside. The clouds were grey and lowering. As they entered the high street, the rain came lashing down, driving away the traders and customers from the stalls. They were soon drenched.

The journey had taken three days. Cowper had returned to his distant, impassive self as if he regretted talking to Rebecca. Nevertheless, he was protective enough; when one of his lieutenants had tried to finger Rebecca's breast, Cowper kicked him in the ribs and had almost beaten him senseless with the flat of his sword. After that she was left well alone.

It had been two years since Rebecca had come here with her father and what a contrast. Then it had been a midsummer fair. Bartholomew, Malbrook and other customers from the Silver Wyvern had laughed, drunk and danced till long after sunset. Now Colchester looked wet and bedraggled, a place of misery and darkness.

Occasionally a beggar scuttled out seeking alms. One look at Cowper's face and the royal badge sewn on his jerkin, and they slunk away.

At last they entered the small parkland which

surrounded the castle, following the pathway across the stinking moat and in through the massive gate-house. Rebecca was dragged from her saddle and led into a chamber where the turnkey and gaolers slouched about. The room was filthy, the rushes wet and covered in muck, the table littered with food. Mangy hunting dogs sniffed and hunted for scraps only to be driven off by their ale-sodden masters. The place stank like a midden. Rebecca's stomach clenched when she saw the brimming chamber pots standing in the corner.

'What in Satan's teeth do you want?' The turnkey rose, a beer jug in his hand.

Cowper took off his rain-sodden hat, at the same time showing the badge on his sleeve. The man sobered up. The rest of his companions fell silent.

'Ah, Master Cowper.' The turnkey's greasy face cracked into a gap-toothed grin.

'Master Turnkey, I have a prisoner.'

The fellow looked at Rebecca and wetted his lips.

'By the looks of her mouth, she's a witch. She'd be pretty if it wasn't for that . . .'

Cowper strode forward and drove his fist straight into the turnkey's stomach. The man collapsed groaning to the ground. A gaoler came forward, head bowed, hands stretched out beseechingly.

'Master Cowper, Master Cowper!'

'St Clair, is he well?'

The gaoler nodded. 'He's in a cell below stairs, not in the dungeon. As you said, clean straw, good food.'

'Give me your ledger.'

The turnkey rose and hurried off. He returned bringing a tray bearing a ledger, inkpot and quill.

Cowper deftly made the entry, his tongue held in the corner of his mouth, reminding Rebecca of a little boy practising grammar or syntax in his horn book.

'The prisoner is Rebecca Lennox. She is to join St Clair! The same cell. I want her kept safe. When I return, I want to find her dry, well fed and ready to answer the Queen's justice. No one is to visit them. If either of them is hurt I'll hang you all from the walls. Now, take her down!'

The turnkey hastened to obey. Rebecca was led out of the gatehouse chamber and down a winding set of stairs. At the bottom two men stood on guard, halberds in their hands. Two more of Cowper's men, sober, well dressed, with the appearance of professional soldiers. They came to attention as Cowper, Rebecca and the turnkey passed them and went down a narrow passageway lit by cresset torches. The turnkey stopped at a door at the far end. He fumbled with his key; after some muttering and cursing, the door swung open. Cowper shoved the man aside and led Rebecca in. The figure seated at a table in the corner rose. In spite of her surroundings, Rebecca's heart leaped as St Clair came forward. He was dressed in a dirty white shirt and a brown woollen jerkin, scuffed and holed. His leggings were the same colour, but his shoes and stockings had been taken away. He was unshaven, his hair bedraggled but Rebecca thought he looked even more handsome than when she had last seen him. The same strong face, kindly eyes and lazy smile. He brushed his hair back as if trying to make himself presentable.

'Why, Master Cowper, what do we have here?'

'You don't recognise her?' Cowper asked.

St Clair studied Rebecca from head to toe.

'The poor wench is soaking wet. Apart from that, what do you mean, do I recognise her?'

Rebecca quietly cursed her own stupidity. Of course, she had forgotten that! She was only pleased that she'd made no sign of recognition, although Cowper must have sensed her pleasure at seeing St Clair again.

'Come, come, Master St Clair,' Cowper quipped. 'Surely you recognise your saviour and rescuer, Rebecca Lennox of the Silver Wyvern tavern which stands in the market place at Dunmow?' Cowper looked over his shoulder at the turnkey. 'Get out! Lock the door behind you!'

The fellow scurried off. Cowper waved St Clair back to his stool behind the rough-hewn table.

'Sit down, Jesuit. You, too, Mistress Lennox.'

Rebecca did so. She had always imagined dungeons as dark, gloomy places, wet and mildewed, full of vermin but this was cleaner than the guard house upstairs. No rushes or coverings lay on the floor but the flagstones were scrubbed clean. The cell was really two chambers. The first part contained a table, some stools and a chest with a broken clasp. A curtain partitioned off the second half of the room but this was slightly pulled aside, and Rebecca glimpsed cot beds and more sticks of furniture while a small window high in the wall provided light and air. St Clair was well looked after. In this part of the cell three candles glowed, one on the table and two in horn lanterns hooked onto the wall. St Clair must be a very valued prisoner and Rebecca wondered what secrets he could tell. Cowper, leaning against the wall, studied St Clair intently before glancing at Rebecca.

'You are very clever, St Clair,' he said. 'You are

going to sit there until the Second Coming and claim you've never seen this wench before?'

'I've told you, Master Cowper: I went to Dunmow. I hid in the Silver Wyvern stables. I disguised myself as a servant, stole some food and a wineskin then saddled a horse and fled the benighted place!'

'Mistress Lennox seemed pleased to see you?'

'Well, of course she does.' St Clair beamed at Rebecca, a dazzling smile, his eyes full of merriment. 'The poor girl is only too relieved to have her name cleared.'

Rebecca stared at this man whose coming to Dunmow had shattered and changed her life. Despite what had happened, she felt happier than she had for many a day. She could have laughed at the irony. She'd lost her life, and what remained of her family, yet she was pleased to be in the presence of this handsome, young man who now claimed he had never met her.

'Mistress Lennox.' St Clair spread his hands. 'I am sorry for any misfortune I have caused. I do have friends in England, so I could arrange compensation be paid for what I stole.'

'My father is dead.' Rebecca blurted the words out. She was going to add more but, despite the sadness which swept St Clair's face, she caught his warning look.

'Dead?' Cowper pushed himself away from the wall. 'Dead, Mistress Lennox? You never told me.'

'You never asked,' Rebecca replied, frightened at the fury in the Judas Man's face.

'But,' he said threateningly. 'I was informed your father had gone to Colchester. Callerton the constable said that he has sworn out information against you!'

'Well, if Callerton says that he must be right. But

145

I believe my father is really dead. He would never turn traitor against his own kith and kin.'

Cowper breathed in slowly, his eyes studying the candle in the lantern horn.

'I'll go back there,' he whispered. 'And I'll hang every man jack of them!'

'Why not take Mistress Rebecca with you?' St Clair intervened. 'She's innocent of any crime.'

'She's as guilty as you, St Clair, and you know it. You're both to be lodged here.'

'Together in the same chamber?' St Clair quipped.

'You are a priest, aren't you?' Cowper snarled. 'You've taken vows of celibacy and chastity. What do I care? You are welcome to her, hare-lip and all!' He must have glimpsed the hurt in Rebecca's eyes. 'I'm sorry, mistress,' he continued. 'I'll get that lazy bastard outside to bring you fresh clothes.'

They both sat until the sound of footsteps faded along the passageway. Rebecca made to get up but St Clair just shook his head. He sat watching the door and Rebecca realised he was counting. Then he crouched beside her and tapped her playfully on the tip of her nose.

'By all that is holy, Mistress Rebecca,' he whispered. 'I am truly sorry. I have told them nothing but they found your father's markings on the saddle and some of the other possessions.' St Clair glanced towards the door.

'Whatever you think of me, don't speak until I tell you. Do you understand that?'

Rebecca nodded. St Clair returned to his seat and, once again, began apologising loudly for the distress he had caused. At the same time miming with his hands and eyes that Rebecca should plead her innocence. When she did so, he put his hands together as if applauding.

'Well, Mistress Lennox, at least take comfort that you are in suitable quarters.' He pulled back the curtain. 'There's a chamber pot and a privy in the corner, which feeds down into the moat so the place won't smell. We have fresh water in a jug and a clean rag to dry ourselves. I've been given every assurances that the blankets and mattress have been fumigated. There's dried bread and light ale in the morning, watered wine or whatever the garrison is eating at noon and hard biscuit with ale at night, so you won't starve or die of thirst. The gaolers are a drunken lot but, they are terrified of Cowper, so they'll leave us alone. As for the future, I don't know what will happen but I suspect we'll be taken to London.'

He paused at the sound of the key in the cell door. Cowper came back bringing a shabby, woollen kirtle, gown, a rather soiled petticoat and two broad sheets of linen.

'You can dry your own clothes,' he said. 'And wear these. Their previous owner doesn't need them, she was hanged yesterday morning.' He walked back to the door. 'Until I decide what's to be done, you'll stay here.' He slammed the door, turning the key in the lock.

Rebecca gathered up the bundle of clothing and went behind the curtain. She changed quickly, drying her hair on the cloth, and swiftly donned the smelly garments Cowper had brought. She hung her gown, stockings, petticoat and other items on pegs in the wall. She peeped round the curtain. St Clair was leaning, hands on the table, playing some sort of game with hardened bread crumbs, trying to get them into a straight line while keeping his eyes shut; customers at the Silver Wyvern had played a similar game with pebbles or coins. She went to join him but he shook his head and pointed at the bed. She went and lay down. She meant to lie there and reflect on what had happened but, within minutes, she was asleep.

St Clair woke her roughly, shaking her. She sat up. Night had fallen. The window was now only a black hole in the wall. He grasped her by the hand and, leading her round the curtains, pointed to the table. The gaoler had brought two battered wooden cups, a cracked jug and a trauncher with pieces of bread, meat and cheese. St Clair crossed himself, blessed the food and urged Rebecca to eat. Every so often he'd help himself but he seemed distracted, as if waiting for someone to approach. The food was barely palatable. Rebecca abruptly felt homesick as memories of the Silver Wyvern flooded back: her father's cooks, the bustling kitchen with its sweet savoury smells. She fought back the tears. She must not think of that! The past was like a room she had left and the door must be kept closed.

Instead she surreptitiously studied the Jesuit's rich hair, sharp features, large, eloquent eyes and full lips. The more she stared the more certain he reminded her of the statue. She'd drunk the wine so quickly, it made her feel depleted and exhausted. At St Clair's urging she went back and lay on the bed. The last thing she remembered was the Jesuit pulling the blanket over her, stroking her hair as she fell asleep.

Later in the night, she did not know whether she was dreaming or awake, she sat up in bed. The curtain was pulled back and the cell was full of sunlight. The Jesuit was sitting at the table, two young men on either side of him. All three were dressed in cloth of gold; Michael's hair had been groomed and oiled as elegant as any courtier's, his face was transformed, shining like burnished gold. His eyes glowed like sapphires, his lips were moving. His two companions, who looked and dressed the same, were staring at the golden, gem-encrusted chalice which hovered in the air between them. All three were praying but Rebecca couldn't understand the language. It was neither Latin nor French, both of which she had a little knowledge of.

The more she stared at the vision, the more certain she became that all three were no longer flesh and blood but fire, yet a fire she had never seen before, like molten gold leaping up out of a furnace. All three were oblivious of her, their eyes on the chalice, glowing red as if a fire burned in its bowl. The room was warm and fragrant. Rebecca was no longer conscious of the walls or any of her surroundings. Behind the three men she could see other shapes, gold and silver, as if a group of knights in full armour stood on guard, their voices, too, joined in the hymn of praise.

Rebecca rubbed her eyes but, when she looked again, there was nothing but darkness. St Clair was asleep on his bed. Through the window Rebecca heard the calls of the sentries. She was cold and, lying down, pushed her knuckles into her mouth like she did when she was a child awake in the night and the tavern was quiet and the shadows clustered.

Rebecca must have dozed for a while until she was awakened again, this time by a voice, harsh and guttural, calling her name.

'Rebecca! Rebecca!'

She sat up and stared in horror at the vision in front of her. She could make out the outline of a cowl, the dark material of the hood trailing down over the shoulders but there was no face, body or head: only fiery holes where the eyes should have been.

'Rebecca! Rebecca!'

'Go away!' she screamed, flailing out with her hands and closing her eyes.

'Rebecca! Rebecca! What's the matter?'

St Clair was up, his eyes heavy with sleep, his hair tousled. He grasped her wrists.

'I don't know.' She fell back onto the straw-filled bolster. 'I had dreams. I woke up, a hood with burning eyes but no face . . .'

'Get up,' St Clair whispered.

She did so, feeling rather embarrassed. She excused herself and, while St Clair went round the curtain, went to the privy. The stone was cold and hard. The corner she had to force herself into was made of rough stone which scored her back. Afterwards she poured water over her hands, splashing some on her face: it smelt brackish and stale. When she pulled the curtain back, St Clair was not seated at the table. All she could see was a dark shape against the far wall.

'Rebecca, come here, sit beside me. Try to make no sound.'

When she nestled down, he drew her close to him. Rebecca felt warm and relaxed. St Clair meant her no harm but why were they sitting in the dark, their backs to the wall?

'I don't think there's anyone at the Judas hole,' St Clair whispered. 'And, if they are, well, I pushed in pieces of rag.'

'What do you mean?'

St Clair laughed. 'You don't think they put us in the same cell out of kindness? There are two peep-holes in the wall near our beds. On the other side is a secret chamber where Cowper has put one of his men. The fellow is probably fast asleep now. I discovered that, if I sit here and talk softly, they can't hear us from the door or the peep-hole. So, if we have anything to say, Rebecca, it will be here and it will be at night, no candles, with as little movement as possible.' He turned smiling at her through the darkness. 'What are these dreams you had?'

Rebecca told him. St Clair laughed softly.

'You're getting me mixed up with a statue. You see me as your knight errant. All I am is a Jesuit on the run.'

'No, you are not,' she said. 'You are hunting Frogmore. You forget, I saw you fighting in our parish church.'

'Yes, yes,' he murmured. 'I am hunting Frogmore and now you are part of that hunt. I can't speak about your first vision but the cowl, the burning eyes, that's Frogmore! It means he's in Colchester trying to discover what has happened to both of us. I am sorry you've been brought to this pass. No, no, I am but, tell me, what has happened since I left you.'

Rebecca did, at first in short, halting sentences. Now and again St Clair would interrupt with a question or a demand to keep her voice low. When she had finished St Clair sat silently.

'What I am going to tell you, Rebecca, will be difficult to believe. I want you to trust me. These are not matters of everyday concern but those things twixt heaven and hell.' He paused. 'How old do you think Henry Frogmore is?'

'Thirty-three, thirty-four summers old.'

'Henry Frogmore,' St Clair declared, 'is at least four hundred years old.'

Rebecca gasped.

'Henry Frogmore,' St Clair repeated, 'was a monk at Glastonbury during the reign of Henry II, a king who died in 1189. Frogmore came of good family. He proved himself a brilliant scholar and joined the Benedictine Order where he was ordained priest. Frogmore had an enquiring mind . . .'

St Clair was about to continue but Rebecca grasped his wrist. For the last few minutes, although cloaked in darkness, Rebecca had sensed an unease. The cell had become very cold. Then she heard it: a slither of footsteps outside. An image flashed across her mind – three men, cloaked and cowled, were edging along the passageway to their cell. One of them had a key.

'We are in great danger!'

'I know.' St Clair sprang up, took down the pole on which the curtain hung and tore this off. Rebecca heard a sound. The key turned in the lock, the door was pushed open. One of the gaolers came in, a fixed smile on his face. He was carrying a torch. He placed this in an iron bracket on the wall.

'Just ensuring everything's well, my dear.'

Rebecca glimpsed the dark shapes behind him.

'Michael!' she shouted.

The Jesuit pushed by her. 'Scream!' he roared. 'Scream as loud as you can!'

The gaoler now dropped all pretence as, drawing a sword and dagger, he joined the other two as they fanned out across the cell, leather boots slapping on the paved stone. St Clair moved with them, bare feet shuffling; he held the pole like a quarter staff.

'Scream!' he shouted over his shoulder.

Rebecca stood transfixed. Why should the gaolers do this? The eyes in their beer-sodden faces looked glazed. Were they drunk? In some stupor? Two of them moved in. Michael lashed out with the pole, catching one a crack in the face which sent him flying back like a ninepin. The other lunged, Michael used the pole to block the parry but the gaoler slipped by him. He walked towards Rebecca like a man dream-walking, sword and dagger out. Rebecca stepped back. She felt the bed behind her. The man leered, forgetful of the mêlée behind him. He dropped sword and dagger, lurching at Rebecca. In the dancing torchlight he looked like some loathsome toad. Rebecca sprang forward, getting inside his guard. The man teetered back and fell, Rebecca on top, nails clawing at his face, scratching his eyes, his mouth, his nose, lashing out with her fists. She could hear someone screaming and realised it was her. She wanted to look up. Was St Clair safe? She glimpsed movement, the whirl of the pole and the glittering swish of steel. The gaoler was now fighting back, trying to draw another dagger. Rebecca bit deeply into the man's fleshy neck, even as the man beat his fists against her ribs.

Suddenly Rebecca found she was no longer in the cell but lying on rushes in a chamber. Frogmore, St Clair and Master Cowper were there. She could hear the distant fury of battle. The pain in her side was becoming unbearable. Abruptly there was a roar like a cannon. Others were bursting into the cell, Master Cowper's voice shouting orders. Another roar. She smelt gunpowder and the gaoler beneath her went still. The top part of the man's head had been shorn away, blood and brains oozing out. His face was shifting, the eyes still moving in their death agony. The smell of gunpowder made Rebecca cough and retch as hands plucked her up and threw her roughly on the bed. St Clair was leaning against the wall gasping, the pole snapped in two at his feet. Cowper held a smoking hand gun. The men behind were similarly armed. All three assailants lay dead. Two had a ball in their skulls, the third had been taken behind, his throat slashed from ear to ear, his blood now gushing out across the floor.

Rebecca felt as if she were in a nightmare. Cowper, dressed in a black quilted jacket, white shirt and leggings, moved among the corpses like some hideous raven, checking that they were dead. He went across and murmured to St Clair. The Jesuit nodded and, crossing his arms, slid down the wall. Cowper glanced across, his face glistening with sweat.

'You are well?' he asked.

'I am, I am.'

Rebecca flailed her hands and started to cry. One minute she had been warm, secure in the darkness then . . .

Cowper came over. He seized her chin between forefinger and thumb. Rebecca caught a look of compassion and something else, then his eyes shifted. He pressed his hand against her cheek and forehead.

'Take them out!' he ordered. 'Take the two prisoners upstairs. Clear the cell. Have it scrubbed.'

'And the corpses?'

'Throw them into the city ditch!' Cowper snapped. 'Tell one of those lazy turnkeys to bring some wine!'

Rebecca and St Clair were hustled out of the cell

along the passageway and up the stairs. They left the gatehouse. The night air was cold, chilling their sweat. They were taken across a cobbled yard lit eerily by torches and into a small panelled room. It had a bed, table and chairs, a shelf of books and, in the far corner, a cot bed with the blankets thrown back. A neat place, it smelt of the herbs sprinkled on the floor, Cowper pushed Rebecca towards the bed.

'Sit there, lie down, whatever makes you feel calm. St Clair, take that chair.'

Rebecca realised she was only in her night shift and took a blanket, to cover herself as she sat on the bed. St Clair had regained his poise. He lounged on a chair, fingers drumming on his thighs, watching Cowper from under heavy-lidded eyes. The Judas Man inspected both of them as if he was a physician.

'No cuts or bruises,' he declared. 'You'll both live!'

A servant came in with a jug of wine and three cups. Cowper snatched it off him. He almost kicked the man out of the room, slamming the door behind him. He sniffed the jug.

'The best claret.' He smiled thinly. 'They are beginning to appreciate who I am.'

'Who are you?' St Clair asked lazily.

'To you, priest, I am a Judas Man. I hunt your kind down. I bring you in, dead or alive, and I collect my reward. To others I'm the Queen's officer in peace and war. I have the ear of Secretary Walsingham. If I say this man goes, he goes. I carry the Queen's warrant. No man, be he high or low, can challenge or stop me. That's who I am, Master Jesuit!'

He served them a goblet of wine.

'Drink,' he ordered. 'It might make you a little sick but it will warm you against the cold.'

'What happened there?' St Clair asked. 'Those men were meant to guard us.'

'No they weren't.' Cowper sat down on a stool, sipping at the wine. 'They murdered the men I left guarding you. If I hadn't heard the wench's screams they would have killed you both. Now, there are no peep-holes here, Master Jesuit, so let's not dance like children round the Maypole. Master Frogmore sent them!'

'You mean bribed them?'

Cowper shook his head. 'Jesuit, if you weren't a priest, you should be a player and stride the boards. You sit there in round-eyed innocence and mock me! Frogmore doesn't bribe people, not unless he has to. You know full well what he did. Do you, Mistress Lennox?'

'I know nothing,' she snapped. 'I do not even know why I am here. For a Queen's man you have poor care of your charges.'

Cowper's smile widened; there was even a twinkle in his eye.

'I do like you, Rebecca, and do you know?' He put the wine cup down. 'I find it hard to decide who I like more, you or the Jesuit. God hates a coward and neither of you are that. I've reflected on what happened. Frogmore was no parson: he is the Soul Slayer.' He pointed at Rebecca. 'I suspect you're the reason he came to Dunmow. Frogmore is a great magus, probably the greatest ever to walk under the sun.'

'You seem to know a lot about him,' St Clair countered.

'What I know and what I say are my business, Jesuit. Frogmore has power over the weak-minded and sinful men. Those three lovelies probably went out to a tavern, their minds and bodies given over to debauchery. Their souls were like derelict houses, the doors and windows hanging open. Master Frogmore could slip in like a shadow. A night-walker is Master Frogmore. They came back to this castle with one desire: to kill you and Mistress Lennox.'

'You are sure of that?' St Clair asked.

'Of course I am. There's no other explanation. Gaolers would not kill you so openly and expect to walk away. What's the use of gold when you are hanging by your neck from the town gallows?'

'But does Frogmore have such power?' Rebecca asked.

'Have you forgotten Dunmow, those parishioners of St Michael? Frogmore was like a fox loose in a hen coop. So, Master St Clair, or that's what you call yourself, are you going to tell me what you know about Frogmore?'

'I know he is a man of evil repute but I am a Jesuit priest serving the faithful in the eastern shires of England.'

'You are also a liar!'

Cowper stopped. The change in St Clair was remarkable. The lazy good humour disappeared.

'I am not a liar, Master Cowper. I simply do not have to tell you my business.'

'Then if you won't tell me, perhaps her majesty's interrogators in London?'

'Oh, you mean the rack, the pulley and the thumb screw?'

Cowper refused to hold his gaze.

157

'I'll have to take you there. Like it or not, Master Walsingham wants words with you.'

There was a knock at the door and Cowper got to his feet.

'The cell is clean, sir.' The soldier nodded at the Jesuit and Rebecca. 'Shall we take them back?'

'Aye, but double the guard. Oh, and Corporal, from now until we go, no one leaves the castle and no one enters.'

Rebecca and St Clair were hustled back to their cell, only a dark stain on the floor showed where the corpses had lain. A new pole had been fixed and the curtain re-hung.

'Go to sleep,' St Clair ordered.

Rebecca, tired from the wine and the shock, needed no second bidding. But, as she drifted off, she woke with a start. If Frogmore had come to Dunmow for her, was that also true of St Clair?

8

'Who are you? Where do you come from?'

It was late afternoon following the violent attack. Rebecca had slept late, roused roughly before noon by Cowper's men bringing in food. Outside, the castle had fallen silent. The priest had taken her to their place against the wall and they now sat with their backs resting against the rough stone.

'I mean.' Rebecca moved her hair out of her face. 'You know who I am, where I come from, my father, my calling.' She smiled. 'A tavern wench. But you?'

'Tell me.' St Clair stretched his legs out and moved the blankets to cover his bare feet. 'Tell me, Rebecca, if a woman has thirteen children and half of them are daughters what are the other half?' He grinned at her bewilderment. 'I love puzzles,' he continued. 'There's nothing like a good riddle to while away an evening. I heard that in a tavern outside Chelmford.'

'What's it got to do with my question?' Rebecca retorted. 'Half of thirteen is six and a half!'

'But that's ridiculous,' St Clair teased.

'Well, I don't know,' Rebecca replied crossly.

'They were all daughters!'

Rebecca shrugged. 'Oh, that's stupid!'

St Clair threw his head back and laughed. 'No,

it isn't. Examine my question carefully, I never intimated that they were never anything but.' He sighed. 'The same applies to your question. Rebecca, I am what I appear to be: a Jesuit priest dedicated to the pursuit and destruction of Frogmore.'

'But where do you come from? Is your family still alive? Do you have brothers and sisters?'

'I have family,' St Clair replied mischievously. 'And I think you would like them, Rebecca. One day you'll see where I come from. I'll take you there. I promise you. Why, who do you think I am?'

'You could be an angel.' Rebecca blurted the words out.

St Clair shook with laughter.

'It's not that funny!'

'Oh, you are correct. Angel comes from the Greek for messenger but don't confuse me with your statue, Rebecca. You saw me fight those villains. I can bleed and hurt as well as the next man.'

'What do you think angels are like?' Rebecca leaned back against the wall.

St Clair pointed across to the candle flame.

'I don't know how to describe one, Rebecca. If I had to speak in parables, I'd think of an angel as pure fire an eternal flame, a spark of divinity with a mind and a will of its own. In that fire burns an all-consuming desire to be with God, be loved by God, to serve God.'

'A flame is only small,' Rebecca countered.

'What does that mean to the good Lord?' St Clair replied. 'He himself became a baby, a man could have put Him in his saddle bag. Large and small, fat and thin, they are human terms and labels. Take that flame.' He pointed again. 'It burns low, but what happens if it had a life of its own? It could remain small or it could grow bigger than this cell, the castle. Indeed, it could consume all of Colchester.'

'And what would this spiritual flame feed on?' Rebecca asked.

St Clair paused. 'The same as the flame inside you, Rebecca. You miss your mother?'

Rebecca nodded.

'You love her still?'

'Yes, of course!'

'If you lived a thousand years, would you love her still?'

'Of course!'

'Then you have answered your own question. The divine fire is pure love: a desire to create, to be in harmony with all things, to love all things and to be consumed itself by love.'

Rebecca pulled the blankets closer. She half closed her eyes, pretending this was her father's taproom. If only Peter the scullion would bring in two jugs of ale and some spiced meat . . .

'Can a devil become a man?'

'Perhaps. More importantly, a man can allow Satan into his soul to control his mind and heart. Frogmore did that.'

'And what about an angel?'

'If Le Bon Seigneur can become a man then why shouldn't an angel? In the book of Tobit, Raphael became a man to rescue Tobit from the wiles of his enemies, to give him good counsel and advice.'

'And Frogmore, you were telling me?'

Rebecca paused at the footfall outside. The key turned in the lock and Cowper strode in. He smiled at them.

'You have discovered the peep-holes?'

'Of course!'

'Well, you needn't worry about them. We are leaving Colchester for London.'

Theodore Ragusa sat in a corner of the taproom of the Merry Pig tavern on the road just outside the old walls of Colchester. On the table before him lay a purse of silver; the wolfs-heads and cutthroats gathered around him gazed at it. They licked their lips and nodded quietly as the mercenary talked about what he wanted and how it would be done.

'The prisoners will be moved soon,' he explained, then stared around.

The taproom was empty except for the shabby chapman who sat in the inglenook. He'd pulled off his battered boots and was warming his feet before the fire. The man had an idiotic expression on his face, bleary-eyed and slack-jawed. Ragusa dismissed him with a contemptuous glance.

'We do not know,' he continued hoarsely, 'when the prisoners will leave the castle. However, they must take the road south through the woods to the river crossing, going through Epping and Woodford before they reach Mile End and the main highway into the city. For each of you, three silver pieces if the two prisoners are safely taken.'

These men had been easy to collect. Ragusa had travelled the pathways and byeways of Europe, it was the same wherever he went. Taverners, particularly those outside the city walls, always knew who to talk to, which men to hire. The great forests which covered Essex still harboured an army of former soldiers, night-walkers, rifflers, naps and foists who had fled

162

from London, well beyond the reach of the sheriff's men. He could trust them because they could trust no one else. True, they could go into Colchester and seek out Master Cowper, but they had no assurances that, once they had given information, they wouldn't be arrested and hanged out of hand.

Ragusa believed he had the measure of Cowper. He'd listened carefully to the rumours in Colchester, Dunmow and elsewhere. He had found the parish of St Michael in uproar, men and women eager to blame each other. He'd heard about the priest, the young tavern wench and how Cowper had arrested them and hauled them off to Colchester. Ragusa had also listened most carefully about Master Frogmore and knew he had found his man, but Frogmore was difficult to hunt. Ragusa regretted allowing the parson by on that lonely road but would it have been so easy to take him prisoner? And was that the best way forward? Prisoner or invited guest of the Ottoman court? Ragusa needed to trap, but then negotiate with this warlock. If he rescued the Jesuit, then he'd have the key to the door and his task might prove all the easier. Ragusa laughed quietly and ordered more drinks for his companions.

The chapman warming himself before the fire drained his blackjack and sighed; he put on his battered leather boots, picked up his fardel and cudgel then walked out across the yard onto the trackway. He walked slowly resting on his stick, head down, hat pulled over his eyes. Now and again he'd stop to take stock of his surroundings. The sky was beginning to darken. A cold breeze still carried the rain as well as the stench of the rotting vegetation from the woods on either side. The trackway was clear of the other travellers. Night was falling and this stretch of the road was notorious for outlaws but the chapman seemed to know where he was going. Just before he reached the crossroads, he turned off, pushing through the wet undergrowth, and climbed the hill. He cursed as his boots slipped on the mud. Halfway up he left the trackway, making his way through the trees into the clearing where his horse, still hobbled, cropped the grass; its saddle and panniers stowed carefully away under a bush. The chapman checked that everything was well and, picking up a saddle bag, resumed his climb.

At the top of the hill he stood and stared out over the valley. He felt at home here. This was an old burial ground where the tribes had once worshipped and hanged their victims from the branches of the trees before throwing them into the marshes which once filled the valley below. The dwelling house of ghosts, of murdered souls; a place where earth met the force of hell. Frogmore sat down. The body of the chapman had been a perfect disguise as he had followed Ragusa around Colchester. He opened the saddle bag and, taking out the leather sack, put the heart of the murdered chapman down before him. He surrounded it with pebbles, built a fire in the circle and watched it consume the heart. Frogmore's eyes closed as he chanted a hymn of malice to his dark masters. He breathed in, feeling his body flex and change, shaking off the shape he had adopted as easily and as effortlessly as a snake shed its skin. Once the fire was out and the sacrifice consumed, Frogmore sat cross-legged, peering down into the darkness.

'Too many pursuers,' he murmured but then smiled. He always thanked his masters for the arrogance of his enemies: Ragusa was as proud as a peacock. A fish out of water, the Venetian had swaggered and blustered. Well, Frogmore would teach him a lesson. Why not let his enemies take care of themselves? He knew the attack on St Clair had failed. Despite Cowper's strictures, the taverns and alehouses round the castle had been full of the gossip, while the corpse of the dead gaolers had been hung on the town's gallows before being thrown into the pit next to the stinking city ditch.

'Ah well!' Frogmore sighed.

He'd sent a letter, words roughly formed in the hand of the chapman, to Cowper who could take care of everything. Frogmore shifted uneasily. For some strange reason he was wary of Cowper. His name stirred memories and Frogmore was growing suspicious. Cowper was proving to be a veritable bloodhound. Many officials could be bought or bribed. Eventually they tired of the chase but Cowper was different. He had a doggedness, a determination which Frogmore recognised as dangerous.

The warlock sucked on his lips. Tomorrow he would enter London by stealth and visit Dr Hermeticus. He stretched out his hands, palms up to the sky. As each year passed his power grew but he had to see the future, he had to take advice, he had to see where the danger lay.

Somewhere at the bottom of the hill, in one of the lonely farms, dogs yapped against the approaching night. Frogmore got to his feet. By dawn he would be on the road to London, where Hermeticus would help. And those who pursued him? Frogmore grinned. In his own good time, and at his own choosing, he'd turn and fight.

*   *   *

The attack occurred within an hour of Cowper's party leaving Colchester. The Judas Man had spent most of the day preparing mounts, writing reports, ensuring his prisoners were fit to travel. New clothes and boots had been provided for both prisoners. Cowper had lashed St Clair's hands to the saddle horn, with his feet tied to his horse's belly. Rebecca was treated more gently. She was allowed to ride free but a rope had been slipped round her waist and tied to a ring on Cowper's belt who rode alongside her, a good dozen outriders flanking them.

At first they made fair speed. The clouds were low and grey but the threatened rain didn't fall and the trackway remained firm under foot. Cowper was vigilant. He seemed slightly distracted, lost in his own thoughts. Now and again he ordered his men off the trackway and into the trees on either side.

In fact the ambush was launched in an unexpected manner. They rounded a bend to find that a cart blocked their path, its wheels lying in the mud. Two men were arguing volubly over whose fault it was. The tired nag which pulled it had been unhitched and was busily cropping the grass. One of Cowper's men rode up. He was the first to die. The dirty sheet covering the cart was thrown back and the outlaw's crossbow, primed and ready, loosed a bolt before the man even fully realised what was happening. Other outlaws jumped from the cart. Cowper cut the rope linking him with Rebecca. He drew his sword and the forest pathway was plunged into a bloody violent fight. Attackers swooped down from the trees, a group of horsemen came from behind. Cowper and his men fought valiantly but eventually Cowper urged his horse off the road, seeking refuge in the trees. St Clair and Rebecca could only sit and watch. As Cowper's men broke and fled, the outlaws seized their horses, closed up around them and galloped along the forest path.

Rebecca had to fight hard to keep straight in the saddle. Her back and thighs ached, her arms grew stiff with trying to manage the reins. Now and again one of the attackers would provide assistance. Ahead of her St Clair bounced and swayed in the saddle like a sack but the outlaws rode so close that, though he slipped, he never fell from the saddle.

The wind whipped Rebecca's breath away. All she was conscious of was the pounding hooves, the horses' heads rising and falling, flecks of foam, the creak of saddle and the shouts of men in that mad headlong dash, the trees whirling by. Now and again a horse would stumble over some pot hole, and a rider came off, but they didn't wait. Rebecca closed her eyes and prayed. Through the darkness they galloped like horsemen from some demonic hunt.

Rebecca wondered how long this nightmare ride would continue when they broke into a clearing. The riders reined in, pulling down their masks and vizards as they brought their horses to a halt, the animals rearing and bucking after such a mad dash. Rebecca saw torchlight, an old tumbledown fence and a pathway leading up to a disused hunting lodge. The windows had long gone, the shutters torn off, while the door hung by one hinge. Shouts of men filled the air. Torches were lit, spluttering against the night air.

Rebecca felt sick, and swayed dangerously in the saddle. A pair of strong hands pulled her down. She didn't even flinch as those same hands roamed, cupping her breats, followed by some whispered lecherous comment. St Clair had already been taken down and was being pushed, his hands still bound, up the pathway. Rebecca followed. Inside, the hunting lodge smelt musty, the floor covered in dust, pieces of wood and shards of furniture. The stairs, however, were still usable. Rebecca and St Clair were pushed up into a large upper room and told to sit in a corner. Rebecca found it difficult to breathe, let alone speak. St Clair seemed semiconscious. Some of their captors stayed in the room. Torches were lit, a fire built in the hearth. From below came the savoury odours of cooking.

'What is this?' Rebecca shouted. 'Why have you taken us prisoner? My companion needs help!'

A man came over, a dark shape. He sat down and took off his broad-brimmed hat. A cruel face, Rebecca thought, olive-skinned, his gaze hard and steadfast. His hair, moustache and beard were neatly trimmed and oiled, and he smelt of leather and sweat. He chucked Rebecca under the chin.

'I'll get a good price for you at one of the ports.' He touched her hare-lip. 'Some men think that's hideous. Others find it attractive.'

'Leave the girl alone!' St Clair raised his head. The Jesuit's left eye was half-closed with a bruise; there was a cut on his chin.

'Cut the girl's bonds and let her go!'

The man shifted in his seat so he squatted and bowed mockingly at the Jesuit.

'My name is Theodore Ragusa, I take orders from no one.' He gently tapped St Clair with his leather gauntlet. 'You are my prisoner but I want to make you my companion.'

'I do not wish to be your companion,' St Clair replied.

'Oh, you will be.' Ragusa narrowed his eyes and stared at St Clair and Rebecca. 'Well, well, Jesuit, so you like the ugly one?'

'Keep your foul mouth shut!'

'I'll tell you what. If you don't cooperate with me, I'll give the girl over to my men. Some of them haven't had a woman for days, weeks. You can sit here and listen to her scream if you want.'

St Clair lashed out with his boot but Ragusa moved sideways, quick as a spider.

'Think about it,' he taunted. He drew his knife and slashed the rope around St Clair's wrists. 'I'll keep your feet tied then you can't run. Have something to eat and we'll talk again.' Ragusa got up and wandered off.

St Clair flexed his arms and stretched his fingers. Abruptly, he looked up in the air and muttered something in a tongue Rebecca couldn't understand.

'What's the matter?' she asked anxiously.

'Nothing! Let's eat and drink and see what this villain wants.'

'Do you know him?'

'I know of him. Theodore Ragusa is a mercenary, a paid assassin, a hunter of men. He is ruthless, bloodthirsty and doesn't suffer any scruples.' The Jesuit shifted to look at her squarely. 'He meant what he said, Rebecca.'

He paused as one of their captors came across and pushed wooden dishes into their hands. They contained some rabbit stew, half a rotting apple and some hard rye bread. Two battered, pewter cups of coarse wine were also served. Rebecca picked at her food but St Clair wolfed his down.

'Eat, Rebecca,' he whispered. 'You never know where the next meal is from. I don't think Ragusa controls this game; I am going to agree to whatever he wants.'

Sure enough a short while later the mercenary returned, smacking his lips and wiping his mouth on the back of his hand.

'Well, priest what do you say? Shall we dance together? Or shall we listen to Mistress Hare-lip pleasure my men?'

'You want me to help you capture Frogmore?'

Ragusa laughed and tapped St Clair playfully on the nose.

'I like you, priest.'

'But not now,' St Clair added. 'I'm tired and exhausted. So is the girl. Night has fallen and there's nothing we can do.'

Ragusa chewed the corner of his lip, gazing slyly at St Clair as if calculating the risks.

'What's the matter, Jesuit? Why wait till morning?'

'I'm tired.'

'Where's Frogmore?' Ragusa snapped.

'On the road to London.'

'What's he doing there?'

'He wishes to visit a warlock, Hermeticus.'

'And where does this doctor live?'

'I'll tell you that in the morning.'

Ragusa nodded. 'Then, sir, I bid you good night.' He came back and threw each of them a shabby rug. 'They have fleas but will keep you warm. If you wish to relieve yourself, crawl to the small chamber next door. Try to leave without our permission or saying farewell and we'll cut the wench's throat!'

He walked away.

'What's happening?' Rebecca touched St Clair's arm.

He just took off his jerkin, rolled this into a pillow and lay down on the floor. Rebecca went to do likewise and St Clair caught her arm.

'You are not ugly,' he said quietly. 'To me, Rebecca, you are as beautiful as any Helen of Troy. Come.'

He pulled her down beside him, cradling her head against his shoulder. At first Rebecca lay there stiff and tense but St Clair stroked her hair and kissed her on the brow.

'Take your rest, pretty one. Say your prayers. Tomorrow is a new day, as Master Ragusa will find out.'

He hushed her whispers. Rebecca felt warm, her body jerking as she relaxed and drifted into sleep.

She woke next morning slightly cold and a little stiff. St Clair was awake, straining up at the great spiders' webs which spanned the rafters above them.

'Stay still,' he whispered.

She did so, listening to the sounds from below, the shouts and cries of men, the clip-clop of horses being led out.

'It's between dawn and day,' St Clair told her.

'St Clair, what are you waiting for?' Rebecca hissed through clenched teeth. 'I am not a child!'

'No, you are not, pretty one. You are a brave young woman, of strong wit and good mind. So, tell me.' St Clair tapped her on the side of the head. 'Let us say, Rebecca, you are the Queen's man and you are in Colchester. You have two important prisoners you must take into London by the securest possible route. How would you do it?'

'I'd . . .'

'No, think!' St Clair urged.

Rebecca would have jumped up but St Clair held her fast. One of Ragusa's men was just outside the doorway.

'Cowper took us along a forest path late in the day,' she said quietly.

'And?'

'If I was he, I would have carried us to one of the ports, used the royal warrants and had a ship take us up the Thames.'

'Precisely.' St Clair chuckled. 'Who'd attack a royal man-of-war, a ship which could dock within sight of Westminster or even further up river? Within the hour we would have been in the Tower. I don't know what Master Cowper intends but he's a soldier and the best time to take an enemy is just before daybreak. When that happens, Rebecca, do precisely what I tell you!'

A guard came in, kicking at their feet, ordering them to sit up. Dirty, chipped bowls of oatmeal were pushed into their hands with a blackjack of ale to share.

'Use your fingers!' the fellow taunted. 'And eat quickly, Master Ragusa wants us out of here within the hour.'

'*Deus volens*,' St Clair replied.

The fellow looked at him.

'God willing,' St Clair translated cheerily.

There was a crack and suddenly the man was staggering back, his eyes rolling up: the ball had taken him full in the temple, and the blood spurted out. Other shots rang out followed by the whirr of crossbow bolts smacking into the plaster outside. The air was shattered by shouts. Pandemonium broke out, men running along the passageways and down the stairs. More shots and cries. St Clair was already pushing himself across the floor. He took the dagger out of the fallen man's pouch and slit the cords round his legs, then staggered unsteadily to his feet and grabbed Rebecca.

'Follow me!'

Instead of going downstairs, he pushed her along into a small room at the back of the hunting lodge. He peered through the window. Men were coming out of the forest. Some were armed with crossbows, others with hand guns and arquebus. A hunting horn brayed. More men left the line of trees, running along the side of the lodge. Rebecca heard the neigh of horses, the clash of steel. At the priest's urging she climbed out of the window and, using the cracked and holed plaster, climbed down the wall. She dropped behind a small fence which ran along the back of the hunting lodge. St Clair followed. He looked through a gap in the fence.

'Now!' he urged and, dragging Rebecca out through the small wicket gate, fled towards the tree line. Rebecca had never run so fast. St Clair was not stopping even when she stumbled. A shot rang out, the ball whistling over their heads. A crossbow bolt splattered the ground in front of them. They heard shouts but they reached the trees, gasping and retching, forcing their way through the tangled undergrowth. Rebecca winced as the brambles tore her legs. She begged St Clair to stop but he tugged her on, deeper and deeper into the cover of the trees, running so hard she thought her heart would burst.

At the hunting lodge Ragusa and his band had been caught totally by surprise. The Venetian, his face mottled with fury, shouted orders, trying to impose some order as his men scattered. Horses reared and plunged. The air filled with the buzz of crossbow bolts and the ominous crack of musket balls.

At first, Ragusa hoped to break out but any of his men who managed to mount a horse was immediately shot down. Two did get through but they ran into a line of attackers armed with pikes and halberds, who brought horse and rider crashing to the ground. Ragusa and his men were forced back into the hunting lodge. The Venetian sobbed with fury; he had been cunningly trapped and he roundly cursed the Jesuit. Now he knew why St Clair had agreed to talk and wait till the morning. The Jesuit must have known all along! Ragusa, armed with sword and dagger, sprang up the stairs but the upper chamber only held the corpse of one of his men, the blood bubbling out of a small hole in his head. From below Ragusa heard the fresh cries of his attackers as they closed, the clash of steel and then the cries for mercy as the outlaws dropped their weapons, kneeling down, hands outstretched. Ragusa ran to the top of the stairs. He glimpsed Cowper's snow-white hair and ran back to the window.

He had one foot on the ledge when the musket ball took him full in the back. The pain spun him round. He tried to walk but found he couldn't even stand, the pain was so intense. He slid down the wall leaving a gushing red trail. Cowper was standing in the doorway, a firelock in his hands. The Judas Man walked over. Ragusa's hand went for his dagger but the Judas Man was quicker. He crouched to remove it and held it up before the Venetian's eyes.

'You tricked me! You allowed St Clair to be taken!'

Cowper nodded, studying Ragusa intently as if he wanted to memorise every detail of his face.

'I should have known.' Ragusa wetted his lips.

'When you hunt,' Cowper replied, 'always look behind you. I received warning of your attack even before I left Colchester. I lost two good men but, there again, you've lost everything!'

'St Clair and the wench?' The blood bubbled at the corner of Ragusa's mouth.

'Oh, I never intended they should reach London. Once Master Walsingham got his hands on them, only the good Lord knows what could have happened.'

'Why?' Ragusa spluttered.

'That's my business.'

And, leaning across, Cowper slashed the Venetian's throat.

9

Despite her pleas, St Clair pulled Rebecca on, the branches lashing her face. She felt as if she was hurtling through a petrified forest, haunted by demons and sprites which jumped out to bite her face, arms and legs. They reached the banks of a small brook. St Clair let go of her hand and, crouching down, lapped at the water, splashing it over his face. Rebecca just lay down. St Clair put his arm under her head and, lifting her up, made her drink. The trees above spun round. Somewhere from the forest, her father was calling her name.

'I must go back,' she muttered.

'Shush now.'

Rebecca found it easier to breathe but, suddenly, her stomach retched and she vomited what she had eaten. St Clair now grasped the back of her head, pressing the heel of palm of his hand against her forehead. He was talking in a language she couldn't understand, harsh and guttural, his eyes no longer merry. They had a strange light. She felt herself go slack, as the nausea in her stomach subsided. She was falling. She was wrapped in blankets, warm and secure. Her mother was pouring something into her mouth. The trees above were coming down as if the branches wanted to pluck her up. The blue sky was

scored with red, her eyes were growing heavy. St
Clair's voice grew louder and louder. Rebecca closed
her eyes and drifted into a deep sleep.

When she awoke, it was dark. She panicked and
turned over, finding twigs and branches clustered
around her. Then she realised that St Clair had made
a bower out of a bramble bush. They were at the edge
of a clearing. St Clair, a few yards away, had lit a
fire. A rabbit, freshly skinned and cleaned, its body
stuffed with herbs, roasted on a makeshift spit.

'You've slept most of the day.' He came forward.
'Come on, you'd best help me.'

'How did you catch it?'

Rebecca stretched. Apart from the cuts and grazes
on her arms and face she felt no other pain after
the tortuous flight from the hunting lodge. St Clair
smiled down at her.

'I'm an angel, Rebecca, I swooped amongst the
trees and saw a rabbit. I put some salt on its tail,
it stopped to lick it off and I caught it.'

'You are a story-teller.'

'Rabbits are easy to catch. I had a knife and the
ropes from the lodge, a tinder in my pocket, the rest
was easy. These woods are full of game and herbs.
So, it will be rabbit meat for us and water from the
brook nearby.'

He sat silently, allowing Rebecca to turn the spit.
Now and again he'd test the meat with his dagger. The
scene brought back memories of the Silver Wyvern.
Rebecca felt pangs of homesickness, for the ordinary
things of life. She took the spit off and sliced the
meat. St Clair had picked evergreen leaves to serve
as platters. They sat for a while popping the scalding,
tangy meat into their mouths.

'Are you a good cook, Rebecca?'

'Father said I was.'

St Clair cleaned his teeth with his tongue.

'Do you miss him?'

'Yes and no.' The words were out before Rebecca could think. 'No, sometimes we were strangers. A gulf had appeared between us. Father kept to himself, with his madcap ideas, his drinking . . .'

'But it wasn't just that?'

'No, it was the tavern wenches. I'd hear the sounds from his bedchamber. I could understand if he had met and loved again.'

'Don't judge him harshly,' St Clair replied. 'Bartholomew was never at peace. It's common enough for a man to find solace at the bottom of a tankard, or between a woman's thighs.'

'You speak as if you knew him.'

'I know his daughter.'

The forest was very quiet. No owl hoot, or night bird cry, no rustling amongst the bracken; only darkness with her and St Clair sitting in this warm pool of light. Was her father's shade out there, Rebecca wondered? One of many in the gloom? Staring hungrily at them, wishing to join them but unable to?

'What will happen to my father's soul?' She put the piece of meat down. 'He had little peace in life. Will he know it in death?'

'I have now prayed for him,' St Clair replied. 'The Soul Slayer can detain a person's soul for up to forty days but I have prayed that Bartholomew be freed to continue his journey.'

'And what then?' Rebecca recalled Parson Baynes' sermons about hell fire and the torment of the damned.

'Bartholomew may have been a weak man, but he was essentially good. He died confronting evil.' He patted Rebecca's hand. 'His soul will travel on unchecked, no challenge will be mounted as he goes towards the place of light.'

'How could Frogmore do that? Control my father's soul?'

'A great warlock, an assassin, Frogmore is steeped in magical powers he has gathered over the centuries. If he takes a man's heart, he can, for a while, control that man's soul, his spirit.' St Clair threw a stick on the fire. 'Bartholomew is now free to face the God who cares.'

Rebecca popped a piece of meat into her mouth. She watched the wood turn white hot, cracking in the heat, the sparks jumping like imps in hell fire.

'It's hard to believe,' she said, 'there's a place of light and a God who cares. If He does, why doesn't He intervene?'

'God is good. A loving mother and father. And the world is a beautiful place but men turn and twist it all. The rich amass wealth and let the poor go hang. But what can God do? He gave us free will, Rebecca. He respects that freedom. If He kept intervening, what would man be but a puppet? And God, some master of the revels telling everyone what to do? He allowed His own son to be reviled and killed. In the end, Rebecca, it will all be transformed: not a tear shed that will not be wiped away, not a child's cry that won't be answered. Not a woman abused that won't be put right. Oh, and it will be a terrible reckoning! God is coming again,' he continued in a whisper. 'He's like the air around us, in all things and yet outside all things. When a poor man starves, God starves with him. When a woman is raped, God is raped. When love is betrayed, God is betrayed.' He spoke fiercely, almost to himself, rather than to her.

'Do you believe that because you are a priest?'

'I don't believe it,' he said. 'I know it. Even evil springs from love: that's the only thing there is. Look at a tree. It loves to grow, a bird loves to fly, to sing. We all love but twist it: instead of loving each other, we love wealth, fine foods, strong drinks, soft flesh. We put these before our brothers and sisters. We betray, we hack, we kill because of our love of self.'

'Even a man like Frogmore?'

'Oh yes, even Frogmore. I've done my studies carefully. In the beginning, in those far-off days of the second Henry, Frogmore was a Benedictine monk, a fine young man, a zealous scholar. He was allowed by his monastery to go out and visit the outlying farms and granges. He met a young woman and he fell deeply, madly in love with her: the only time Frogmore has ever really loved in his life. Her name was Katherine. She became the cause and centre of his existence. He renounced his vows as a monk, left his order and lived with Katherine. They became handfast, man and wife.'

Rebecca shivered. St Clair threw more bracken onto the fire.

'Frogmore really loved her. Not lust, Rebecca, and, in that, I suppose he found pardon. She conceived and bore a son whom he called Michael. Frogmore proved himself to be a good clerk and husband. He found employment with the manor lords. Even his order forgave and forgot him; then the pestilence swept through Somerset. Katherine and Michael died hideously, suppurating boils, terrible fevers. Frogmore spent his wealth on physicians and medicines but they proved to be of no avail. Both died.' St Clair stared into the darkness. 'A priest came down. Frogmore drove him off, cursing and yelling. He then took a torch and set fire to his house, burning the corpses and everything he owned. According to legend, he went into a nearby chapel where he publicly denounced his faith in Christ, the Mass, the Church. And then he withdrew. You've never been to Somerset?'

Rebecca shook her head.

'Marshy land,' he replied. 'A mysterious place, especially round the Tor near Glastonbury, a den of great wizardry. Frogmore returned to his studies of the occult. He steeped himself in all the lore, never had the black arts such a zealous student. He rose through the ranks of wizardry and began his travels. One thing drove him, a desire to learn more, to become skilled, to become a great lord of the darkness.'

'And his powers?'

'He acquired them piecemeal: first, a growing protection against death. Then power over minds. He grew more skilled. He indulged in bloody sacrifice and murder, plucking the hearts out of sinners and offering them to the masters of the shadows.'

St Clair paused. Rebecca moved closer to the fire; the wind was cold and the forest seemed a more threatening place.

'In return,' St Clair continued, 'Frogmore can control the souls of his victims for a short period, some say up to forty days after their death. More importantly,' St Clair grasped her hand, 'and this explains how Callerton could produce that letter allegedly written by your father, Frogmore can shift his appearance, adopt the guise of the person he killed.'

'Impossible!' Rebecca gasped, fearful of these horrid terrors of the night.

'No, it is true.' St Clair released her hand. 'I did not want to tell you in Colchester, your despair would have only deepened.'

'My father?'

'Your father, old Mother Wyatt, all for a while until Frogmore releases them into darkness. He is truly the Soul Slayer.'

'But my father appeared to me?'

'A divine intervention by the powers of light. Your father co-operated with these and, because of that, he'll find pardon.'

'And Frogmore must kill?'

'Constantly, to replenish his power. As we need red meat to nourish the body, Frogmore must murder and perform the dark sacrifice. His victims are usually people in a state of sin, who have left themselves open to the powers of darkness.'

'But he can be destroyed?' Rebecca was no longer aware of the noises from the forest, just these hideous revelations.

'Yes, he can be destroyed but, with every year that passes, this becomes more difficult.' St Clair took Rebecca's hand once more. He squeezed her fingers before releasing them. 'Put your trust in me, Rebecca. One day I will tell you how he can be destroyed; you will have a role in that.'

Rebecca did not object. She knew her life was now inextricably entwined with this strange priest and whatever terrors they had to face.

'I have pursued Frogmore through Russia and

across the principalities of Europe,' St Clair continued. He breathed in slowly. 'Frogmore has now returned to England.'

'So, he has been here before?'

'Oh yes, the last time was in the final years of the old king's reign. He comes to hide, seek victims. He even has his own secret cavern in the ancient sewers and tunnels beneath London!'

'But why has he come now?'

'Frogmore has many powers but one he lacks. He cannot divine the future. Now the world is full of quacks and cunning men, seers and fortune-tellers but few really have that gift.'

'I have,' Rebecca intervened. 'Is that why he came to Dunmow?'

'No, Frogmore came to Dunmow for a different reason, but in London resides a Dr Hermeticus who truly has the gift of seeing the future. Frogmore knows of him.'

'But why must Frogmore know the future?'

'He's becoming frightened.' St Clair chose his words carefully. 'He fled from Moscow where he had a house near the Kremlin, the place they call the Tsar's Palace. The monastery of St Michael, which lies within the Kremlin walls, contains a very ancient manuscript called the Book of Secrets: this gives detailed instructions on how a demon like Frogmore can be killed. Frogmore knows of that book. He may have even read it. Now he's come to London, not just to hide, but to consult Hermeticus, to see what dangers await.'

'And after that?'

'Frogmore will return to Moscow. The kingdoms of the west are more organised. Their princes take note of men like Frogmore but Russia is different.'

'There is another reason?'

'Oh yes, more than one.' St Clair smiled into the darkness. 'I nearly caught Frogmore in Moscow. I received help from some holy monks from the monastery of St Michael's. Frogmore had to flee his house. I suspect there's something hidden there which he wishes to collect. Years ago, when he burned his house and the corpses of his beloved ones, Frogmore first removed certain prized possessions: a lock of hair from his wife and child, letters, small artefacts. I believe he has them hidden away in Moscow and will return to collect them.'

'And secondly?' Rebecca asked.

'While in Russia Frogmore attracted the attention of spies from the Ottoman Empire, which wants to hire his services. Frogmore was not ready. He snakes and curls like smoke in a wind, backwards and forwards. However, despite his powers, I suspect Frogmore is tired of being pursued. He may well decide to throw in his lot, at least for a while, with the Ottoman prince whose territories lie just beyond the Russian borders.'

'And Master Cowper?' Rebecca asked. 'He is not what he appears to be!'

'A strange one is Cowper. He has his orders but there's something else. Cowper allowed us to be taken then permitted our escape from the hunting lodge. I don't understand why. He will undoubtedly want to kill Ragusa, he'll want no rivals. I suspect Cowper has concluded that he won't break me in the Tower so it's best to let me go and follow on.'

'Into London?' Rebecca asked anxiously.

'We have to. Frogmore is going there.'

Rebecca got up. The fire had grown strong and she wanted to savour the cool of the evening. St Clair sat back on his heels, hands on his thighs. Rebecca went across and kissed him on the brow.

'Thank you,' she said.

'Oh, the rabbit was nothing,' he teased.

'No, back at the hunting lodge. You called me pretty.'

'And I was wrong?' St Clair seized her hand. 'You are beautiful, Rebecca.'

She blushed and tugged but St Clair held fast. He stretched up and touched her hare-lip.

'Perhaps, when you were a baby, an angel kissed you?'

'Do angels kiss?'

'Oh yes, Rebecca, they constantly kiss God, kiss each other.' His smile widened. 'And they can't keep their hands off the children of men. Remember Christ's words? How the angels of children constantly see God in heaven?'

'I have always been afeared of my hare-lip, always shy . . .'

'Then keep on being shy, Rebecca Lennox, be yourself. I shall call you Chrysogona, it's Greek for "golden-mouthed".'

'I hear you say things in a tongue I cannot understand, it's harsh and guttural. Is that Greek?'

'No, it's a more ancient language: one I have studied over the years.'

'Do you flatter every woman you meet?'

'All women are attractive, Rebecca. Haven't you read in Genesis, how the angels of God fell in love with the daughters of men?'

'You are a cozener,' she retorted, squatting down to face him squarely. 'You are a cunning man with a silver tongue. You shouldn't have become a priest!'

'Haven't you read again, Rebecca?' St Clair kept his face solemn. 'How the good Lord Himself enjoyed the company of women? They were the only ones to stay with Him when the rest fled!' He placed his finger against Rebecca's hare-lip. 'I am sworn to be celibate, to be chaste; not to lust, either in mind or body, thought, word or deed. But you, Rebecca Lennox, are still beautiful. There's no sin in revelling in the glory of God.'

'But you are a priest!'

'We are all priests, Rebecca. Is not a priest someone who brings God to man? And was not the Virgin Mary the first priest? Her body the first cathedral, her womb the first altar? Did you not show God to me when I was cold, starving and hiding in that stable?' His eyes grew soft, the tears brimming full. 'For I was hungry and you gave me food; I was thirsty and you gave me drink! I was a stranger and you took me in. You also gave me snowdrops.' He smiled. 'You did that for me, Rebecca. You put everything to the test. If you'd been taken, you could have been hanged out of hand. You still could face a terrifying death. Yet food, drink, a horse and, above all, snowdrops for a stranger, were more important. Believe me, Rebecca Lennox.' His voice grew hoarse, his eyes shifted as if he was speaking to people behind her. 'The angels in heaven saw what you did. You were tested and were not found wanting.'

'What do you mean?' Rebecca broke from her reverie of warm flattery.

'Like gold in a fire, like silver in the furnace.'

'Don't talk in riddles, St Clair.'

An owl hooted from the trees.

'*Tenebrae factae sunt*,' the Jesuit said. '"And darkness fell and it covered the face of the earth." Well, we must sleep.'

'I wish you wouldn't talk in riddles! It would make life a great deal easier!'

St Clair laughed and pointed to the bower he had created.

'Obey your elders!'

She sighed in exasperation, and went down to cross the brook where she went behind a bush and, having relieved herself, stopped at the brook and washed her hands and face. St Clair also was moving about and, by the time she returned, he was lying down by the fire. Rebecca went to her own makeshift bed. All she could see was St Clair's outline and she wondered if he was asleep or awake. The events of the day teemed in her mind. Ragusa's face; Cowper staring fixedly at her; that mad gallop through the forest; the escape from the hunting lodge.

'Rebecca?'

'Yes, St Clair.'

'A deaf man was drowning and he saw a passerby. How could he call for help?'

'St Clair, stop your riddles!'

'I heard that in Chelmsford,' he replied. 'Why do people think that deaf men can't shout?'

'Oh, go to sleep!'

The last thing Rebecca heard, before drifting off herself, was St Clair laughing softly to himself as if intrigued by the childish riddle.

They awoke just after dawn, cold and stiff. St Clair built up the fire.

'Aren't you frightened of pursuit?' she asked. 'Cowper could bring in dogs.'

'Our Judas Man has better things to do than hunt two fugitives on a cold January morning. First, we finish the rabbit.'

They squatted by the fire.

'So, we go on into London?'

'No.' St Clair threw away the bone, the meat cleaned off. 'We need to rest and prepare. Lady Pelham at Owlpen Grange will help.'

He led Rebecca off at a brisk walk. They came to a trackway but St Clair kept to the trees and followed it as it wound round. Now and again they hid as travellers, merchants, tinkers, pedlars and packmen passed them by. Late in the afternoon they came out of the woods and crossed open fields. Rebecca espied columns of smoke drifting over the brim of a hill.

'Owlpen Grange!' St Clair announced.

The old manor house stood in the lea of a hill across a small valley – a pleasant enough place with its black beams and white plaster, tall, red-bricked chimneys, the mullioned glass in its bay windows reflecting the weak afternoon sun. St Clair paused, studying the front of the hall before pronouncing himself satisfied. He led her down through a fringe of trees and onto the patch which led up to the front of the manor. A few servants passed them but did not stop to question them. He took Rebecca in through a small postern door which led into the kitchens. Here a startled scullion stopped them to ask their business.

'Tell Lady Eleanor,' the Jesuit replied, 'that Michael is here. Go on now! She's expecting us.'

The boy scurried off. A short while later a tall, grey-haired woman, dressed in a dark-burgundy gown,

a light gauze veil over her head, swept like a queen
into the kitchen. She was followed by a small,
vivacious, red-haired young woman dressed in green
and white, the veil over her head slightly awry. She
took one look at St Clair.

'Michael!' she cried and ran forward to embrace
him, kissing him on each cheek.

Rebecca felt a pang of jealousy and stepped back,
looking at both women under lowering brows.

'Mary, step back! St Clair is a priest!'

Michael, however, was laughing. He grabbed the
young woman by the waist and kissed her roundly
on the lips.

'Sweeter than the honey comb,' he declared. 'Better
than wine, the full young lips of a woman!'

'Flatterer!' Mary Pelham accused.

For a while all was confusion as two great shaggy
hunting dogs came bounding in. They, too, went for
St Clair, leaping up and licking his face. Servants
scurried in shaking the Jesuit's hand. Lady Eleanor
eventually restored order, banging her silver-topped
cane on the stone floor.

'Michael, we heard you were taken!'

'Like a rabbit down a hole,' he quipped. 'There's
not a prison which can hold St Clair.'

'Boaster!' Mary accused.

'Speaker of the truth,' St Clair retorted.

He introduced Rebecca. The two women immediately became concerned. They embraced her, exclaim-
ing in horror at the cuts on her face and hands, the state
of her dress, her hair greasy and still bearing traces of
the mad flight through the woods. She was taken to an
upper room, a wooden tub provided, servants bringing
up jugs of hot water. Rebecca took off her clothes and

sat in the warm herb-scented water, making herself relax. In the gallery outside she heard laughter and exclamations as St Clair also was hustled up to be bathed and changed.

Rebecca closed her eyes. She must not be jealous. The Pelhams apparently adored St Clair, seeing him as a kinsman rather than just a Jesuit priest. She closed her eyes and dozed, allowing the hot water to slop around her, then awoke with a start as St Clair came in. Rebecca sank deeper into the water, her face red with embarrassment. If Lady Eleanor and Mary hadn't accompanied him, she would have given him the rough edge of her tongue but she could see the time for jesting was over. St Clair held a bundle of clothes in his hands, not women's but men's: a white linen shirt, a bottle-green jerkin, breeches, boots, even a sword belt with a dagger in its sheath. Lady Mary carried a large pair of scissors.

'I've explained to our hosts.' St Clair wasn't a whit embarrassed that she was naked as a baby in the water. 'I apologise if I embarrass you, Rebecca, but you came here as a woman yet you must leave as a man.' He held a hand up. 'It will help us all.'

Rebecca was about to object but St Clair's eyes and face were hard and she realised that he spoke the truth. Cowper could already be in London, issuing warrants for the Jesuit and his female companion.

'As you wish.' She brought her hands up to cover her chest. 'And, as you've probably noticed,' she added tartly, 'there's very little to hide here!'

St Clair bowed mockingly, put the clothes on the floor and left the chamber.

Lady Eleanor and her daughter fussed around her. They dressed the cuts and bruises but they were insistent on following St Clair's instructions. Lady Mary seized Rebecca's long hair and began to cut it. She cropped it so close Rebecca yelped.

'It has to be so,' Lady Mary explained. 'Michael has told us how brave you were. You must become a man in everything: thought, word and deed. Otherwise you'll be taken again.'

Afterwards Lady Eleanor and Mary dressed the raised welts on the back of Rebecca's hand.

'You know St Clair well?'

'He's been here twice,' Lady Eleanor replied. 'We give him refuge and provide him monies. I am a widow. I still adhere to the Church of Rome.'

Rebecca started; Mary was holding her hand firmly and she had a picture of the young woman in a garden with a tall, blond-haired man. They were sitting in a flowered arbour watching two children play beside a carp pond. Rebecca felt sad yet happy. Mary, apparently deeply in love, sat close to the man, her head on his chest, his arm round her shoulder.

'What's the matter?'

Rebecca opened her eyes. 'You will have two children,' she said. 'You and the blond-haired man you love so much.'

Lady Mary's face paled. 'How do you know George Beauchamp?'

Rebecca closed her eyes. Cowper was walking up the pathway to the hall, his white hair floating out from underneath his black, broad-brimmed hat.

'A man will come here. His name will be Cowper. He'll ask you if you have sheltered us.'

'Oh him!' Lady Eleanor couldn't hide the contempt in her voice.

'No, no, tell him the truth,' Rebecca insisted. 'Tell

him we came here and travelled on. He will leave you alone.'

'But he's a Judas Man! One of Walsingham's creatures!'

'No. This one's different. He means you no harm. He just wants to know if we've been here. Tell him the truth and he'll go immediately.' She smiled at the young woman. 'And then you'll marry George.'

'St Clair said you had the second sight. But come.' Lady Eleanor brushed Rebecca's shoulders. 'You've been in the water long enough.'

She brought a fresh jug. Rebecca stood and Eleanor poured the water over her shoulders, washing away the hairs. She felt so strange, no hair down the side of her face or the nape of her neck. Lady Eleanor brought a piece of burnished steel even as her daughter wrapped a cloth around her.

'I look so different,' Rebecca exclaimed. She hardly recognised her reflection: the eyes yes, but her high cheekbones were emphasised as was her cleft lip. 'I look like a man.'

'Yes and no,' Lady Eleanor replied comfortingly. 'But you are a fugitive from the law, not someone going up to the court of St James.'

Rebecca muttered her thanks. She put on the shirt, clouts, breeches and stockings, pushing her feet into long leather boots. She then wrapped a broad war belt round her waist, pulling it tightly. She liked the way she felt, stronger, freer. She began to walk up and down, clumsily at first until she remembered the swagger of the gallants in the taproom of the Silver Wyvern: head slightly forward, eyes narrowed, thumbs stuck into the belt. Lady Eleanor and Mary laughed but Rebecca was now in her stride. She growled at them to keep quiet and raised a fist threateningly. The door was flung open and someone began to clap. St Clair leaned against the doorjamb.

'You look like a city punk, a roaring boy. One of Walsingham's bully lads.'

'I'm Rebecca Lennox,' she replied tartly but she burst out laughing at the way she'd growled her name.

'Time for Mass,' Lady Eleanor announced.

They gathered in the chapel, a small Romish place with stained glass windows, statues in the niches and a small altar on the dais.

'The sheriff's men rarely come here,' Lady Eleanor whispered. 'And, when they do, we hide all this away.'

Rebecca was about to reply when the door opened and St Clair came in dressed in white and gold vestments. Despite the priestly garb, he looked even more like the statue in the parish church, younger, more vulnerable, his face shaved, his hair groomed in oil. Rebecca stole a glance at Mary Pelham. Surely she, too, must think this young man was beautiful? But Mary had her eyes closed, lips moving in silent prayer.

'*In Nomine Patris et Filii* . . .' The Mass began.

Rebecca watched fascinated. She had heard about this rite. She felt a pang of loneliness; once upon a time her father must have been like St Clair, celebrating Mass in some chapel with the woman who had fallen in love with him staring soulfully from the congregation. St Clair, however, was absorbed in the mystery, lifting up the bread and the wine, reciting the Latin canon of the Mass. He bowed down over the altar.

'*Hoc est Corpus Meum!* This is my body.' He then breathed into the chalice. '*Hic est Sanguis Mea!* This is my blood.'

At the communion Rebecca remained kneeling when Lady Eleanor and Mary went up to receive the sacred species but St Clair, his face solemn, came down carrying the host. He stopped before her.

'*Ecce Agnus Dei qui tollit peccata Mundi!* Behold the Lamb of God who takes away the sins of the world!'

'I am not a papist!' Rebecca breathed.

'Behold, Rebecca,' he said quietly. 'The Body and Blood of Christ!'

She closed her eyes and opened her mouth. The thin wafer bread dissolved on her tongue and she sipped the sweet wine. St Clair returned to the altar.

After the Mass they all gathered in the small wainscoted parlour below for a delicious meal of sliced venison, eels cooked in a spicy sauce and the best wine from the Pelham cellars. St Clair entertained them all by telling them stories of his travels. Rebecca half-listened, distracted by a strange, distant beating of a drum. Mary's face paled slightly though Lady Eleanor continued with her questions. Michael answered as best as he could but Rebecca could see that he, too, was concerned. Lady Eleanor was informing him how his money belt was still there when St Clair tapped his meat knife against the wine goblet.

'I promised you, didn't I?' he asked.

The room fell silent. The servants were also disturbed by the rattling of that drum, like some malignant child intent on causing as much noise as possible.

'It's more frequent, Father. More noisome. After dark, no one dare approach the chamber.'

'What is it?' Rebecca asked.

'It's a haunting,' Lady Eleanor replied. She smiled thinly. 'You mustn't think, Rebecca, that all Pelhams were good, Christian folk. My late husband's great-grandfather.' Lady Eleanor sipped from her wine goblet, finding it hard to control the tremor in her hands. 'He was a fierce lord. This part of Essex has always been a wasteland and the Pelhams were a law unto themselves. Edmund was a man of dark passions and fiery tempers. He had a wife Anne whom he loved to distraction. She was his pride and joy. However, he was a violent man, fearing neither God nor man. The road to Owlpen was festooned with gallows where he'd hanged those who trespassed or poached on his estates. In the war between the houses of York and Lancaster Edmund went to fight for Henry Tudor. He came back earlier than Lady Anne realised and found his beloved wife in bed with one of his retainers.' Lady Eleanor refilled her wine cup. 'According to legend, Lord Edmund pursued the man through the house to a chamber far at the top. He then dragged him out and hanged him over the balustrade. His victim strangled to death slowly; Lady Anne begged for mercy but her husband was deaf to her protests.'

Rebecca stole a glance at St Clair. He was sitting so fixedly, his face so grave, that she realised this was not just some family story.

'Once the man was dead,' Lady Eleanor continued, 'Lord Edmund sawed off his head, and Lady Anne became his prisoner. Every night they would have dinner here. Before the meal began, Lord Edmund had two of his henchmen bring down the decapitated head and made his wife kiss it on the forehead and lips. This happened every night, day in and day out. Months passed into years; the grisly ceremony always took place even as the head decomposed until it was nothing more than a skull. Eventually, Lady Anne could stand no more. She hanged herself on the same spot where her husband had executed her lover. A year later Lord Edmund himself was killed in a hunting accident.'

'The years passed.' Mary Pelham took up the story. 'The Pelhams made reparation for the sins of Lord Edmund. Masses were said, offerings made, pilgrimages to shrines. However, when Henry VIII broke from Rome and the Mass became a much rarer ceremony, the hauntings began in earnest.'

'How?' Rebecca asked.

'What you hear is the sound of the drum as the head is taken downstairs for Lady Anne to kiss. This is often followed by terrible cries from the chamber. Sometimes the bodies of Lady Anne and her lover are seen still jerking and struggling at the end of their ropes. Voices at night, cries for pity.'

Lady Eleanor grasped St Clair's hand. 'You did promise, Father, that the next time you came, you would exorcise the room.'

'And I will.' The Jesuit rose to his feet. 'I want you to bring some holy water and the chalice I used.'

'Can I come?' Rebecca pushed back her chair.

St Clair was about to refuse.

'We've shared everything so far,' Rebecca pleaded. She was intrigued by what was going to happen. Perhaps this frightening incident might reveal more about this enigmatic priest.

'We shall stay down here,' Lady Eleanor announced.

197

She pointed to the fire roaring in the hearth. 'We are not cowards but that is a dreadful place.'

Her daughter returned with the chalice half-full of consecrated water. St Clair took this in one hand, murmured a prayer and crossed himself. They left the hall, Lady Eleanor's principal manservant going before them carrying a torch. The sound of the beating drum was now an ominous rattle which echoed through the house. They went up two flights of stairs. The servant led them along the cold, moonlit passageway and stopped at the foot of another set of stairs. The drum beating had stopped. Rebecca shivered at the cold.

'This is as far as I will go, sir.'

'Give the torch to the girl,' St Clair said softly. 'And thank you.'

Rebecca took the torch, keeping the flame away from her face, even though she welcomed the blast of heat and the light it provided.

'You can stay, Rebecca.'

She stared up into the darkness. Her mouth felt dry, the wine she had drunk turned acidy in her stomach, her legs felt heavy. She recalled that dreadful night in the charnel house, the oppressive evil, the horror lurking in the shadows.

'I will go up.'

'Good!' St Clair replied. 'Because you have nothing to fear. Put your trust in God.'

Rebecca climbed the stairs. The air smelt musty, the wood was chipped and broken. A rat brushed her boot and hurtled, squeaking, into the darkness.

'Oh, for mercy's sake, have pity!'

The voice, a man's, boomed from the darkness. Rebecca stepped back so violently she nearly missed her footing. St Clair steadied her.

'Oh, pity, pity!'

The sound of knocks and scufflings. Something hit the stairwell above her, crashing against it as if a heavy piece of leather had been thrown over. Rebecca was about to continue when the heart-rending gurgling and gasping began, the awful groans, the creak of wood as the man fought against the life being throttled out of him. More hideous sounds followed, a woman screaming. Again the sound of someone falling, soul-searing cries and choking. Dark shapes rippled before her. Rebecca realised she hadn't moved at all, that St Clair was prodding her on. She did so carefully, her hand shaking so much the shadows danced all around her.

At the top an oppressive silence had replaced the hideous sounds. Rebecca pressed down the latch of the metal-studded door and went inside. The windows were unshuttered and the light of a full moon streamed in through the dirty, cracked windows. No furniture could be seen except a bench against the wall and a small table. St Clair found a rusting iron sconce for the cresset torch. He then sat on the bench, pulling Rebecca close.

'St Clair!' The voice came like a whisper. 'Oh, for Jesu's sake, Domine, help us! For pity's sake, let us go free!'

The voices were a man and woman speaking in unison.

'Pox-ridden priest!'

St Clair replied in a language Rebecca couldn't understand.

'Oh, I'm sorry, I'm sorry!' The voice was throaty, hoarse, wheedling.

St Clair rose and took the chalice. He blessed the

four corners of the room. All the time he spoke gutturally and harshly. Rebecca grew aware of shadows, not thrown by the torch, flitting about the chamber like bats in a lonely church. They moved so quickly she could hardly follow them. All the time St Clair was talking. Sometimes he would pause, and the voice which had wheedled and begged, was replying but no longer in English. It seemed to be echoing the phrases St Clair used; all the time, as the Jesuit continued his exhortation to the demon or evil spirit which dwelt here, Rebecca could hear the man and woman sobbing. They spoke in English, begging contrition, asking pardon. St Clair replied sharply and they, too, spoke the tongue he used. The atmosphere in the room changed imperceptibly. St Clair was now blessing the chamber, lifting his hands in prayer, the torchlight glistening in the sweat on his brow. The other voices subsided, the oppressiveness receded.

Rebecca felt tired, as if the wine and the food she had eaten suddenly took effect. Her eyes grew heavy. She tried to get up, to fight against the sleep but she couldn't. She didn't know whether she was dreaming or awake; St Clair no longer seemed to be standing on the floor but a few inches above it. The moonlight streaming through the far window strengthened, as if the sun had risen. The chalice, too, was moving of its own accord, going between St Clair's outstretched hands. Rebecca watched, fascinated by this dream. Other voices were joining St Clair's prayer. Rebecca watched the chalice receding into a pinprick of light. Her head drooped down.

'Rebecca!'

Her eyes flew open. St Clair was crouched down beside her.

'Well, you are a fine one to summon as a witness to an exorcism! Did I bore you so much?'

'I was frightened,' Rebecca said.

The moonlight was still streaming through the casement window but now the room just looked like an ordinary, disused, dusty chamber. The chalice was still on the table. St Clair's eyes looked tired.

'I had a dream,' she went on. 'What has happened?'

'Very little.' St Clair smiled. 'This chamber was inhabited by Lord Edmund and his two victims, bound by a circle of hate. That circle had to be broken. All three must now go on. Answer the challenges that face them, seek contrition, give and grant pardon.'

'And if they do not?' Rebecca asked.

'Then they will stay in their hell and think it's heaven.' He tapped the side of Rebecca's head. 'It's all here, Rebecca. Inside our souls, the kingdom of God or the kingdom of hell and, when a man dies, he enters either one.'

10

Henry Frogmore, a pitch torch in his hand, scurried like a huge spider along the disused tunnel which had once served as a sewer when the Romans first built London. Frogmore had entered the tunnel in a derelict graveyard outside the disused church of St Dunstan-in-the-Fields. A veritable catacomb ran under the city, tunnels, sewers and underground rivers. Frogmore knew every inch of them. He had threaded his way along them many a time, to escape the sheriff's men or the others who had pursued him over the years.

Frogmore had stayed outside the city for a number of days, going down to Cripplegate, Aldgate, Newgate and even round the Tower. He had not been reassured. Cowper and his bloodhounds were there. Frogmore had recognised them: sharp-eyed men, fingers drumming on the hilts of their swords or the long stabbing daggers in their belts. Cowper's master, Walsingham, had the city of London in the palm of his hand. Not a dog could enter or a cat could leave once Master Walsingham had put his mind to it. His bully-boys now patrolled the streets, slouched in taverns or lounged at gateways. They had distributed handbills. Silver must have crossed hands. Taverners, landlords, ostlers and grooms asked: 'Have you seen this man? You have not? Good, then remember his description!'

Of all cities, Frogmore distrusted London the most. It was a warren of streets, a maze of alleyways, but the city itself was narrow and confined. A man could walk swiftly from Aldgate to Newgate, or from St Giles in the north and soon arrive beside the black waters of the Thames.

Frogmore had waited and watched, laying his plans carefully. He'd thought of travelling on but he needed to see Dr Hermeticus, ask that warlock to read the cards before taking ship to the cold north. He would have to leave from London. The Cinque Ports, as well as those along the east coast, were too small and confined. A stranger would be recognised; even the Jesuits with all their subtle skill, disguises and friends, found it nigh impossible to penetrate such a net so Frogmore had used the tunnels. He only hoped that the passing of the years had kept them open. A fall of masonry or a swollen stream and the way could be blocked.

Frogmore hurried on. Beside him the dirty waters slopped as black-coated rats slipped in and out. These kings of the underworld, lords of this black domain, did not scurry from his path. Some even stood on their back paws and looked up as he passed, wrinkling their noses, their slit eyes winking in the torchlight.

Frogmore paused as the passageway ended. One tunnel to the left, another to the right. Frogmore examined the stonework. He saw the markings etched there so long ago. He sat down and smiled. So many years! He couldn't even remember the last time he had been here. Or why he had gone scurrying along. Those were more halycon days when Frogmore, like

Hermeticus, used his powers to amass wealth, a fine house in Cheapside, sable furs, golden cups, the best wines, the softest and sprightliest of wenches. It had, eventually, all turned to ashes in his mouth. Month following month, year following year and, of course, there were always those who were prepared to comment, to whisper, to point the finger.

Frogmore eased the saddle bags off his shoulder. So much time had passed! He leaned his head against the wall and stared into the darkness. He had made the sacrifices. He recognised he was in great danger. St Clair and Cowper were different from the others and that wench, the Lennox woman? She was dangerous.

He must not fall into their traps. Everything was so easy, so near. If only he was sure. A visit to Hermeticus and then down to the quayside to compound with some captain for a safe passage along the Thames and up, through the frozen seas, to a Russian port. Once there, he'd slip across the snows into Moscow. He must visit his house in the shadow of the Kremlin, retrieve what he had hidden. Frogmore, who knew no pity, let his head droop, his body relax. So long ago! Yet it was like yesterday. The spacious, half-timbered house amid the green fields of Somerset; his wife and child chattering beneath stairs; he in his chamber staring out at the sunshine.

A rat scurried across his hand. Frogmore didn't even flinch. If he could only bring them back! If he could only recreate those times. He heard a whisper from the darkness around him. He was sure it spat out the word 'Remember!' and Frogmore had to. There must be no regrets. He had made his compact, signed his accord, delivered his soul. No regrets! So why this crawling fear? In Dunmow he'd been the master. St Clair was a bothersome fly, no more vexatious than the vermin scurrying around him. However, at every turn and twist, St Clair seemed to survive, even those assassins in Colchester. Frogmore scratched his chin.

'Am I alone?' he shouted. 'Do I have anything to fear?'

Years ago in Cologne he had visited a great magus who had warned him: 'Remember, Master Henry, you have acquired great powers. But, as the years roll on, these will attract adversaries. Beware of God's messenger! Beware of the virgin!'

Frogmore had scoffed. He had later killed the man but now he wondered. Had St Clair gone to Dunmow for a purpose? To seek out that hare-lipped virgin with her meagre powers of second sight? Frogmore unbuckled a saddle bag and took out a small wineskin. He pulled the stopper and poured a little between his lips, then stretched up, straightening the torch he'd pushed into a niche on the wall.

'If I had my way,' he muttered, 'she'd be no virgin!'

Absentmindedly, Frogmore pushed the stopper back into the wineskin. He watched a rat, sleek and slimy, crawl out of the water.

'I am like Cain,' he addressed it. 'I wander the face of the earth.'

That, too, must come to an end. He needed powerful patrons. Frogmore thought of Ivan Ivanovitch, Prince of Moscow.

'No, no!' he whispered.

He recalled his pursuers, those envoys of the Ottoman Turk. He could hide there, away from the eyes of these western princes. And when he tired, perhaps take the silk road and revisit the fabulous cities of the East.

Frogmore put the wineskin away, picked up his saddle bags and torch and continued on his journey.

When he came to the end he paused until he found the narrow aperture and squeezed through. The chamber inside was musty. Lifting the torch, Frogmore recognised the signs of his previous stay – shards of pottery, scraps of leather. He continued on up the crumbling steps, hoping that the slab which lay in the old leper corner of St Paul's graveyard had not been built upon. Frogmore pushed with all his might at the stone but it held fast. He pushed again and again. The stone didn't move. His face covered in sweat, he sat upon the steps, his eyes closed, lost in his own macabre prayer. He drew his dagger and ran it along all four sides of the slab. He pushed again, felt movement and, putting his whole shoulder under it, lifted the slab. At last it moved. As Frogmore stepped back and pushed the slab sideways, the cold night air rushed in, extinguishing the torch. He pushed his head out. The sky above was cloud-covered, not a star in sight. The place was as derelict as usual though, across the cemetery, he saw the fires of the outlaws and landless men who hid in St Paul's churchyard.

Frogmore threw out his saddle bags and eased himself up. He pushed the slab back, realising as he did so that he would never come this way again. The thought made him pause. A premonition or warning? He slipped into the darkness following the wall around the cathedral. Two figures stepped out from behind a buttress, but Frogmore pulled his dagger and the bully boys scuttled away.

Eventually he was out of the cemetery, going down a narrow alleyway which led into Paternoster Row. He paused outside a tavern. Hermeticus lived in Lamprey Lane off the Poultry. Hermeticus! Frogmore grinned. It was now fashionable to use such names and it did sound grander than John Devereux. The door to an alehouse opened and two whores staggered out. Frogmore let them go and stepped in.

A short while later, Frogmore, pretending to be drunk, his arm round a young whore, staggered up the Poultry past the watch and the bully boys standing on the corners and into Lamprey Lane. The girl was soft and warm, stinking of some cheap perfume.

'Where are we going?' she lisped. 'Does the master have a chamber?'

Frogmore paused. His eyes searching the end of the alleyway. If Hermeticus could see the future then he must expect Frogmore?

'Come on,' he slurred. 'Just a bit further down.'

They went the whole length of Lamprey Lane. Above him the upper stories of the houses towered up, blocking out the sky. Frogmore studied every window, every doorway. He passed the apothecary's shop, where a light glowed in an upstairs window. At the end of the lane he turned round again. The whore protested.

'Shut up!' Frogmore hissed. He pressed a silver coin into her hand. 'You are going to be well paid for this evening's work!'

The whore tried to gain a closer view of this man whose face was hidden so deep in the cowl but the feel of silver comforted her. If this stranger wished to stagger up and down the lanes of London and pay so generously, who was she to object?

When they reached the apothecary's shop, Frogmore thrust another coin into the girl's hand.

'Go across there!' he urged. 'Knock on the door!'

'For what?'

'Ask for some love philtre,' he replied, dropping another silver coin into her hands. 'Tell him you'll pay well.'

The girl scurried across the street and rapped on the door. A woman's voice called out. The door was opened on a chain. The girl spoke quickly, holding up the silver coin. The chain was loosed and the girl went in. A short while later she came out.

'Well?' Frogmore asked. 'Who was there?'

'Just the old man and his pretty young wife.'

Frogmore slipped another coin into her hand.

'You may go, my dear.' He smiled. 'And consider yourself very fortunate. I want words with this man.'

The whore stood back in surprise. 'Is that all?'

'What more do you want? Now go, and tell no one!' He pushed by her and rapped on the door.

'What now?' The man's voice was strident, sharp and high-pitched.

'It is urgent,' Frogmore called. 'More gold, Dr Hermeticus, than you've ever seen!'

The door immediately opened.

'My name is Henry Frogmore.'

In the pool of candlelight he could see the old man's face, waxen white, needle-bright eyes, the thin nose twitching like that of a rat sniffing cheese. The man was dressed affectedly in a fur ermined robe and a skull cap on his thinning hair.

'Why, Master Frogmore, I wondered if you'd come!'

'What are you going to do?' his visitor asked. 'Call the watch? They'll wonder why I came to your house.' He jingled the coins in his purse. 'As I said, more gold than you've ever seen. All I want is for you to read the cards.'

The shop inside was small with a counter against the far wall; above stood shelves of jars and pots, their contents giving off strange, rather unsavoury smells. Hermeticus led him through into the small parlour beyond. Frogmore gazed appreciatively at the wainscoting halfway up the wall; the plaster above it was clean and pink-coloured. Beeswax candles stood in candelabra on tables and cupboards, the window seat overlooking the gardens was cushioned and quilted. Two fine high-backed chairs stood before the fire, a wire mesh protecting them from sparks. Thick rugs covered the floor.

'John, who is it?'

A young dark-haired woman with a pretty, doll-like face came into the room.

A pretty young doxy indeed, Frogmore thought, with her alabaster-white neck and merry eyes. She was plump and toothsome. Hermeticus must be making a handsome profit!

'Go back to bed, Cecily. Our visitor has business.'

The woman was about to protest but Hermeticus shoved her quietly out, shutting the door behind her. He waved his visitor to a table in the corner. Frogmore sat down, loosening his purse and tossing it on the table. Hermeticus undid the three locks on a leather trunk. He took out a small coffer, the bronze clasps gleaming and bright, which he put on the table to unlock. The cards he took out were about nine inches long and five across, their backing made of hardened parchment glazed and coloured. Hermeticus put the cards between him and Frogmore.

'You can tell the future?' Frogmore gazed disdainfully at this little man, resentful of the gift he owned.

'I can see the future. And you believe that, Master Frogmore, otherwise you would not be here!'

'But how do you see it? In visions? Did you know I was coming tonight?'

'Yes and no,' Hermeticus replied guardedly. 'I read the cards. I read night and darkness. I read secrecy and a powerful stranger.' The seer's head came up. His eyes, not so watery now, were hard and calculating.

A dangerous man, Frogmore concluded, a real threat.

'And how did you acquire this gift?'

Hermeticus looked as if he was going to protest. Frogmore undid the purse and tossed a mixture of gold coins on the table. The seer swallowed hard, his pride with it.

'Why is one man built stronger than another? Why is a woman more kind? More loving? Why is one dog more fierce, another timid?'

'You talk in riddles.'

'I don't talk in riddles!'

Hermeticus scrutinised the stranger closely. He recognised him both by name and reputation and he also knew that Master Walsingham's men were searching the city, but that would wait.

'I don't talk in riddles,' he continued more speedily. 'To put it bluntly, Master Frogmore, I was born with the gift. Other men can write poetry, compose a madrigal, etch out a sonnet, build a cathedral, plant a garden . . .'

'And you can read the future?'

'I can divine it as through a glass darkly, the shape and shift of time. Most men make the path they follow.' He lowered his head but Frogmore glimpsed the cunning in the man's eyes. 'We always reap what we sow, Master Frogmore, and, for each of us, harvest time comes.' He tapped the cards. 'Sometimes it's the cards, sometimes it's a pool of water or a glass. I have to be careful. My customers are, how can I put it, very discreet? It is a gift we do not trumpet abroad. I do not want to end my days lashed to the stake in Smithfield or doing the Tyburn dance. And now, sir, I have answered your questions. Why don't you answer mine?'

'I am a customer,' Frogmore taunted back. 'I am very discreet.'

Hermeticus knocked the pile of cards so they fanned out across the table.

'Then let's go to it. Pick up a card, Master Frogmore.'

The warlock did, slowly. He felt a pang of disappointment. It showed a castle on the hill. One of those fairytale buildings with pointed towers and crenellated walls, standing in a field of snow.

'Study it, Master Frogmore. Look at it carefully. What do you see?'

The magus was experienced in every trick and game of the counterfeits and cranks, the jacks of the roads, the mummers, the cunning men. Frogmore saw them as no more vexatious than a buzzing fly or a piece of ill-digested meat. Yet, the more he studied that card, the more he grew aware of being in the presence of a great magus: the card was not what it seemed. It was like studying a painting or a portrait, where the more you looked, the more you learned. The castle did not look so angelic and innocent. Blood seeped between the walls. Indeed, it held the bricks together. Its gateway looked dark and cavernous. He could see small faces at the window as if he were looking at a prison house. In the snow, a tree stood with a man hanging from its black branch; underneath it, wolves gazed up hungrily. Horsemen dressed in strange furs and metal spiked hats rode towards the castle. A woman and two men were also approaching. Frogmore sensed these were St Clair, Cowper and that hare-lipped wench. For the first time in his long life, Frogmore experienced a real sense of fear.

'What does it mean?' he rasped, throwing it back on the table.

'What do you think it means?' The magus had his hands covering his mouth.

Frogmore felt a spurt of rage at being taunted.

'I pay you good silver.'

'That is a place you will visit. And, if I read that card as well as the expression on your face, it will be the very antechamber of hell. A place of blood, narrow and close. Violence within the walls, violence without, pursuit and danger.'

'But not death?' Frogmore asked.

'Death can come in many forms. We will arrive at that. Take another card, Master Frogmore.'

Frogmore did. He turned it over. Again a building, but this time broken down, the walls tumbled, the gate loose. It stood on a rocky escarpment surrounded by a sea of grass. In the gateway stood a man dressed in the armour of a knight, a red cross on his tunic. Behind the knight was a woman and, coming from the sea of grass, what looked like a giant, his face burned black, a turban on his head. In one hand he carried a scimitar, in the other a round shield and behind him stood an armed camp with banners furled.

'Another place of danger!' Hermeticus whispered.

Frogmore glanced up. Hermeticus' face was younger, smoother; the wrinkles seemed to have disappeared.

'All places are dangerous,' Frogmore mocked. 'A lane in Cheapside or a country road outside Paris. They all hold horrors.'

'Play the cards,' Hermeticus insisted. 'Six you shall draw. Each room has four corners, a ceiling and a floor. We are all bound by four corners as well as what covers and supports them.'

The third card was more simple, the picture of a knave. This one had white hair, as if bleached by the sun, and his costume was black. In one hand he held a book, in the other an upraised sword. Frogmore held the card up.

'And this?'

'A man pursues you,' Hermeticus replied enigmatically. 'A man with authority, the power of the book as well as that of the sword.'

Frogmore pulled a fourth card. His heart skipped a beat. It represented a virgin or maid, her hair dark brown. Her face would have been beautiful if it hadn't been for the cloven lip. In one hand she held a chalice and in the other a dagger. Above her an angel flew with outstretched wings.

'What is this?'

Hermeticus' face was now pale, covered in a fine sheen of sweat. He was gnawing on his lip, running fingers through his straggly moustache. His eyes moved towards the doorway. Frogmore grasped his hand, which felt ice cold.

'What does it mean?' he asked.

'Death!' Hermeticus murmured. His eyes held Frogmore's.

'Beware of the virgin! Beware of the virgin and the chalice!'

'What are you frightened of?' Frogmore asked.

'I don't know,' Hermeticus stammered. 'I feel cold, I feel uncomfortable, I wish you had not come!'

'But you can divine the future,' Frogmore replied soothingly. 'Here we are in your comfortable little mansion, with your rugs and your furs, your wine and your sweetmeats. Upstairs, between silken sheets, your plump little palfrey is ready to ride.'

'Don't talk like that!' Hermeticus replied. 'Pull the cards and be gone!'

Frogmore did. This time it was a pair of scales hanging between heaven and earth. Hermeticus relaxed, the colour came back into his face.

'Good news!' he breathed. 'Good news indeed, sir!'

'Why?' Frogmore asked.

'The cards lay out the possible paths. You, sir, shall travel to places of great danger but these will not, and shall not, threaten you. You are pursued by the knave, a man of the law, but he, too, poses no danger. The virgin, however, is your nemesis. This card,' he tapped the scales, 'shows that nothing has been decided. Some men's deaths are preordained, at a certain time in a certain way on a certain date.' He got to his feet. 'Come, Master Frogmore, I'm not your enemy.' He went to the table, filled two large goblets with wine and brought them back. 'Let's toast your good fortune!'

Frogmore was puzzled by Hermeticus' dramatic change in behaviour. He waited until the seer sat down.

'This is my future,' he said. 'Yet, Dr Hermeticus, you seem relieved?'

'I thought you'd draw some other card, I don't know, something quite terrifying. I just had a feeling, an impression, images in my mind.'

Frogmore sipped at the wine.

'I will just speak to my wife.' Hermeticus sprang to his feet.

'No, sir, don't leave.' Frogmore pressed him back into his chair. 'You've read the handbills, haven't you?'

Hermeticus nodded.

'My description issued by Master Walsingham. Why didn't you send to him?' Frogmore continued. 'Why not claim the reward, Dr Hermeticus?'

Frogmore lifted up the beautifully engraved cup. He studied the jewels and amethysts along the stem.

'Were you frightened of this?'

And, without even looking down at the cards, Frogmore drew the sixth and turned it over. He heard a moan. Hermeticus was now staring down at the picture, his hands shaking so much he had to put his goblet down.

Frogmore himself couldn't bear to look. Ever since St Clair had appeared, a suspicion had grown slowly but surely, probing his soul, disturbing his sleep. 'Nothing ever remains the same,' had been the maxim of one magus. 'All things act and react.'

'What do you see, Dr Hermeticus?' he demanded harshly.

'I see a young man coming out of the rising sun.

On his head he bears the mark of the Living God. In one hand he carries a sword and in the other a chalice. He hangs between heaven and earth, above the princes of this world and their master.'

Frogmore, without even looking at the card, tossed it aside.

'*Alea jacta*, "the die is cast",' he murmured. He stared across. 'Why, Dr Hermeticus, you are shaking.'

'Drink your wine,' the seer replied thickly. 'Drink up and begone!'

'Can you foretell your own death?' Frogmore asked.

'You know I can't. That is one path which is closed. Obscured by eternal night.'

Frogmore sniffed at the wine. 'I'll tell you what.' He put the goblet down and pushed it across the table, his hand going beneath his cloak. 'You drink from my cup and I'll drink from yours.'

Hermeticus licked his dry lips. 'This is foolishness. Get you gone, sir!'

'Without drinking my wine? Shall I tell you what, Dr Hermeticus?' Frogmore pricked the man under the chin with his dagger. 'You've given me a wine with an opiate in. Somewhere in this chalice is a little button which you press. While you went upstairs to visit your sweet, little wife, I was to drain this cup. You'd return and I'd be in a sleep close to death. You'd take my wealth then hand me over to Master Walsingham and so find greater fortune and favours at court.'

'You are moonstruck!' Hermeticus whispered. He made to rise but the dagger point nicked his throat.

'That's the way of the world, Dr Hermeticus. You

read the cards. You knew I was coming here but you dared not go to Master Walsingham. If I suspected a trap I would never have knocked on your door. So you thought you'd play your tricks, wait then afterwards act the hero! How you'd been roused in the dead of night and tra, la, la, la!' Frogmore waved his hand.

'Just take your gold! Take the cards! Anything! Go, I won't say . . .'

'Anything I want?'

Hermeticus nodded. 'Agreed!'

Frogmore pressed in the knife and, in one quick slash, tore Hermeticus' throat from ear to ear. The seer jerked back in his chair, hands going up as if he could stop the rush of blood bubbling from that terrible wound and filling his mouth. He lurched from the chair. Frogmore caught his body and lowered him gently to the floor. He waited for a while but there was no sound from the chamber above or from the street. He ensured the door was locked, then pulled Hermeticus' corpse out into the middle of the floor. He lit two candles and secured the door to the stairs. As an afterthought he picked up the cards and turned them over. He gasped in astonishment, his blood ran cold. They were all blank, white as sightless eyes. Frogmore went and knelt behind Hermeticus' corpse. He tore the man's gown apart and pressed down his knife, cutting deep into the flesh around the heart.

In the once-pleasant room, amid all the luxuries Dr Hermeticus had collected, Frogmore performed his macabre rites. Lost in his own reverie, his own ecstasy of evil, he conjured up his powers. When the sacrifice was finished and the candles guttered out, Frogmore, now guised as Hermeticus, sat down at the small writing desk.

He had decided what to do. The net was closing in here and abroad. He'd return to the wilderness of Russia, to his house in Moscow, before travelling south to offer his sword, his powers, his services to the great Sultan himself. Picking up a quill, Frogmore wrote in a cipher he knew the Ottoman would understand. He signed and sealed the letter with blobs of wax. He would take ship as soon as possible and have this despatched to Aeneas Vicoli, a Venetian merchant in the pay of the Great Turk.

'Husband? Husband?' The cooing voice became more strident.

Frogmore smiled. He opened the door to the stairs.

'Don't be frightened,' he called. He made out the outlines of the young woman. 'Take off your shift.'

Frogmore, still in the guise of the great Dr Hermeticus, left an hour later, saddle bags slung over his shoulder. Before he went, he took oil from the kitchen, sprinkled it over the floor and furniture and watched the candle flame turn it into pools of fire. Upstairs Dr Hermeticus' wife lay sprawled naked on the bed, her throat slashed from ear to ear. Her husband's corpse still sprawled in its gory mess on the floor. As Frogmore walked down the street, the flames took all this and turned it into black, cindery ash.

11

St Clair and Rebecca left Owlpen Manor under the protection of the Minions of the Moon, a troop of Egyptians or gipsies who travelled the highways and byeways of the kingdom, protected and favoured by people such as Lady Pelham. They travelled in carriages and carts, swarthy-faced men and women, bold-eyed and garishly dressed in a motley collection of coloured rags adorned with cheap bracelets and earrings. They moved to a cacophany of bells attached to their horses, carts and garments, jabbering in a tongue Rebecca couldn't understand though St Clair seemed to have no difficulty with it. Their leader, the Jackman, treated St Clair with great respect: outside Owlpen he gathered his men and pointed at Rebecca.

'He's telling them to treat you with dignity,' St Clair explained. 'Their word is their bond. They steal like magpies but, to their friends and those who have taken the blood oath, they are steadfast.'

St Clair spoke the truth. The Minions of the Moon knew she was a woman dressed as a man. They gazed at her sloe-eyed and, now and again, when their curiosity became too much, pinched her arms and thighs. However, they left her alone, more interested in scouring the countryside. Woebetide any farmer or peasant who let his sheep or chickens roam. The Moon Minions scooped these up in the twinkling of an eye; throats were slashed, carcases gutted, chopped up and stowed away in barrels of salt or pickle on top of the carts.

As they passed through villages they earned money by performing tricks, spitting fire, pulling coloured ribbons from their noses, juggling and acrobatics. The villagers treated them with disdain though fascinated by their tricks and cajolery. The Moon Minions always moved on quickly, fearful that their thefts might soon come to light. At night they'd shelter in some copse or open field, feasting on the meats, breads and wine they had stolen, laughing and joking. Sometimes, in their wild exuberance, they performed strange dances to the sound of the tambours and flute.

Rebecca was fascinated by them. She helped load the babies in wicker baskets slung on either side of the horses, clean the meat or build the fire. St Clair tended the horses and the Jackman seemed in awe of his herbal knowledge. They called the Jesuit 'Petichio' which, St Clair explained, meant 'pattering priest'.

'Have you travelled with them before?' Rebecca asked.

'Not here, but in Germany and France. They hold Pelham in awe while my knowledge of their tongue and work with horses always stands me in good stead.'

'A man of many talents,' Rebecca teased.

St Clair just shook his head. 'Thank God they don't ask me to cook. I can't even crack an egg without causing a mess while my oatmeal.' He pointed to a stone farmhouse. 'It's little better than mortar and lime.'

'How long will we stay with them?' Rebecca asked.

St Clair stared up at the greying sky. They were travelling in the middle of the column, close up against the biting wind.

'We've been with them two days. By tomorrow evening we'll be on the outskirts of London.'

St Clair proved correct. The following morning they reached the main highways leading into the Bishopsgate. More travellers joined them, merchants, lawyers, soldiers as well as the flotsam and jetsam of the highways, the whores, doxies and bawdy baskets, the peasants with their carts and barrows, wandering scholars and landless men.

St Clair grew more nervous and wary. He and Rebecca stayed in the wagon fearful of being noticed by some Judas Man who, St Clair believed, must surely be patrolling the highways and gateways to the city.

'Cowper let us escape,' he declared. 'We are the lure to trap Frogmore. Sooner or later he must yank the line in. It would be nice to travel on.' He leaned against the side of the gaudily coloured wagon, stretching his legs out, and quoted something in Latin.

'What's that?' Rebecca asked.

'I'm sorry,' St Clair apologised. 'I am showing off my knowledge.'

'No, I have heard those lines before,' Rebecca insisted. 'When we were sheltering in the wood after we fled the hunting lodge and again at Lady Pelham's.'

'There was a poet, a Roman called Ovid. He wrote a collection of poems called the *Tristia*. These poems

223

were written on the sorrow of exile. Ovid was a brilliant man. The Emperor Augustus exiled him to the Black Sea. Anyway, he wrote a marvellous line: "Those in love recognise their own destruction but embrace it." And again: "I am deeply in love with the weapon which has wounded me."'

'And?' Rebecca leaned across and tapped him on the nose.

'Well, I'm an exile,' St Clair replied. 'Well away from home.'

'And where is that?'

'One day I'll show you. And you'll love it, I promise you.'

'But what about this love which hurts?'

'Love always hurts, Rebecca and, in time, burns itself up. My exile will end when that whom I love decides my life has run its course.'

'Whom do you love?' Rebecca asked.

'Why, love itself.'

Rebecca kicked his foot. 'Riddler! Do you always speak in riddles and parables?'

St Clair laughed.

'Have you ever been in love?' Rebecca asked. 'I know you are a priest,' she added hastily. 'Sworn to cel . . .'

'Celibacy and chastity,' St Clair finished the phrase for her. 'But the act of love is only the expression of love. Of course priests fall in love.'

He pushed his head back so it was hidden in the shadows, as if he wished to conceal his face.

'Have you ever lain with a woman?'

'Oh yes, on a number of occasions.'

Rebecca felt her heart lurch.

'And was she beautiful?'

'Oh very.'

Rebecca caught the bubble of humour in his voice.

'Who?' she said accusingly.

'Why with you, Rebecca Lennox! Have we not lain under the stars together?' He moved his leg before she could kick him. 'And you? Hasn't some swain or handsome youth had his way?'

Rebecca blinked and looked away. She remembered the hot eyes of the men in the Silver Wyvern. When her father was absent, they tried to claw her breast or put a hand down her bodice or up her skirt.

'I always thought, I always thought one day perhaps . . .' She tapped her upper lip. 'I was the hare-shotten. The mummers' freak.' She couldn't stop the tears brimming in her eyes. 'Oh,' she sighed. 'I suppose some yeoman would have offered to marry me. Do me a favour in turn for a handsome dowry.'

'And in a cold bed beside cold flesh,' St Clair added.

'Aye,' Rebecca replied absentmindedly.

She steadied herself as the cart swayed over a large pothole, then distracted herself by pulling back the awnings and staring out. It was late afternoon. She watched the gipsy children skipping and dancing beside the cart.

'What will happen to the Silver Wyvern?' St Clair asked, eager to change the course of the conversation.

'Well, my father is dead. His will made me his heir but, of course, I am now accused of treason. I suppose the Crown will seize it and sell it to the highest bidder.' She let the awning drop. 'What does it matter?'

St Clair shuffled towards her and seized her hand.

'You need not come any further, Rebecca. You've done more than enough. I could send you back to Lady Pelham or others who would shelter you.'

Rebecca studied his face, the crinkles round his eyes, his tousled hair, the stubble on his chin and side of his face which glittered like burnished gold. She moved her hand in his, relishing the soft warmth.

'Don't send me away,' she said quietly.

'I didn't say I would but it's a dangerous path you tread.'

'Where you go, I will go,' she replied. 'Where you lie, I will lie. What you eat and drink, I shall share and, whatever comes, I can face.' She squeezed his fingers, gripping them tightly. 'I can do so as long as you are with me.'

He raised her hand to his lips and gently kissed the tips of her fingers.

'Are you sure, Rebecca Lennox? There is a point where there is no turning back. It's hand in hand for both of us. Against all the terrors hell can spit out!'

'I am sure,' she replied. 'In life and in death.'

'They are the same.' He smiled faintly. 'The gipsies have a word, "murripen": it means the same, for life and death. There is no difference. Life does not end, it simply changes.' He squeezed her hand. 'Do you know what a blood oath is, Rebecca Lennox?'

She shook her head.

'Well, now you do, you've just taken one.' He grasped her face between his hands, pulling her gently towards him. 'We are no longer two,' he said fiercely, 'but one.'

He kissed her long and hard on the lips. She did not resist, but hoped his hands would slide down, grasp her, pull her towards him. Then he brushed her brow with his lips and let her go.

'We'll be near the ruins of St Mary of Bethlehem soon,' he said. 'And from there it's only a short distance into the city.' He picked up his cloak and their saddle bags. 'Now we should leave.'

'Without saying goodbye?'

St Clair took a rag from the bottom of the cart. He took two silver pieces off his belt, put them in the rag and tied a knot.

'To these people you never say goodbye, they'll understand. Moreover, if one of Cowper's men is about, it would only mean danger. Come on!'

St Clair helped her out of the back of the wagon. For a short while they walked behind it. Just before they rounded a corner, St Clair grasped Rebecca's wrist. They left the trackway and made their way to a lonely farmhouse which stood on the lea of the hill behind a small copse of trees.

Secretary Walsingham sat in the small two-roomed chamber in the Wakefield Room at the Tower of London. The lieutenant of the fortress had always had these chambers set aside and furnished for her majesty's Secretary of State. Walsingham was a man who liked to come and go, like a thief in the dark. Now he was seated beside the roaring fire, cradling a cup of posset and staring across at his protégé Master William Cowper. Secretary Walsingham pulled his cloak around him because, despite the fire and the braziers, the shuttered windows and the woollen cloths against the walls, he was still cold. He was also curious and angry.

'I don't understand it, William,' he said. He watched

Cowper unhitch his coat and throw it over the table, his broad-brimmed hat on top of it. 'You would like some wine?'

Cowper shook his head. He watched his master intently. If Walsingham had had him brought here, the only place where the Office of the Night might meet, free of an eavesdropper, then it must be a serious matter. The Commons were sitting at Westminster, her majesty was at Eltham, so for Master Walsingham to travel up river in such freezing weather meant that Elizabeth's master spy was a deeply troubled man.

'I don't understand,' Walsingham repeated, glowering at Cowper from under his eyebrows, angry that his agent had not even bothered to reply. Walsingham lifted his cup to shield his face. He glanced sideways at the roaring fire. 'You are my best limner, Cowper, cunning and swift. Yet you take two of my prisoners by road with a pitiful escort and allow them to be rescued.'

'I wanted them rescued.'

'Continue!'

Cowper beat his gloves against his thigh.

'What would have happened, sir, if I had brought them into London? Do you think we would have broken a man like St Clair? Would that have brought us any closer to Frogmore? All we'd have would be a dead Jesuit and a simple-minded girl who'd swoon away with fear. Master Frogmore would dance, like the wizard he is, along the roads to the nearest port and go wherever he wished. It could take us years to track him down.'

'It might still do.'

'I doubt it. Frogmore has considerable powers. He can disguise himself. He has a neverending source of wealth. He can move like a will-o'-the-wisp, lie low in some culvert or find protection with some foreign prince. It's much easier, Secretary of State, to hunt a Jesuit who is running hand-in-hand with a country wench with a hare-lip. No one will forget them. St Clair is only valuable,' Cowper continued, throwing his gloves onto his cloak, 'when he is pursuing Frogmore. He's our bait.'

Walsingham nodded. He turned to the side table, thumbing through a sheaf of parchments.

'Why the interest, William?'

The question was so abrupt, Cowper lowered his eyes.

'As you said, sir, I am your most faithful limner.'

'Come, come, don't dance round the Maypole with me!' Walsingham glanced up. 'Did they ever find Master Ralph Cowper, the kindly leather merchant who took you in?'

Cowper stared unblinkingly back.

'How old are you, William?'

'Thirty-four years.'

'In the last months of our Queen's father's reign, the most noble Henry VIII. The year 1547.' He let the words fall like a schoolmaster lecturing a recalcitrant scholar. 'What happened in Gloucester?'

'Sir, you asked me not to dance round the Maypole. You know what happened in Gloucester.'

Walsingham smiled, his upper lip curling like that of a dog. 'You tell me, William, in your own words!'

'I was sixteen years of age and about to leave for the Halls of Cambridge. My mother and real family would have nothing to do with me. Ralph was my mother, my father, my brother, my sister, uncle and aunt. Sometimes I am full of self-pity but, at others, I feel most fortunate to have been loved like that. It was a warm summer. I wasn't looking forward to leaving for Cambridge. Gloucester had been my home; the cathedral, the abbey buildings. Sometimes Ralph would take me to visit Berkeley Castle or across the Severn to the Forest of Dean, a dark mysterious place.

'One day, late in July, he sent me to friends in Stroud. I was absent for two or three days. I came back and Ralph wasn't in the house. None of his apprentices or journeymen could tell me where he was. He'd gone out into the town. I went there. Ralph had visited a tavern, then left. He'd told the landlord it was so pleasant that he would go for a ride along the country lanes. It was the last anyone saw of him. Oh, I petitioned the mayor and the corporation. Searches were made, brooks and streams were dragged, foresters paid to forage in the undergrowth.' Cowper clicked his tongue. 'Nothing, as if he had just vanished off the face of the earth. I was inconsolable. Ralph had drawn a will up making me his heir. I went to Cambridge. Do you know, sir, I paid a considerable part of my inheritance to cursitors and searchers but not a trace was ever found.'

'But there's more to that, isn't there? You discovered a great deal in your enquiries?'

'Yes, sir, I did. At the same time, horrible murders had been committed in and around Gloucester. The same had been reported near Tewkesbury and Cirencester: men and women, their corpses horribly mangled, their hearts plucked out . . .'

'Continue,' Walsingham whispered.

'I left Cambridge and became a clerk. I entered

Secretary Cecil's service and later yours. I am fluent in French, Italian, Spanish and some other languages. I am a consummate swordsman and a good horseman. I do not drink to excess. I keep my mouth shut and I fight the Queen's enemies here and abroad.'

'Yes I know that. And you also have access to private memoranda and documents under the Privy Seal.'

Cowper smiled thinly. 'Then you know that I have been through those accounts for the years 1546–1548. The late King Henry was much interested in Master Frogmore – even then he had won a reputation as a wizard and a warlock.' He sighed. 'I also discovered that, at the same time my stepfather disappeared, Master Frogmore was back in England, prowling along the marches of Wales.'

'And you think he was responsible for your step-father's death?' Walsingham wagged an admonitory finger but smiled. 'You played us like a fish, William! How clever you were! You brought Master Frogmore to her majesty's attention. You wanted him captured for your own good reasons.' Walsingham put his goblet down. 'And there's more, isn't there? Our good man Andrew Cavendish. You had few friends, William, but he was one.'

'I told him to be careful. I wish he had followed my advice. Master Secretary, I have done nothing treasonable. Master Frogmore is a threat to the security of this country, to the security of any Christian prince and to the faith. He has to be hunted down, trapped and killed. What would you prefer? Someone who has no interest in the matter? Lacklustre in his efforts, ready to cry halt and return to the kennels?'

Walsingham stared down at the amethyst ring on his little finger.

'But you'll bring him back, won't you William?'

'Master Secretary, my heart and soul will sing their own song when Frogmore's rotten carcase shrivels in the fires of Smithfield.'

'Good! Good!'

Walsingham played with the ring, slipping it on and off his finger. Cowper sat tense. He knew this most secretive man. Others would think Walsingham was finished but Cowper knew there was worse to come. Walsingham sipped from his cup.

'It's very good wine,' he commented. 'Hot and spiced.' He tapped his brocaded stomach. 'Keeps the rheums at bay and the humours balanced. Do you know, William. Sometimes I understand the papists. Confession is good for the soul, is it not? Here we are in the Tower, where many men have confessed, broken on the rack, torn, cut up by boiling hot pincers. Others get tired of the loneliness, the darkness, as days and nights slide into each other. Time seems to stand still but it's a secure place.'

'Which is why the records of the Secret Seal are kept here,' Cowper added.

Walsingham laughed, a short barking sound. 'William, I do enjoy talking to you. You've been there, haven't you?'

'I have every authority.' Cowper tapped his wallet. 'I carry the Queen's warrant.'

'And tell me what you found?'

Cowper shrugged. 'About what?'

'Not about Frogmore. The other one. St Clair. Tell me! I want your judgement, William, I value it.'

'St Clair is the same age as myself. He's of Irish

stock, his father was a prosperous Dublin merchant. He had warehouses along the River Liffey and was the owner of trading ships. A member of the reformed faith, Michael St Clair was given the best education society could offer. His parents died when St Clair was young. He was sent to France to study, at the Sorbonne in Paris. Later he journeyed to Montpelier to study medicine.'

'And?' Walsingham asked.

'St Clair became a convert. Deeply interested in theology, he fell into the hands of the papists; the Jesuits, a new Catholic order, were busily seeking recruits among the young and educated. He was sent to Rome where he finished his education. He took his vows, entered the Society of Jesus and was eventually ordained a priest.'

'And his connection with Frogmore?' Walsingham asked.

'St Clair proved to be a brilliant theologian. He specialised in what the papists call demonology. He wrote several papers which excited the curiosity of the Inquisition. On a number of occasions St Clair was invited before their tribunal to defend what he had written, he did so brilliantly.'

'So, why was he in trouble?'

'From what I gather,' Cowper continued, 'the finger of accusation was pointed at him claiming that St Clair had dabbled in the black arts, an accusation commonly used by the Inquisition against their enemies. The Jesuits withdrew him and put him in seclusion. He disappeared for a while then, according to reports from merchants across the Adriatic, he was seen at Tirgoviste in Wallachia, a travelling companion to Master Frogmore.'

'I've read the documents,' Walsingham intervened silkily. 'But, William, you bring them to life, express it so succinctly.'

'According to our agents in Rome, St Clair may have fled the Jesuit Order. There seems to have been a deep friendship between him and Frogmore. What its precise nature was I don't know. About four years ago both Frogmore and St Clair returned to Italy where there seems to have been a great falling out. The news is sparse, very little evidence, only rumour and gossip. According to this, St Clair and Frogmore were involved in a savage duel somewhere in the Alban Hills outside Rome.'

'And?'

'If this rumour is to be believed, St Clair fell over a precipice, and his body was never recovered. After that there is silence. Then about two years ago St Clair re-emerges, this time as Frogmore's implacable opponent, hunting him the length and breadth of Europe.'

'But what conclusions have you drawn? Is St Clair a practitioner of the black arts? An accomplice turned enemy?'

'I don't know,' Cowper replied. 'I really don't. I tell you, sir, I'd give everything I had to know that.'

'Umm!' Walsingham leaned back in the chair. 'The only people who can help us would be the Jesuits themselves. But we've got as much chance of achieving that as I have of becoming a cardinal in Rome. And you believe Frogmore's in London?'

'I think so.'

'There was a fire,' Walsingham continued. 'A house in Lamprey Lane burned to the ground. It belonged to a Dr Hermeticus. Both he and his wife, or what was left of the corpses, were found amongst the charred remains. Hermeticus was an astrologer, a proclaimed seer. The fire may have been an accident or the work of Frogmore.'

Cowper pulled a face. 'I know nothing of that, sir. I am waiting for St Clair and the Lennox woman to arrive.'

'You won't let them slip through your fingers?'

Cowper just stared back.

'I hope not,' Walsingham murmured.

He picked up a small bell from the table and rang it. The door opened and a short, squat, young man entered; his smooth Italianate face was clean-shaven, his hair carefully oiled and swept back over his head. He was dressed in dark green. Cowper glanced at him and looked away.

'You know Pandolfo?'

Cowper breathed in deeply and rubbed his nose as if he'd smelt something unsavoury, bit the quick of his thumb and spat the dry skin out. Walsingham smiled. He was used to such rivalry amongst his dogs.

'Pandolfo here will help you.'

'Pandolfo's an assassin,' Cowper replied.

He glanced at the half-Portuguese renegade who now worked for the English secret service. Cowper truly hated Pandolfo not because he killed but because he enjoyed it so much.

'Where you go, Pandolfo will follow! And no, William, don't accuse me of not trusting you. I just think you need help.' Walsingham put his hands together and clapped softly. 'You may go!'

Cowper bowed, collected his cloak, hat and gloves and walked out of the chamber. Pandolfo followed, trotting behind like a dog. When they reached the Lion

Gate, Cowper turned and stared up at the Tower. He would never see Walsingham again, nor this place, yet he didn't feel sad.

'You don't like me, Master Cowper?' Pandolfo spoke in a whisper, his face full of hurt innocence.

Cowper beckoned him closer. 'Come with me. I want to show you something. Where I go, you follow, yes?'

Pandolfo nodded, slipping his arms up the sleeves of his gown till he looked like some jovial friar.

'Let's strike while the iron's hot!'

Cowper led Pandolfo out of the Tower but, instead of going to the quayside, he turned abruptly left along a narrow trackway which skirted the buildings of the Tower. Pandolfo objected to Cowper's pace and questioned where they were going.

'Don't worry!' Cowper called over his shoulder. 'If you are to go with me wherever I want, then this is important.'

They crossed a ditch, walking out across an open field and into a thick clump of trees. Pandolfo's agitation grew. He did not like the countryside, these silent, gloomy paths. Pandolfo was a man of the street, a denizen of the alleyway, expert with the garotte and the knife, his back always to a wall. Cowper, however, was striding purposefully ahead deeper into the trees; the silence was only broken by the snap of twigs and the call of some lonely bird. They entered a clearing. Cowper stopped, took off his cloak and unsheathed his sword and dagger. Pandolfo gazed in consternation.

'What nonsense is this?'

Cowper drew his sword and dagger, flexing his muscles.

'Do you like killing, Pandolfo?'

Cowper was now moving around him. Pandolfo shifted his stance.

'You do like killing, don't you?' Cowper taunted.

Pandolfo, throwing his cloak back over his shoulder, also drew sword and dagger.

'What is this?' he repeated.

'I'm here to kill you,' Cowper said quietly. 'I can't afford to have you at my back. I am in a hurry! I don't trust you. I don't trust the orders you've been given. How will it end? A dagger in the back? Doesn't Secretary Walsingham trust me any more?'

Before Pandolfo could reply, Cowper closed in, boots slapping the hard, wet grass, sword snaking out. Pandolfo countered. He couldn't hide his surprise. One minute they were in the Tower, Walsingham's men. Now this. Had Cowper gone mad? Was Secretary Walsingham right? Had Cowper been bribed and corrupted? More interested in his own affairs than those of the Office of the Night? Pandolfo responded using sword and dagger to drive his opponent back. As he did so, he became afraid. Pandolfo was used to fighting in a group, like a pack of hounds tearing their victim down. Cowper was a superb swordsman. Pandolfo's mouth went dry. He began to panic and lashed out with his sword, but Cowper moved sideways. In that brief moment, Pandolfo realised he had made a terrible mistake. Cowper's sword came slicing in, piercing deep into his fleshy throat.

12

On those windswept, salt-spattered marshes which ran along the Thames estuary, Henry Frogmore crouched and stared out at the rakish, sinister smugglers' sloop standing off the coast, ready to take him abroad. He watched intently as its bum boat was lowered; two sailors, straining at the oars, headed towards the small fire Frogmore had lit as a signal.

The warlock felt content. He had despatched his letter and changed his mind. The wharves and quaysides of London were under careful scrutiny, particularly the Steelyard where ships sailing to and from the Baltic were berthed. Frogmore had glimpsed Walsingham's spies pretending to be sailors, merchants, beggars, but he could see through their masks and mummery. If he had approached any captain, he would have been arrested immediately.

Frogmore had gone back into the city, slipping along Fleet Street, across the open countryside past Westminster and into the tawdry inns and shabby ale shops along the Thames estuary: the denizen of smugglers, river pirates, men who had as much to fear from the law as Frogmore. Silver had been exchanged, a rendezvous arranged. Frogmore would travel to the Low Countries and go on from there. He would reach Moscow, take what was his and then journey southeast, crossing the borders into Moldavia or Wallachia, to seek out the local Turkish commander.

During his short stay among the smugglers, Frogmore had listened to the rumours from crews returning from the Middle Sea. According to them, and it was only gossip, the Ottoman Emperor, Suleiman, was collecting a massive fleet in the Golden Horn. He was determined once and for all to set out against the Knights Hospitaller in Malta and wipe out that nest of hornets which plagued Turkish shipping.

Frogmore gazed up at the cold, lowering sky.

'It would be good,' he said, 'to feel the sun.'

Blue seas, perfume-filled gardens, to rest and not to be constantly looking over his shoulder. However, before he left, Frogmore had unfinished business. He had communed and he had meditated. St Clair and his tavern wench were not far behind him. As he waited for the craft to beach, Frogmore closed his eyes and continued his satanic prayer, using all the powers at his disposal to call up the Dark Lords of the Air, to give St Clair a reminder of who was the master. Frogmore rocked backwards and forwards, picturing the Jesuit's face and that of Rebecca Lennox. They were his sworn enemies and had to be stopped.

Rebecca wrapped her arms against the cold and stared back over her shoulder. She could make out the outlines of the farm where she and St Clair were hiding: the small pointed gable, the night candle glowing in one of the windows. In the faint moonlight she glimpsed the door she must have left open. She looked across the field which stretched up to a line of trees; the night was cold, the biting breeze tugged at her hair and thin shift. Rebecca heard a nightjar, a dark shape scurried across the field in front of her. The stars were faint pinpricks of light in a black sky. Rebecca was so startled she couldn't move.

She and St Clair had been at the farm, looked after by Mistress Bloxham and her simple-minded son Robert. For the last three days, she'd gone to sleep in that little cot bed and now she was awake, here in a freezing field at the dead of night.

'I must have sleep-walked.'

She wanted to go back to the house but found she was rooted to the spot. Some part of her soul recognised that she was to meet someone here, an assignation, mysteriously arranged, though she couldn't remember the details. Rebecca drew a deep breath and tried to assert her common sense. She started to walk back towards the door.

'Rebecca!'

The voice was soft, just above a whisper. Rebecca shook her head. She was having a dream, a nightmare.

'Rebecca!'

She stubbed her bare toe against a stone and winced at the pain. This was no dream. Sweat started in panic. Someone was coming out of the darkness towards her, squat and waddling, a mob cap on her head, a thick shawl around plump shoulders, the hem of the skirt tattered.

'Old Mother Wyatt!' Rebecca pleaded.

The old woman shuffled forward.

'Rebecca. So good of you to come.'

Wyatt was not the plump, friendly, old woman she'd known. Those twinkling eyes were now staring and dark-rimmed, the jowls sagging, the lips wet and slobbery. Mother Wyatt lifted her arms as if she wanted to hug Rebecca close.

'Rebecca, we've come to see you.'

'Go away!' Rebecca screamed, crossing herself quickly. 'Go away!'

A movement caught her eye. Someone else was approaching, walking with a pompous swagger.

'It's Malbrook the constable!' Old Mother Wyatt's voice was calm and comforting. 'See how your friends miss you!'

Rebecca's throat was dry. She couldn't move her tongue, found it difficult to swallow. She wanted to run but her legs were weak and she didn't have enough breath. Malbrook was ambling closer, his tattered, dirty clothes giving off the stench of the grave. Other figures were appearing, so that any escape back to the house was closed off. Some of the faces she recognised. Wasn't that Simnel's daughter? Her body moving langorously, hips swaying, hands by her sides. Rebecca started to run, but then she bumped into someone. The man had an old, scrawny face, a neck like a chicken. He tried to grasp Rebecca but she struggled free. She was aware of the chilling cold, the terrible reek as if she was in a midden, full of ordure and rottenness. She wiped the sweat from the palms of her hands on her nightgown. The figures lingered about her, ghoulish-faced. Malbrook had a dagger in his hand.

'Who are you? In God's name, who are you?'

'Come with us!' Malbrook's hand was extended. 'You are safe, Rebecca. We mean you no harm. Come with us!'

'Where to?' Rebecca asked.

'Trust me.' Old Mother Wyatt edged forward. 'Just a short walk, Rebecca. Come on now!'

Rebecca saw the red gash in her throat, closed her eyes and screamed, flailing out with her hands. She was rolling in the dirt, trying to bury her face in the ground; her name was being called, hands grasping her, but she fought back. Then a resounding slap scored her cheek, and she found herself staring into St Clair's face.

'Rebecca, what on earth?'

She gazed round: the field was empty, she had been dreaming! She had sleep-walked out here and experienced some nightmare. St Clair had come for her. He was speaking that strange language as he helped her to her feet. She looked towards the doorway. Mistress Bloxham was standing, lantern held high.

'Come on,' he said. 'Walk back one step at a time.'

She shook herself free. St Clair had brought a lantern out and placed it on the ground. She picked it up and, ignoring his protests, surveyed the ground. Then she saw the footprints: here a thin shoe; another, those great boots Malbrook always wore. St Clair caught up with her and prised the lantern out of her hands.

'It wasn't a dream!' she exclaimed. 'They were here! Malbrook, old Mother Wyatt . . .'

'Come back to the house,' St Clair ordered.

She let herself be led on. Mistress Bloxham threw a blanket around her.

'For heaven's sake, child!' the widow woman exclaimed. 'You'll catch your death of cold!'

She led them into the stone-paved kitchen, making

243

Rebecca sit in the large box chair before the fire. Robert came downstairs, tousled-haired and heavy-eyed, but his mother shooed him back to bed. St Clair pulled up a stool and sat beside Rebecca and, taking her hand, stroked her fingers soothingly.

Mistress Bloxham made her eat something and warmed her a posset cup. Rebecca sat watching the flames leap, the sparks floating up into the darkness. Mistress Bloxham would have done more but St Clair thanked her and asked her to leave. Once she had gone, St Clair faced Rebecca.

'Tell me what happened?'

Rebecca did in slow halting phrases. She didn't know whether she was fearful or angry for giving away to panic.

'It wasn't a dream,' she declared defiantly. 'I was out there, Michael, and people dead, murdered by Frogmore, were all around me.'

'You didn't see your father?'

Rebecca closed her eyes and shook her head. 'I wasn't dreaming.'

'No, I don't think you were!'

She glanced up quickly.

'You weren't dreaming. Frogmore can do that,' he continued. 'He can conjure up phantasms. Invade your mind, entice you into danger.'

'What danger?' Rebecca leaned forward.

'Those phantasms would have killed you. They were real people. Ghosts, but substantial ones, whose souls are still in Frogmore's power. He can summon them up to do his bidding.'

'To kill? To murder in the dead of night?'

'No, no.' St Clair shook his head. 'They asked you to go with them?'

Rebecca nodded.

'If you had . . .'

'What do you mean?'

St Clair pulled his stool closer. 'Rebecca, forget about the body, about your arms and your legs. Think about you, Rebecca Lennox.' He tapped her on the forehead. 'Your mind, your soul, your will: that is what they wish to control! Provided you said no, provided you resisted, they had no power. If you had lost your faith and your strength, given way to that panic and gone with them . . .'

'Then what?'

'Oh, it would have been an accident. In the woods are marshes, quagmires. In some other place it would have been over the edge of the cliff, down the crumbling bank of some roaring river or, if it had been a castle, some high wall or tower!'

'And I would have slipped?'

'Yes, you would have slipped.'

'But he can't have that power.'

'Oh yes, he can,' St Clair replied. 'Remember how Satan tempted Jesus? He took Him up to a high mountain then to the roof of the temple. The good Lord did not resist that but His will resisted Satan's temptations. Frogmore has similar power but he can only use it sparingly. Tonight's phantasms would drain his cup and he must refill it.'

'How do you know so much?' Rebecca asked. 'How well do you know Frogmore? When I saw you fighting that duel, he called you an old friend?'

'He was mocking me.'

'As you are me,' Rebecca accused, pushing back the chair.

'Rebecca, Rebecca!' St Clair grasped her hands. 'I

know Frogmore. I have studied him. You have to learn all about your enemy in order to deal with him.'

'Why you? You are a priest. You should be celebrating Mass, caring for souls.'

'I do that.'

'So, who are you?'

'Rebecca, I am what you see. Someone chosen by God to carry out this mission. Like the good Lord, I must fight human evil on human terms. Frogmore is what he is because others allowed him to become what he is.' St Clair let go of her hand. 'I suppose,' he added despairingly, 'that if I prayed and if I fasted, if I asked for a miracle, God might reply but He is not a puppet master. We can't expect God to intervene and block every evil act. We must oppose it ourselves. God works through your will and mine.'

Rebecca watched his eyes. He had a pleading look, anxious, even frightened.

'What do you fear now?' she asked. 'Tell me, you are frightened now.' Rebecca rubbed her eyes. 'You are frightened that I will leave, aren't you?'

St Clair nodded slowly.

'You didn't come to Dunmow by accident. You came looking for me, didn't you?'

'I have hinted at that,' St Clair replied evasively.

'Why? And Frogmore?' she continued. 'How could Frogmore pretend to be a parson in the church of England? Didn't anyone object?'

St Clair shifted on his stool and glanced sideways at the fire.

'England is a turbulent place, Rebecca. The present queen has only been on the throne less than seven years. Those priests who supported her Catholic half-sister have been thrown out of parishes and benefices. All is confusion. Ah well.' St Clair got to his feet, stretching himself to ease the cramps. 'I will tell you the full story.

'The last time I met Frogmore was at Dordrecht in Hainault. For a short while, he turned hunter and I became the quarry. I knew he was coming to England. He would hide here then slip into London to see Dr Hermeticus. Whether he has or not I don't know. One night, in a tavern near Dordrecht harbour, my chamber was broken into. I had left to secure passage across the sea. Frogmore rifled through my possessions. He found a make-shift map.' St Clair spread his hands. 'It's the only mistake I made. That map showed very clearly that I intended to travel to Dunmow. Frogmore knows that he is in danger; he also suspects how he can be destroyed. Anyway, to cut a long story short, he landed at one of the eastern ports, slipping through the countryside like a weasel. For some strange reason, probably Cowper, the English authorities were alerted. A man called Cavendish began to pursue him. Cavendish was one of Cowper's men. Frogmore certainly killed him. He then journeyed into south Essex where he learned that Parson Baynes was retiring. Frogmore exploited the opportunity. He is versatile, cunning, charming with an ever-ready wit. He simply appeared in Dunmow as the new parson. It would have taken months for Baynes' replacement to arrive, or for the ecclesiastical authorities to discover that this new vicar had appeared from nowhere and had taken up residence.'

St Clair went to fetch a cup of wine. He came back and sat on the stool.

'And who would care? The local bishop would just think some wandering priest was carrying out parish duties. Dunmow is a small, poor parish. No one would object.'

'But Frogmore wanted to discover what was so special about Dunmow?'

'Yes,' St Clair replied.

'And what is it, Michael? Please.' Rebecca brushed the hair from her face. Even in the few days since leaving Owlpen Hall it had grown again.

St Clair picked up one of the rushes from the floor and broke it between his fingers.

'If you look at the Bible, Rebecca, God always intervenes in history through a woman. In the Old Testament, Sarah bore Abraham Isaac. Moses' sister saved him from the wrath of Pharaoh. Judith drove off a pagan king. Ruth married Boab from whom the line of David descends. The mother of the Maccabees raised her sons to be heroes. Finally, Mary acceded to God's will and bore the Lord Jesus.'

Despite the warmth of the fire Rebecca felt a prickle of cold.

'What are you saying?'

'Frogmore can only be killed by a virgin who gives him the blood of Christ.'

'I am a virgin,' Rebecca replied.

'Yes you are.' St Clair smiled. 'And your hare-lip is not a disfigurement. As a child in the womb you must have been kissed by an angel. Its burning lips have sealed you with the mark of the living God.'

'But why me?' Rebecca asked. 'How did you know about me? That I lived in Dunmow? That I had a hare-lip?'

'Do you ever dream, Rebecca?'

'Of course! Everyone dreams!'

'Then so did I. One night I was asleep, lying in

a field on the road between Fontainebleau and Paris. I dreamed I was in England. I knew that because my dream was so clear and distinct. I was on a road, people were passing, ordinary travellers. I asked them where they were going. They replied to Dunmow, so I followed them. In my dream I entered a church, sitting at the back in the shadows. A young woman came in, the top half of her face was hidden in shadows but I could see her mouth, her hare-lip. She carried something in her hand. She went across the shadow-filled church. I saw it was a posy of flowers. She placed these at the base of a statue and a voice said: "This is she". I woke up but, unlike other dreams, it never faded. I remembered every detail.

'When I landed in England I immediately went to Owlpen Hall. Through Lady Pelham I asked tinkers and pedlars. I learned a great deal about your home.' He smiled. 'The Silver Wyvern, its good cooking; Master Lennox the taverner and his strange daughter, the one they called hare-lipped.'

Rebecca rubbed her arms.

'So, this is all preordained? We are puppets on a string?'

St Clair sipped from the wine.

'No, no, Rebecca. When I sheltered in that stable you could have refused to help me. You could have ignored me. You could have even turned me over to the authorities, allowed Master Cowper to have his will. God may have chosen you but that does not mean you have chosen Him! You responded according to your nature, Rebecca. You never thought about yourself. You never knew who I was except a man beaten, tired, thirsty and hungry. You brought me flowers, food, drink and protected me. You took a horse out of your father's stable and led it through the night to that graveyard. Yes, you are the one, Rebecca Lennox! However, you can change your mind whenever you wish.'

'The door behind me is sealed and locked,' Rebecca replied. 'There can be no going back. Frogmore murdered my father. He has my blood on his hands and he must be brought to justice. I will not waver.'

'The cost will be great, before Frogmore is brought to justice and destroyed.'

'How do you know?' Rebecca interrupted.

'How do I know what?'

'How do you know that Frogmore can only be destroyed in the way you described?'

'It's in scripture. In Genesis, God promised how the descendants of Eve will crush the head of Satan. In the Apocalypse, the last book of the Bible, a woman clothed in the sun, magnificent as an army in battle array, defeats the great dragon. Salvation always comes through a woman, this is no different.'

'Is my virginity so important?' Rebecca tried not to let the question sound like a taunt.

'Virginity is not just a physical state, Rebecca. It is easy to be virtuous when you are never tempted. True virginity is strong and powerful, of the mind and the soul, a dedication to an ideal.'

'Did Frogmore want to end that when he invited me into the priest's house at Dunmow?'

'Frogmore was suspicious. By turning up as a parson in Dunmow he would be immediately apprised of local gossip. He would be able to sift the wheat from the chaff; in such a small place he'd soon discover if there was anyone who might threaten him. He would hear about Rebecca Lennox, the girl with the harelip, the daughter of a taverner.' St Clair tweaked her nose. 'An indomitable young woman, with a mind of her own as well as the gift of second sight.'

'And if he'd ravished me?'

St Clair's face became grave. 'It would not have made any difference. I do not wish to be coarse about your feelings,' he continued, 'but virginity is a matter of the will, not the act. Oh no, what Henry Frogmore would have intended was not ravishment but seduction.'

'In which case he'd have been laying siege for many a year.'

St Clair bellowed with laughter.

'You've got a tongue as sharp as a knife.' He sighed. 'And Frogmore would have realised that. You are no country wench to be tumbled in a barn.'

Rebecca was about to continue her teasing but she bit her lip. 'You still have not answered my question, St Clair. You are so good at evasion. I don't want any of your riddles. How do you know that Frogmore can be destroyed in the way you described? Who told you? Where did you learn it?'

St Clair murmured something in Latin.

'I said no riddles!'

'It's a line from Ovid's "Metamorphosis",' St Clair explained. 'It means it's right to learn, even from an enemy. Moscow is a strange place, Rebecca: built out of wood, it surrounds the Kremlin, the Tsar's palace, which is really nothing more than a collection of churches and monasteries. Now the Tsars of Russia make great play of the fact that they are descended from Byzantine emperors who fled from Constantinople when it fell to the Turks.

251

The Kremlin houses many manuscripts once held in the libraries of Constantinople. The Book of Secrets was written many centuries ago to counter the likes of Frogmore. It describes, in great detail, how a great magus or warlock can be destroyed. That's where I found it. I suspect Frogmore knows of it and will renew his acquaintance with it.'

'And who will help us?' Rebecca asked.

'We are on our own. Who would believe us?' St Clair added.

'Cowper might.'

'Ah yes, William Cowper! Sooner or later he will show his true hand.'

Rebecca was about to ask further questions when she jumped at a loud rattling on the door. She made to rise but St Clair pushed her back and quickly sketched a cross in the air. Again the loud knocking.

'Mistress Bloxham will hear it,' Rebecca hissed.

'No, she won't.' St Clair was now listening intently.

'What is it?'

As if in answer the rapping now moved to the shutters where it turned into a scrabbling as if some wild animal was struggling to break in. Rebecca held her breath.

'They are back, aren't they?'

'Yes they are. They still have power,' St Clair said slowly.

The knocking and scrabbling continued until it seemed as if a whole legion were outside rapping on the walls, battering to get in. Rebecca seized St Clair's hand but he prised it loose.

'Don't do anything,' he warned her hoarsely.

He got up then abruptly knelt down, head bowed,

hands joined. As the rapping and scrabbling continued, St Clair prayed in that strange tongue. Rebecca heard the word 'Adoonai' and remembered her father once said that was Hebrew for Lord. The more the rapping and knocking grew, the greater his urgency, as if he were trying to drown it out. Then there was silence. St Clair lifted his sweat-soaked face.

'They have gone,' he said. 'They will not trouble us again. We should sleep and build our strength.'

13

The next morning, after they had broken their fast on oatmeal mixed with milk and honey, St Clair became restless, going out of the cottage, gazing down the trackway. Rebecca knew he had sent young Robert into the city soon after their arrival and that St Clair was waiting for someone. She helped Mistress Bloxham with the household chores, then picked some plants and formed them into a crown for Robert who clapped his hands, eyes full of glee. St Clair sat on a bench outside the cottage door.

'Who are you waiting for?'

St Clair didn't reply. Rebecca followed his gaze. An old pedlar was making his way across the field, a battered tray slung round his neck. He walked slowly, now and again stopping to draw the broad-brimmed hat lower down his face. Mistress Bloxham came out armed with a broom.

'Go away!' she shouted. 'There is nothing we want to buy!'

'Hush!' St Clair whispered.

The pedlar came on. Rebecca got to her feet. When the man tipped back the brim of his hat Rebecca was surprised that the face beneath was lean, dark-eyed, the moustache and beard jet-black, the teeth white and strong.

'Good day, mistress, a ribbon, a geegaw?' He straightened up as St Clair approached. 'I am the Darkman,' he announced. 'But don't shake my hand or greet me in case I was followed. Tell Mistress Bloxham to invite me into the house.'

St Clair and Rebecca followed him into the kitchen. Once inside, the tinker took off his hat, tray and tattered cloak and threw them on the ground. He stretched his thin, wiry body and undid the ribbon which kept his oily hair tied in a queue at the back of his head. He was dressed in a needle-stitched leather jerkin with metal-studded guards at the wrists and on the shoulders. The shirt beneath was snowy white, clean and crisp. The leggings pushed into the battered boots were of good wool and around his waist he wore a thin, brown belt on which two daggers nestled in embroidered sheaths. He sat down in Mistress Bloxham's chair at the top of the table and rubbed his face.

'Who's here?' he asked, sharp eyes never staying still. St Clair explained.

'So you are the Jesuit and this is your companion? Dressed as a man but anyone can see that she has no need for a codpiece.' He smiled at his own humour.

St Clair sat down on the bench facing him. Mistress Bloxham served tankards of ale from the barrel inside the buttery. The Darkman stretched out his hand.

'I was promised gold. For each of you, three pieces.'

St Clair handed the coins across. The Darkman got up and brought across his tray, lifted up the false bottom and took out two square pieces of parchment.

'Licences to go beyond the seas.'

St Clair undid both parchments. Rebecca, looking over his shoulder admired the creamy-white texture of the manuscripts, the clerkly hand, and the forged seals at the bottom.

'They are issued,' the Darkman declared, 'in the name of Richard Boynton and his manservant Gervase Tabard.'

'They are only useful,' St Clair said, 'if we are stopped.'

'I have a ship,' the Darkman replied. 'The *Rose of Lübeck*. A German, two-master, a seaworthy cog. Its master, Jacob Vogel, now waits to sail from East Watergate. You are to be there before midnight. If you are not, they'll sail tomorrow without you. He'll take you into the frozen seas as far as Varody. Once you are ashore, you are on your own.'

'I know, I know.'

'You'll bring your own clothes and arms. A bum boat will take you out and Vogel will hide you until the ship clears the Thames.' The Darkman sipped at the ale then wiped his mouth on the back of his hand. 'If a warship intervenes, Vogel will hand you over.'

'And how much will it cost?'

'For me, two gold pieces to take you into the city and then you'll have to pay Vogel.'

'How can I trust you?' St Clair asked.

'You have no choice. Walsingham's men are combing the city. Every spy, every Judas Man, plotter, cross-biter, counterfeit-man, crank, even the idiots from Bedlam are looking for a Jesuit and the wench who accompanies him.'

St Clair handed more money over.

'I'll stay with you until tonight.'

'Who are you?' Rebecca broke in. 'And how do we know we can trust you?'

The Darkman stabbed a finger at her. 'Shut your mouth. As soon as you speak it's obvious you are a wench! He slipped the gold coins into his purse. 'Yes, I'm a wealthy man but, if you are taken, if Walsingham's agents, particularly those from the Office of the Night, finger my collar, I'll dance at Tyburn alongside you. Do you know how long it takes to strangle at the end of a rope? And then you're cut down, still alive, and your body slit from neck to crotch.'

'Hush now!' St Clair lifted a hand. 'Rebecca. This is a Jark, a counterfeit man. He calls himself the Darkman because he keeps to the shadows. He's an expert forger, that's what Jark means in the London cant. You want a licence, letter or charter, the Darkman will draw it up.'

The Darkman was staring, bold-eyed, at Rebecca.

'He also knows every alleyway and runnel in the city. He'll take us down to the riverside, past London Bridge to East Watergate.'

The Darkman leaned over and ran his thumb along Rebecca's hare-lip. 'You'll wear a muffler,' he said. 'That hare-lip will attract every sharper.'

Rebecca stared at his soulless eyes. She did not like or trust this man. 'If you could dance at Tyburn?' she asked. 'If the hunt's so close . . .?'

'The Darkman,' St Clair intervened smoothly, 'is well paid by leading Catholic families in the city. He does a busy trade with Jesuits and priests in and out of the kingdom. He's never lost one yet. But come, Rebecca, it's time to pack, the day is drawing on.'

Rebecca agreed and left St Clair and his visitor

talking, heads together. She still felt deeply uneasy, a prickle between her shoulder blades, a feeling of danger. When St Clair joined her in the small bedchamber they shared above the kitchen she said as much, but St Clair just laughed.

'You are as sharp as a barber's razor, Rebecca, the Darkman is now implicated. If we are taken, he'll hang!'

'What happens if he's reached a private accord with Cowper? And what is this Office of the Night?'

'You've answered your own questions,' St Clair replied. 'The Office of the Night is a special committee led by Walsingham and chosen agents. They answer directly to the Queen. The Office of the Night investigates cases of black magic, witchcraft, devil worship, anything which might threaten the Queen. The Office of the Night does not compromise. Men like Cowper are ruthless and rule by fear.'

'But surely Walsingham and Cowper will have men like our visitor closely watched?'

'Oh, they can watch but they have to catch him. By the way, our visitor, as you describe him, brought us news. Dr Hermeticus and his wife were killed in some mysterious fire.'

'Frogmore's work?'

'I think so. Frogmore never leaves people to answer questions or give information to those who might pursue him.'

St Clair came over and grasped her hands. 'Before we start, Rebecca, I want you to remember this. Whatever happens, whatever dangers we face, flee to the far ends of the earth, but never believe that you can negotiate with Frogmore.'

'But you have?'

'Ah yes.' St Clair smiled. 'But that's another story!'

They left shortly after dark. St Clair and Rebecca whispering their thanks and good wishes to the Bloxhams while the Darkman was already halfway down the hill. St Clair and Rebecca followed him into the wood, keeping to the countryside as they made their way down towards the Thames.

They avoided the outlying farms and manor houses, wary of disturbing dogs or the curiosity of villagers and peasants. They passed the ruins of the hospital of St Mary of Bethlehem. In the distance they could see the lights from the city. Their guide swung further east. They crossed Hobb Street, skirted East Smithfield and went along the river bank into the city. The Darkman padded like a cat before them. Now and again he would stop and draw them into the shadows. In the area near the Tower Rebecca felt exposed and vulnerable.

The Darkman now changed his pace. He whispered they should walk slowly, pretend to be pedlars going into the city. As they continued Rebecca stared around. She had heard men talk of London but had never been here. It was so strange, with the different smells from the river and the alleyways leading down to it, the soaring fine houses. She gaped in astonishment at the huge outline of London Bridge, its lofty arches through which the river tumbled noisily and the houses along it which stretched up into the night sky. She also glimpsed the poles jutting out over the rails of the bridge, grisly bundles tied at each end, the decapitated heads of traitors. Now and again they were accosted by whores with painted faces and gaudy wigs who slunk out of the shadows. The Darkman, speaking the cant, bluntly answered the invitations of these ladies of the night.

Other figures also slipped out of the blackness, hooded and visored, cudgels and daggers in their hands. The Darkman explained these were members of the gangs which controlled the river quayside. They posed no danger as long as they were paid the toll they demanded. St Clair did this, a clink of coins and they were allowed on.

They passed lines of ships moored at the quayside: fishing smacks, fat-bellied cogs, warships and merchantmen. The wharf was busy with sailors and porters either unloading holds or getting ships ready for the morning tide. At one point the Darkman espied customs officials, torches held high, walking along the quayside. He immediately forced St Clair and Rebecca down some steps, wet and slippery and stinking of rotten fish and other odours. Rebecca looked up, her eyes drawn by the light. If her mouth hadn't been covered by the muffler, she would have screamed. She had wondered why torches had been lit and placed on poles in that particular spot. Now she saw the reason. Three men hung by their necks from the quayside, the ropes round their necks tied to hooks in the paving stones.

'River pirates,' St Clair whispered. 'They are strangled and their corpses left here for three turns of the tide.'

Rebecca gazed in horror at the tortured, twisted faces of these men. Clad only in loin cloths, they dangled like dolls, their heads still yanked by the ropes which had cut off their breath.

'They just put the ropes round their necks and toss

261

them over,' The Darkman told her. 'You'll find very little pity along London's river.'

He stole back up the steps, Rebecca and St Clair following on. They passed Queenshithe, Paul's Wharf, the ruins of Castle Baynard and East Watergate where the quayside was stacked with barrels and great sacks of English wool. The Darkman left them for a while in the corner of a doorway of a disused house. A few minutes later he came scurrying across the cobbles.

'All is well,' he whispered.

He led them out, past a group of sailors who'd paid a whore to perform a wild drunken dance for them, porters with barrows, beggars searching for alms or anything thrown away. A jostling midnight crowd where people did not meet each other's eyes. At the quayside the Darkman led them down to the boat bobbing at the bottom of the steps, two hooded men at the oars. St Clair climbed in. As Rebecca turned and grasped the Darkman's hand an image flashed through her mind: the Darkman was in a chamber dressed only in his shift, a woman with long black hair was sprawled on a bed, wine cups lay on the rush-covered floor. Men, hooded, booted and spurred, were bursting in, swords drawn. She felt dizzy. The Darkman grasped her by the shoulder.

'Steady there!' he said. 'You are not yet aboard ship and you are seasick.'

'Did you betray us?' she asked.

The Darkman's gaze shifted.

'If you did, God help you!' Rebecca let go of his hand. 'And beware of drinking with a whore!'

She stepped into the small boat.

'Remember what I have said!' she called out, but the Darkman was already going up the steps and the boat was sliding away across the black choppy Thames.

The *Rose of Lübeck* was a sturdy, two-masted craft with a high fortified stern and raised bowsprit. The rest of the craft lay low in the water. It reminded Rebecca of some hunting dog, slinking in the grass stalking its prey. She glanced at the rowers but their cowled heads were bent over the oars. When she turned and looked back towards the quayside, the Darkman had gone. She felt the first drops of rain, heard the faint rumble of thunder and glanced up. The clouds which had been threatening all day now blotted out the stars: the rain splattered the river, ominous in its angry swell.

'Are you sad?' St Clair asked.

'It's part of my life!'

St Clair put his arm round her shoulders.

'I'll tell you the truth, Rebecca Lennox, and the good Lord is my witness, you'll never see it again.'

Rebecca tried to see his face but it was dark and his hood was pulled full across. She rubbed her stomach, queasy not only because of the river swell but with a mixture of fear and nostalgia. The wherry bumped into the side of the *Rose of Lübeck*. Rebecca heard shouts and the patter of feet. A rope ladder came hurtling down out of the darkness, one of the rowers deftly catching it. St Clair pushed Rebecca up.

'Climb, Rebecca, don't look down! One foot after the other!'

Rebecca obeyed. The rope was harsh and smeared with oil. She thought she'd never reach the top when arms seized her and pulled her over the rail. She steadied herself against the side, surprised at how broad the slippery deck was. In the light of lanterns hung from the mast and elsewhere, she glimpsed heaps of cordage, two cannon, men asleep in every nook and cranny. The huge main mast soared up into the blackness. The door in the small cabin beneath the stern opened and two men came over, one thin as a bean pole, with scrawny hair and beard, the other small and plump, a weather-beaten face under the flat cap, a shabby gown round his shoulders. Both men were armed. Rebecca heard the clink of their weapons; they walked with a swagger. The small, fat one pushed his cap back and poked his face closer, a friendly gaze, small, merry eyes, his breath reeking of onions and wine. He said something but Rebecca shook her head. The man stepped back as St Clair joined her on the deck.

'I am Jacob Vogel,' he said in broken English. 'This is my first mate, Arnold Brecher.'

'I am Michael St Clair, and this is my companion Gervase Tabard.'

'I don't give a rat's turd who you are! And if she's Gervase Tabard then I am Queen to Cham of Tartary!'

Vogel stamped his feet and looked up at the sky.

'There's one of your English storms coming.' He spread his hands. 'Pay the fee or I'll throw you over the side!'

St Clair unloosed the money belt round his waist. Coins exchanged hands. Brecher excused himself and left shouting orders. Vogel inspected the coins in the lantern light and grunted.

'Come in! Come into the dry, you'll be soaked!'

The cabin was nothing more than a small cupboard. It contained a board which served as a bed, a table, and a chair with two or three stools. The table was covered in charts heaped around a dish of meat and a half-drunk goblet of wine. Vogel offered the dish to St Clair and Rebecca but they both shook their heads.

'Ah well.' Vogel filled two tin cups from a jug of wine he brought from a small recess. 'Sit down! Sit down!' He pocketed the coins and squeezed back behind the table to finish his meal. He ate slowly, thoughtfully, staring at both of them. 'You are a woman, aren't you?'

Rebecca nodded.

'I didn't know you had a hare-lip. Sailors are superstitious – they'll say it will bring us ill fortune.'

'Tell them,' St Clair countered, 'that on board ship a hare-lip is the sign of good luck.'

Vogel's face cracked into a smile. 'Don't worry, I've already thought of that. You'll each have a rug below deck: it's smelly, dark and ruled by rats, and some of the men aren't much better. Never be alone with them. They'll soon discover you're a woman.' He popped an onion into his mouth. 'But, to many of them, it wouldn't really matter if you were a boy. When you use the latrines make sure no one's about. The voyage will take a month, it will be hard and cold. I can sell you cloaks, smeared with whale oil, which will keep you warm.'

St Clair agreed.

'We'll be sailing north into the Baltic. There'll be rocks, icebergs and pirates.' He leaned across the table, eyes wide. 'And there are most terrible monsters. If you fall ill, there's bugger all I can do. If you die, within an hour you'll be wrapped in your cloak and tossed overboard. On this ship I am master and God Almighty. If I tell you to jump, you jump! If I find you plotting against me, I'll hang you from the yardarm!'

'You're a terrible man,' St Clair replied. 'Or at least you pretend to be.' St Clair pointed to the cross nailed on the bulkhead behind Vogel. 'But you are a good man and a fair captain.'

Vogel hid his face in his wine cup.

'I think you'll treat us fair.'

Vogel sipped at his drink. 'Why are you going to Russia?' he asked.

'To meet someone.'

'I'll land you at Varody?'

St Clair agreed.

'I won't stay very long,' Vogel continued. 'The Russians are cruel bastards and their port officials are corrupt. Also, the harbour at Varody freezes and thaws at the turn of a tide. I don't want to get locked in. It's a strange place you're going to. You've heard the rumours?'

St Clair shook his head.

'Last time I was there, Prince Ivan, Duke of Moscow and Tsar of the Russias, seemed a just enough man.' Vogel put his elbows on the table. 'But, all things change, Master St Clair.' He tapped his head. 'They say Ivan's gone mad, worse than Nero of Rome! He's hanging and burning his subjects by the thousands. He's fortified a new winter palace in the southeast of Moscow and surrounded himself with demons.'

'Demons?' St Clair asked.

'The Oppritchina. You are conversant with the Russian tongue?'

'The Oppritchina can be Russian for gargoyle.'

'It's the Tsar's private army,' Vogel replied. 'They

dress in black, ride black horses, their standards are a decapitated dog's head on the end of a broomstick. They call themselves the Tsar's hounds, sent by God to keep Russia clean of . . .'

Vogel stopped. The ship creaked and swayed beneath them. Rebecca, chilled by Vogel's words, heard the shouted orders, the sound of the anchor being raised, the patter of feet on the deck. She was in a nightmarish world, swaying here in this narrow, little room, listening about the terrors St Clair was leading her into.

'No one's safe,' Vogel continued. 'Four months ago, Ivan who has now taken the title of "the Terrible", executed some of his leading nobles in the square before the Kremlin. He impaled one prince on a stake through his fundament. The man took fifteen hours to die. Another was doused alternately in hot and freezing water until his skin peeled off him like that of an eel.' He paused. 'Are you sure you wish to go there, Master St Clair?'

'Are foreigners still allowed in?'

Vogel laughed till his shoulders shook, his fat cheeks streaming with tears.

'Allowed in? Good Lord, man, of course they are allowed in! It's getting them out that matters!'

Rebecca steadied herself as the ship moved.

'Don't worry, little one.' Vogel gestured with his hand for Rebecca to drink the wine. 'We are not under way yet, just moving into mid-stream. We'll go on the morning tide.'

Rebecca sipped at the wine, which was smooth and rich.

'You'll get seasick,' Vogel warned her. 'But try to eat and drink. It's worse to vomit when your stomach is empty. It clenches the muscles.'

Rebecca froze as she felt something scrabble across her boot.

'You'll get used to that as well.' Vogel looked under the table, a dagger in his hand. 'I can never see the bastards,' he muttered.

There was a knock and the door swung open.

'Captain, a barge displaying the royal arms . . .'

Vogel jumped to his feet. St Clair and Rebecca followed him out across the deck, which was so slippery she ran into the taprail. Above her the thunder crashed. The rain drummed down and the lightning lit up the quayside in lurid flashes of yellow-blue light. She glimpsed carts, stacks of barrels, a three-branched gibbet on which corpses dangled. She found it difficult to follow Vogel's direction, the river was black and threatening.

'There!' St Clair shouted.

Rebecca's throat went dry. A wherry, a long, sinister-looking craft with a lantern horn on its poop, was making its way through the darkness towards the ship. A man stood in the prow. Rebecca couldn't clearly make out his features or form but she knew it was Cowper. She narrowed her eyes. A flash of lightning lit up the craft. She glimpsed the blue, red and gold pennant flapping on its stern, the men bending over their oars; the man in the prow had lifted his head and she glimpsed his snow-white hair.

'Cowper!' she groaned. 'God have mercy on us!'

'Can't you drive it off?' St Clair asked.

Vogel gave a short bark of laughter.

'For the love of God, man, this is the Queen's river! We wouldn't reach the mouth of the Thames before the warships were around us. They'd sink us or I'd have to strike my colours. My ship would be lost and a stinking dungeon would be for us until we're ransomed!'

'They could go over the side.'

Vogel's lieutenant came up behind him. The captain shook his head.

'The current's too strong. They'd drown.'

The wherry had almost reached the ship. Faint orders rang out and it swung sideways, coming crashing in against the rail.

'I carry the Queen's commission.' Cowper's voice came full and strong. 'Allow me on board!'

'Piss off!' Vogel shouted back.

'Allow me on board or I go back and the river will be sealed!'

Vogel muttered an order. The rope ladder was lowered. St Clair and Rebecca stepped back, watching the rail. A pair of heavy saddle bags was tossed over and Cowper climbed on board. He leaned against the rail, took off his hat and wiped the sweat with the back of his hand. He seemed impervious to the rain. Lightning flashed. Rebecca thought he looked younger, not as sinister as when she had first glimpsed him in the Silver Wyvern. Vogel went to protest, but Cowper thrust a piece of parchment into his hand.

'You harboured the Queen's enemies, Captain! Michael St Clair and Rebecca Lennox!'

'There's no such . . .'

'Answer the question. Are they on board or are they not?'

'You know they are!' Vogel snarled. 'But I didn't know they were the Queen's enemies.'

Cowper walked across the deck. He grinned slyly at Rebecca then at St Clair.

'I'm glad,' he said. 'I'm glad I found you. Master Captain, come here!'

Vogel came lumbering across.

'How much, sir, for another passenger?'

Rebecca's astonishment was only equalled by that of Vogel who gazed, slack-jawed, at Cowper.

'Is this some English joke?'

'No, sir, it isn't. It's a bargain. You either take my money and me or I ask my bully boys to come on board. It would take weeks for you to answer all our questions.'

'For you, three pieces of gold and the same conditions as these two. Once we are clear of the Thames, it's my ship.'

'Oh, don't worry, Captain.' Cowper's gaze had never left Rebecca. He seemed unaware that she had cut her hair or disguised herself as a man. 'I no more want to go back to England than these two do.'

'You can't come with us.' St Clair stepped forward, his hand going to his sword hilt.

'Let him go!' Rebecca pleaded. 'Michael, it's a small price to pay. He either comes or we never go.'

Cowper leaned across and gently touched her cheek.

'It's good to see you again, Rebecca. Well?' He stretched out his hand. 'I promise you, St Clair, clasp my hand and I am your man, in peace and war. No tricks, no subtle deceits, no lies!'

'What about your punks on the wherry?'

Cowper smiled boyishly. 'I'll tell them to go back to the quayside and wait for my signal. They'll never get it.'

St Clair clasped Cowper's hand. 'A l'outrance!' he said.

'Yes,' Cowper agreed. 'Until death!'

Part II

Russia: Spring 1565

At Death's Gate
The Slayers wait,
In dark, massed might,
For the Soul's bright light.

Anon

14

Henry Frogmore, a furred kolpek on his head, an ermine-lined robe about his shoulders, stepped out into Vronsky Street, shading his eyes against the early spring sun which turned the snows of Moscow into a shimmering mass. As a sled pulled by four horses passed, he retreated into a doorway, allowing it to go skidding by in a clop of hooves and the jingle of fairy bells. The woman in the sled caught Frogmore's gaze and her eyes wrinkled in amusement. Frogmore raised his hand as the woman turned in the sled. Such pleasures would have to wait. The women of Moscow were noted for their beauty and, in some cases, their licentiousness. He stepped back into the shadows.

A group of young fops, their courtesans with them, came running along the street, red-faced, their bodies still steaming from the bath-houses near the river. Frogmore wanted them to go; he felt refreshed, despite his long but swift journey across northern Europe. His forged passes, and his neverending supply of gold and silver, had opened doors and gates, silencing the questions of border officials.

He'd spent three days in the heavily fortified monastery of the Holy Trinity just outside Moscow, the guest of its black-garbed monks, but now he judged it right to return to his house. Nevertheless,

Frogmore was uneasy. Throughout his journey he had chosen victims and made his sacrifice, pleading with the Dark Ones to help. Nevertheless, Frogmore believed he was in danger, insubstantial, shadowy but still threatening.

During his previous stay in Moscow, Frogmore had skulked like a bear in the woods, keeping out of the eye of officialdom. Now he was even more determined to be discreet. Abrupt and violent changes had occurred. Tsar Ivan had declared war on his nobles or boyars. Frogmore had half listened to the chatter of his guide who had driven him by sledge from the Russian frontier to Holy Trinity monastery. Sheltered beneath the bearskin, sharing the man's food, ground millet and salted pork, Frogmore had discovered that Ivan was intent on a bloodbath. His favourite wife had died suddenly and mysteriously: Ivan blamed the boyars and would brook no opposition from them.

In his journey into the city, Frogmore had passed a mounted corps of Oppritchina on their black war horses, dressed like death, their garish banners above them, severed dogs' heads still dripping blood on the end of broom handles. Frogmore did not wish to become involved. He had considered appealing to Ivan for protection, but how long would the Tsar survive? Moreover, Ivan had a love for all things Western; it might only be a matter of time before some prince demanded Frogmore's surrender.

Frogmore gazed up at the red-walled Kremlin, a stone battlemented triangle of fortifications on an island above the Moscow river. A cold, forbidding place with its block house, towers, barbicans and drawbridges. The sixty-foot walls bristled with heavy cannon. Beneath them scores of gun loops had been cut and, along the parapets, Frogmore glimpsed the twinkle of armour. On the top of the arsenal tower, which soared a hundred feet above these high walls, Frogmore saw the corpses dangling there by their necks. The Kremlin stank of death! Across from him stood the Saviour Gate, and the Place of the Brow, a huge circle dominated by a dais with a stone balustrade. This was the Tsar's execution ground, which looked like the forest of the damned. The gallows bore grisly burdens and corpses rotted on the end of stakes. Yet, beneath this, the people of Moscow bartered and sold, impervious to the ghastly sights above them.

The market was busy, the lines of collapsible stalls arranged according to what was being offered: sheepskins, bear pelts, bones for buttons, walrus tusks for knife handles; silks, cloths, foods, different wines and beers: gingerbreads; melons grown sweet in horse manure; precious cloths from Cathay; woven tapestries from Samarkand. The people milled about: men in their fur kolpeks, sheepskins around their shoulders, baggy trousers tucked into heavy boots. The women of Moscow, hair hidden under veils, were conspicuous by their long, coloured dresses, woollen capes and yellow or red buskins on their feet. Of course, the market was also a magnet for the poor peasants in their rags. Everywhere were hordes of monks and priests in their tall, black hats, sombre gowns, long hair and beards, which moved in a flash of light as the sun caught the gold chains and silver crosses at their necks.

Trumpets blared from the crenellated walls. The Saviour Gate opened. A troop of Oppritchina galloped out, beating the people aside with their knouts, screaming for silence in the name of the Tsar. More executions were to take place. Long lines of prisoners staggered out, some down to the river to be drowned in cages. One woman, bound like a hog and thrown over a donkey, was to be led out to the outskirts of the city and buried alive for the murder of her husband. The rest, their bound hands carrying lighted candles, were hustled up into the Place of the Brow to be decapitated, hanged or boiled alive. The crowd left the market and surged to watch the Tsar's justice being carried out.

Frogmore seized his chance and made his way along the row of houses. He watched his step; the streets and alleyways were still precarious, the wooden shavings on the ground of little use. Rain and snow had seeped through turning them slippery, more of an obstacle than an aid. Frogmore found it difficult to know where he was. Moscow's houses, causeways and bridges were built of wood; fire was an ever-present danger. There had been a conflagration since he had fled the city and he congratulated himself on burying his treasure deep in the cellars of the house he had owned.

He went down an alleyway and paused, staring back. Moscow was full of spies and paid informers. He was sure he was being watched, followed. Yet, who could it be? He pushed open the wicket gate. The house before him was boarded and shuttered, untouched by the fire. Frogmore found the key where he had secreted it. He knew the house would have been visited by vagrants, scum from the city slums, but he didn't care. They would never have found what he had hidden so carefully. He opened the small postern door and slipped in. The tang of salted fish and the faint fragrance of perfume wafted towards him and he recalled the herb-pots he had bought to keep the house sweet and smelling. Memories flooded back of St Clair and those fighting monks who had nearly trapped him here. Leaning against the damp-soaked wall, a thought crossed his mind. Should he secure admission to the monastery of St Michael in the Kremlin and, once more, study that Book of Secrets? Frogmore listened to his own breathing. Or should he take what he had come for and flee? He heard a sound outside and his hand fell to the sword in his belt but the moment passed.

Frogmore went down the passageway. He opened a small door concealed beneath the wooden staircase and went down into the darkness. When he reached the bottom he fumbled about until he found the oil lamp with the tinder beside it and struck a light. Frogmore walked deeper into the cellar, an underground cavern of a palatial house long since destroyed.

At the far wall he took out his dagger, worked bricks loose. He stretched inside it, pulled out the thick leather bag and, sitting down, pressed it against his face. This was his weakness, for which he had travelled back. Now he had it, he must travel on. The Book of Secrets could wait. Once he was out of Moscow who could stop him? He would rest in some lonely farmstead or shelter in a cottage; their very loneliness would provide enough victims. He would acquire the strength he needed and, in a matter of days, cross the border into Turkish-held territory. The court of Constantinople must have received his letter. Frogmore cursed quietly. What did they all matter?

He undid the cord of the neck of the leather bag

and shook the contents out onto the floor. He caressed each item. A ring, a necklace, a roll of vellum, a faded piece of clothing and a child's toy, a wooden knight on a horse. Frogmore held this between his hands, moving his fingers along the worn, smooth wood. Tears pricked his eyes. Memories flooded back. Warm, sunlit days, his son playing on the cobbled courtyard behind the house.

'If only . . .' Frogmore whispered.

He ran the horse along the ground as if the very movement could bring back his long-lost son. Frogmore's heart seethed with rage. If only they had not died! If only he had the power to bring them back! Yet they had gone into the darkness and Frogmore had begun his own long journey.

At first he had not planned what had happened. He had done it out of rage yet his chosen pathway had led deeper and deeper into a forest where there was no ending, no turning back.

He placed the contents back into the sack.

Others would scoff at something so petty, travelling for weeks to reach this spot. Yet it would not have been necessary except for St Clair pursuing him like a dog, yapping at his heels. In the beginning it hadn't been like that: St Clair had been a friend, a man with powers. Frogmore had even viewed him as the son he had lost so many years before. In the past Frogmore had had companions, disciples yet St Clair had been different – witty, amusing, clever and astute. Only when Frogmore tried to draw him along the same path he'd travelled had the truth emerged. St Clair was a spy bent on his destruction.

Frogmore stared down into the pool of light. And yet that sword fight? Harsh and violent, whirling steel under an Italian sun. Frogmore had felt the power seethe within him. He had pushed St Clair over the edge of the precipice. No man could survive such a fall! Only later had he found out that St Clair was a Jesuit, a Catholic priest. Frogmore smiled ruefully. He was rarely duped and yet . . .

'Within a year!' Frogmore whispered. 'Within a year!'

St Clair had reappeared, dogging his heels like a mastiff.

Frogmore went back up the stairs and closed the cellar door behind him. He extinguished the oil lamp with the toe of his boot, and went out to the garden. The place was full of soldiers, archers and members of the Streltsi, the imperial guard: a silent wall of steel. In front of them, sabres drawn, their faces hidden behind black masks, stood three members of the Oppritchina. Frogmore's hand went to his sword.

'Welcome to Moscow, Master Frogmore!'

The Oppritchina in the middle stepped forward, pulling off his mask. His face was young, almost girlish, smooth-shaven, his black hair close cropped.

'We are here on the orders of his imperial highness, God's regent and vicar, Ivan, Duke of Moscow and Emperor of the Russias. If you draw that sword you are dead. If you keep it in a sheath you are the Tsar's friend.'

Frogmore took his hat off and bowed mockingly.

'I am as always,' he smiled, 'his imperial highness's most loyal subject.'

'Good!' The Oppritchina waved him forward. 'The Emperor awaits!'

'He was a good man!' St Clair declared.

Rebecca, standing on the ice-covered quayside of Varody harbour, quietly agreed. She watched the *Rose of Lübeck* turn carefully, wary of the chunks of ice which still floated under the spring sun. A puff of smoke rose as Vogel fired a cannon in salute. Its main sail dipped and the ship, true to its master's word, left Russia's northern harbour as quickly as possible. Rebecca felt her legs wobble and she had to sit down on their belongings heaped in the dirty slush. She grasped her stomach and stared at where Cowper and St Clair were busily doing business with the harbourmasters. The fur-capped officials in their dirty robes pretended to examine the documentation. At the clink of coins one official grunted, snapped his fingers and a clerk with a wooden tray round his neck trotted forward. Passes were issued, stamped and sealed and the officials strode away.

St Clair then did business with a number of seedy men dressed in rags who offered their services as porters.

The Jesuit came striding over.

'It's as Master Vogel says,' he reported. 'Easy to get into Russia it might be, but very difficult to get out.' He crouched down. 'You are well?'

'You've got sea legs,' Rebecca groaned, holding her stomach.

'I've been on ships before.' St Clair's eyes twinkled in amusement. 'And I think the same is true of Cowper.'

Rebecca looked at the Judas Man. A crowd of tattered children had gathered round, looking curiously up at his snow-white hair.

'It's a month,' Rebecca breathed. 'Since we left England. Almost a month to the day.'

282

She shook her head and stared round at the tattered, wooden buildings, the slush-filled trackways. The harbour was a collection of log cottages. Rebecca noticed the roughly hewn icons fixed to each door post. There was no glass or wooden doors, just flaps of deerskin. In front of many of the cottages cauldrons of reeking blubber simmered and their salty steam, like a thick veil, hung in the icy air. Figures loomed in and out of this mist. Men, in coloured caftans over collarless shirts and baggy trousers, knives and spoons in their belts; women in dowdy gowns, shawls or capes over their shoulders.

Rebecca started as a cold hand pressed against her cheek. She turned and recoiled at the man standing there naked as a baby. Long, shaggy hair and beard covered his chest and back, a leather collar encircled his neck. He patted her cheek again, smiled and said something and started to dance, shaking what looked like a baby's rattle. Round and round he cavorted and, as he did so, sang, a low wailing sound. Every so often he would stop, come back and press his fingers against Rebecca's face. St Clair came over.

'Stay still,' he warned her. 'The dancer is a Yurydivey, one of their holy fools. Even the Tsar treats such men with respect.' The Jesuit crouched down beside her. 'He appears to like you.'

The Yurydivey abruptly stopped and stared at the small metal cross at Michael's neck. He came forward fearfully, his hand going out to caress the Jesuit's face like a mother would a baby.

'Are you in any danger?' Cowper asked.

The Yurydivey, now on all fours, approached St Clair like a dog, shuffling forward slowly, belly down, head forward. His eyes were rounded in amazement, his head going from side to side as if he couldn't believe what he saw. Abruptly he prostrated himself, banging his head three times on the ground. St Clair touched the man's hair and said something in Russian. The Yurydivey jumped to his feet, clapped his hands and danced away singing at the top of his voice.

'Well, you've made one Russian happy,' Cowper said drily. He stared down at them. 'What's so special about you? I thought Russians only did that to icons and sacred objects?'

'I'm wearing a cross,' St Clair replied defensively. 'And in Russia a hare-lip is seen as a sign of divine approval, that Rebecca has been kissed by an angel.'

Rebecca would have objected but she held her tongue. The Yurydivey had apparently been taken by her, but it was St Clair the holy fool had paid real reverence to.

'Come on!' St Clair got to his feet and shouted at some porters. 'We'll stay at a kibak. It's Russian for a tavern. Hot baths, some good food, then we'll travel on.'

He led them down from the quayside into the thin, winding streets.

'In Russia,' he explained, 'most houses are made of wood so be careful of fire.' He kicked at the wooden shavings lying thick along the street and pointed up to the wooden causeways and bridges connecting the upper stories of houses. 'In summer, when this dries out, a mere spark can turn a town into a conflagration.'

The kibak stood in a small causeway just off the town squares. It reminded Rebecca of an English tavern, though more shabby, the rooms narrower and, instead of rushes on the floor, wood shavings and sawdust. The smells were different. Everywhere reeked of fish blubber and oil though Rebecca caught the faint smell of soap and St Clair explained there were hot baths behind the tavern. These were nothing more than large, paved ditches, filled with hot water piped in from nearby springs. The landlord took them upstairs; the wooden balustrade was intricately carved and, wherever she looked, stood small statues or icons.

'The Russians believe that demons are everywhere,' St Clair whispered.

'You don't have to be a Russian to believe that,' Cowper interjected.

The landlord showed them two rooms, a small, narrow one for Rebecca whose bed was simply boards put together and covered in sacks of sawdust with a thin straw mattress laid over the top. Cowper and St Clair shared an adjoining one. Rebecca wondered, now they were off the ship, how these two enemies would fare. She still felt unreal. Her legs ached and trembled, her stomach pitched and, when she stood still, the floor seemed to move under her as if she was still on board ship.

Rebecca lay down on the bed and immediately fell asleep. When she woke, it was dark and she was cold. At first she thought she was back on the ship and the knocking was the sound of sailors running up and down the deck but it was St Clair rapping against the bed boards. He was shaved, his hair cropped and dressed in the Russian fashion, with a thick woollen caftan over his shirt, baggy trousers and new fur-lined boots.

'Cowper looks the same.' He patted Rebecca on

the shoulder and, from behind his back, brought out a huge pair of shears. Rebecca groaned.

'Your hair's got longer!'

St Clair made her sit on the edge of the bed and cropped her hair. Afterwards, a maid, a red-cheeked, giggling wench, took Rebecca down to the baths, steaming pools of water in a long, shabby shed. An old man sprawled in one of the baths, leaning against the side. When Rebecca objected, the maid shook her head, pointing at Rebecca's clothes, and Rebecca realised that, in Russia, male and female bathed together. She quickly took off her clothes and, shivering, slipped into the pit of hot water. She tried to hide her small breasts but the young maid just giggled and pointed to her own, large and luxurious. St Clair came in but stood at the door, almost hidden by the rolling steam.

'How do you feel, Rebecca?'

'Like a piece of fish being boiled!' she exclaimed, splashing the water and tasting the salt.

'It's very good,' St Clair assured her. 'It cleanses the body and you'll sleep like a babe. I've brought a sack of fresh clothes for you, shirt, trousers, boots, stockings, even a woollen cap. I don't care if they know you're a woman here but, in Moscow, try to act the man.'

As soon as he left Rebecca got out of the bath. The woman dried her quickly with a rough, hard cloth and helped her dress. From her chatter, Rebecca gathered she was to join her companions but she felt very faint and sleepy and insisted on returning to her own chamber, where she fell asleep within minutes.

When she awoke the tavern was quiet but someone had placed an earthenware bowl with slices of salted fish, bread, a small pot of honey and some strange fruits on the floor wrapped in a cloth against the mice which Rebecca could hear scurrying about in the darkness. She got up and ate the food slowly. On the windowsill she found a small cup. It tasted like the beer her father served but was thinner.

Afterwards, Rebecca lay back on the bed staring up into the darkness. The voyage had taken a month. For the first two weeks Rebecca had been so ill, all she could do was lie below deck and be sick. St Clair had tried to force food down her but, time and again, Rebecca would bring it back, retching so violently her stomach became sore. Cowper, too, was there. Now and again she'd wake to find him staring down at her, dabbing at her brow with a wet cloth. Vogel himself, perhaps alarmed at how long her sickness lasted, brought a herbal drink and forced it down her throat. After that Rebecca got better. She kept food down but then became aware of the freezing cold, the awful stench of the hold, the slops, the rats' urine, the waste and the ordure of men forced to live, eat, drink and sleep in that small, dark pit. She was glad when St Clair allowed her on the deck. Now used to the pitching ship, she was amazed at the grey, silent sea around her. Ice glistened on the shrouds, the ropes and rails were freezing to the touch and the wind cut like a whip. Nevertheless, Rebecca preferred to be there.

The crew soon realised she was a woman yet, perhaps because of Cowper's presence, his eerie appearance, the way he constantly drummed his fingers on the hilt of his sword, they kept their distance. Indeed, they showed her great kindness, often helping her up and down the steep steps into the hold or showing her where to stand, how to roll with the pitch of the ship and not fight against it.

The food was usually cold: a mess of pottage and hard biscuit which contained weevils, plus rancid meat, heavily salted and spiced, washed down with cups of strong ale. Cowper and St Clair had become members of the crew, helping out in different tasks. Both men, so they claimed, had taken part in voyages and were used to discomfort and hardship. St Clair proved himself able with maps and charts while Cowper, when the ship was challenged by Frisian pirates in their low, evil-looking fishing smacks, manned one of the *Rose of Lübeck*'s cannon. He put a shot so perilously close, the pirates soon changed their minds and quickly slipped away into a bank of mist.

The hard conditions, the iron routine of the ship, prevented much discussion. One night, about a week before they sailed into Varody, they were all sitting in the hold. Cowper began to talk about Frogmore but St Clair shook his head warningly.

'We've been together for three weeks,' he whispered hoarsely, his eyes bright because he was a little feverish. 'It's best if we do not discuss such matters. Sailors are very superstitious, the slightest hint of what we are involved in and they would have us over the side.'

Rebecca, free from immediate danger, had agreed with St Clair but the loneliness had heightened her sense of unreality. There she was, a tavern wench from Dunmow, sailing across frozen seas under grey, lowering skies. She was in a boat adrift upon waters where there was no glimpse of shore, travelling to a country at the far end of the earth. Her companions were equally bizarre, a secretive Jesuit priest and his erstwhile enemy, the Judas Man Cowper! And for what? To hunt down a great magus who had taken her father's life.

Rebecca stiffened as she heard the howl of a wolf, long and undulating like the cry of a ghost. She went to the small window and pulled back the strengthened piece of deerskin; the blast of cold air made her flinch. She glimpsed torchlight and heard sounds of revelry from the other end of the village. Shapes, dark and indistinct, loped along the street, huge shaggy dogs or some wild animals from the nearby forest. Rebecca let the flap fall and went back to bed. She recalled her father, the warmth of the Silver Wyvern.

'God forgive me!' she said to herself. 'But it's not just that!' True, she wanted justice but her presence here was for more than one reason. She recalled St Clair's words about coming to Dunmow to choose her, something she had accepted, so quickly, so easily. Why?

'Because I'm supposed to be here,' she whispered into the darkness. Yes, that was it! It was almost as if she had been born for this; her previous life, certainly since the death of her mother, had only been a time of waiting and now that was ended. Where would it lead? A wolf howled. Rebecca slipped deeper between the covers. She must never forget that somewhere out in the darkness, Frogmore was waiting.

15

Late the following morning, when the tavern had emptied, St Clair brought Cowper into Rebecca's room. She had risen late, freezing cold, and devoured bowls of hot boiled millet in goat's milk, some dark rye bread which made her teeth ache and a fiery drink which had turned her giddy, much to the giggles of the watching maidservant.

Rebecca had gone back to her room as St Clair and Cowper had left to hire sleds and guides to take them south to Moscow. As soon as both men entered, Rebecca could tell from St Clair's face that they had exchanged ill words. The pact of silence and conspiracy imposed on them by conditions on board the *Rose of Lübeck* had now gone. Rebecca's heart sank at the prospect of clashes between her two companions even though she realised that she had been living in a fool's paradise. Cowper was a Judas Man, St Clair a Jesuit, inveterate enemies brought together because they hunted the same quarry. Moreover, Cowper had not explained his change of heart and St Clair had only taken him under duress.

'You've been quarrelling, haven't you?'

'No,' Cowper replied lazily, sitting down on the floor, his back to the wall. He took his hat off, shuffling the brim between his fingers. 'We've been walking arm in arm to watch the fishing smacks in the harbour.'

'I want Cowper to leave us,' St Clair said.

'Why?' Cowper leaned forward. 'Why should I leave you? You know I am at a disadvantage. I don't know this country, the tongue, its customs.'

'You should have thought of that before you boarded the ship!'

'I did, Jesuit. There's no going back! If I do, it will be to a gibbet or living as a hunted man for the rest of my life. Master Walsingham never forgets.'

'Then tell me, Master Cowper, why have you come? Why have you, one of Secretary Walsingham's lovely boys, decided to kick over the traces and throw in his lot with a Jesuit and a tavern maid? Oh, I know what you are going to say.' St Clair unbuckled his sword belt and threw it menacingly on the floor between them. 'That you want Frogmore's capture as much as I, but you are a Judas Man. You capture the likes of me and hand them over to the executioners. How do we know that you are not playing one of Secretary Walsingham's games? Get close to the Jesuit and his tavern wench and, when the time is ripe, when Master Frogmore is within our grasp, seize him yourself for your Queen back in London.'

'And I can do that in the middle of the snows of Moscow?'

'Don't fool me, Cowper. England's ties with Russia are growing stronger by the year. A Russian ambassador has visited London, there are Englishmen visiting the court of Tsar Ivan. His imperial highness, if given English assurances, might only be too willing to hand over Master Frogmore, not to mention a wanted Jesuit and an attainted tavern wench, to the English authorities. We'd be put on some sled and taken to the nearest port. Once we are aboard an English ship, we might just as well be back in the Tower of London or the keep of Colchester Castle.'

Cowper leaned his head back against the wall and stared up at the timbered ceiling. St Clair stood, stony-eyed, adamant. Rebecca could accept the logic of his argument. Why had Cowper sacrificed so much? Was it all a game? A charade? She got up, stamping her feet as if they were cold but, in truth, she wanted to break the tension. If this continued, both men would draw their swords.

'Why are we here?' she asked.

'I've told you,' St Clair replied. 'Frogmore had to come back to Moscow. He had certain possessions he wished to collect. He may also want to study the Book of Secrets held by the monastery of St Michael.'

'Book of Secrets?' Cowper queried.

'Yes, Book of Secrets. If you travel to Moscow, they'll tell you all about it.'

'Why?' Rebecca insisted. 'Why are you so sure that Frogmore is in Russia, Moscow or anywhere else?'

Cowper tapped his foot. 'Good question, tavern wench, and one I've been wondering about. You can sit there, Jesuit, and hug your secrets to yourself but I'll give you a little knowledge. Master Frogmore never took ship from the Thames, at least not to Russia. I suspect he fled across the Narrow Seas to France and travelled overland. He is well equipped and cunning. He had no baggage or impedimenta. He probably arrived in Russia at least seven to ten days before we did. He could have collected these possessions, read that book, stolen it for all I care, and be lost in the icy wastes or travelled south to warmer climes.'

'Michael,' Rebecca added warningly, watching the stubborn set to his jaw.

'I knew Frogmore would come to Russia!' St Clair replied. 'Before I left Dordrecht, I wrote to my good friend the Abbot Sylvester of the monastery of St Michael. I begged him, for the sake of our friendship and for the love of Christ, to have Frogmore's house watched day and night. Sylvester is a good and honourable man among a pack of thieves. He recognised Frogmore's great evil. Sylvester is respected by the Tsar. If Frogmore returns he will be taken. However, our adversary is so honey-tongued, he may well use the situation to his advantage. We must reach Moscow before Frogmore slips out of the net Sylvester has cast.'

'Ah!' Cowper sighed.

'I still think you should go your own way.'

'I saved your life in London. I could have had you both arrested . . .'

'But you didn't.'

'Michael.' Rebecca crouched down beside him. 'What's the danger? If Cowper isn't with us, he's against us. Either way, he's now in Russia. He poses no threat.'

'Then why doesn't he tell us why he pursues Master Frogmore so hotly?'

Cowper scrambled to his feet. St Clair picked up his sword belt. Rebecca stepped between them.

'Tell me!' St Clair demanded.

'I will if . . .'

'Stop it!' Rebecca cried. 'You are like two boys in a game. You both know the truth. Frogmore is a demon who kills men, takes their hearts and imprisons their souls. You, Michael, are sent by your order to destroy him because of the evil he can and will do.'

Cowper's face was freshly shaved and scrubbed, his strange light blue eyes like pieces of ice, the full lips a thin mean line. A man who feels he has been cheated, Rebecca concluded.

'I'll answer your questions, Jesuit,' Cowper said hoarsely. 'I am an albino. An ugly, misshapen entity, spawned at midnight and rejected by his own mother. To some I am an oddity, to others I am cursed by God.' He blinked, glancing quickly at Rebecca. 'Yet I have a heart like any other man, feelings which can bruise as quickly as the next man's. I was taken in by a leather worker, a Master Cowper. Twenty years ago, this man disappeared. Never found again. Frogmore was in the vicinity at the time, committing his usual horrible crimes. I vowed, even though a youth, eternal vengeance on the man who killed the only family I had.'

'I don't believe that,' St Clair interjected.

'Are you calling me a liar, Jesuit?'

'Stop it!' Rebecca cried. 'Michael.' She shook her head. 'Michael, he's telling the truth. I can feel it and so can you!'

'I have served as a soldier,' Cowper continued tonelessly. 'On ship and on land. I have studied law at Cambridge. I have climbed the greasy pole of preferment but one thought, Jesuit, remained constant: vengeance on Frogmore! Ever since I entered the Office of the Night, I have listened to reports from spies, informants at this court and that. I began the whispers, inciting Secretary Walsingham's interest, depicting Frogmore as a threat to both the Crown and Church in England. Walsingham rose to the bait. We nearly had him.' Cowper raised his hand and clenched his fingers. 'A man I trusted and liked, Andrew Cavendish, nearly trapped Frogmore. Cavendish's body was found in a ditch, his heart ripped out.' He shook his head. 'I do not work for Secretary Walsingham. I work for William Cowper. I intend to track Frogmore down and kill him or die in the attempt God knows, Jesuit, I don't want to argue with you.' He chewed his lip. 'I knew Ragusa would try and free you. I let him succeed, at least for a while. Walsingham grew suspicious. He put one of his assassins to watch me but I killed him. There's no going back for me!'

'Michael,' Rebecca pleaded. 'He speaks the truth.'

'But I haven't finished,' Cowper interjected. 'Why are you, St Clair, so hot on Frogmore's heels? Why does the Jesuit Order want Frogmore brought to justice so desperately? Don't they have enough on their plate combating the Lutherans and the Calvinists?'

'I am one man,' St Clair replied. 'This is my task.'

'Is it? You forget, St Clair, I have read the reports of spies and informants. You were once Frogmore's disciple, his friend?'

'Mere trickery. To draw closer!'

'Then you quarrelled?'

'Yes. We quarrelled.'

'According to my spies, St Clair fell over a precipice. He was killed.'

The Jesuit laughed. 'Well, Master Cowper, you shouldn't believe everything you see or hear.' The

Jesuit buckled on his sword belt. 'But there's something else, isn't there, Master Cowper.' St Clair's gaze shifted to Rebecca.

'Another reason you wish to join us?'

Cowper put his hat on, holding the brim down as if to hide his face.

'I am not a papist, Jesuit. You want to hear my confession?'

'One day perhaps.'

Rebecca didn't know if St Clair was being bitter or just teasing.

'Then we are allies.' He stretched out his hand. 'I have your word, Frogmore is to die?'

Cowper clasped it. 'As I promised on board ship, this hunt, Master St Clair, and all who take part in it, is to the death!'

'Good!' St Clair stepped back. 'In which case we need one extra sledge. You'd better pack. We can make some distance before dark.'

St Clair strode out of the room. Cowper made to follow but closed the door and turned, leaning his back against it.

'Why, Master Cowper, shouldn't you be busy?'

Cowper took his hat off and bowed mockingly.

'Are you the Jesuit's wench?' He sighed noisily. 'I'm sorry! That was unworthy of you, St Clair and myself.' He walked back into the room but stared at the floor, playing with his hat.

'In Dunmow I knew St Clair was hiding in your stable. I knew you were feeding him, giving him sustenance!'

Rebecca's heart beat a little quicker.

'The same is true outside Colchester. I was glad that you escaped. Two of the men in Ragusa's band were in my pay. They had strict instructions, no harm was to come to you.'

Rebecca blushed. 'What are you saying, Master Cowper?'

'Can't you call me William?' A muscle high in the Judas Man's cheek quivered. He stepped closer. 'I love you, Rebecca Lennox.' The words came out in a rush. 'I loved you the first time I saw you. Remember? I was standing in the doorway of the Silver Wyvern. You were talking to your father. Your hair was slightly untidy, you looked as if you had slept long and deep. It was your eyes which held me.'

'Why?' she interjected hotly. 'Why do you love me, William? Because I am like you, different? Because of my hare-lip?'

Rebecca caught the deeply wounded glance in Cowper's eyes and bitterly regretted her outburst.

'You know that's a lie. Who cares about the candle if the flame burns bright? And it burns bright in you, Rebecca Lennox. Can't someone like me love? Must there always be a difference between me and the next man?'

'You said you had no heart, that it was stone, not flesh and blood.'

Cowper gave a lopsided grin. 'That's one of the reasons I love you, Rebecca. I found I was wrong.'

'Why now?' she asked.

'I don't know. We are together. Tomorrow, we might die. God knows what dance Frogmore will lead us. But, I want you to know.'

Rebecca stared into those pale eyes. She put her hand gently on his shoulder and kissed him on the cheek.

'We must go now.'

They left at noon. A watery sun, high in the blue sky, did little to offset the cold, biting breeze. St Clair had hired three sleds each drawn by two sturdy horses, shaggy-haired, small but tough. Rebecca noticed how, as on all horses in Russia, their harness and traces were intricately carved and decorated. Their drivers were small, pot-bellied men, swathed in furs; their grizzled, weather-beaten faces almost hidden by the great woollen caps. The drivers were fascinated by these foreigners. They gathered around Cowper, staring at his snow-white hair, and muttered under their breath. St Clair whispered that they thought Cowper was a devil, a snow demon from the forest. They also studied Rebecca. Their suspicion about her male attire was forgotten in their curiosity about her hare-lip and they chattered excitedly amongst themselves. St Clair, pretending to know only a little of the language, smiled as he tucked the evil-smelling bearskin round Rebecca.

'They regard you as good luck.' His smile widened. 'Isn't it strange, in Dunmow you were cursed.'

'And in Russia,' she replied tartly, 'I'm freezing!'

St Clair brought out a little flask which he had offered to Cowper. 'Drink a little of this,' he said. 'It's a Russian drink, vodka.'

He poured it between her lips. Rebecca coughed at the burning sensation at the back of her throat. The drivers laughed.

'It will keep you warm,' St Clair whispered. 'Remember, Rebecca. Fingers, toes, ears and noses, keep them well hidden from the biting wind! If they freeze they will turn black. Frostbite can disfigure in a matter of hours.'

The drivers lashed their baggage onto the back,

299

climbed into their seats and cracked their whips. St Clair's sledge went first, Rebecca's second, Cowper's bringing up the rear. Once the horses got into their stride, Rebecca felt she was gliding across the snow. St Clair had informed her how the roads in Russia were good with an excellent imperial post system.

'But if we get lost, then heaven help us!'

Rebecca settled back. Now and again she was jolted as the sledge swayed when it hit a rock or pot hole. They reached the outskirts of Varody and soon they were speeding along the road. Rebecca pulled the bearskin up to her eyes, pushing the thick gloves up to cover her wrists, moving her toes in the heavy leather boots. She recalled her dream. On either side vast expanses of snow stretched up to a dark-green line of forest.

'This is my dream,' she said quietly.

Yet it was different. She felt peaceful and rested, pleased to be off that swaying ship. Above her huge eagles soared in the wind. Now and again, above the drumming hooves and the crack of the whip, she heard that mournful, heart-rending howl of wolves. She fell asleep and woke cold and stiff. The sledge was still moving but darkness was falling. The stars in heaven glittered like little candlelights. Looking to the left Rebecca realised how the snow turned the night bright, catching the light of the moon so it shimmered like a sheet of silver.

They entered the forest, a wall of trees on either side stretching up blocking out the sky. Animals crashed in the thickets. On one occasion the sleds had to stop as two huge bears lumbered across. St Clair turned.

'They are not dangerous,' he called out.

His guide said something. St Clair nodded. The

whips cracked and the sleds continued. They re-entered open countryside and Rebecca wondered where they would stay for the night. Peering through the gloom ahead, she saw the driver stiffen while the sled in front also slowed down. Then Rebecca saw the grey shapes on either side of the sled, running silently like ghosts.

'Wolves!' Cowper shouted.

All three sleds stopped. The drivers got down and brought out bows and a quiver of arrows. They stood, arrows notched, but the wolves disappeared as silently and as mysteriously as they had appeared, shattering the silence of the night with their hungry howls.

On they went until they reached a small village. The guides negotiated with the Headman for fodder and room in a draughty barn. The next morning, after breaking their fast on gruel and hard bread, the journey continued. A snow flurry made the day darker than it seemed.

By now Rebecca was becoming tired and bruised with the jolting of the sled, her eyes sore at the neverending whiteness. In the evening they sheltered at the edge of the forest, building up fires, hobbling the horses and breaking into other precious supplies. The guides were uneasy, nervous. In the darkness, beyond the firelight, Rebecca glimpsed shapes shifting and moving, the glow of an amber eye. Like the rest she had to take her turn on watch, prepared to seize a fire brand, jump up and scream at the wolves slinking in, attracted by their cooking smells and the hot, plump flesh of the horses.

On their third day out, just as they left the forest, the guides stopped, shouting in alarm. St Clair got out and peered along the roadway. Rebecca followed his gaze. A sledge stood by the roadside, surrounded by wolves which kept darting in and running away. Others were joining them, coming in with their long, loping strides through the snow. Armed with bows and drawn swords, St Clair, Cowper, Rebecca and one of the guides edged forward, while the other two stayed to guard the sleds. The wolves turned as they approached. Bigger than mastiffs, their long pointed snouts soaked in blood, a huge ruff of fur high on their shoulders, they growled menacingly. Cowper released the catch of his small crossbow; the bolt skimmed one of the wolves bold enough to edge forward. It yelped, turned and fled, the others joining him. Then they turned in a semi-circle and crouched watching him.

The sled they attacked had apparently left the track and its two horses were dead, their carcases badly savaged. The driver sat frozen in his seat, eyes open, staring sightlessly across the snow. He was covered in hard white frost: an old man, the ice had wrinkled his skin even further so the veins stood out in his pale, pinched face. One of the guides chattered excitedly to St Clair.

'One of the horses probably became lamed,' The Jesuit explained. 'And, instead of cutting loose, the man remained. He froze to death!'

They examined the back of the sled. The troika carried a small cargo of cloths and bric-à-brac.

'A tinker,' St Clair declared, 'who believed he could cover the distance. It's a common fate out in the wastelands.' He gestured to the ever-watching wolves and stared up at the grey, lowering sky. 'There's nothing we can do. If we bury the corpse, they'll dig him up and we'll waste time.'

They returned to their sleds and, in a cracking

of whips, the horses neighing at the smell of the wolves, they sped by the ghastly sight. Rebecca looked over her shoulder. Already the damaged sled was hidden in the whiteness and the wolves were closing in.

They stayed that night in the monastery of St Athanasius which stood overlooking a frozen river. It was protected by a high, turreted wall, its onion-shaped domes and towers a beacon for those travelling along the Moscow road. Inside the walls stood a collection of wooden cottages, outhouses, granges and barns, all grouped round a large stone-built church.

The guestmaster and the monks, dressed in black, high hats, their faces almost masked by their luxuriant beards and long hair, grouped round them, chattering volubly. St Clair replied giving what news he could. Rebecca looked about and noticed the women in their flamboyant gowns and dresses. One passed her by, a pot on hips which swayed provocatively. On the steps of the church, another monk sat, chattering and kissing a girl who appeared young enough to be his daughter.

'Is this a monastery?' Rebecca asked, sidling close to Cowper.

'Russian priests can marry,' he replied tersely. He had grown aloof since he had opened his heart to her in the tavern. 'And their rule, perhaps,' he shrugged, 'is not as strict as it should be.'

'They are friendly enough,' St Clair said, jingling the coins in his hand. 'We'll get board and bed and be out of here tomorrow. We'll have to share the same chamber. Some of the reverend fathers,' he added drily, 'have already taken a liking to you,

Rebecca, and they don't care whether you are male or female.'

St Clair finished his haggling over the price of their stay. They were shown to one of the small cottages, dank and musty, its beds nothing more than wooden boards raised off the floor and covered with straw mattresses. A fire burned in the centre, the smoke escaping through a hole in the roof. A monk brought in a small pot which smelt fragrantly of herbs and stewed fish. They ate hungrily, St Clair going out to check that the guides, too, had a place to shelter and that their sleds and baggage were safe. While he was gone, Cowper ate moodily, picking at the pieces of fish from the wooden plate and popping them into his mouth, chewing slowly, lost in his own thoughts.

'Are you sorry about what you said?' Rebecca asked.

'It's the truth. I can only tell you the truth, Rebecca.'

She bowed her head, playing with the piece of fish in her bowl, moving it around with her fingers. During the ride across the wilderness, she had thought about what Cowper had said, but how could she respond? How could she tell this man that he was a threat, a danger? A man who hounded them, threatened her as well as her beloved St Clair? Without even thinking or reflecting, she regarded St Clair as her beloved, someone she could not be parted from, whatever the cost. Did Cowper suspect this? Is that why he had jibed so cruelly? She glanced up.

'I never thought it would happen,' he said. 'William Cowper in love. How Walsingham and the others would laugh and mock. Do you ever think of me, Rebecca?' he added softly.

'I don't know,' she replied. 'I'll be truthful. I don't know anything any more. Here I am in this strange monastery, in the middle of a wilderness where wolves prowl and all manner of danger awaits us.'

'Have you ever loved?' Cowper asked.

Rebecca sighed with relief as St Clair lifted the deerskin covering.

'All is well,' he said cheerfully. He glanced at Rebecca, then Cowper. 'Come, I'll show you their church. It's better than staying here and being smoked to death over that fire.'

They followed him out into the darkness, across the slush-filled courtyard, towards the side door. The church was lit with candles down each side. Mosaics along the wall glowed in a wild variety of bright colours, blue, red, green and gold. Icons stood in niches, diamond-eyed angels hung from silver chains attached to the roof. The air was sweet with incense which curled round the high, elaborately carved altar, beneath a broad mosaic of Christ in Judgement. Michael led them round, pointing out different scenes from the Bible, explaining the importance of icons and angels. Cowper wandered away, attracted by a huge gold eagle which had been carved and placed in one of the side altars.

'Is he a danger?' St Clair asked abruptly. 'He seems so withdrawn, solemn. I thought he'd be happy to be with us.'

Rebecca paused. 'He claims he loves me, Michael.'

St Clair turned away and walked deeper into the shadowy alcove.

'Don't do that!' Rebecca hissed, following him. 'Are you trying to hide?'

'No.' St Clair kept his back to her. 'I thought as much. Cowper wants revenge, but I watched him on board ship. He cared for you, Rebecca, like a mother would a baby.'

Rebecca's heart skipped a beat. She couldn't imagine Cowper being tender and passionate. His strange white hair falling down from his shoulders, he was staring up at a painting, lips slightly parted. Rebecca felt a surge of pity. He was no longer the Judas Man, one of Secretary Walsingham's lieutenants. He looked like that little boy waiting to meet his mother, only to be cruelly slapped in the face. Cowper glanced across and smiled nervously, as if he was sure of nothing anymore. Rebecca waved him over.

'Were you ever a papist, William?'

Cowper put his hands on his hips, and bowed his head, tapping his boot against the wooden floor.

'It's beautiful,' he said. 'Probably the closest to God I'll ever get!'

'You seem so certain of that?' St Clair asked.

'If there is a God,' Cowper retorted. 'I don't think, Jesuit, that He has anything to do with burnings, lynchings, racking and torture, be it the fires of Smithfield or the scaffold at Tyburn.'

'So, you believe in nothing?'

'Oh, I believe there is a God and I'm His little joke.'

Rebecca jumped as the church door crashed open. A monk came running in, his hair and beard flying around him. He gestured at them. Rebecca had never seen a man so frightened. The monk joined his hands in supplication and she caught the word he repeated time and again: 'Oppritchina! Oppritchina! Oppritchina!'

16

St Clair, Rebecca and Cowper exited through the church door onto the steps. The front of the church was surrounded by a semi-circle of horsemen. They carried torches which spluttered as drops of fire fell onto the snow. The monastic compound was now deserted. The riders were dressed alike in black fur caps with spikes on top and long fur robes of the same hue. Only the glint of teeth and the flash of naked weapons showed in the silent wall of dark cowled men seated so silently on their great warhorses. Some held standards, horse-tails and fox-tails; a number wore the skins of wolves and bears, the heads of the animals covering their helmets and turning them into grotesque and ghoulish demons.

Their leader rode forward, on either side of him two standard bearers. Each carried a broom, twigs lashed to one end and, on the other, against the evening sky, a decapitated head. At first Rebecca thought these were human but, on closer inspection, she realised they were dogs' heads. Cowper's hand went to the hilt of his sword.

'Don't be foolish!' St Clair warned. 'You'll be dead before your blade ever leaves its scabbard.'

He sauntered down the steps. The leader pushed

his horse a little closer. He pulled down the edge of his cloak.

'My name is Dmitri Gorlyaev.' He spoke English haltingly. 'I am a commander of his imperial majesty's Oppritchina. You are the Englishman St Clair?' He pointed at Cowper. 'The agent of the English Queen?' A lazy smile crossed the Russian's unshaven face. 'And that must be the tavern wench who pretends to be a man! A pretty boy with thighs and bottom like that.' He turned and translated his remarks into Russian which provoked guffaws amongst his companions.

'We are subjects of the English Queen,' Cowper declared hotly.

Dmitri snapped his fingers. 'You are nothing but dirt under my horse's hooves! In Russia you are the subjects of God, and God's beloved son, Ivan Ivanovitch, Emperor of the Russias!' He smiled. 'I know your tongue. I have done business with your merchant at Varody. I am instructed to bring you into the august presence of our Tsar. We have collected your baggage.'

He stood in his stirrups and waved his hand. Three horses were brought forward. A terrified monk slipped through the line of horsemen and threw their cloaks onto the dirty slush.

'Do as he says,' St Clair said.

They hurriedly dressed, putting on gloves, hats and cloaks. St Clair helped Rebecca into the saddle.

'For God's sake!' he whispered. 'Do nothing untoward. The same goes for you, Cowper. These men will kill you out of hand!'

'How did they know we were here?' Cowper whispered back.

'I told you. Russia has good roads and a post system. As soon as the *Rose of Lübeck* appeared off Varody, messengers were sent to Moscow.'

'Hurry up!'

Dmitri, his horse's hooves skittering on the ice, led the group across the monastery compound and out through the main gate. Here they paused, a long line of horsemen, their three prisoners in the middle. Dmitri shouted again and Rebecca gazed in horror as the monks pushed their three sledges out into the snow. The horses had been unharnessed but the drivers were now lashed to these sledges, their bodies stripped naked. The weals and cuts where they had been savagely whipped glittered in the torchlight. The sledges were put in line, the drivers moaning and twisting at the cruel cords biting into them.

'This is not right!' St Clair shouted.

One of the Oppritchina smacked him in the mouth. Dmitri rode down the line, turning his horse to face St Clair. He drew his sabre and placed the naked blade flat against his shoulder.

'You spoke, Englishman!'

St Clair dabbed at the blood seeping from the corner of his mouth.

'These are poor men,' he declared.

'They had no right to take your money and bring you into Russia without a licence from the Tsar and his officials!'

Now he was up close, Rebecca could see that Dmitri was very young. Dark hair escaped from under his hat, his unshaven face was smooth, slightly olive-skinned, the eyes slanted.

'They had no licence,' he repeated. His horse came closer. 'But I'm sorry you are bloodied, Englishman.'

311

Dmitri stood in the stirrups and, bringing his sword round in a cutting arc, expertly sliced the neck of the Oppritchina who had struck St Clair. The head bounced off, blood spurted up in a fountain and the carcase shifted sliding to the right, spattering Rebecca with its blood before tumbling into the snow. Dmitri rapped out an order. Two Oppritchina dismounted, took the severed head and placed it between the legs of one of the drivers lashed to the sleigh. The dismembered carcase was then thrown on top of another driver, making them look like two grotesque lovers. Rebecca closed her eyes, fighting hard not to vomit. The Oppritchina round her simply murmured and laughed. Dmitri turned his horse.

'He shouldn't have struck you, Englishman. He did not have my permission.' He smiled at Rebecca. 'If he'd struck you, he'd have died more slowly. I would have put his genitals in his mouth before taking his head.'

Dmitri rode off back to the monastic gateway. Again he shouted. Five of the brothers ran out carrying large leather pigskins between them. One was placed on each sled. Dmitri slashed them with his own sword and the oil spilled out. The drivers, realising what was going to happen, screamed and yelled, struggling against their binding ropes. Torches were then thrown on and, within a matter of minutes, all three sledges and their contents turned into a roaring inferno. The flames lit up the darkness, filling the air with the stench of burning flesh.

Rebecca closed her eyes. She wasn't here. This was a nightmare! She was in the woods outside Dunmow, holding her mother's hand. They were going to collect wild flowers. Beside her she heard St Clair whispering a prayer in that strange tongue. She opened her eyes, averting her gaze from the burning sledges. Cowper, on the other side of St Clair, sat rigid in the saddle. She could only make out the outline of his face. He was staring impassively ahead. Dmitri rode up to him and said something, but Cowper didn't reply.

'He's calling you a white-haired demon,' St Clair told him.

'In which case,' Cowper answered, 'tell him that I am in good company.'

Dmitri asked St Clair to translate. The Jesuit replied slowly. Dmitri laughed and smacked his thighs.

'I think he likes you,' St Clair whispered. 'You've learned your first lesson, Cowper, about this land and these men. In their eyes, there's no vice and only one virtue, courage in the face of death! Never forget it!'

They waited until the fire began to die. The abbot and most of the community came out and prostrated themselves before Dmitri's horse, banging their heads three times on the ground in silent submission. Dmitri shouted at them, cracking the air with the whip he carried over the horn of his saddle.

'Oh Lord, not more deaths!' Rebecca whispered.

'No,' St Clair replied. 'Dmitri says he's in a good mood. They had no right to harbour strangers without permission from the Tsar. If they do it again, what happened to the drivers will be nothing to what happens to them.'

Dmitri finished his harangue. He twirled his whip, ordered the torches to be doused and led his men, their three prisoners in the centre, in a mad gallop away from the monastery of St Athanasius.

Rebecca could only grasp the reins and grimly

hang on. All around her the Oppritchina, heads down against the wind, rode like demons through the night. They stopped now and again to rest the horses and eat a little food: rye bread, some salted pork or dried fish. Rebecca did not know whether she was awake or dreaming. She was aware of the sky lightening above them, the pounding horses' hooves and these dark shapes which stank of blood and smoke.

In the morning, just as the sun rose, they entered another monastery. She was taken into a smoke-filled room and laid on a bed of straw covered with sacking. Later in the afternoon she woke, aching in every joint, her neck sore, her mouth dry. She was in a small cottage. St Clair and Cowper sat before the fire, sharing food with the Oppritchina. Dmitri walked across and crouched beside her.

'Be careful what you say!' St Clair shouted from the fire.

Dmitri stretched out one gloved finger and touched her hare-lip. He whispered something in Russian. Rebecca just held his gaze. Dmitri lowered his hand and gently squeezed one of her breasts. Rebecca did not flinch. Dmitri, a smile on his face, dropped his hand between her thighs. He turned and said something to his companions. Rebecca held her breath. St Clair was getting up, Cowper stared furious. She spat with all her force, the spittle catching Dmitri's cheek. The entire cottage fell silent. Dmitri's men were going for their swords and daggers. Dmitri picked up the smelly horse blanket and wiped the phlegm from his cheek.

'Is this the first time you've touched a woman?' Rebecca asked. 'Don't you know what we are like?'

Dmitri shouted something in Russian, asking St Clair to translate. The Jesuit just shook his head.

'Tell him!' Rebecca ordered. 'Tell him exactly what I said!'

'And tell him that if he does it again,' Cowper added, 'I'll kill him!'

Dmitri repeated his order. St Clair translated. The Oppritchina gazed coolly at Cowper then back at Rebecca. Her heart was thudding, her mouth so dry she thought she couldn't breathe and swallow. Dmitri started to laugh. He grasped Rebecca's cheek and tweaked it playfully. The rest of his men joined in the laughter and Dmitri, holding Rebecca's face between his hands, kissed her fiercely on the brow. He got up snapping his fingers. One of his men brought across a small wineskin. Dmitri held it to his lips and poured some of the fiery substance into Rebecca's mouth.

'It's good,' he said haltingly, trying to control the laughter which had brought tears to his eyes. 'It will ease the pain!' He patted Rebecca on the cheek, wagged a finger playfully at Cowper and walked out.

The following morning they continued their mad ride. When they reached the highway into Moscow, scouts rode ahead clearing a path with their knouts and the flat of their swords. They thundered through the gates of the city. Rebecca, now recovering from the bruising ride, glimpsed wooden houses, two or three stories high; narrow alleyways, wooden bridges and causeways across the slush; nobles in their frogged coats; merchants and peasants like those she had seen at Varody and elsewhere; monks and priests as numerous as crows in a field. The red walls of the Kremlin loomed above them. Rebecca averted her gaze as they passed the Place of the Brow with its scaffolds, stakes, racks, stocks and pillories.

Once inside the Kremlin, the Oppritchina threaded their way more carefully along the cobbled trackway past churches, halls and stately houses with rose-brick walls and shingled roofs. These were interspersed by gardens and small copses of yellowing birches, firs, pines and serried rows of rowan bushes, their berries still scarlet. On every corner, in every doorway and at the foot of every staircase stood soldiers in damascene helmets and coats of mail with blue and silver tunics laid over them. Groups of Cossacks, or so St Clair described them, their Tartar-like faces hard and grim, patrolled in groups. The air was thick with the mingled scents of incense, sandalwood and horse dung. Cooking smells billowed from the many kitchens and, through all this, a sense of watchful terror prevailed.

The Oppritchina dispersed. Dmitri took them into one of the houses and handed them over to a small, grey-bearded man. The place was clean, the wood polished, the walls decorated with furs. They were shown to a room on the first gallery, told to rest and sleep and, when the bell tolled, to go down to the kitchens for food. Their baggage was also brought up though Cowper and St Clair were denied their weapons. The old man just shook his head and muttered something in Russian. Rebecca followed him out and noticed how two Oppritchina had taken up guard at the top of the stairs. She went back, closed the door and surveyed her surroundings. The room had four beds, chests and a few sticks of furniture. Fox and bear pelts hung against the grey stone walls; in every corner stood a small icon fitted on a niche, small boiling pots underneath providing warmth as well as some fragrance from the incense sprinkled on top.

'Why don't they kill us?' Cowper asked bluntly, sitting down on his bed.

'I don't know,' St Clair replied.

'How do you know their tongue?'

'I spent some time in the monastery of St Michael but that's neither here nor there.'

'And what now?' Rebecca asked.

'We are in the hands of God,' St Clair replied. 'And those of the Tsar.'

The following morning, after the servants had brought up oatmeal and some sweet-tasting white wine, Dmitri appeared. Apart from his hat and helmet, he was dressed the same, menacing as ever.

'His imperial highness will see you now,' he announced. 'When you go in, whatever you think, and that goes for you, white-haired demon,' he almost jabbed a finger in Cowper's face, 'go on your knees and bow three times against the ground. Swallow your pride and swallow some dust.' He looked them up and down. 'This is not a formal occasion – your clothes are not too clean.' Dmitri grinned. 'But acceptable to an ascetic prince.' He stood aside. 'Now, St Clair, you have a visitor.'

The monk who came in was dressed in dark purple, his hair and beard a silvery-grey. A Byzantine cross hung on a silver chain round his neck; his eyes were red-rimmed from crying.

'Abbot Sylvester.' St Clair spread his arms and they embraced, exchanging the kiss of peace.

Rebecca's heart warmed at this saintly-looking old man. He gazed at her and Cowper, sketched a blessing, then said something to Dmitri. The Oppritchina just shrugged and left the room. Abbot Sylvester grabbed St Clair's hand and spoke quickly, earnestly, every so often squeezing St Clair's hand tightly to emphasise his advice. There was a rap on the door. Sylvester bowed and left as quietly as he came.

'Compose yourself,' Dmitri anounced, coming in. 'You will leave in a few minutes.'

Once he had gone, St Clair beckoned Cowper and Rebecca close.

'Abbot Sylvester came to warn me. Russia has changed: he knows Tsar Ivan well, he believes his Emperor is possessed by a demon with the blood lust of a Nero. Frogmore is also in the palace. Ivan does not know what to do with him but Turkish envoys have demanded that Frogmore be handed over to them. Frogmore is being treated like an honoured guest. Sylvester believes that Frogmore has also demanded that we, too, be handed over to the Ottoman Turks. Their envoys are sheltering in a palace outside Moscow.'

'And Ivan?' Cowper asked.

'Thankfully Ivan does not like being dictated to but the Turks control his southern border. Ivan is also frightened of Frogmore. The Emperor will stay in Moscow for a while but Sylvester has heard terrible stories coming from the palace Ivan has built for himself two miles to the northeast, Aleksandrova Sloboda. A former hunting lodge, Ivan has turned it into a macabre monastery where he, and commanders of the Oppritchina, dress like monks and swing from an orgy of prayer and asceticisms to torture and bloodshed.' St Clair sighed. 'Sylvester warned us to be very careful.'

Cowper made to continue the questions but there

was a hammering at the door. Dmitri, dressed in chain mail, sabre drawn, beckoned them out. The corridor outside was lined with black-garbed soldiers. Each held a naked blade. Rebecca and her two companions were led along the passageway, down the stairs and out into the weak sunshine. Soldiers thronged every gully and alleyway. They passed churches and halls, Rebecca growing nervous at the ominous silence, the oppressive atmosphere.

Eventually they were led into a long, dark hall, the door slamming shut behind them. Brands of pitch burned in iron sockets along the walls. There were no carpets or wall hangings, only two lines of Oppritchina on either side. At the far end was a raised dais with a carved stone throne. A man dressed in the garb of a monk lounged there. On the steps before him, kneeling with their backs to him, were what looked like more Oppritchina. Behind the throne Rebecca glimpsed a yellow-haired dwarf dressed in motley rags. The dwarf kept peeping out and staring down at them.

'That's Vaslov,' St Clair murmured. 'The Emperor's jester and holy fool. Ivan calls him his conscience.'

'The place is like a barn,' Cowper said.

Rebecca had to agree. Above her stretched dark, heavy beams, the only decorations the usual icons in their alcoves and a sombre cross which hung from the rafters above Ivan's throne. The dwarf came out and clapped his hands. St Clair, Rebecca and Cowper walked forward. The dwarf clapped his hands again and stopped, then looked expectantly at them, shaking a small leather club. St Clair got down on his knees, Rebecca and Cowper followed. They touched the ground three times with their foreheads.

Rebecca felt her hair being pulled and looked up. The dwarf was standing there. He was hideous, with a misshapen face, thick fleshy nose above podgy lips, no eyebrows above muddy, brown eyes. His skin was sallow and pitted with the pox, the greasy hair dyed a garish yellow. He was dressed in green and brown with red buskins on his feet. He tapped Rebecca on the head with his small leather club and, before she could stop him, crouched and kissed her on the lips, licking her hare-lip with his tongue.

'Please!' St Clair whispered. 'Smile!'

Rebecca did. The dwarf smiled back and kissed her again: his teeth were rotting, his breath smelt fetid. He moved to Cowper and felt his eyes then examined his snow-white hair, chattering excitedly to himself. Finally he went and stood squarely before St Clair. The Jesuit kept his head bowed. Vaslov grew angry, stamping the floorboards until St Clair looked up. Vaslov came closer. Rebecca had never seen such fear transform anyone. The dwarf's jaw sagged; putting his hand to his mouth, he ran across the hall behind the lines of the Oppritchina and was violently sick.

Ivan on his throne was leaning forward, watching curiously. The Tsar's dark reddish hair hung down like lank flax on either side of a thin face: his eyes were deep-set. He had high cheekbones and a curving beak of a nose above a mouth which reminded Rebecca of a carp, the lower lip jutting out; the likeness to a fish was heightened by the way the Tsar tilted his head slightly back.

Vaslov came hurrying back but, instead of being angry with St Clair, he went down on all fours, cringing like a dog and banging his forehead against the floor. The Tsar barked an order. Vaslov indicated they stand and they moved to the bottom of the steps. The Oppritchina kneeling there didn't even look up and Rebecca stifled her scream. She had thought they were soldiers but they were cadavers which had been cut up, cleaned and stuffed with straw, their corpses re-dressed with cloak and cowl. They had been placed like statues, pallid-faced and glassy-eyed, emanating a strange smell of perfume mixed with rottenness.

'Lord God save us!' Cowper breathed.

Ivan leaned forward and talked excitedly to St Clair. St Clair replied in monosyllables.

'What's happening?' Rebecca asked, trying not to look at the mummified corpses arranged along the steps.

St Clair sank to his knees, head bowed, and said something at which Vaslov clapped his hands and replied. St Clair then rose and turned.

'The Tsar has given me permission to translate but, be careful. There may be people here who fully understand the English tongue. He asks why you are frightened, Rebecca? These corpses belonged to a group of friars who tried to poison him. They have been placed here as a warning to all who approach the Imperial Throne. Ivan, however, is more interested in why Vaslov kissed you and bowed before me.'

'And?' Rebecca asked.

'I explained that I was a priest and that both of you were marked by God. It might be enough to keep us safe.'

The Emperor interrupted, talking excitedly to St Clair. The Jesuit replied, talking volubly with his hands. Ivan's fascination seemed to grow: his soulless eyes sparkled with life; he would tap his knees and chatter at Vaslov, who would nod slowly. Eventually Vaslov, threading his way through the corpses, came down the steps and ran across to a side door.

'Frogmore's here,' St Clair said in a low voice. 'The Tsar wishes to decide between us. For God's sake, whatever you do, do not upset the Tsar or his creature. Vaslov is a sorcerer-priest, a magician. I suspect he's jealous of Frogmore and the powers he claims.'

Rebecca tried to control the shuddering terrors which pressed on her mind. She wanted to flee this dreadful place.

Vaslov came bounding like a dog back into the hall. She heard slow measured footsteps. A door behind the lines of Oppritchina opened and shut and Frogmore swaggered out of the shadows. He was dressed like a priest, in a dark, furred gown and polished leather boots. A white cord circled his waist. Rebecca saw the jewelled rings flashing on his fingers, possibly favours from the Tsar. Ivan rose, hands extended in welcome. Vaslov, however, had retreated from behind the throne and was watching Frogmore balefully.

The Soul Slayer stopped and bowed. His hair, beard and moustache had been cut and dressed with oil, his face was plumper, the sheen of a well-fed man. He looked younger and much more dangerous. He bowed mockingly.

'Why Michael, Master Cowper.' His smile widened at Rebecca. 'My little girl. Welcome to Moscow!'

'Does the Tsar really know who you are?' St Clair asked abruptly.

'I think so. I've cured him of a fever. He's mad, you know, Michael. He has a hunger for human blood but he's frightened of me. He thinks I can fly like a night bird and drop fire on his palaces.'

'And what do you want with us?' Cowper declared hotly.

'Oh, I have asked the Tsar to lift your heads and stick them on poles.' He grinned evilly. 'Or take Rebecca into his bed and fondle a woman kissed by an angel, eh, Rebecca?'

Rebecca forgot her fears at the impudent arrogance of this evil man. She had travelled to Russia because of St Clair. Now she confronted Frogmore, all she could think of was her father, bumbling, sometimes drunk, but kind and well meaning, walking like a fly into this grotesque spider's web. The Tsar said something but Rebecca didn't care. She pushed her face close to Frogmore's.

'One day,' she breathed, the tears starting in her eyes, 'I will take your heart, Master Frogmore, like you took my father's!'

She wasn't sure but those dark eyes changed. Was it fear? The Emperor spoke again. Rebecca felt St Clair's hands on her shoulder, dragging her back. The Tsar was glaring at her but Vaslov was smiling slyly, nodding slowly. Again the Tsar spoke, his voice rising to a shout, hands flailing the air. He jabbed a finger at Frogmore, then at St Clair.

'Lord save us!' the Jesuit whispered. 'He says we are two magicians. He demands a demonstration of our powers!'

The Tsar fell silent and sat back on his throne. Vaslov came forward and spoke in sharp, harsh sentences.

'We must do something,' St Clair translated wearily. 'To astonish and dumbfound the Tsar.' He splayed his hands. 'I'm no conjuror but Frogmore has already taken up the challenge.'

One of the Oppritchina brought the magus a burning brand. Frogmore held it up. All eyes were on him as he began to blow gently. The flame went out. Some of the soldiers began to snigger. The Tsar gazed under heavy-lidded eyes. Vaslov clicked his tongue like a schoolmaster disappointed with a scholar. Frogmore held the brand up; the ash still glowed red and white. Eyes half-closed, he was whispering to himself. Then he blew on the ash. Sparks burst out. They rose like fireflies in the air and drifted above their heads. They broadened, shining like bubbles of soap. One drifted by Rebecca's eyes and she gasped as the Tsar did. She glanced at one of the corpses: the face in the bubble was one of the executed friars but he was living, lips moving as if begging for mercy. Frogmore was now blowing like a child would bubbles, so that more and more rose through the air.

Rebecca stared open-mouthed. Now some of these small circles of fire contained faces she recognised: Malbrook, old Mother Wyatt. The Tsar, too, was recognising faces, clapping his hands in glee. Frogmore dropped the stick onto the floor and ground it beneath his boot. The bubbles disappeared in small sparks and drifted down as white flakes of ash. Vaslov, his face contorted with jealousy, shook his leather club in St Clair's direction.

Rebecca watched. Was St Clair a Jesuit? Or was he a magus, a magician? Or an angel in disguise? Now surely he would prove himself, outdo Frogmore in his feats of magic? The Jesuit stepped forward. He spoke in Russian then translated it.

'I must confound the Tsar, puzzle him?'

Vaslov nodded. The Tsar glanced up.

'Something,' he said slowly in English, 'which intrigues me, priest.'

'You mean like bubbles of fire?' St Clair replied mockingly. 'But I shall tell you a story. In a town in Russia . . .'

The look of annoyance on the Tsar's face disappeared and he leaned forward.

'In this town,' St Clair continued. 'A barber had control of the mayor and forced him to issue an edict that no man could shave himself or cut his own hair.'

Ivan pulled a face.

'But in Russia, your majesty, as your wisdom dictates, no one is above the law.'

The Tsar made a sound, his face puzzled.

'Well, your majesty, if no one is above the law, who shaved the barber?'

Ivan leaned back, clapping his hands. Vaslov looked puzzled. Frogmore stared uneasily.

'But the Tsar wants magic!' the Soul Slayer complained.

'No, he doesn't,' St Clair replied, quickly translating for the Tsar. 'He asked me to puzzle him, to intrigue. I have obeyed the Tsar's instructions.'

Ivan rapped out an order.

'His Majesty is intrigued,' Vaslov said. 'What is the answer to your riddle, priest?'

'Oh, it's quite simple,' St Clair replied. 'The barber was the mayor's wife!'

Rebecca drew in her breath. A simple, stupid riddle! St Clair was playing with all their lives. She had learned a little about these people, their love of courage, of impudent insolence, but surely St Clair had gone too far? Vaslov looked at the Tsar, who stared back.

Even Frogmore looked surprised. Vaslov laughed, a loud neighing sound, the Tsar, too, grinned, the harshness disappearing from his eyes and mouth. He giggled like a little girl, covering his mouth with his fingers. St Clair's story must have been repeated amongst the guards, for they also joined in the laughter. Vaslov was now jumping from foot to foot. The Tsar was sitting up, bellowing at the ceiling. Cowper looked so relieved his whole body sagged. Vaslov's malice was apparent: flushed with anger, Frogmore realised St Clair had publicly made a fool of him while, at the same time, answering the Tsar's challenge.

Abruptly, Ivan clapped his hands and the laughter died. Vaslov, shoulders still shaking, crept behind the throne. Ivan turned and whispered something to him. Vaslov hopped down the steps into the centre of the hall. One of the guards brought a copper dish of glowing charcoal. Vaslov sprinkled something on this. At the back of the hall a drum began to beat. The dwarf started a macabre dance round and round the glowing charcoal, faster and faster, his little body twisting and twirling. One of the Oppritchina stepped forward, a garotte string in his hand. As Vaslov whirled, the Oppritchina slipped the garotte around the dwarf's neck, turning the small stick at the end. The dwarf's grotesque face turned red, eyes popping, tongue protruding. Just when Rebecca thought Vaslov must surely choke to death, the garotte string was loosened and Vaslov fell on all fours, breathing noisily like a dog which has run too far. He breathed in the sacred fumes, his eyes rolling back in his head. When he spoke, his voice sounded like the bark of a mastiff, low and throaty, the words coming out in short gasps.

Rebecca went to whisper to St Clair but the Jesuit shook his head. The Tsar was listening intently to his dwarf. Now and again he would glance at Frogmore then at St Clair. Vaslov stopped speaking and collapsed on the floor. The Oppritchina brought forward a woollen blanket. Vaslov's body was put in this and he was solemnly carried from the hall. Tsar Ivan spoke quickly and quietly. Frogmore was not pleased. He objected, pointing at St Clair. The Tsar made a cutting movement with his hand and sat back on his throne.

'At least we are not going to die,' St Clair translated. 'Vaslov is a sorcerer-priest. He went into a so-called sacred trance and gave the Tsar his advice. Ivan will take us to his hunting lodge at Aleksandrova Sloboda. Frogmore will be handed over to the Ottoman envoys. Frogmore has demanded that we, too, as his enemies, be handed over, either to the executioners, or as a gift to the Ottoman Emperor.'

'And?' Cowper asked.

'The Tsar has refused, at least for the time being.'

17

'That was very, very dangerous.' Cowper mounted his horse, still glaring at St Clair.

They had been taken out of the audience chamber by Dmitri, given their cloaks and hats and told to be ready to leave immediately: their baggage would be brought along later.

'Dangerous? What do you think I am, William? A magus or a sorcerer-priest?'

'Or an angel?' Rebecca interposed.

'Angels don't play tricks,' St Clair retorted. 'To satisfy the likes of the Russian Tsar or wizards like Vaslov and Frogmore. But I tell you this: we are now going to the Tsar's hunting lodge. I assure you, William, we will need all the magic in the world about us, for this, truly, will be a descent into hell.'

They left Moscow an hour later, riding at the tail of the great column which wound its way out of the Kremlin through the slush-covered streets of Moscow. The Tsar was carried in a litter, its gold-fringed curtains pulled back so Ivan could smile and bless his subjects. They, of course, were not allowed to look upon God's anointed. Whenever the litter passed, his subjects, be they boyars or merchants, or the poor, prostrated themselves in the mud, banging their heads three times as an act of obeisance. Moscow became like a city of the dead, total silence reigning as the procession, led by hundreds of priests carrying banners and swinging censers, accompanied the Tsar out of his capital.

Of Frogmore there was no sign. St Clair said that the Tsar, wishing to humour the magus, had bestowed the great privilege of allowing Frogmore to ride behind him.

Every crossroads and open stretch of land they passed bore the marks of Ivan's bloody tyranny. Gallows and gibbets, heads on spikes and, on one occasion just outside the city gates, rows of impaled corpses black and stinking. Rebecca pulled her hood over her face and lowered her eyes; she prayed eagerly, invoking memories of sweeter, calmer days.

At last they were in the open countryside. The villages they passed were empty, the people fleeing from the path of their Tsar. Now and again the procession stopped so the Tsar might carry out punishment. One small hamlet, where the people were supposed to be organised by the local boyar to greet their Tsar, was found empty. The boyar came out, prostrating himself in the snow, begging his Tsar's forgiveness. Ivan had the man immediately decapitated and sent Dmitri with the Oppritchina to burn every house to the ground, kill all the animals, destroy the barns and hunt the peasants down. By the time the tail end of the procession reached the hamlet, the boyar's decapitated corpse, its head tucked between the legs, was spreadeagled on the snow while the village was being consumed by a sheet of fire which roared up to the lowering grey clouds.

They reached Aleksandrova Sloboda just as a weak sun set, casting dark shadows over the snows. A great black mass of sprawling buildings stood surrounded by a high curtain wall. St Clair explained this was the capital of the Oppritchina kingdom.

'A place of terror,' he added. He leaned across and squeezed Rebecca's hand. 'God knows how long Frogmore will stay here. The Ottoman envoys will undoubtedly arrive within days. You, Rebecca, are in great danger. Abbot Sylvester told me that Frogmore has consulted the Book of Secrets in St Michael's monastery. Frogmore will certainly try to kill you. Be on your guard!'

'Where she goes I will follow,' Cowper promised.

'And I pray heaven help us,' St Clair declared, adding something in that strange tongue.

Rebecca was going to question him further but St Clair began to describe the forbidding fortifications of Sloboda. The hunting lodge had been turned into a fortress. Its various approaches were guarded by stone blockhouses and high watchtowers. They crossed the drawbridge which spanned the icy moat and into the compound which included a huge stone citadel, a harem where Ivan kept his women, warehouses, barracks, chancery offices, cells and dungeons. It also possessed a new church dedicated to the Virgin, a cross osten-tatiously etched on every brick. The compound itself was a morass of mud and snow so wooden causeways had been built connecting every door. Black-garbed Oppritchina stood guard everywhere.

By the time Rebecca and her companions entered, the Tsar had gone to his palace. The compound was packed with grooms and ostlers milling round the horses and carts. Suddenly, Rebecca heard a scream. The light was fading, torches fixed in the walls allowed the shadows to dance and shift. At first Rebecca thought a huge dog had slipped out from behind one of the stables, pursuing an ostler who had blood streaming down from a wound in the neck. The Oppritchina were laughing. The animal stopped and came back and stood up on its hind legs. It was not a dog but a young black bear; its great paws flailed the air, mouth open in a formidable roar. The groom was helped away by companions, one of whom came forward with a stick threatening the bear. The Oppritchina didn't intervene.

'Lord in heaven!' Cowper exclaimed. 'What is this place?'

'The groom is fortunate,' St Clair replied. 'That bear is only a cub. Ivan allows the beasts to wander the palace at their will. If you stay wary, you are safe, the groom must have disturbed that one.'

The bear fell back on all fours and shuffled away.

One of the Oppritchina came up and snapped his fingers. St Clair, Rebecca and Cowper were taken into the stone citadel, up the narrow, spiral staircase into a cavernous chamber on the third storey. Arrow slits served as windows, candles and torches fixed in niches flared fitfully. A fire burned in the hearth, the smoke seeping through a vent in the outside wall. A cold, grim place. Its three beds were nothing more than pallets on which furs had been thrown. Water to wash was provided together with some rags tossed on the table. The chamber also contained two stools, a bench and some pegs on the door to hang clothes. The man gestured, muttered something in Russian and left.

Rebecca immediately got onto the bed and pulled one of the furs around her. It smelt stale, so moth-eaten the fur had begun to peel off. A groom came up with their baggage. Cowper demanded their weapons but the man just shrugged and St Clair told Cowper to keep a civil tongue in his head.

'The Tsar does not allow weapons,' he said. 'And be very careful what you say. This room has been specially chosen.' He grinned at Cowper. 'Colchester Castle is not the only place where there are gaps in the brickwork for people to listen and watch.'

'Are we prisoners?' Cowper asked.

'It depends entirely on Ivan and probably Vaslov.' St Clair knelt down beside his bed and crossed himself. 'This is not the time for comforts. Any day here could be our last.'

Rebecca found that St Clair's words about the hunting lodge were more than true. Over the next few days the Jesuit kept his distance: he was cold to the point of harshness, never allowing them to talk or discuss why they were here. Instead he would openly praise the Tsar's hospitality.

They were confined to the chamber, food and drink being brought up from the kitchens, and they were only allowed out to use the latrines further up the citadel. Now and again Rebecca would catch St Clair staring at her. He would wink and, on one occasion, passed across a quotation from one of Ovid's poems. When she looked puzzled, he just smiled and raised his eyes heavenwards.

Cowper also tried to comfort her. On one occasion he sat by her on the bed holding her hand.

'Believe me, mistress,' he whispered, turning his face away, as if looking at a point behind her. 'If it comes to the hurling time, you must escape.'

'And do what?' she hissed. 'Walk through the snows back to Dunmow?'

'There will be a time and place,' he replied. 'And we will seize it.'

After a few days of such captivity, they were released

from their chamber to witness the blasphemous and hideous routine of Tsar Ivan's court. Of Frogmore, they saw no sign. St Clair became deeply agitated, thinking the warlock had been whisked away but Vaslov, who increasingly saw Frogmore as a rival, informed the Jesuit that the magus was living in luxurious isolation at the far end of the compound.

Over the next few days Rebecca noticed how St Clair and Vaslov became firm friends, often whispering together in corners. Cowper became concerned and wondered what trickery the Jesuit was involved in. However, such anxieties disappeared as they were caught up in the hideous life of Sloboda. Tsar Ivan now considered himself both a priest and a monk. He indulged in the most profane parody of the monastic life. He was the abbot, the Oppritchina his brethren; courtesans from the city were encouraged to take up the post of prior, sacristan, librarian and other offices.

These 'brethren', as Tsar Ivan called his coterie, went about in dark cassocks and cowls of rough red serge. They divided their time between exhausting church services and atrocities. St Clair, Cowper and Rebecca had no choice but to be unwilling observers of these. They were awoken at three in the morning for Matins and gathered in the small basilica for a service which lasted until well after dawn. Ivan sang, read and prayed, sometimes with such ardour that his forehead turned a bloody mess from beating it on the ground before some icon or picture of a famous saint. After Matins the Chapter was held, in reality a parody of a trial for all those who had offended Ivan. St Clair, Rebecca and Cowper, dressed in the monastic habits Ivan had sent them, were forced to watch a whole line of miserable unfortunates be shouted at, punched and kicked before Ivan would spring to his feet shouting:

'*Hoida! Hoida!*' 'Get on with it! Get on with it!'

The prisoners would be dragged out to the execution ground just beyond the main gate. The punishments were diverse and many. Hanging was a simple matter but others included impalement, being boiled alive or pegged out on the snow and left to die.

On another occasion, five priests, accused of immorality, had their boots filled with burning charcoal and forced back on their feet. Ivan and his Chapter then laughed till the tears streamed down their faces at the wretched prisoners dancing in agony as the fiery coals seared them. A boyar, accused of improper remarks, was treated more harshly. He was sewn up in a bearskin and beaten with sticks from the Chapter House to the gates. He was then told to run for his life while being pursued by ravenous mastiffs.

After the Chapter, Ivan and his 'brethren' would gather for the first banquet of the day. During this the Tsar insisted on reading from the lives of the saints or some other edifying work. In the afternoon he would hunt with his brethren (Rebecca and her companions were never invited), before going down to the dungeons to witness the torture of prisoners. Ivan would come up from these, blood splashed on his hands and face, his eyes bright with excitement.

In the evening the 'brethren' would be summoned to prayer and more banquets. Afterwards the Tsar would be lulled to sleep by tales from three blind story-tellers.

Rebecca found such horrors difficult to understand or accept: blood splashing for the sake of blood, screams and groans, terrible tortures and grisly executions. Sometimes, as in a dream, she'd become confused and wondered if her wits were wandering. At night she would get up and sleep-walk and climb into bed with St Clair, on other occasions with Cowper. They would just lie there stroking her hair.

Of Frogmore there was no sign. By now St Clair was very busy with Vaslov, refusing to tell Rebecca or Cowper what he was plotting. One afternoon, about ten days after their arrival at Sloboda, St Clair went missing. Rebecca, fearful that something might have happened to him, ignored Cowper's warnings and went wandering round the hunting lodge. She was used to the huge, shaggy, black bears which prowled about. They were well fed on scraps from the table and the kitchen and, unless vexed or irritated, scarcely bothered Ivan and his court.

Rebecca kept away from the execution ground and the huge, cavernous doorways leading down to the dungeons. She became lost in a corridor but eventually arrived at a small postern door. It swung open of its own accord, allowing in a silver of daylight. Rebecca gratefully hurried out onto the wooden causeway which spanned the compound nine feet below. The bridge stretched to another postern door. Rebecca paused, wondering if it was open, when the door behind her slammed shut. She pushed against the wood but the door refused to move. A black she-bear, dozing with a cub in the far corner, lurched to its feet, paws scything the air, its yellowish snout sniffing. It roared its anger at this intrusion and possible danger to itself and the cub. Rebecca ignored it. She walked along the makeshift wooden bridge. The bear shuffled towards her on all fours. The bridge was too high but its claws scraped the wood and Rebecca trembled at the mad, red glint in its eyes.

The walk seemed to take for ever. The bear, half-tamed and sensing that this potential threat would walk away, followed, growling softly. Rebecca reached the door but, when she turned the iron ring, found it was locked. On the ground the bear was once again pushing itself up, angry at Rebecca's shouts and repeated knocks. Rebecca backed away. Perhaps she should return? Only then did she notice that the ropes connecting the causeway to hooks embedded in the tower wall were thin and fraying. Even as she moved, one set of strands snapped and the bridge lurched dangerously. Rebecca screamed, the bear charged, the rope snapped and the bridge crashed down into the mud.

All Rebecca was aware of was that large, black, dangerous shadow shambling towards her. It was bigger than she had thought, great shoulders of muscle rippling under the black fur, its stubby head, glaring eyes, lips curling over white jagged teeth and those great unsheathed claws. The bear was angry but not sure so it stopped. Rebecca kept still. The bear sat and watched, then charged in a flurry of mud. Rebecca screamed and backed away. Again the bear stopped. One vicious swipe of its paw and this danger to itself and its cub would end. Rebecca, the cold mud seeping in through her dress, backed away slowly. Abruptly a door, the one Rebecca had tried to flee through, was thrown open. The mother bear turned in a wild flare of rage, rearing up to face this new danger. Cowper was there, two of the Oppritchina behind him. Cowper pointed down, jabbing his finger. The Oppritchina shook their heads. Cowper grasped one of their spears and jumped down into the pit. The bear, more wary of this new danger, and fearful for its cub, shuffled backwards roaring its rage. Cowper followed, jabbing the air with the spear. When it was safe, he beckoned Rebecca forward. The bear went to charge between them but again the spear jabbed. Rebecca reached Cowper.

'Don't faint! For the love of God, don't faint!' he shouted behind her. 'And that goes for me too,' he added wryly.

The bear was now confused, more frightened than angry. Its cub was safe and these two strangers were now backing away towards the door. The bear gave one last roar of defiance and shambled away while the Oppritchina hoisted Rebecca and Cowper up onto the ledge. The Russians were much impressed by Cowper and Rebecca's courage. One even gave Cowper a dagger, telling him to hide it beneath his cloak.

Rebecca felt giddy. She didn't know if her encounter with the bear was a dream or reality. The cuts on her hands and face, and her stained gown awoke her to the living nightmare she was ending. Once back in her chamber, she just crouched on her bed, face in hands, trying to control the tremors of her shaking body. Cowper came over, a cup of Rhenish wine in his hands. He explained he had won it from the Oppritchina in a dice game, which was what he had been doing when he had heard her cries. He gently coaxed Rebecca as he wiped some of the mud from her hands and face, urging her to drink.

'I'm sorry.' Rebecca pulled back her hair and retied it with ribbon. 'But this is the very pit of hell!' She raised the cup and toasted Cowper. 'You were very brave,' she said. 'The bear could have killed us both.'

The Judas Man's face had lost its harsh severity. If the truth be known, Cowper, too, looked frightened: a tightness of lips, the creases round the eyes, a slight trembling in his hands. Rebecca felt confused about this strange man not just because he had rescued her but because, since their arrival at Sloboda, he had proved to be a pillar of strength, curbing his fiery temper, more concerned with her than himself. If St Clair was Rebecca's handsome prince, then Cowper was her squire. The Jesuit was vivacious, sharp, ever-helpful. Sometimes Rebecca couldn't accept this optimism. Cowper, on the other hand, reminded her of some of the good men she had known in Dunmow: dour but brave and dependable. She also regretted her own show of weakness.

'I fear too much,' she confessed. 'I tremble and I'm sick.'

'Hush now.' Cowper leaned across and tweaked her hair. Rebecca glimpsed the tears in his eyes. 'For God's sake, you are a tavern wench from Essex! You have seen horrors which would turn other men's hair as white as my own. This is not just cruelty, Rebecca, demons prowl here. Now, have you noticed,' he continued, 'how many of them are frightened of St Clair? They hide it well but they are wary. Treat him with respect.' He sipped from his cup. 'Do you know much about our Jesuit?'

'Do you?' she countered.

'What I know,' Cowper narrowed his eyes, 'is that he's Irish-born, trained abroad and, according to all the evidence, he should have died in Italy yet, here he is, flesh and blood. Do you still consider him an angel?'

Rebecca shook her head. 'I used to. Some strange things have happened but I watched him with Frogmore. There were no tricks, just subtle wit. I think he's a

Jesuit, committed to Frogmore's destruction by fair means or foul.'

'And afterward?' Cowper asked. As soon as the words were uttered, he regretted them.

Rebecca edged further back on the bed. She rarely thought of that! She accepted that St Clair would always be with her and she with him. She wanted justice for her father but, if the truth be known, she really wanted St Clair.

'I apologise.' Cowper took Rebecca's hand between his, rubbing them, trying to clear away the chill. 'The blood should beat strongly in someone like you.' He kept his head down. 'Rebecca, whatever happens after Frogmore is dead, I shall stay with you.' He glanced up and smiled. 'Whatever you do! Wherever you go! Turn around and you'll see Cowper's shadow! I love you, Rebecca!'

'William, you told me that in Varody!'

'Do you love me?'

'What is love?' Rebecca stammered. 'Men in my father's tavern, bellies full of beer, said they loved me. My father said he loved my mother but he tumbled slatterns and maids.'

'Aye and my mother should have loved me and I should have loved her,' Cowper intervened mockingly. 'I don't know what love is. At Cambridge I read a story of how God takes a piece from each soul and scatters them around. Some people fill what is missing with something else. Others are more fortunate. They meet a person who holds that missing piece from their soul, who can fill the void and make them whole.'

'And I am that?' Rebecca asked.

'For me you are. From the first moment I saw you. I knew it when you walked out across that stable yard, ready to put everything at risk, your life, your honour for the sake of a stranger.' Cowper shook his head. 'You are unique, Rebecca! I've seen men and women betray others for a few shillings. You are stronger than you think. You are whole, you are healed. Never once did you break at Colchester, when taken by Ragusa the mercenary or on that voyage out. So, you can shiver and tremble at Ivan's court.' He lowered his voice. 'But even an angel would be frightened. I am not going to ask you for this or that.' He brought her hands to his lips and kissed the tips of the fingers. 'I love you, Rebecca, for many reasons: your courage, your beauty, but above all the way you've healed me. I will not let such a talisman go lightly. I'll no more forget you than I can my heart, or my tongue, the flesh of my body, not even death!' Cowper's eyes held hers. 'Even there, I'll charge the gates of hell for you!'

'You are so sure that you are damned?' Rebecca replied quickly, hoping to tease herself away from the searing passion in his eyes and face.

Cowper was about to reply when St Clair came into the room. He had a leather bag in his hand and immediately hid this among his own possessions. He was jumping about like a boy who has found something precious, his eyes bright with excitement. Rebecca's heart danced. St Clair was like that. A window bringing in warmth and light to this cold, dank chamber. She turned her face away so Cowper wouldn't glimpse her pleasure. St Clair now studied Rebecca.

'What has happened?' he asked.

She told him quickly. St Clair grasped Cowper's hand. 'You are a gentleman, a scholar and a warrior. That was no accident,' he explained. 'Locked doors, bridges snapping, a she-bear ready to tear you to pieces. That's Frogmore's work, him and his subtle magic!'

St Clair sat beside her. Cowper winced and looked away.

'There,' St Clair murmured and kissed the top of her brow. As if he was aware of Cowper's fervent jealousy, he let her go. 'Frogmore could do that,' he repeated. 'His parting gift before he leaves, destroy you so he can relax, sink into the luxuries and softness of the Turkish court.' St Clair sighed. 'I knew he would attack, I could not guard you every second but I prayed, fervently, for you.'

'And now?' Rebecca asked.

'I am now firm friends with Master Vaslov and Captain Dmitri. They both hate Frogmore and see him as a potential rival. Tomorrow morning Frogmore will be handed over, of his own free will, to Turkish envoys. A short ceremony outside the compound gates; we will not be allowed to see.'

'And us?' Cowper asked.

'The Tsar is in a quandary. He does not like to bend to the Turks but he doesn't want to offend them. Tomorrow morning Ivan intends to be absent when the Turkish envoys arrive. Vaslov and Dmitri have inveigled him to invite us to a hunt. Vaslov and Dmitri will furnish us with food and good horses.'

'We can escape?'

'Yes. North to Finland or Livonia or west to any of the German or Polish states.' St Clair got to his feet. 'The hunting lodge is to be prepared for the envoys. Thanks be to God there'll be no blood shed tonight!'

'And what have you hidden?' Cowper asked.

'A lure.' St Clair grinned. 'To bring Frogmore back into the trap!'

18

Under St Clair's direction they spent the greater part of the evening preparing to leave. Vaslov came whispering at the door to St Clair. The dwarf also brought saddle bags, food, smoked meat and millet.

'But won't they be suspicious?' Cowper asked. 'I mean, if we ride out tomorrow with saddle bags packed behind us?'

'We are allowed weapons for the hunt,' St Clair replied. 'But Vaslov will take these bags. He will take us to where they are and, God willing, we ride to freedom!'

The hunt began late the following morning. St Clair informed them that Frogmore had left with his Turkish hosts, given safe passage out of the Tsar's territories. Ivan now wanted to celebrate by arranging a wild ride through the forest hunting bears and stags.

'Anything which moves,' St Clair added wearily. 'Ivan has a hunger for blood which can never be sated.'

Dmitri came to collect them, returning their war belts. He poked Rebecca playfully in the chest and fingered her hair.

'You should get it cut.' He tapped her on the cheek. 'You become more womanlike every day.'

Cowper seemed pleased to have his war belt,

strapping it on, drawing out sword and dagger, testing their points and cutting edges. St Clair was more concerned about what clothing they took. He urged his two companions to put on warm undergarments and the heaviest jerkins. Vaslov also supplied them with items but Rebecca wasn't convinced. The dwarf, the little she saw of him as he came flitting back to their chamber, seemed happy enough. Frogmore had gone but there was a cunning look in his eyes while Dmitri smirked to himself as if savouring some private joke. Cowper, too, was suspicious.

'Why?' he demanded of St Clair. 'Vaslov and Dmitri are as steeped in blood as their master. They are members of the Oppritchina. True, they wanted to see the back of Frogmore but what else? Jesuit, I'm talking to you!'

St Clair straightened up, leaving the saddle bag he was filling unbuckled. Rebecca noticed that whatever he had brought so secretly into the room the previous day was now concealed beneath his jerkin.

'Why is Vaslov helping you?' Cowper asked quietly. 'You can see he regards you as someone special.' He grabbed St Clair by the arm. 'Answer me!'

'I don't know.' St Clair pulled his arm free. 'I am a priest and perhaps Vaslov is frightened of that. Perhaps he views me, the woman with the hare-lip and the demon with the white hair as possible threats. Perhaps, one day, I might replace this priest sorcerer with another. Anyway, Vaslov wishes to see us go.'

'I am not satisfied with that,' Cowper retorted.

'Master Cowper, I couldn't really care whether you are satisfied or not. Dmitri waits on the stairs, the die is cast. Within an hour we will be riding for our lives.'

A short while later, swathed in their cloaks, astride powerful Polish horses Vaslov had brought from the stables, Rebecca and her companions joined Tsar Ivan and the Oppritchina in a wild, mad gallop out of the hunting lodge. They charged down the broad thoroughfare before turning east onto the trackways into the forest.

Rebecca recalled the ghost stories told to her in Dunmow. About the devil's hunt, how Satan and his legion of damned angels hunted on fiery horses across the wild wastes of Essex. In her eyes Tsar Ivan and his followers were a fitting parallel. They were dressed garishly in a mixture of monastic garb, dyed boots, and coloured scarves round their necks. Their saddles and harness were caparisoned with decorations and little jingling bells. Coloured banners flew above them; their huntsmen carried birds of prey pinioned to leather straps on their wrists or wooden perches: eagles, hawks, peregrines and falcons. Huge mastiffs bellowed and ran alongside them, leaping up and snapping while one of the Oppritchina even brought a black bear, muzzled and harnessed, like one of the dogs.

Sometimes they galloped, other times they slowed down so Ivan could loose a bird or, taking bow and arrow, shoot at any animal, hare, fox and, on one occasion, even one of the hunting dogs which had displeased him.

'It's a nightmare,' Rebecca said quietly, staring across the frozen snow to the dark edge of the forest. 'St Clair, this is a nightmare which has gone on too long. I want to wake up!'

St Clair patted her on the shoulder then pulled down the woollen muffler which protected his nose and mouth.

'Hang back now,' he said.

Ivan's huntsmen sped off into the forest, charging along shouting and screaming. Rebecca, St Clair and Cowper were left alone: no guards, no huntsmen. In the distance they could hear the silence of the forest being shattered by the blast of horns and horses neighing, the receding hoof beats of the Tsar's mad gallop and the hollow baying of the dogs. Rebecca looked over her shoulder to where a sturdy sumpter pony stood, the provisions piled high on its back, protected by a furred coverlet.

'Now we ride,' St Clair ordered.

He grabbed the sumpter pony and they charged back across the snow-covered meadow towards the highway they had left.

The day was clear, spring was making its presence felt, the snows were starting to melt, the sky cloud-free. By noon even the sun felt warm. They paused to eat and drink, allowing the horses some rest and fodder before continuing their flight. Now and again St Clair would rein in and look back over his shoulder. On one occasion Cowper even rode back to the brow of a hill.

'What are you frightened of?' Rebecca asked.

'The unworthy thought crossed my mind,' Cowper replied drily, 'that perhaps Ivan wanted a different quarry to hunt. When we were at the lodge, Dmitri told me, and he smiled all the time, how the Tsar liked to hunt his prisoners, watch them being torn to pieces by his mastiffs. If there is no sign of pursuit, we are safe.'

They continued their journey. Rebecca realised, as they covered the snowy wastes of Russia, that this was what she had seen in a vision years before.

She, Cowper and St Clair travelled south before turning west. Vaslov had provided St Clair with maps and passes. The further they travelled, the more Rebecca's hopes rose that they truly would be allowed to leave this dreadful land.

'And when we do?' Cowper demanded. 'What then? Sail to Constantinople and demand that the Emperor hand Frogmore over to us?'

St Clair refused to be drawn, lost in his own thoughts. He did confess that he mistrusted Vaslov and Dmitri and was surprised at how easily and smoothly their escape had gone.

They travelled a further six days before Vaslov's trickery became apparent. They were approaching a frontier post when the ambush was sprung. A group of masked men burst out of the forest. St Clair and Cowper tried to draw their swords but Rebecca watched helplessly as their attackers closed in. Cowper was knocked from the saddle; St Clair, standing high in the stirrups, lashed out with his sword. All around, his assailants, armed with clubs, tried to unhorse him. When this failed, one of them drew a dagger and thrust it straight into the horse's withers. The poor animal, neighing with pain, reared up, throwing St Clair off. Rebecca screamed, dismounted and tried to force her way through. A figure loomed before her. Rebecca went to claw his face. She saw the club swinging down and tried to step back but a violent blow to the temple sent her spinning, as if falling deep into a pit. Beside her other bodies fell like birds tumbling from the sky.

She struggled to remain conscious. She was moving, but not on horseback, carried in a rough, ready-made litter. On one occasion she pulled back the deerskin cover and saw St Clair and Cowper riding, hands tied before them. It was not so cold, the sun was strong, voices chattered in a tongue she could not understand. Rebecca fell asleep, fainting into a sea of fire where her body burned and she had a terrible thirst. In her fevered state she thought she was back at the hunting lodge, sitting on a bed with a huge she-bear towering above her or dancing before the Tsar in a hall splashed with blood. Dmitri grinned at her from behind the throne. Vaslov was whirling like a bird round and round, blinding her with his speed and the varied colours of his garish garb. Then she was back on ship, travelling silently through a sea of ice. No one was aboard. The ship was empty but the sails billowed full and the wheel turned of its own accord. She cried for St Clair but the door to the cabin just opened and shut. She heard footsteps and knew that Frogmore was present. She tried to run but, when she climbed the shrouds, the ice made her slip. Water poured into her mouth and she could feel Frogmore's hands biting into her shoulder. She struggled and screamed, only becoming calm when she heard St Clair murmuring softly to her.

Other visions followed. Somehow or other the ship took her to Dunmow and she was walking along the corpse path into the church. Constable Malbrook was shouting from his grave and old Mother Wyatt stood at the door of the charnel house. When she entered, instead of a statue, Tsar Ivan was standing on the plinth, his face like a gargoyle, blood spurting out of his eyes.

'Oh, no, no!' Rebecca groaned.

She turned round. Parson Baynes, holding her father's hand, was shuffling forward. Two boys burst in. They were shouting obscenities. Rebecca could see the charnel house had disappeared; instead the graveyard was covered in snow. She shook her head, fighting hard, then opened her eyes. St Clair was looking down at her while smoothing her face.

'I'm trapped in the church,' she whispered. 'Is Frogmore near?'

'Hush now!'

Rebecca felt as if she were soaked in water.

'I am so thirsty,' she whispered. 'So very, very thirsty.'

'Of course you are.' St Clair stood back.

A small, wizened man was now bending over her. He wore a white coif about his head, his face was burned black by the sun. He chattered to her and the most cool and fragrant drink was poured between her lips.

She was falling again but this time she knew she was asleep. She kept waking fitfully, sometimes when it was dark, at other times when the room was full of sunlight. Sometimes she was alone, at others Cowper, St Clair and that strange wizened, old man were next to her. She heard herself being talked about, then she opened her eyes and knew where she was. The bed, the bolsters behind her, the white gauze veil which hung around the bed. She panicked, thinking it was a corpse shroud, and cried out. The veil was pulled aside to reveal St Clair and Cowper standing anxiously over her.

'Where am I?' she asked. She pulled herself up. The linen sheets felt crisp and clean. She dabbed at her neck, wiping away the sweat. 'How long have I been asleep?'

'Have a guess,' Cowper joked.

Rebecca noticed his white hair had been cropped: he looked leaner, fitter. St Clair, too, looked well rested, the dark rings beneath his eyes gone. Rebecca rubbed her eyes.

'A few days,' she hazarded. 'I remember the attack in the forest.' She looked up at the window, at the bright sunlight.

'Where am I?'

'At Karenska, a Russian fortress near the Turkish border. We are, once again, in the hands of Dmitri. Dmitri sent for a wise man and he, I and Cowper,' St Clair put a cup to her lips, 'nursed you through your fever. You've been ill for weeks.'

'And Frogmore?'

'Oh, sooner or later, he'll be here!'

Frogmore, dressed like on Ottoman prince, in a red, high-collared coat interwoven with mother-of-pearl and gold thread, scarlet buskins on his feet, his hair and beard oiled and perfumed, followed the Janissary guard out of the small villa which had been put at his disposal by the Imperial Chancery in Constantinople.

Frogmore had been treated with every respect since his arrival in the city. Garments and gems, slaves, food and wine, the personal favour of Suleiman. Nevertheless, Frogmore hid his raging fury. The Jesuit had tricked him yet again – the leather bag containing his most precious possessions had been removed and replaced with one similar. As he walked, Frogmore breathed in so long and hard that the Janissary officer turned, frowning. Frogmore sighed and smiled. He could not betray his anger to his new masters, who would not understand why a great warlock or magus was so easily upset by the loss of a few paltry possessions. Moreover, it might make them wonder how a man with such great powers could be so easily tricked. Nevertheless, Frogmore was determined to exact his own vengeance: to recover what was his, to remove from his heels those yapping curs St Clair and Cowper and, above all, to slay that hare-lipped tavern wench. The Book of Secrets had confirmed how dangerous she was, a deadly weapon in St Clair's hands. They, however, would have to wait.

'Relax and soothe your temperament,' Frogmore said to himself. He used those skills, learned in the east, to clear his mind to balance the humours in his own body. He must be prepared for whatever trick or stratagem the wily emperor had prepared.

Frogmore was pleased to be out of the icy wastes of Moscow, away from Ivan and his jealous dwarf Vaslov. It was good to feel the sun, to walk in a place of real power. Frogmore gazed appreciatively around at the gardens on either side of him, a mixture of beauty, grandeur and magnificence where every imaginable kind of plant and fruit tree grew and locks of brilliantly plumaged birds flew and sang. The air was fragrant with different perfumes as well as the sweet odours from the pots of burning incense and herbs placed along the path. Coloured candles glowed brilliantly in alabaster jars placed on raised stone plinths or into specially dug holes along the path.

They passed through gleaming white marble porticoes full of gold and silver ornaments, their walls decorated in bizarre motifs formed from clusters of precious stones and pearls. Soldiers stood everywhere. Janissaries in their distinctive yellow garb and ornate white turbans, decorated with heron plumes which dipped and danced in the morning breeze. Black-skinned mamelukes swathed in white robes, drawn scimitars against their shoulders. Sipahi horsemen, in gold chain mail, guarded every gateway and the entrances to courtyards. Nevertheless, despite the many people, an unnatural, almost religious, stillness permeated the palace. Perhaps it was the soldiers, or the occasional terrible reminder of the Emperor's power. Now and again they would pass pillars, tall marble columns festooned with golden hooks. On each of these, tied by the hair, hung the severed heads of those who had displeased their Emperor.

They went through the Gates of Salutation, a massive fortification, its every approach dominated by gunholes and arrow slits. Inside the palace proper, beyond the formidable great iron gates, cobbled paths radiated out to different entrances to the Imperial quarters. They passed the Gate of Bliss, the entrance to the harem; and the Hall of Divan where Suleiman met his great council. Frogmore knew they were being watched through eye-slits and peep-holes.

The Janissary officer led Frogmore along a cavernous, shadowy passageway. Halfway down, two shadows slipped out of the porticoes on either side. The Janissary bowed and walked quickly away. Frogmore looked at the two Gardeners in their tall, conical hats, garotte strings wrapped in their belts. They joined their hands, bowed then stepped back. One of them clasped a hook in the stone floor, pulled up the paved slab and waved Frogmore down the torchlit steps, along secret passageways into the bowels of the palace.

It was deathly cold, the walls wet with slime. Frogmore hid his unease. He'd expected to be met with great pomp and grandeur; now he suspected the Emperor wished to test his powers. One of the Gardeners, his soft-soled feet slapping on the mildewed, rocky floor, went ahead carrying a torch. The other, a yard behind Frogmore, slipped along as silently as a shadow. Now and again they would pass the occasional sentry garbed in black from head to toe, their faces hidden behind vizards which stretched up to their eyes. They stood like statues, a rounded shield in one hand, a sword in the other. Frogmore walked slowly, eyes ahead, watching the tunnel wind and turn, the torchlight throwing grotesque shapes. Occasionally, from his left and his right, he heard groans and moans, cries of pity, and realised that, along the galleries leading off, were the pits and oubliettes housing the imperial prisoners.

The passageway ended at a small gateway built into the wall of rock. The Gardeners swung this open and gestured for Frogmore to enter. The chamber inside was large and cavernous, well lit by torches and oil lamps. On a throne at the far end sat the Emperor Suleiman. He was dressed imperially: golden-edged robes, a jewel-studded pure white turban with purple curved slippers on his feet. On a stool to Suleiman's right sat his Grand Vizier, his monkey face tense and watchful. Frogmore remembered protocol and, falling to his knees on a cushion in the centre of the room, pressed his head three times against the paved stone floor.

'Welcome to our court.' Suleiman spoke in the lingua franca.

'Your imperial highness does me great honour.'

353

'And I will do more, Master Frogmore, if the reports I have heard about you are true. You may sit.'

Frogmore clambered to his feet. Dark-garbed servants came out of the shadows bringing more cushions. The magus sat down, crossing his legs, and stared up at the impassive, hawk-like face of the Emperor. Suleiman rubbed the open ulcer on his thigh and idly wondered if the magus could cure this.

'Can you read men's thoughts, Master Frogmore?'

'No, your excellency,' Frogmore replied. 'I can only guess.'

'A good answer, Master Frogmore. Men who boast about what they can do are usually liars.'

'My master has brought you here,' the Grand Vizier said as he got to his feet, 'because he wishes to see for himself the powers you claim.'

'I am not some mountebank,' Frogmore replied, 'a mummer come to entertain in some bazaar!'

'Then what are you, Master Frogmore?'

'I am a man who has studied the secrets of the Cabala: the mysteries of the ancient ones. I have called on the powers of the Lords of the Air and they have answered.'

Frogmore's eyes glazed over. The Grand Vizier shivered with fear.

'Show us these powers, Master Frogmore.'

The Sultan raised his fist to his mouth and bit his finger.

'Show us now!'

Frogmore's eyes moved: the torch, blazing in its brackets on the wall above the Grand Vizier, fell in a splutter of sparks, igniting a cushion. A slave ran across, beating it then kicking it away. The Grand

Vizier paled and put his hand up the voluminous sleeves of his robes. Suleiman scarcely moved.

'I have heard of such tricks,' he declared drily, 'being performed in the bazaar to entertain children.'

Frogmore smiled and bowed. He had many things he could do. Powers which would delight or horrify but he sensed Suleiman was not interested. In the bazaars of the Ottoman Empire swarmed an army of wizards and warlocks who could transform a stick into a snake or conjure up a myriad of illusions.

'You are the Soul Slayer,' the Emperor declared. 'Prove to me, Master Frogmore, that you are!'

Frogmore covered his eyes and recited a short, swift prayer to the Lords of the Air.

'You can have whatever you need,' Suleiman added quietly.

The Grand Vizier backed away, going to stand beside the Emperor's throne. The Grand Vizier felt nervous. Here he was, in the secret passageways and caverns beneath the Imperial Palace with an army of soldiers at his beck and call, yet this dark-faced infidel filled his soul with terrors and the Grand Vizier did not know why. Had the room grown colder? Were those shapes dancing in the flickering torchlight mere shadows or something more substantial? Was it safe to have brought a man like Frogmore here? Would he not seal them here like a genie in a jar?

'I need a man,' Frogmore replied, lifting his head. 'A victim for sacrifice.' He surveyed the room, noticing the guards who stood hidden in the shadows. 'And when I say this chamber must be cleared, it must be cleared, apart from you, your excellency.' Frogmore smiled, his eyes catching those of the Grand Vizier. 'And your closest adviser.'

Suleiman rapped out an order. Frogmore heard the door behind him open and shut. He sat, hands loosely in his lap, looking down at the floor. If the Prince wanted a demonstration of power, then he would give it. Once they had seen it, they would accede to his every demand. He had enough power, though he would need to replenish it, to dazzle their souls.

The door behind him opened in a clink of weapons and a long, drawn-out moan. The mamelukes threw the bound body of the prisoner to the floor. He was dressed in rags, his hair and beard one long, grey, shabby mess tangled with dirt. He lay there struggling against the ropes which pinioned him, his eyes crazed with fear, his toothless mouth opening and closing: begging in Arabic, he tried to crawl towards the Emperor's throne. The Grand Vizier clapped his hands. The soldiers withdrew but Frogmore pointed and took the dagger one of them carried. When the room was empty, Frogmore slashed the prisoner's ropes. The man struggled to his feet. Frogmore, talking soothingly, pressed his middle finger against the man's forehead and the prisoner lay back. Frogmore leaned over, staring into the man's eyes. He felt a flicker of compassion at the fear raging there.

'Sleep!' he soothed. 'Sleep! All will be well!'

He swiftly drew the dagger across the man's throat, recoiling as the blood spurted out. He ignored the Grand Vizier's gasp. Frogmore rose and took two torches from the wall and laid them on the ground, one at the head and one at the foot of the corpse. He grasped the dagger and, in one incisive movement, sliced deep into his victim's chest and pulled out the still faintly pulsing heart. He laid the two torches together and, impervious to the heat, placed the heart at the centre of the fire. The iron stench of blood and burning flesh filled the chamber. Suleiman sat unmoved; his Grand Vizier took a perfumed pomade from the pouch at his girdle and held it to his nose.

Frogmore dried his hands on the prisoner's shabby clothes and knelt before the fire, head up, hands extended, his eyeballs rolled so far back the whites of his eyes glowed eerily in the firelight. He swayed backwards and forwards as he fell deeper into the trance, lips mouthing the ancient ritual. The fire turned a blueish-orange; the Grand Vizier started to shiver as if the chamber had been seared by some cold, biting wind. He glanced quickly at his master. Suleiman had paled, a bead of sweat ran down his hooked nose. The magus was now shrouded in smoke and fire but when it shifted, the Grand Vizier exclaimed in terror. The man who stood up and walked towards them was no longer Frogmore but the prisoner.

'In the name of Allah the Compassionate!' The Grand Vizier covered his face, peering through his fingers.

The prisoner's body still lay there, the great bloody gash in his chest, so who was this?

'Shape-shifter!' Suleiman whispered hoarsely. 'You can adopt the guise of other men!'

He touched the face of the figure before him. The skin was ice-cold like that of a fish but, the mouth, the hair, the emaciated body . . .

'Impossible!' Suleiman whispered.

He looked at the eyes. These did not reflect the soul of a beaten man but glowed with a power Suleiman had never seen before. The figure turned and walked away, passing the corpse into the shadows. Suleiman watched and waited. The figure came back; it was

Frogmore, face slightly pale, eyes blinking. Suleiman sat, hands in his lap, and watched the flame die. He had seen the greatest magicians from the East – the fakirs, the wise men, the warlocks, the wizards – but never anything like this. If he sent his troops against Malta, or against any fortress, what would he not give to have a man who could move in and out in such disguise.

'Anything,' Suleiman grated. 'Anything you wish and it will be yours!'

Frogmore knelt down. 'Your imperial excellency, I have enemies who are also yours . . .'

19

The fortress of Karenska stood on a slight promontory about ten leagues from the Russian Turkish border. A new fortress, built by Ivan's engineers, it possessed high, soaring walls of grey granite; a gatehouse, protected by square towers; the same on each corner and in the middle of the four curtain walls. The parapets were broad, the walls were ringed with gun loops and embrasures. The Tsar had bought expensively, importing cannon from the Germans of Hamburg and elsewhere. Inside this protective ring was a hall, outhouses, stables, granaries and cellars where provisions had been stocked. If the fortress was breached, a huge stone keep of grey cut-stone soared a hundred and sixty feet into the sky, affording further protection.

The land around Karenska was open steppe or pasture land frequented by nomads, tribes and gipsies who wandered across with their flocks. It was now late spring, the beginning of May. The green grass, once fresh and wet from the melting snows, was beginning to fade but the wild flowers grew profusely in a glorious array of colour. Above it, the hawks and kestrels soared seeking prey; the song birds nesting in the long grass would sing their hearts out until autumn came. A wild, lonely place. To the south the land slipped away towards the river which marked the border and to the north and east it was bordered with the dark fringe of forests.

Rebecca was taken by the savagery of the place and recalled her visions: this would be a place of bloodshed but she felt too weak, too bemused, to care. She had recovered but it had taken days to regain her strength. Teased and coaxed by St Clair and Cowper to take this dish or that, she still felt nauseous and light-headed.

'We thought you were going to die,' St Clair told her, sitting on a stool at the side of her bed. 'We really did think we had lost you. You were soaked in sweat, your skin boiling to the touch.'

'But what happened?'

St Clair pulled a face. 'Ivan and Vaslov deceived us. The envoys who took Frogmore also wanted us. Ivan, however, hates to bend the knee to the Turk or be told what to do.'

'So he pretended that we had escaped?'

St Clair nodded. 'Vaslov let us run like children in a game. We were approaching Kiev when the horsemen surrounded us. You received a blow to your head.' He scrutinised the bruise on her temple. 'And they brought us here to Karenska.'

'For what?' Rebecca asked.

'Ivan will wait. If the Turks press their suit we are near enough to be handed over. If they forget us,' he shrugged, 'we might be released but, we could spend the rest of our days here.'

Rebecca closed her eyes and sighed.

'Frogmore wants us dead,' St Clair continued. 'He wants St Clair and Cowper to stop yapping at his heels. But, above all, my Chrysogona, he wants to destroy you. Once that's done, he'll rest safely with his Turkish masters.'

'Am I so important?' Rebecca felt a qualm of fear.

'Yes, you are. Frogmore is a magus but he knows the law of Nature: no one is allowed to run free for ever. He knows he is approaching a time of confrontation. He sees you as a great danger.'

'It must end,' Cowper declared, beating his fist against his knee. 'And it can only end in Frogmore's death.' Cowper sat on the other side of the bed. 'While you were in your fever, St Clair told me how Frogmore can be destroyed. I . . .'

'He finds it difficult to accept,' St Clair intervened. 'But it is the truth, William.'

'Did you plan all this?' Cowper accused.

'All that has happened, William, could not have happened, without the consent of the human will: yours as well as Rebecca's.'

Cowper shook his head. St Clair lifted Rebecca's hands and spoke softly in that strange guttural tongue. Cowper glanced at Rebecca. She saw the glow of jealousy and quickly nipped St Clair's fingers.

'What are you jabbering about?' she teased. 'Why do you say things in that strange tongue, as if talking to someone we cannot see?'

'It's Aramaic,' he replied. 'And I am praying.'

'For what?' Cowper snapped. 'A legion of angels to help us?'

St Clair laughed and shook his head.

'You're happy, aren't you?' Cowper got to his feet, thumbs in his belt. He paused as he heard the sound of footsteps outside but they faded away. 'Answer me!' Cowper insisted. 'Your mind teems like a box of worms. We've been here two weeks and you've never mentioned escape. You think Frogmore will come here, don't you?'

'I know he will.'

'But not just for Rebecca,' Cowper persisted. He gazed round the room as if looking for something. 'Where's that leather bag?'

'What else does Frogmore want from us?' Rebecca asked.

St Clair rose and went across to where their saddle bags hung on the wall. He undid the buckles and took out a leather pouch whose contents he shook out onto the bed.

'What!' Rebecca exclaimed. 'They are nothing but bric-à-brac: items you can find on any tinker's stall.'

She stretched out and sifted among them: a ring, a brooch shaped in the form of a twisting snake; a piece of faded samite. She pulled across the rest: a woman's leather glove, holed, but the mother-of-pearl clasp on the back still glittered; a jerkin for a boy; a toy, a battered wooden knight on a horse holding a lance; a small scroll of parchment.

'What are these?' Cowper insisted. 'No wonder Dmitri wasn't interested.'

'Frogmore's a demon,' St Clair replied. 'But, once, he was a man who loved deeply.'

'And these belong to him?'

St Clair covered Rebecca's hand with his.

'Yes, Frogmore wishes to have us back in his power but he also wants these.'

'How did you get them?'

'That evil dwarf Vaslov hated Frogmore, so I bribed him. Not that it took too much to steal and replace these with a duplicate. I told Vaslov that, if these were handed to me, Frogmore's powers would weaken.'

'A Jesuit priest telling a lie?' Cowper mocked.

'No, to a certain extent it is true. Frogmore's power is exaggerated. He is powerful in a lonely village like Dunmow, killing the likes of old Mother Wyatt. He is a subtle assassin. However, in the full glare of day, Frogmore is really more like a snake. Dangerous because of his stealth, speed and surprise. He is half-man, half-demon, floating between heaven and earth with no place to call his own. Sometimes, deep in his heart, he must wish to be ordinary, he might even regret what he has done. He must look back on days when he knew happiness and was satisfied and these trifles are memories of such times. He will come back for them, he'll crawl out of his dark hole.'

'Do they mean so much to him?' Rebecca asked.

St Clair picked up the piece of greasy parchment, blackening with age, and unrolled it.

'If life is love,' he read. 'And love is life, then your life is my love.' St Clair tossed the parchment on the bed. 'Frogmore wrote that to his beloved many years ago.'

'While Rebecca was in her fever,' Cowper said, 'you told me much about Frogmore and his powers. How he can be destroyed. But, Michael,' he added softly, 'you told me little about yourself. Did you know, Rebecca, he comes from Ireland and once served Frogmore as a disciple?'

'I've explained that,' St Clair replied coolly.

Cowper leaned across the bed. 'But you've never really explained,' he hissed, 'how in a fierce duel with Frogmore, you slipped, fell over a cliff yet lived to tell the tale.'

'I didn't fall,' St Clair replied slowly. 'Not as far as Frogmore would have wished.'

'And when this is over,' Cowper insisted. 'Where to then, St Clair?'

'Why, Master Cowper, to home!'

'To home,' Cowper jibed. 'To be hanged at Tyburn?'

'Stop it!' Rebecca intervened, wary of a fight breaking out between them. She touched the piece of parchment. 'Does this mean so much to Frogmore?'

'If you died, Rebecca, and all I had,' St Clair replied as he picked up the small pouch, 'was a lock of your hair, that fragment would be more precious to me than all the silver in the world.'

Rebecca heard Cowper's sharp intake of breath. She looked away at the hurt in his eyes.

'I would like to sleep again.' She squeezed St Clair's fingers, then, stretching out, took Cowper's hand. 'If either of you die then my heart would break. You are my flesh and blood.' She collected the mementoes and slipped them back into the leather bag. 'We must stay together,' she continued. 'If the confrontation's coming then we must be prepared.'

Rebecca was pleased to be interrupted by a knock on the door. Dmitri swaggered in. He was dressed in a black-and-red surcoat which fell to his knees; the baggy pantaloons beneath were tucked into high-heeled, leather riding boots. His hair was brushed back from his forehead, his thumbs stuck arrogantly into his sword belt. He stopped before the bed and bowed mockingly, scrutinising Rebecca through half-closed eyes. She became aware that all she was dressed in was a thin linen shift and pulled the blankets higher.

'Why, Mistress Lennox.' He spoke slowly, making a flowery gesture with his hand. 'You can see my English has improved.' He flicked at a piece of parchment stuck into his belt. 'Messages from Moscow, Master Cowper, your absence from England has been noted. The Tsar now has received a demand that, if you are in his realm, you must be returned!'

'That won't happen,' St Clair replied tersely.

Dmitri testily gestured round the chamber. 'You are guests here. Look, you have a fire, food, warm coverlets on the walls.' He tapped his boot. 'The same on the floor. Well-stocked kitchens serve good food, better than you'll eat in your misty island.'

'We are still prisoners,' Cowper replied.

'Guests.' Dmitri had trouble pronouncing the word. 'You are not prisoners, Master Cowper, you are guests.'

'Then why the trickery?' Rebecca asked.

Dmitri laughed, sucking his teeth with his tongue. He reminded Rebecca of a hunting dog which had just eaten.

'I've told your companions, mistress, you are safe here. The Turks wanted you, but we have told them that you have escaped.'

'So why not let us go?' Rebecca demanded hotly.

'Well.' Dmitri rubbed his hands together. 'I have difficulty with your language but, if you escape too easily the Turks will become suspicious. Yet, time rolls by . . .'

'Time is of the essence.' St Clair got to his feet. 'Dmitri, I have told you before, Frogmore will discover where we are.'

'Impossible!'

'He will discover where we are,' St Clair insisted. 'We are not far from the Turkish border. You should send a message to the nearest governor, yes even the Tsar himself, and ask for reinforcements.'

Dmitri, hands on his hips, shook his head and laughed softly.

'It would take them months. Tomorrow we hunt, yes?'

And, without waiting for an answer, Dmitri strode off, slamming the door behind him.

'Tomorrow, Rebecca, you must walk and exercise.' St Clair kissed her on the brow. 'But sleep now.'

Cowper patted her on the shoulder and both men left the chamber.

Rebecca snuggled back down between the coverlets. She felt warm, sleepy and soon she was dozing. She wasn't really sure whether she was awake or asleep when she heard her name called, insistently, like her father would when she was in her chamber at the Silver Wyvern and he wanted her downstairs in the taproom. She sat up. The room was darkening, the thick, tallow candle on the table at the far end of the bed had burned low. The chamber had grown cold. The windows were still shuttered.

'Michael! William!'

Nothing but silence. She heard a sound in the far corner but dismissed this as a hunting rat. She got out of the bed, her legs weak. She went across to the fire. It had burned low so she poked it with the iron rod and threw on more kindling, which the fire caught in a rush of sparks. Shapes and shadows danced round the room. She heard her name called again, looked at the fire and stifled her scream. Frogmore's face had appeared, quite distinct in a tongue of flame, his eyes mocking, as if he knew her secret thoughts and fears. Rebecca lashed out with the iron rod until a rush of sparks made her jump back. St Clair was right: Frogmore knew where they were!

Rebecca spent the next few days recuperating, wandering round the castle, often going up the parapet walk and looking over the sea of grass. She recalled the vivid dreams she had had at Dunmow. Karenska brought back memories of the flat countryside of Essex, the lonely call of the birds, the wind bending the grass, sending the seeds fluttering, yet Rebecca found Karenska a formidable place. The garrison was manned by members of the Oppritchina: cavalry, foot soldiers and bombardiers, all hardened cut-throats. These watched her slyly and jabbered in their own tongue whenever she passed. Nevertheless, she was treated with respect, as were Cowper and St Clair, who joined the soldiers in the drill ground. Cowper, in particular, demonstrated his prowess as a duellist. The Oppritchina would sit on their haunches in a circle, their flat, high-boned faces impassive, and watch the albino who, time and again, in his foot-stamping dance, would disarm this or that swordsman.

Other women were there, camp followers, prostitutes, but the routine of the castle echoed that of Ivan's hunting palace, a mixture of monastic routine and orgiastic revelry. The great hall was a large, high-beamed place, the hunting trophies along the wall interspersed with swords and shields, icons and banners. The kitchens behind this were always busy. Rebecca would wake in the early hours and hear the sounds of revelry, the shouting and carousing, the cries and shrieks of the women. Sometimes, she heard the neighing of horses and the quick thud of hooves, as one of the Oppritchina, his belly full of raw spirits, galloped wildly round the castle. On a few occasions at night, the drawbridge would be lowered and the Oppritchina would thunder across to raid one of the outlying villages.

Both St Clair and Cowper became worried about how long Dmitri would keep them at Karenska. Rebecca prayed daily that the order to take them back to Tsar Ivan's hideous court would not arrive.

One evening, just after they had retired, St Clair insisted on celebrating a Mass in their chamber. Cowper stood, arms folded, and coldly watched. Rebecca knelt before the improvised altar as St Clair, with bread and wine filched from the kitchen, performed the sacred ritual. He insisted that she take the consecrated bread and wine, even offering them to Cowper, but the albino shook his head.

'It would be blasphemous,' he declared. 'I believe in no God. If there is one, why should I insult Him by believing just because I am in danger?'

St Clair smiled and withdrew the chalice.

'Whatever you say,' he answered quietly. 'You are a good man, William Cowper.'

Once he had finished the Mass, St Clair took a minute leather wineskin, no more than six inches long and half that in circumference. It was neatly stitched along three edges, and the narrow funnel top could be closed with a clip and a piece of string. He poured some of the consecrated wine into this and tied it securely. He then put the white cord round Rebecca's neck, hiding it beneath her jerkin.

'What are you doing?' Cowper asked.

'Rebecca will know.' St Clair's eyes held hers. 'When the appointed time comes, she will know what to do. If Frogmore drinks this wine, his power will be diminished.'

'And then what?' Cowper jibed.

St Clair ignored him. 'She will do what her heart tells her.'

'Magic against magic!' Cowper jeered. 'Do you really believe that, St Clair? If there is a God why doesn't He send some of His angels to fight on our behalf?'

'If He did,' St Clair retorted, 'you still wouldn't believe.'

'Perhaps I would!'

St Clair finished the wine in the goblet, washed it thoroughly and put it back on the table. He paused to listen to the singing coming from the hall.

'If an angel came,' he asked, 'what do you think, William, he or she would be like? A knight in shining armour? A person with magical powers? Read the scriptures: Le Bon Seigneur, Jesus Himself, was flesh and blood, bound by the laws of time and space. In His trial, passion and death He could have called upon a legion of angels, but He never lifted a finger. No.' St Clair started cleaning up the altar. 'Man's evil must be countered by man's good.'

'Do you love the woman?' Cowper blurted out.

Rebecca gasped at his bluntness.

'Do you love Rebecca Lennox?' Cowper insisted.

'William!' Rebecca gasped.

'Because I do,' Cowper continued hotly. 'And when this is over I shall ask her to marry me. Where she goes, Jesuit, or where you take her, I will follow!'

St Clair went across and took Cowper's hand.

'William, William, when this is all over, God knows what will happen!'

He turned and beckoned Rebecca across. Still grasping Cowper's hand, he took hers in the other.

'Here we are,' he said, 'in a place of darkness. All around us, through the eyes of our souls, we see the glowing camp fires of our enemies. We are three, yet we are one! We are bound by love and loyalty. We reflect the power of the Great Three, Father, Son and Spirit.' He lifted his voice and Rebecca's skin prickled at its power.

'May the power of the Three be with us!' he intoned. 'May we all see the length of days but, if the darkness falls and we must yield to the night, then let the Three who live in eternal light send Their envoys to greet you.' He squeezed their hands and let them go, then gestured towards the window. 'Dmitri is a fool, he will not heed my warnings. It is about to begin!'

The next morning St Clair, Cowper and Rebecca climbed the narrow, winding stairs to the top of the keep. St Clair brought some wine, bread and dried meat. The sun was strong and the parapet gave them a view over the countryside beyond. Rebecca could make out small villages, the occasional farm; the fields stretched like a sea of green to the far horizon.

'Why are we here?' Cowper asked. He sat down against the parapet and stared up. 'I know, it's a beautiful day.'

'Wait and see,' St Clair replied.

They sat and talked for a while. Cowper, his sullenness apparently dissipated by St Clair's words and appeal to unity, chattered about his life at court: the foibles of Queen Elizabeth; the sly treachery of Walsingham; the scandal surrounding the sudden death of Dudley's wife at Cumnor Place.

After a short time Rebecca got to her feet and peered over the wall. She stiffened. Was that some farmer's fire? But then Rebecca saw another long wisp of black smoke rising up against the blueness. The two men scrambled to their feet. Other puffs of black smoke were rising, fading up against the blue sky.

'The Turks have crossed the border,' St Clair said. 'They are burning the outlying farms.'

'How did you know?' Cowper asked.

'I guessed! Rebecca told me about her vision some two weeks ago. Frogmore would act quickly once he knew where she was.' St Clair pulled a face. 'It was a matter of calculation: Frogmore and a Turkish general would be despatched in haste to a local governor who would already be forewarned. Today, tomorrow, what does it matter, they are here!'

He opened the trap door and they scrambled down the narrow steps. By the time they reached the inner bailey, sentries on the curtain wall had also glimpsed the smoke. Horns were sounding, Dmitri was bringing the horses out of the stables. The gates were thrown open and the scouts thundered out.

'You knew they were coming, didn't you?' Dmitri screamed at St Clair. He rubbed his wine-sodden eyes and muttered something in Russian. 'You knew they were coming.'

'I told you they would,' St Clair replied slowly. 'The Turks are across the border, they'll be burning and pillaging but they have really come to lay siege to Karenska.'

'So, you are a prophet as well?' Dmitri jibed. He hawked, spat and beat his riding crop against his thigh. 'I won't cry like a maid,' he added. 'What do you propose?'

'They'll be here by nightfall. Send men on your

fastest horses. Order them to ride north and seek whatever help and assistance they can.'

Dmitri agreed and shouted out a spate of orders. The whole garrison was now aroused. Arms and equipment were taken up to the parapet, cannon prepared. St Clair and Cowper joined Dmitri on the gatehouse and, despite their protests, Rebecca insisted on joining them.

As the day wore on, the scouts returned, agitated and nervous. They came up and knelt before their commander, talking heatedly about what they had seen.

'This is no raiding party,' Dmitri said. 'But an army. Two thousand Janissaries, about three thousand support troops, dervishes who eat the hashish and believe they must die in battle. About one and a half thousand Sipahis or cavalry. They are well provisioned and they have siege artillery. St Clair, this will be a bloody siege.'

Dmitri callously ordered that many of the women and camp followers be driven out of the fortress. They were given horses and provisions and told to flee in the opposite direction to the advancing Turks. The drawbridge was raised; the walls bristled with armaments. Powder and ball were brought up from the storerooms and stacked beside each of the bombardes; tuns of oil, wild-fire and wooden hoops soaked in tar were made ready. The privies were emptied into the moat, along with the corpses of rats and cats, to pollute the water. Sheets of leather soaked in water were placed over the cannon. Small braziers full of glowing charcoal were also prepared. By late afternoon Dmitri ordered the castle to be sealed. Postern gates were taken down and burned, the entrances bricked up, then they waited.

At first it looked like a long line of ants which appeared through the shimmering heat on the far horizon. This long, black line stretched as far as they could see. As the day wore on, the line grew closer. Rebecca could make out the glint of weapons, the different colours, the great flapping banners. A huge army was swarming towards them, foot and cavalry, while behind them trundled cannon and carts.

By the time darkness fell, the night was filled with flaring light from the fires and torches of their enemy. St Clair insisted that Rebecca return to their chamber. She did so and slept fitfully, her mind plagued by nightmares where Frogmore hovered like a great, evil bat. Even in her dreams, Rebecca knew: the time of reckoning was at hand.

20

Rebecca woke just after dawn. St Clair and Cowper were gone. She dressed hurriedly, throwing her cloak around her. The castle was silent. She fitfully wondered if all this was a nightmare. Had everyone fled and left her to Frogmore's mercy? In the castle yard, however, she found the Oppritchina and other soldiers, quietly massed, all staring up at the parapet. Rebecca forced her way through, scrambling up the steps which led to the tower overlooking the gatehouse. She reached the top to find Dmitri, St Clair and other officers assembled there, staring in silent wonder at the great army which now encircled them.

During the night the Turks had set up camp. St Clair pointed out the Janissaries in their yellow coats, the white-garbed mamelukes, the Sipahis, horsemen and the hordes of black-garbed dervishes. The enemy camp was orderly, well out of range of Karenska's guns. The air was smoky and, even from where she stood, Rebecca smelt the odours of their cooking pots. Beyond the troops, at different places, stood the silken pavilions of their officers, as well as the carts and horse lines. Cannon were already being brought forward as well as a formidable siege tower. Dmitri pointed out the crosses which stood on the edge of the Turkish camp. Rebecca shaded her eyes against the sunlight and wondered what these were. Her throat went dry: they were crosses and, to each of them, was nailed a writhing naked man or woman.

'Peasants!' Dmitri exclaimed. 'They must have caught the poor bastards and nailed them up!' He looked over his shoulder at St Clair. 'It's a warning to us what will happen if Karenska is taken!'

He crossed the gatehouse and shouted down. Rebecca heard the jingle of harness, the neigh of horses.

'What are you going to do?' St Clair asked.

Dmitri tightened his sword belt and put on a steel-pointed helmet, with chain mail guards to protect his cheeks and neck.

'Why, priest, I am going to welcome our visitors. They won't expect us.'

Rebecca was about to turn away when one of the officers shouted a warning. Three horsemen had left the Turkish camp and were galloping towards the castle. The one in the centre carried a white banner lashed to his lance. Dmitri leaned over the crenellations. The three Turks reined in at the edge of the moat. The one in the centre raised himself in the stirrups and shouted out in the lingua franca. Dmitri heard him out and grinned at St Clair.

'They say they'll retreat as quickly as they came, on one condition. We hand the foreigners over: the devil with white hair, the priest and the hare-lipped wench.'

'And?' St Clair asked.

Dmitri hawked and spat. 'The Prince would have my head. Russians do not bend the neck to those who cross their frontier, sack villages and lay siege to one of the Tsar's fortresses. Secondly, Englishman.' Dmitri smiled wickedly. 'I rather like you.'

He looked over his shoulder. 'Give the Turks my answer!'

Three archers notched arrows to bows, leaned over the walls and fired a volley of arrows. Two of the Turks slumped in their saddles, one of the bodies rolling into the moat. The third turned, dropping the white flag: he had only gone a short distance when two arrows took him in the back. He threw his hands up and slipped from the saddle, one foot caught in the stirrup. His body bounced along in the dust as the horse careered back into the Turkish camp.

'They were under a white flag,' Cowper pointed out.

'White flag! White flag!' Dmitri snarled. 'Tell that to those nailed to the crosses!'

He hurried down. In the courtyard the horses were being brought out and saddled. The Oppritchina were ready, swords in hand, black shields clipped over their arms. Dmitri shouted an order. The portcullis was winched up, the drawbridge lowered and Dmitri and his cavalry thundered across, aiming like an arrow direct for the Turkish camp. The Turks were completely surprised. They were here to lay siege, not to be attacked. Dmitri, riding like a demon, pounded along, his men fanning out behind him. Great white clouds of dust rose; a cannon roared, shots were heard, the air rang with the clash of steel and the cries of men locked in terrible battle.

St Clair shook his head. 'St Paul,' he said musingly, 'said that love was the greatest virtue but, in the eyes of Dmitri, courage is paramount. He may have a heart as dark as night but his bravery cannot be doubted.'

They couldn't see what happened. The gunsmoke and dust, like a thick, white curtain, hid the conflict which raged in the Turkish camp. Now and again a horse would break loose and race back. Foot soldiers, massed in the gateway, guarded the approach to the drawbridge, ready to raise it at a moment's notice.

'What does Dmitri hope to achieve?' Rebecca asked.

'Terror, fear,' Cowper replied. 'The Turks and Master Frogmore are now being informed that it is a battle to the death. No pardon will be given and none asked.'

He had barely finished speaking when they heard the sounds of the Russian hunting horns. The sound of fighting died. The dust cloud thinned as Dmitri's horsemen, their mounts blown, lathered and covered in foam, reappeared. They galloped back towards the drawbridge, thundering across it to the courtyard below. Many were unscathed, but some had lost their horses and were mounted behind companions. Others came running on foot. Many had scratches, minor cuts, others terrible wounds. Rebecca offered to go down to help but St Clair told her to stay on the battlements. Of Dmitri there was still no sign. Just as they gave up hope, a group of horsemen appeared out of the dust. Behind them came a group of mailed Sipahi horsemen, cloaks billowing out, lances set, but they had no hope of catching the Russians. Dmitri came last, as if he wished to ensure that none of his men would be wounded or fall behind.

At the entrance to the drawbridge, while his companions charged across, Dmitri abruptly turned, forcing his horse back on its hind legs, hooves scything the air. Rebecca watched, heart in mouth, as the Russian commander, sword out, charged back towards the enemy. She thrilled at his courage as well as his cunning. The leader of the Sipahis had galloped far ahead of his companions so that he was vulnerable, alone. Dmitri met him in a clash of sword against spear then he was round, bringing his sword down in a cutting slash, deep into the Turk's shoulder. Horse and rider crashed to the ground and Dmitri continued his wild gallop back across the drawbridge. His men cheered, those along the parapets jeering and insulting the Sipahis grouped around their fallen commander.

The sun was now high in the sky and a strong breeze had sprung up. The dust cloud separating the castle from the Turkish camp cleared, revealing the swathe of damage Dmitri's horsemen had caused. Tents, wagons and carts were burning; corpses strewed the ground; cannon lay overturned and a black pall of smoke rose from the stores and horse lines.

Rebecca, her hand clasped firmly by St Clair, went down into the courtyard where Dmitri and his men were jubilant, passing wineskins round.

The Turks, however, soon made their anger felt. By late afternoon they brought their cannon up under heavy cover to pound the walls on either side of the gatehouse. Throughout the night the cannonade continued, the darkness lit by brilliant flashes and tongues of fire. At dawn the first wave of attacks began: urged on by their imams, dervishes, shouting their war cries, raced to the edge of the moat. Wooden bridges were flung across, ladders set up against the walls.

The dervishes climbed like a horde of ants. The Russian cannon had answered but, as the Turks drew close, they prepared small barrels of wild-fire, burning hoops, cauldrons of boiling water. These were set up on the parapets and, as the enemy climbed, Dmitri ordered this barrage of scalding fire down onto the attackers' heads. Rebecca, on the gatehouse tending the wounded, could only watch, her ears dinned by the screams, the clash of weapons, the roar of guns and, as the curling smoke cooled, the stench of burning flesh. She worked as in a dream, bathing the wounds of those who were still capable of returning to the fighting. Most wounds were caused by musket balls and arrow heads: under Cowper's and St Clair's direction, she learned how to dig deep, ignoring the screams and contortions of the wounded men, pushing the wine-soaked rag back into their mouths.

The attack lasted well into the early afternoon. By the time the Turks withdrew, a carpet of dead and wounded lay on either side of the gatehouse. Dmitri and his men had now lost their first jubilation. Clothes were rent and burned, faces black with smoke and soaked in sweat. They stumbled from their defences to eat, drink and doze fitfully before returning to the walls.

During the late afternoon, the Turks gave a respite as they collected their dead and withdrew. However, in the evening, the cannonade began again. The walls were thick, the stone hard and firm but Dmitri became concerned and, under the lash, a second wall was built up in case the Turks forced a breach. Rebecca, St Clair and Cowper were relieved of their positions and told to sleep. They hardly spoke but dragged themselves back to their chamber.

Rebecca woke to the sound of gun fire and pulled herself up. Her companions slept on. The chamber was very cold and the smell! What was it? It reminded her of the charnel house in Dunmow! A rottenness! A feeling of desolation!

'Cowper,' she whispered, but he was lying on his back snoring like a child.

Rebecca, feeling rather foolish, pushed back the covers and stood up. Her body ached. She recalled the events of the day; her hands were still bloodstained. Memories flooded back, of the soldiers writhing beneath her, screaming, their eyes full of pain.

The fire had burned very low so she placed a couple of logs on and, leaning down, blew at the embers. Flames shot up, catching the dry wood in a spray of sparks. Rebecca stretched her hands out. She tried not to recall the vision she had seen there. The wood crackled merrily, a reassuring sound, and she was grateful for the growing warmth. Nevertheless, her unease remained. Once the fire was burning vigorously, she got up and walked across to an arrow-slit window. She could see little except for patches of light and the flame bursts of the Russians' cannon. She heard a sound.

'Who's there?'

Only one candle burned on the table beside Cowper's bed. She glimpsed Cowper's sword lying in its scabbard on the floor, its hilt winking invitingly. Again she heard the sound. Someone was shuffling towards her, breathing deeply. She gazed into the far corner: it was coming from there! Rebecca walked slowly across.

'Who's there!' she repeated.

She cursed her own stupidity. She should never have gone to sleep without a dagger or a pistol by her side. What if the Turks had broken into the castle? She glimpsed the shape, shadowy, indeterminate.

'Cowper!' she screamed. 'St Clair!'

The figure came out of the gloom. Rebecca didn't wait but ran across, screaming at Cowper to rise. He rolled over, muttering and sucking his lips. Rebecca pulled the sword out of its scabbard and turned. The man standing in front of her should be dead. He looked like a living corpse, those dark eyes, that livid pallor, the gaping mouth: Ragusa! The mercenary who had attacked Cowper on the road outside Colchester. He was standing there as if dragged from his grave in a shabby, dust-covered jerkin, soiled shirt, scuffed boots and hose. Rebecca didn't know if she was asleep or awake. She lunged with the sword but it sliced thin air. When someone grasped her arms, Rebecca lashed out again.

'Hush girl!' Cowper held her. 'Rebecca, for the love of God, drop the sword!'

She did so.

'What's the matter?'

St Clair, rubbing his face, stumbled towards them.

'He was here,' Rebecca whispered. She broke free of Cowper's hold and walked across the chamber. 'He was here, I tell you!'

In the dancing light of the candle she could see nothing. She pinched her cheek and turned round.

'I was not sleeping!' she protested. 'I saw that man Ragusa, the one who took us prisoner on the road outside Colchester. He was here, standing in this chamber!' She sat down on a stool. 'I wasn't dreaming. I got up. Look, I built up the fire. He came from the shadows, shuffling towards me, a living corpse!'

St Clair brought a cup of wine across and made her drink. He looked back at Cowper.

'He's coming,' he said. His warm hand cupped Rebecca's cheek. 'One of Frogmore's tricks. He's used his power to see where we are and what we are doing! Be on our guard, it will not be long before he comes himself!' He stared across at Cowper. 'Remember, for the love of God, Frogmore can be injured, wounded – at least for a while, yet he will recover quickly.' His gaze now held Rebecca's. 'There's only one way he can die. You, my Chrysogona, will be Frogmore's nemesis!'

In the Turkish camp, Frogmore, dressed in a golden sable robe, sat comfortably on the cushions cradling a fluted glass of sherbet. He stared across at Bayezl the Ottoman commander, the fury seething within him.

'What are you saying? That the will of the Emperor will be frustrated?'

Bayezl stroked his moustache and kept his voice steady. He just wished the Emperor had chosen someone else.

At first it had seemed so easy. He had been provided with crack corps of the army for the operation: a raid across the Russian border, a speedy siege, the capture of the three hostages and a victorious march back to Constantinople. Now everything teetered on the brink of a nightmare. The magus, through his secret powers, had divined where the three hostages were held. Bayezl had been confident that the Russians, at the very most, would only put up a token resistance. They had been proved horribly wrong. The killing of the envoys, the attack on the camp and the stout defence by the Karenska garrison had clearly demonstrated that this would be a fight to the death.

'I have told you sir.' Bayezl measured his words carefully. 'The garrison is well provisioned. The walls are thick, built of pure stone while the ground beneath is rock-hard and cannot be mined. The Russians have refused even to consider our demands. I have sent an envoy back for more troops but . . .'

'But what?' Frogmore asked testily.

'The news of our invasion, that we have crossed his frontier, must now be speedily sent to the Tsar. Reinforcements could well be on their way.'

Frogmore sipped from the sherbet.

'Nevertheless,' Bayezl added slyly, 'you, sir, are a great magus, a man of power.'

'Aye, remember who I am.' Frogmore put the glass down. 'And, Bayezl, remember that I have the ear of the Emperor. My powers are my own. I cannot make walls vanish or turn the Russian soldiers into a horde of croaking frogs. The destruction of Karenska is your responsibility.'

Bayezl paled and bowed his head.

'How long do you think it will take you?' Frogmore continued.

Bayezl shrugged. 'Ten days, perhaps even longer.'

Frogmore chewed his lip. He knew where his enemies lay. He would grasp the opportunity and demonstrate to this incompetent what he could achieve. He would enter Karenska and bring back the heads of his enemies in a sack. Frogmore swilled the sherbet and watched the bubbles burst. He recalled the cards he had studied in Hermeticus' chamber: Karenska was the fortress, now was the testing time! He smiled faintly, for he recognised St Clair's cunning: he had studied, once again, the Book of Secrets in the monastery of St Michael. The tavern wench! She must be destroyed and he would do it, finish this once and for all and, when he returned to Constantinople, this poltroon Bayezl would know the full extent of his anger and power.

'You have a prisoner?' he asked.

'We have a number taken from the walls.'

'Have them bound,' Frogmore replied, 'and brought to the darkness beyond the camp.'

He got to his feet, contemptuously knocking the glass over.

'This time tomorrow the siege will be ended.'

The Turks swarmed to the attack early the following day, clambering over a breach in the wall, locked in hand-to-hand fighting. Dmitri, St Clair and Cowper beside him, launched a counter-offensive and drove the Turks off. No sooner had they withdrawn than a great cry went up. Rebecca, on the gatehouse, peered over the parapet and saw that the great siege wooden tower was being pushed towards them. Five stories high, each platform was packed with Janissaries. Dmitri screamed out orders and huge casks were brought up from the castle cellars. The cannon were primed with chain shot, half-cannon balls fastened together by chains. The master gunners did their work and the chain shot sliced, pulped and pounded the wooden structure.

Meanwhile, a group of musketeers on the gatehouse, the best marksmen in the castle, picked off the Janissary officers on the top storey of the siege tower. Finally, one of Dmitri's men, wild-eyed and clutching a pot of wild-fire, was lowered down the wall. He landed on the kindling and rocks with which the Turks had filled the moat; clutching the small barrel of oil, he ran towards the great wooden structure. The Turks tried to shoot him down but the man had a charmed life. He reached the bottom of the siege tower, splashing the wild fire into the wooden structure at the bottom. He was running back when a Turkish ball took him in the back of his head but his work was done. Archers with fire arrows aimed for the bottom structure. Some arrows missed but the others found their mark so that the siege tower was soon consumed in a sheet of flame trapping the Janissaries inside. The screams of the men were hideous. Many found their way out blocked and had to jump, risking life and limb. Those who fell towards the castle were immediately killed by archers and marksmen.

The Turks withdrew but, early in the afternoon, they launched another cannonade, concentrating every single gun on the small breach they had made. As dusk fell, a general advance was ordered. The entire Turkish force streamed towards the castle walls: some against the breach, others, with ladders, across the moat to scale the gatehouse.

'Go back!' Dmitri crouched before Rebecca.

She was nursing a young soldier who had received terrible belly wounds. There was nothing she could do for him except stroke his face and listen to his pitiful moans for his mother.

'Let me wait!' she replied.

Dmitri muttered something to the young man. The soldier nodded and, quick as a striking snake, Dmitri cut the man's throat in one slash from ear to ear; the hot blood spilled out onto Rebecca's knees, soaking her gown.

'A quick death,' Dmitri declared. 'We could not move him and the Turks may find a footing here.' He wiped his mouth on the back of his hand. 'Cowper! St Clair!' He yelled at Rebecca's companions who were helping load a cannon in one of the embrasures. 'Go on!' he screamed. 'Back to your chamber! The Turks must not capture you! If the walls are breached, we'll make a final stand in the keep!'

Reluctantly Cowper and St Clair agreed and, holding Rebecca between them, they hurried down the steps, across the yard full of wounded and dead, into the keep. Once in their chamber, Rebecca dressed the minor wounds they had received and measured out some of the dried food and wine. Now and again Cowper would go out to watch the fighting, returning with a despondent face.

'The Turks have reached the walls,' he moaned, sitting on the edge of the bed, face in his hands. 'If this continues, Dmitri will fall back on the keep. St Clair, what shall we do?'

But the Jesuit was lying fast asleep.

'William!' Rebecca said urgently to him. Cowper looked up.

'If the keep is forced, if it appears there is no salvation, you must not let me be taken!'

Cowper's pink-rimmed eyes smiled. He stroked her hair and kissed her on the brow.

'None of us will be taken,' he reassured her. 'Believe me, Rebecca, as in life so in death. I do not wish to dance to Turkish fifes and drums.' He sighed and let her go. 'I don't think Dmitri will either. There's gunpowder stored in the base of the keep. Once the Turks are in, we'll fire the lot.' He grasped her hands. 'Rebecca!'

She looked at his tired, lined face and recalled the dangerous man who had swaggered into the Silver Wyvern. Beneath it all Cowper was the young boy in Gloucester eager to be accepted, wanting to be loved.

'Do you love me, Rebecca?'

'I could say no,' she replied, withdrawing her hands. 'But, in a way, yes, William.' She got up and sighed. 'I am so tired, so distracted, I am not too sure of anything now. I thought it would end differently.' She pointed across at the sleeping St Clair. 'At one time, William, I really thought he was an angel in disguise. I even wondered if he was St Michael come to rescue us.'

Cowper laughed bitterly. 'If there is a God, He's either laughing at us or busy with something else.' He picked up his sword and put it in the scabbard. 'Under heaven, Rebecca, there's nothing but this, a man's courage, the strength of his arm and the sharpness of his sword.'

Rebecca went back and sat on her bed. She was about to lie down when there was a knock on the door. One of Dmitri's officers entered, wearing a pointed helmet whose chain mail flaps covered his face; he was carrying a wineskin. The man flung it at Cowper but came on towards Rebecca. On the bed St Clair murmured, thrashing about in his sleep. Rebecca stiffened. She'd thought the man was also bringing something for her but his shirt was unbuttoned and, as he moved, it billowed open. She saw the inverted cross on the left side of his chest, his hand going towards the dagger hilt.

'Frogmore! Frogmore!' She screamed and rolled across the bed even as he lunged at her.

Frogmore had now pulled the helmet off, his eyes blazing with a murderous fury. He was coming round the bed, dagger held low, and Cowper was moving: at first stunned by her screams, he had drawn his sword but Rebecca knew he would be too late. Frogmore seized her by the throat, pulling her up. He was too strong. Her hands flailed out, trying to strike at the dagger, but she knew it was futile, then St Clair crashed into Frogmore. Rebecca was dropped like a sack. Both men went rolling across the floor. Frogmore clambered to his feet. St Clair rushed in again. The Soul Slayer side-stepped, a sudden quick movement; as he did so, he stuck his leg out and tripped up St Clair who tried to regain his balance but failed, his head hitting the wall with a sickening thud.

Rebecca ran across. A great cut was opening on the Jesuit's temple, the blood running down his face. She felt for the pulse in his neck, relieved to find it was still strong and vibrant. She turned, expecting Frogmore, but Cowper now blocked his way. He stood with sword and dagger ready. Frogmore was unhitching his cloak, letting it fall on the ground before him.

'So, so Master Cowper.' He drew his sword as with the other hand he unbuckled his sword belt. He let that fall, kicked it away and picked up his dagger. 'Shall it be to the death, Master Cowper? Sword against sword, dagger against dagger? I'm going to kill you.' Frogmore grinned. 'I'm going to stick you like a pig and listen to you squeal. And then I'm going to prop you against the wall while I and the tavern wench enjoy ourselves.'

Cowper remained silent, moving slightly backwards and forwards, determined to keep himself between Frogmore and Rebecca. Frogmore's sword and dagger came up as he assumed the fighting stance, then he sighed in mock exasperation and let them fall.

'My friends on the walls will take care of Dmitri and his Russians. However, before I kill you, Cowper, answer me one question?'

Cowper stared silently back.

'I mean, you are an ugly, unfortunate bastard,' Frogmore continued. 'A freak of nature with your pink rabbit eyes and snow-white hair. So, do you lust after the tavern wench? Is that why you are here? A pair of tits and a woman's arse?'

'I'm going to kill you,' Cowper grated. 'First, because of what you are, a piece of dirt spat up by hell. Secondly, because of Rebecca: while you live, she'll never be safe.' He took a step closer. 'And, finally, because of my father, Ralph Cowper. Do you recall him, hell's spawn? A leather worker in Gloucester? You took his heart and broke mine!'

'Dear me, dear me!' Frogmore breathed. 'What a state the world's fallen into, eh?' He peered round Cowper. 'Are you ready for me, Rebecca? Do you feel the wetness between your thighs?'

Then he struck, sword and dagger up, snaking out for Cowper's exposed chest and neck. Cowper was ready, stepping sideways, he blocked Frogmore's weapons. The two men circled. Rebecca knew that as long as Cowper lived she was safe. Frogmore would never turn his back on so dangerous an opponent. She dabbed at the wound on St Clair's head with the hem of her dress and realised it was only a cut.

'Michael!' she whispered. 'Michael, for the love of God!' St Clair moved his head, groaning softly. Rebecca crawled across the room, closing her mind to the clashing steel, quick indrawn breaths, the slap of leather on the flagstone floor. She seized Cowper's wine cup and came back to force it between St Clair's lips but it was to no avail. She looked around in desperation. Frogmore and Cowper were locked in their duel. Cowper's blackened face coursed with sweat, his chest was heaving but he was holding his own. Frogmore had lost some of his arrogance: more watchful, wary of this Englishman who knew every trick, sudden thrust and subtle ploy a duellist could use. Rebecca recalled St Clair's warning. Cowper might wound but could he kill Frogmore and, if she intervened, might Cowper lose his poise?

The two duellists met time and again in a whirling arc of steel, thrust and counter-thrust, parry and feint. Sometimes they fought up close, sword and dagger locked. At others they drew apart, circling, looking for a weakness, an opening. At last, Frogmore, driving Cowper off with his dagger, lifted his sword shoulder-high, its point tilted downwards towards Cowper's chest. The Soul Slayer moved sideways like a dancer on the balls of his feet. Cowper responded. Frogmore struck but, this time, instead of meeting Cowper's sword he abruptly stopped halfway. Cowper surprised, stumbled, and his sword blade went too low. Frogmore, like a hawk closing for the kill, moved in, driving his blade deep into Cowper's chest. Cowper, doubled in agony, dropped sword and dagger to the floor, hands clutching the bubbling wound in his chest. He staggered towards Rebecca, and collapsed on his knees, eyes narrowed in agony at this killing thrust. Rebecca crawled across the floor, catching him as he tipped sideways, and laid him gently down. She retrieved the wine cup and held it to Cowper's lips but the wine only mixed with the blood bubbling out of the corner of his mouth. Rebecca glanced across the room. Frogmore had withdrawn, resting on the hilt of his sword.

'I am sorry.' Cowper's eyes blinked.

He stared up at the face of this woman he so

passionately loved yet he could not concentrate. The pain had receded but he felt cold and recognised the freezing touch of approaching death. He was back in Gloucester surely? And the door was open and the sunlight coming through. He opened his eyes and tried to lift his head. Rebecca leaned down.

'Oh, Rebecca.' The words were a red bubbled whisper. 'I love you.' Cowper coughed. 'But, oh, it's grown so very, very cold . . .'

Rebecca grasped his face. Even as she did, Cowper gave one final shudder, his face went slack in her hands, eyes half-closed in a sightless gaze as the blood rushed out through his parted lips.

21

Rebecca's hand went to her throat, where she felt the small pouch St Clair had given her. She tore it from her neck, undid the cord and poured the wine into the cup beside her. Frogmore had not noticed. He was picking up his cloak, fastening it about him, all fatigue and exertion from the duel had vanished.

St Clair still leaned against the wall, eyes closed. She drained the wine, which tasted sweet and full. She could feel it in her mouth and throat. She no longer felt frightened. It wasn't the wine, consecrated or not, nor the distant sound of fighting from the walls, but Frogmore. He was standing as arrogant as a barnyard cock, leering at her as if he hadn't a care in the world; as if he didn't realise whom he'd killed or what he'd done. He resheathed his sword and held out his hands. Rebecca got up and walked towards him.

She hated this man. He had killed her father, shattered her life and brought everything to destruction. He pulled her close and his mouth came down on hers, his tongue thrusting between her lips. Rebecca responded, forcing her saliva between his lips, licking at his teeth with her own tongue. He thrust beneath her gown, grasping one of her breasts, squeezing it savagely till she winced with pain. His claw-like fingers tore at her dress, scoring her skin. Rebecca's hands clasped his neck, her mouth eagerly taking his until Frogmore stopped. He staggered back, face ashen, as if struck by a musket ball.

'Rebecca!' he gasped. 'What have you done?' His eyes went to the wine cup on the floor.

Behind her, St Clair moaned. Rebecca saw that the Jesuit was now conscious, face in hands. Frogmore drew his sword in a clumsy, staggering movement; his face was sheened with sweat, like a man poisoned. He looked old, weaker, shoulders bowed.

'You whoreson bitch!' he rasped. 'You whoreson bitch!'

Rebecca picked up Cowper's sword without anxieties or scruples. All her life had come down to this moment confronting this mocking, evil man. He lunged at her. Rebecca stepped back and in one swift thrust she drove straight for his heart. The sword sank in, splintering flesh and bone. Frogmore screamed at the pain. Rebecca turned the sword and drew it out. Frogmore was rocking backwards and forwards on his feet. He tried to lift his sword but Rebecca, moving sideways, again drove her blade into his chest, digging deep. Frogmore collapsed to his knees. Rebecca let go of the hilt as Frogmore clawed at the blade.

'Rebecca!' he gasped.

Behind her St Clair was getting up. She grasped the hilt, kicking with her boot at Frogmore's body, and drew it out. His eyes rolled heavenwards, the blood spouting out of his mouth like wine as he collapsed, face down, onto the floor. Rebecca dropped the sword and crouched beside Cowper's corpse. Lifting his hand she kissed it and caught some of the warmth still there. St Clair touched her shoulder. She didn't respond but allowed him to draw her close, kissing her softly on the side of her head.

'It's over,' he whispered.

'Cowper's dead,' she replied. 'He has gone out into the dark.'

'No.' St Clair spoke something in Aramaic. 'He's in the light, Rebecca. No objection will be raised to his passing. Whatever his life, his death was given for love, and there's no greater sacrifice than that.'

Rebecca kissed the priest on the lips.

'You knew it would happen, didn't you?'

St Clair pulled over Frogmore's corpse. The magus's face was contorted in the dreadful rictus of death – eyes open, staring in horror, his gaping mouth soaked in blood. The priest knelt beside it and again muttered something in Aramaic.

'The Lords of the Air have him. Frogmore made his compact with them and, for eternity, he will be in their camp. He can do no more evil. Many will rejoice in his passing and a host of accusers stand waiting for him.' The Jesuit raised his head. 'Listen!'

Rebecca did and realised the sound of fighting had died away. Footsteps crashed in the passageway outside and the door was flung open. Dmitri, covered in blood from head to toe, his hair wild and matted, his chain mail cut and battered, strode into the room, his captains behind him. He stared at Cowper then at Frogmore and, falling to his knees, bowed his head and raised his hands in prayer.

'The Turks have been driven from the wall. They are regrouping but we held them.' He rose and kicked the dead magus' leg. 'I wonder if they knew?'

One of his captains said something but St Clair didn't wait for Dmitri to translate.

'That was the reason,' he said. 'They may even sense something has gone wrong. Frogmore used his powers to hide his shape and disguise his form; he must have sacrificed one of the prisoners and used his appearance. Once on the parapet it would have been easy for him to pretend he was a Russian.'

'What do you mean?' Dmitri narrowed his eyes. 'Change his appearance?'

'He was a devil-worshipper!' St Clair snapped. 'And to the devil he has gone!'

'And we shall show the enemy!' Dmitri rapped out an order.

Frogmore's corpse was seized, stripped of all its clothing. The terrible wounds in his chest were purple-red, great ugly gashes. Rebecca couldn't believe she'd had the strength to wreak such terrible damage.

Dmitri pointed to Cowper.

'Did he kill him?'

St Clair shook his head and gestured at Rebecca. The Russian commander leaned down and kissed Cowper on each cheek and then on the forehead. Rebecca studied St Clair: the cut on his head had stopped bleeding but his skin was white as chalk. He staggered slightly and she helped him back onto the bed.

'Lie and rest,' she whispered.

St Clair shook his head. 'It's finished,' he replied, as if to himself. 'And my time has come.'

Rebecca felt Dmitri's hand on her shoulder. When she turned the Russian was smiling and she didn't resist when he grasped her face in his hands, kissing her full on the mouth.

'A woman of courage.' His eyes gleamed. 'A mother of heroes. I salute you, Rebecca Lennox!'

He snapped his fingers. Frogmore's corpse was lifted.

'He doesn't look so powerful now, does he?' St Clair asked. 'Look at it, Rebecca.'

The magus's skin was a dirty white, his head lolled, the terrible wounds in his chest gaped, his thighs and legs were cut and dirty.

'We'd best see this,' St Clair said to her.

They followed Dmitri and his officers out and across the yard full of soldiers resting in the shade. Immediately these sensed something had happened. Dmitri spoke quickly, pointing back at Rebecca. The soldiers received a new lease of life. They sprang to their feet, swords clashing against their shields. Frogmore's corpse was hoisted up onto the gatehouse. A rope was slung round his neck and it was thrown over the battlements, one end of the cord being tied to the crenellations. The body dangled and danced, face turned towards the Turkish camp. Soon the whole castle rang with a raucous chorus of praise.

A group of mailed Sipahis, shields up, ran towards the edge of the moat. They surrounded and protected a Turk dressed in exquisite silks.

'Their commander,' St Clair whispered.

Dmitri leaned over the battlements: crowing with triumph, he pointed at Frogmore's corpse and then at the Turks who seemed uncertain. On Dmitri's orders the rope was loosened and the corpse lowered further. The group of Turks sat for a while, all eyes on that naked, macabre cadaver twirling in the breeze, then they turned, hastening back towards the camp. The whole garrison was now standing to arms and Rebecca, despite feeling weak and rather faint, stayed with them.

An hour later the Turks gave their reply. The cannon were withdrawn. Tents and pavilions were taken down, carts were hitched and the Turkish army, slowly but surely, retreated from the hideous devastation around Karenska.

By nightfall they had gone. All that was left was a swathe of darkened earth, now the hunting ground of birds of prey. Dmitri sent out a party of horsemen to harass and observe the Turkish retreat. Burial parties were organised and, by nightfall, the darkness was lit by the leaping flames from the great funeral pyre built on the other side of the moat. The Russians were too exhausted to celebrate but slept where they lay on the parapets or in the castle bailey below.

St Clair took Rebecca back to their chamber where they prepared Cowper's corpse for burial. Early the next morning, St Clair brought two great sheets of leather in which to wrap their former companion's body. It was then lifted onto a cart and they took it out beyond the battlefield into the great sea of grass. Dmitri sent some soldiers, armed with spades and mattocks. A deep grave was dug and, after St Clair recited the office of the dead, the corpse was buried and a wooden cross set at its head.

Rebecca did not weep or mourn. She could not think of a better resting place for a man who had travelled so far in pursuit of justice and given his life so she could live.

By the time they returned to the castle, Dmitri and his officers were organising a victory celebration. She and St Clair ate a little food, drank some wine and returned to their chamber where they slept for most of the day.

It was growing dark when St Clair awoke her. He watched Rebecca pull herself up, then he thrust the deep-bowled goblet into her hand and lifted his own in a silent toast. She sipped: the wine was rich and full.

'It's claret,' St Clair said. 'Dmitri found it in the castle stores. He broached a cask and sent us some. They want us to join them but . . .' He shrugged and looked towards the window. 'The daylight's failing,' he went on. 'The shadows fall and we must all, Rebecca, yield to the night.' He drank, Rebecca likewise. 'Drink deep,' he urged. 'My Chrysogona, Rebecca the maid with the heart of a lion.'

She smiled. She found that she couldn't really discuss what had happened. It had been too searing, too quick. She still half-expected Cowper to come swaggering through the door, his eyes full of soulful glances. And what now? Frogmore was dead, her father avenged. She was now alone, thousands of miles from Dunmow, sipping wine with a Jesuit priest. And tomorrow? Rebecca drank again. She felt warm and at peace. If only St Clair would say something: reveal what might happen.

'The wine makes me sleepy,' she said.

Her heart beat a litle faster as St Clair drew closer and leaned over her.

'You will sleep, Rebecca, long and full. The powders I put in the cup will soon take their effect.'

She dropped the cup and tried to struggle up but St Clair gently pushed her back.

'I am finished so I must go,' he announced. 'And there is no other way of leaving you.'

'Why?' Rebecca's heart was thudding, scalding hot tears seared her eyes. 'Oh, Michael, don't leave me.' She fumbled for his hand. 'You can't leave me! You are my love, my life!'

'I have no choice,' he replied. 'It is all finished.

Frogmore is dead. While you were sleeping, Dmitri scattered his ashes to the winds of hell.' He squeezed her fingers. 'I'll always love you, Rebecca Lennox. I always have. I chose you. I came to Dunmow because of you. You were put to the test and were not found wanting. You risked your life for me.' He paused. 'I knew you, Rebecca, even before I met you, I knew you. I kissed your lips when you were in your mother's womb.'

'Who are you?' Rebecca asked, fighting back the waves of sleep.

'I am Michael. I stand before the throne of God and on my head I bear the mark of the living God.'

'No, you are St Clair the Jesuit.'

'At the moment of death St Clair the Jesuit gave me his body, his mind, to continue the struggle.'

'Why?' Rebecca pleaded. 'Why?'

'Frogmore's evil had to be destroyed by human means, by someone bound by the limits of weakness. To bring Frogmore to confront his nemesis, you, Rebecca Lennox. Now it is done, I have a journey to make and it is a long one. No trace of me will remain.'

St Clair's face was changing, skin glowing like molten gold; his eyes were no longer dark but sapphire-blue and his voice seemed to come from afar off.

'But I love you!' The tears were streaming down her cheeks.

'Love is still love, Rebecca, even more so when it is unconsummated. Love never finds fulfilment. It always hungers for more. It lasts for all eternity. It is, indeed, the weakness of God.'

She tried to grasp his face but he gently pushed her hands back.

'I shall never leave you. And, when you call, I will come to you. In the end, you shall be with me.'

Rebecca tried to speak but her lips wouldn't move. She was falling, a pleasant, soothing sensation, into a velvet darkness. St Clair was holding her hands, his lips pressed against hers.

Rebecca woke late the next morning fully refreshed and alert: all the aches and pains from the siege had disappeared. The chamber was empty. St Clair's bed had not been slept in. The clothes he had worn were neatly piled at its foot; his sword belt hung from a peg on the door. Perhaps she had been dreaming? Perhaps it was all a mistake? She shouted his name, her voice echoing round the chamber, then she saw them, lying on the table, tied with a ribbon, freshly cut snowdrops. She picked them up. Memories of the forest glades outside Dunmow flooded back and she knew, in her heart, that St Clair had gone. She sat and quietly wept until her soul, her eyes, her heart could weep no more.

Afterwards she dressed hurriedly and hastened down to the castle yard. The great gates now stood open, the drawbridge lowered. Only a few sleepy-eyed guards were on duty, and they saluted and raised their hands as she passed.

Rebecca left the castle, her feet scrunching on the charred earth. She pinched her nostrils at the acrid smoke wafting from the funeral pyre. The remains of the battle still lay scattered about: spent shot, broken weapons, scraps of cloth, pieces of steel glinting in the grass and, now and again, the occasional bloody corpse, overlooked by the burial parties.

Rebecca went and sat on the small hillock, gently stroking the freshly turned soil over Cowper's grave. She felt as if her heart would break. Cowper was dead. St Clair was gone. All she had were her memories. Rebecca put the snowdrops on Cowper's grave, where she would have remained all day, but a shadow fell over her and she stared up into Dmitri's face.

'He has gone.'

The Russian gently pulled her to her feet. He took off his great, fur-lined cape and wrapped it round her, clasping its silver chain at her neck.

'Rebecca, you may go where you wish,' he declared. 'You may come to Moscow and, I swear by all that is holy, you will be treated as a princess, a heroine of the people. Or, if you wish to go elsewhere, I give you my blood oath, you will travel comfortably and free. Anything you wish shall be yours.' The Russian's hard eyes softened. 'You are angel-kissed.' He gestured at the grave. 'I do not know what happened yet I truly believe you've been touched by the shadow of God's wing.'

Rebecca didn't reply. Dmitri led her back into the fortress where the entire garrison had assembled. These redoubtable soldiers, veritable wolves in human flesh but men of great courage, drew their swords and clashed their shields. They saluted Rebecca as a true warrior, a heroine who had fought the power of evil, brought them victory and rescued them from the hands of the Turks. Time and again the swords clashed, time and again their paean of praise rang throughout the fortress.

Rebecca stood, dry-eyed. Her thoughts were back at Dunmow, with a soft-eyed priest hiding in the stable loft and Cowper, his eyes full of desire, striding through the taproom towards her . . .

Rome: September 1565

Father Roderigo Bastini sat back in his great throne-like chair and stared across the desk at the English-woman sitting opposite him.

'Do you hear the bells, Mistress Lennox?'

This important official in the Jesuit Order cocked his head, listening to the clarion call of the bells pealing across Rome. They filled the air with their rejoicing, spreading the news of how the Emperor Suleiman's forces had been driven from Malta. After a long and fierce siege, the Hospitallers had held their island, inflicting a great defeat on the Turks.

'A great victory,' Bastini declared.

He picked up the quill and just wished this disconcerting Englishwoman wouldn't look at him so intently. She was attractive, in a strange sort of way; her face was slightly burned by the sun but her hair was thick and lustrous, the eyes ever-watchful. Out of courtesy he did not stare at her lip. Was that a flaw in her beauty or did it enhance her? He picked up the letter.

'A perilous journey, Mistress Lennox. You were escorted by Russians to a port across the Adriatic, treated like a princess; your escort didn't leave here until they reached Rome. And where are you staying now?' He spoke slowly, his command of English was not as perfect as he wished.

'With the Sisters of Sancta Severina, on the other side of the Tiber.'

'Ah yes, the lady nuns.' Bastini leaned forward.

'Severina is a convent used to looking after, how can I put it, ladies with the means to retire from the frenetic hurly-burly of life?'

Rebecca smiled and Bastini thought how sweet her face was.

'I do not wish to retire from the hurly-burly of life, Father, though I have come well provisioned.'

'So, you wish to return to England?'

Rebecca shook her head. 'The letter, Father, tells you what I want.'

'Ah yes.'

Bastini picked it up and studied the cursive elegant script. It was written in perfect Latin by a high-ranking official in Venice who traded with the Russian court. The letter introduced Rebecca Lennox, 'friend and kinswoman of Ivan, Tsar of all the Russias. A woman of deep courage who had rendered great service to the Russian court', to Bastini and the Jesuit Order in Rome.

'So, what do you want, Mistress Lennox?'

'Rebecca, my name is Rebecca.'

'Very well, Rebecca.'

'Michael St Clair?'

'Ah yes.'

Bastini looked across the room at the stark crucifix on the opposite wall. He had received this letter the previous evening and had searched the records. Now Bastini felt slightly uncomfortable about discussing the secrets of his Order.

'All I can say, Rebecca,' he replied slowly, 'is that Michael St Clair came from Ireland. He was educated in France and joined the Jesuit Order . . .'

'Frogmore!' Rebecca broke in. 'I know all about Frogmore!'

Bastini swallowed hard.

'Please!' Rebecca toyed with the silver chain round her neck. 'Please, Father,' she repeated. 'I know everything!'

'You say you were with St Clair in England and Russia?'

'Father, I helped him escape when he was trapped in England. I travelled with him into Russia.' She saw the shift in the Jesuit's eyes. 'No, Father, our relationship was . . .' She smiled. 'Let me put it this way, you have no need to hear my confession.'

Bastini laughed: the more he talked to this serene, enigmatic young woman, the more he liked her.

'Enough games.' Bastini put the quill down. 'A few years ago the Jesuit Order in Rome was asked by the Holy Father to track down a warlock, a great magus called Frogmore. My superiors chose Michael St Clair, a very personable young man of deep piety: learned, skilled in the ways of the world, a duellist.' Bastini picked up the quill and stroked his cheek with it. 'A true Jesuit, a man of many parts.' He sighed noisily. 'St Clair became close to Frogmore. I never met Michael personally but, I understand, he was a man of great charm who insinuated himself into Frogmore's company.'

'He was to kill him?' Rebecca intervened.

'Yes, he was to kill him. Lawful execution on behalf of the Church. They came back to Italy. According to rumour, Frogmore discovered St Clair's true identity. There was a duel and St Clair allegedly fell to his death, but his corpse was never discovered. By that time the Holy Father had died and been succeeded by another. The Jesuit Order had done what it could.

'Then, about two years ago, we heard that St Clair

was still alive, ruthlessly hunting Frogmore across Europe.' He spread his hands and shrugged elegantly. 'But we had no dealings with him and he had no dealings with us.'

'So, St Clair could have survived the fall?'

Bastini's eyes became guarded. 'If he did, it was a miracle.'

'What are you saying, Father?'

'I don't know, Rebecca. Did St Clair survive? Did someone else take his name?'

'Do you believe, Father, an angel could have taken his place?'

Bastini's eyes widened in amazement.

'What are you implying, Rebecca?'

'Nothing, Father.' She half-smiled. 'But, tell me,' she continued. 'What else do you know about St Clair?'

Bastini rose and led Rebecca down out of the chamber along a passageway whose wooden floor-boards were polished and gleaming, the walls painted a brilliant white: a stark, austere place except for the crosses on the walls and statues in their niches. They continued across a broad, sweet-smelling garden, where flower beds still bloomed and cypress and olive trees afforded some protection against the hot autumn sun until they reached the small church of St Michael which served as the Jesuit chapel. This, too, was austere with white washed walls, black timbered beams and wooden supports. It smelt sweetly of beeswax and incense; halfway down, Bastini stopped and took Rebecca into a small side chapel. She glanced up at the statue of St Michael and the tears started in her eyes.

'It's just the same,' she whispered. 'It's like the

statue in my parish church in Dunmow. Look, the
dark hair, that face, the armour of a knight . . .'

'We don't know who carved it or where it comes
from,' Bastini replied, touched by the sheer passion
in Rebecca's face. 'St Clair had a great devotion to St
Michael, his namesake. According to the records he
celebrated Mass here and often came to sit and pray
or just talk to the statue. He used to make the other
brothers laugh.'

'Can I stay here?' Rebecca asked. 'Father, I was
given treasure before I left Russia. I am of the Catholic
faith now. I cannot return to England and to be locked
up with the Sisters . . .'

Bastini chewed the corner of his lip.

'I am a good cook,' Rebecca continued. 'I can clean
and sew.'

'But people would talk.'

'I am a virgin,' Rebecca replied. 'I would take an
oath on the sacrament that I will remain so, dedicated to
God and the service of your Order.' Her eyes wandered
back to the statue. 'It's all I have left.' She grasped
Bastini's hands. 'Please! You'll never regret it!'

Father Bastini conferred with his colleagues, who
also met Rebecca. They pronounced her strange but,
there again, people from that far misty island were
noted for their eccentricity. Then they voted and the
result was unanimous. Rebecca Lennox, an Englishwoman consecrated to God and the service of the
Order, became their housekeeper.

Never once did they regret such a decision. Rebecca
proved to be an excellent companion: a most ingenious
cook, a woman who became a friend as well as a
housekeeper. They admired her mordant wit and sharp
observations. She was often found in the chapel of

St Michael seated at the foot of the statue or in their library studying manuscripts. They teased her about this, her scholarship and passionate devotion to St Michael the Archangel, but she only smiled and would not be drawn.

The years passed and Father Bastini died, as did most of the brothers who had been there when Rebecca Lennox first arrived. Others succeeded them. They, too, grew to love and respect this ageing Englishwoman who asked nothing more than to stay in their house and worship in the chapel of St Michael.

On the feast of the Archangel, 29 September 1605, Father Verleto, the newly appointed superior of the Jesuit house in Rome, was standing in his chamber overlooking the gardens. The season was changing: the sun was not so strong and the garden was showing all the signs of autumn. He watched Rebecca Lennox, grey-haired, rather stooped, come out into the garden, a basket on her arm. Verleto smiled, the Englishwoman so loved flowers! He watched her crouch and cut at a rose bush; he was about to turn away when he heard a voice, clear on the breeze.

'Rebecca!'

Verleto was sure the word 'Chrysogona' was called across the garden. The Jesuit felt a shiver go up his spine. Something was about to happen. The Englishwoman was standing up, the rose and cutters she carried had slipped from her hands. She was staring open-mouthed at the church but, from where he stood, Verleto couldn't see what she was staring at.

'Michael!' Rebecca's hand went to her lips. 'William!'

The Jesuit watched, fascinated. She hurried across, running like a young woman. Verleto closed the window, ran along the passageway and down the stairs.

When he reached the garden, he found it empty but the door to the church was slightly ajar. He pulled it open and quietly slipped through. The chapel was in darkness but Verleto was sure that, as he went in, he glimpsed, at the far end of the church, three figures moving hand in hand: a man with black hair, the other with hair as white as snow and, between them, a young woman laughing and joking.

'Rebecca!' Verleto called.

He went into the chapel of St Michael. Rebecca Lennox was lying at the foot of the Archangel's statue. At first the Jesuit thought she was asleep, her face was so composed, so serene. When he tried to revive her, he could find no pulse in her neck. Stranger still, in her hand was a small bunch of snowdrops tied with a piece of blue silk ribbon. Verleto picked them up and smelt their fragrance.

To his dying day, the Jesuit could never answer the mystery of why such flowers came to be in a dead woman's hand: snowdrops, fresh and sweet, which the harsh soil of Rome could never produce.

If you enjoyed this book here is a selection of other bestselling titles from Headline

Headline books are available at your local bookshop or newsagent. Alternatively, books can be ordered direct from the publisher. Just tick the titles you want and fill in the form below. Prices and availability subject to change without notice.

Buy four books from the selection above and get free postage and packaging and delivery within 48 hours. Just send a cheque or postal order made payable to Bookpoint Ltd to the value of the total cover price of the four books. Alternatively, if you wish to buy fewer than four books the following postage and packaging applies:

UK and BFPO £4.30 for one book; £6.30 for two books; £8.30 for three books.

Overseas and Eire: £4.80 for one book; £7.10 for 2 or 3 books (surface mail).

Please enclose a cheque or postal order made payable to *Bookpoint Limited*, and send to: Headline Publishing Ltd, 39 Milton Park. Abingdon, OXON OX14 4TD, UK.
Email Address: orders@bookpoint.co.uk

If you would prefer to pay by credit card, our call team would be delighted to take your order by telephone. Our direct line is 01235 400 414 (lines open 9.00 am–6.00 pm Monday to Saturday 24 hour message answering service). Alternatively you can send a fax on 01235 400 454.

Name ....

Address ....

....

....

If you would prefer to pay by credit card, please complete:
Please debit my Visa/Access/Diner's Card/American Express (delete as applicable) card number:

Signature .... Expiry Date ....